HUSBAND OF HITWOMAN

Jeffrey A. Pitts

Moonshine Cove Publishing, LLC

Abbeville, South Carolina U.S.A.
First Moonshine Cove Edition Sep 2020

ISBN: 978-1-945181-900
Library of Congress PCN: 2020914988
© Copyright 2020 by Jeffrey A. Pitts

Edited by Chase Nottingham; cover illustration by Ryan Lanz (AWP, A Writer's Path), back cover, interior design, and additional editing by Moonshine Cove staff.

To Mom and Dad, thank you for instilling the value of reading and storytelling in me at an early age. I love you very much.

About the Author

Jeffrey A Pitts grew up on farms in Oregon and Washington, and spent most of his time in whatever backcountry he could reach on horseback or afoot. Now, this dedicated storyteller's  characters walk in the same tracks. Seldom does he utilize a wilderness setting he hasn't hiked, camped, fished, or hunted. Jeff loads, tests, and maintains important ballistic data of his own ammunition, because the harvest of wild game is a way of life to him, not a hobby.

After graduating from high school, Jeff worked as a carpenter, log home builder, logger, and heavy equipment operator. Fascinated by the roughest wilderness areas the US has to offer, he's spent much of his life exploring the wildest country possible, sometimes living off the land as he traveled. From the Goat Rocks Wilderness of Washington state, the Bob Marshall of Montana, to the Frank Church River of No Return Wilderness of Idaho, he's hiked thousands of miles on and off trails.

After the loss of a special German shorthair pointer, he filled the void with wirehair pointers and adds dogs into much of his writings.

An avid powerlifter, Jeff enjoys the big loads of squatting, benching, and deadlifting. He is married to Jodi, his childhood sweetheart, and they have two children, Tyrel and Terin, and three grandchildren, Noah, Hayden, and Kody.

A lifelong reader, he began writing stories when they could no longer be contained in his head and spilled over onto paper and computer screens.

Jeff derives pleasure from a slow rural life, enjoying friends and family, crafting his stories, growing a garden, and living off the grid in the Pacific Northwest with wife, two German wirehairs, and a flock of chickens

www.jeffreyapitts.com

HUSBAND OF HITWOMAN

Chapter I

God, I love watching my wife. Five-foot nothing and rarely cracking a hundred pounds, I couldn't imagine anyone prettier. Until she smiled. Then, Julia transformed into the most beautiful woman in the world. Didn't figure she knew I watched from the porch steps. Still in her school clothes after returning home from work—a dress reaching her calves with a waist-length jacket over top—no one would guess she carried a holstered Glock beneath her left arm. Watching her toss cracked corn to her flock of hens and a rooster—she called it scratching her chickens—brought me nothing but joy. Julia loved all her animals but especially Jake—a three-year-old German shorthaired pointer I sometimes worried she loved more than me.

The coop door slammed, and she disappeared toward her bunny cages, but I was ready. They weren't visible from where I waited. Standing slowly and backing onto the porch, I waited for her to appear with a basket of eggs in the hopes of catching her by surprise. A minute passed, then two, before I leaned out far enough to catch a glimpse. "Gotcha!"

I damned near folded when her voice came from behind through the open window. "Christ, Jules. You're gonna feel awful someday when my ticker stops." I should've suspected what might happen after she took it upon herself to lubricate the door hinges.

"Thought you might already be dead, honey." She stepped out to give me a kiss. Jake shot between us to check his markers and warn encroachers he remained vigilant. "You were sitting so still on the stoop I figured you fell asleep or kicked the bucket." Her hands went over my shoulders and mine circled around her. Soft lips met mine. "Is that a gun, or are you happy to see me?" Our teeth clicked when we grinned.

I shifted the revolver on my belt. "I might ask the same, Mrs. Pelletier. Do I feel a third boob, or are you packin' heat?" My elbow tapped the Glock hanging down her side.

She giggled. "Don't need a third. I'd be happy growing enough to fill a training bra." Her small bosom didn't matter to me. I loved her exactly as she was—a tiny blonde spitfire with more energy than any of her middle school students. "What's for supper?" She left me wanting more by returning inside.

I followed, enjoying the view of her backside on our way to the kitchen. "Scotty invited us out. Swears he's payin' this time. Seems he got a check for a short sightseeing tour into the hills." Scotty Rich was the owner of Wannabe Rich? guide service offering horseback rides into the Frank Church wilderness area. He spent summer months until the beginning of September cleaning trails and taking clients on photo excursions and high lake fishing trips. October until early December were filled with guided big-game hunts.

Jules ran a glass of water and sipped at it while she headed to the bedroom. "How's your friend doing? I haven't seen him since...." Julia stopped, and her face grew cold. Hanging her jacket in the closet, she slid the shoulder harness off and tossed her gun on our bed.

"Been a while," I said. "He caught me leaving the feedstore this morning. Said he wanted to buy steak dinners tonight, probably hopin' you'll give him the kiss and dance you owe." I winked to lighten the atmosphere.

"You're probably right," she grumbled. "He's going to wait a long time before I pay up. Forgot about that damned bet." My wife—barely an acquaintance then—bet Scotty she was older than him. He won by only a few months. I'm the elder of both by some half-dozen years.

"Likely kids on your brain." She'd been back teaching only three weeks since summer ended and almost six since she killed Manny. We spent the summer hunting the man who was her handler while she worked as an assassin for an entity known as The Company. I voted for whacking him at eight hundred yards and calling it good. Not Julia. Like any respectable hired killer harboring a personal grudge, she wanted to look the double-crosser in the eye, so he knew who terminated him. The simple act was important to her. No small wonder she didn't recall mundane details from a time she fought to stay alive in a war—one she wasn't entirely sure had ended.

She let the dress pool around her ankles. I found it difficult to keep my hands to myself. Standing in her bra and panties, my wife was a sight to behold. Knowing her thoughts drifted to a difficult and dark time, I maintained a respectable distance. Besides, there's nothing like watching a woman draw on a snug pair of jeans. Jules stepped into them to dance and shimmy until they were buttoned. Our weather still warm, she chose a tank top. Her feet went into a pair of nearby moccasins, but she didn't leave the room without a firearm.

Her sigh took me unaware when she opted for her Colt Diamondback in .38 Special. "Guess I'll always carry a gun. Might as well stay used to it."

Something was eating at her. "Jules? You okay?"

She sighed again. "No..." I heard a sob and then hiccups. "M-Mr. Windward died last night. We held an assembly this morning to-hic-let the kids know." She shook her head. "I think it was t-hic-tougher on the faculty than students. I stopped to see your aunt before leaving. Bess thought a lot of him."

"Shit." Our day was ending on a sour note. Mr. Windward taught me in junior high and high school. "Any news of when his service is planned?" I drew her against my chest to soak my shirt.

"Saturday in the gymnasium," she said. "Bess said the venue because of so many present and former students and their families...they loved him."

The news left me with little to offer. "I'm sorry, Jules. I really am. If I haven't fattened too much, my suit should still fit." I owned one three-piece, and appropriately enough, it was somber black.

She pulled away and wiped her face. "I'll be sure to iron your shirt between now and then."

Oddly enough—for a woman with such a violent past—Julia harbored a tender heart. She cried when it came time to butcher rabbits or a chicken. A sad song was enough to cause tears on occasion. Conversations about her family—all three murdered—were few and far between simply because she battled strong emotions. I wondered how she would respond during a funeral she didn't cause.

* * *

My old buddy waited with a table ready. Not one to feel self-conscious, Scotty stood when he saw us and waved his Stetson high overhead. Noise was intense in the restaurant and lounge on a Friday night. The live band struck a slow song as we moved through the crowd. Rather than continue, I swept Julia into my arms and onto the floor. I led, and she surprised me by following my waltz. Although I rarely danced, I found it simple and relaxing, but my wife proved to be lighter on her feet than me. When she didn't attempt to pull away, I kept us on the floor until the song ended.

"Hot damn!" Scotty said when we reached the table. "Never guess you danced so well, Julia." I didn't miss his wink. "Am I next?"

Her response was typically prim. "Mine are saved for my husband, Scotty Rich." She thrust out a little hand in greetings. "How are you these days?"

"Pissed," he said. Instead of shaking, he raised her knuckles to plant a kiss. "Can't believe I heard about you getting hitched through the grapevine. What sort of shitty friends are you?" Bastard slid a chair out and seated my wife, grinning over her head at me.

"Busy ones," I said.

"Figured." Scotty lifted a glass of something I guessed mixed heavily with vodka. After a healthy pull, he returned the mug to the table and spun it in a ring of condensation. "Either of you going to explain what happened when you needed Dad's truck?"

I shrugged when Jules looked to me. "Nope."

"Julia?"

She surprised me with a try to dazzle him with a smile. "Dawson wanted to take me to a romantic spot in a nice truck and ask me to be his wife." It changed to a lopsided grin while she waited.

Scotty stared for a moment before snorting. "You must think I'm dumb—"

"You are," I said.

"Not dumb enough to swallow a giant load of horseshit like your beautiful bride just shoveled." My longtime friend leaned across the table. "Dawson, you haven't looked so serious since coming home from overseas and first heard shots fired. I watched you grab for a gun you didn't carry anymore." He stopped when our server arrived.

"Hey, Allison," I greeted while she passed out unneeded menus. "How's Mike?"

"Sad and needing a shoulder tonight," she said.

Scotty appeared mystified until I cleared the air. "Mr. Windward passed away last night." A stolen glance gave me insight as to how Julia would handle Saturday. Her face fixed with a cold stare while she gazed into the crowd. I shivered—it wasn't much different than when she worked a job.

"Ah, shit." Scotty stared into his glass. "Loved the guy...my homeroom teacher the first year after moving here in middle school. Any idea of when the service will be held?"

"Mike said Saturday at eleven in the gymnasium," Allison said.

"Figures." He stared into space for a moment. "Got a couple nights with a party of eight Thursday through Saturday. Need the money, so I won't be home in time."

"Have a card and flowers delivered," Julia said. She pitched her proposal in a flat tone. "No sense in missing a payday. I'm sure Mrs. Windward will understand."

Our order was taken before Allison left without a menu opened. Jules took me by surprise when she ordered a cosmopolitan. Even Scotty raised an eyebrow. "Hey, it's been that kind of day," she said.

Scotty and I made short work of our dinners while Jules barely touched hers. Instead, she ordered another two drinks after finishing her first. I left mine untouched, knowing alcohol was something she avoided. My friend gave me a nod when I slid it to him instead. We told stories of Mr. Windward while we were kids. Jules laughed for a while before clamming up after her third cocktail arrived. I left for the restroom sure she waited in good hands. Scotty was talking on my return. "I'm sure you'll like it. It's short, light, and someone replaced the plastic recoil pad with a rubber one."

"What's going on?" I asked.

"Julia mentioned she'd like to hunt over Jake but doesn't own a shotgun. I took a Browning in on trade a few weeks back. It's a twenty-gauge Citori, and someone shortened the stock too much for me. Probably a perfect fit for her."

Julia's grin was crooked. "He offered it for a grand, honey."

Knowing they sold at twice the price of Scotty's offer, I wasn't averse to looking. "Bring it over when you get a chance." Jake constantly looked for a reason to point at any bird, even robins. The dog was born to hunt and would do anything to please his mistress.

"Probably not until I get home with my clients. I'll find a day to wander past your place and let Julia try it out first. I'd hate to see her buy only to find it didn't fit." Scotty was all business when it came to any sort of outdoor pursuit.

"Sounds good," I said. Allison stopped by to box Julia's dinner before I poured her into the Wagoneer. Scotty followed.

"Never seen her like this." He watched me get her in the Jeep and buckled.

"She didn't know him long, but Mr. Windward was a favorite. Hit her hard." We heard her giggling to herself inside.

Scotty stopped me at the driver's door. "You owe me a story, buddy, and I aim to collect."

He wasn't going to let our use of his dad's truck drop, so I nodded. "One of these days, my friend. But don't push it, okay?" I whispered. "There's a side to Julia you can't imagine."

* * *

She did better at the funeral than me. She wept into a handful of Kleenex, while I dried my eyes with a kerchief. Aunt Bess and the Windwards' minister handled most of the load. A potluck was held afterward where I took a dish of my best fried chicken. Julia raised dark

Cornish bantams with a new batch needing butchered, but I cooked store-bought rather than use the tiny chickens she liked best. I wasn't surprised when Scotty didn't show, but we were pleased with the overall turnout. The teacher was beloved in the community.

Julia strode stiffly from the Wagoneer to the house when we returned home, not offering a half-dozen words on the way. Her soft heart was made plain by eyes swollen after a morning of tears. I dropped to the couch and scratched Jakes ears after her disappearance into the bedroom. He looked at the closed door with questioning eyes. "I dunno, boy. Momma's hurting right now. I suggest we leave her be if she takes a nap." We waited quietly until the door flew open after a few minutes. Julia stalked out—her .38 belted on—with the tool of her old profession tucked in her waistband, another in her hand, and her M4 slung over a shoulder. Under one arm was a box I knew to be laden with ammunition. "Jules?"

She didn't stop on her way to the backdoor. "Leave me alone."

It wasn't Julia I observed leave the house. Instead, she was someone I hoped to never see again. The gray woman needed a violent release of emotion. The door slammed, and I hurried to watch her disappear behind the chicken coop. I knew where she preferred to target practice if it could be construed as such. Past the chicken house and rabbit pens, she continued toward the base of the mountain to where I'd built a shooting bench—far enough so her chickens would continue laying but wasn't so distant to be a nuisance carrying gear.

I left Jake inside while I made my way near a couple pines offering shade for her critters. Perhaps a hundred yards farther back, she piled her gear on the benchtop. Stacks of ammunition were sorted from the cardboard box along with spare magazines. She preferred a silhouette to a bull's eye. An old post worked perfectly, and she stapled a target to the horizontal slats left nailed from an earlier session.

While Jules appeared quiet and demure to others, a side unseen by anyone still alive but me occasionally appeared. Julia became J—her pseudonym during years spent as a professional killer. After her family was murdered by drug dealers, she'd been approached and hired by an organization known only as The Company. Julia then routinely carried out hits against drug dealers and importers. Quickly identified as an efficient killer, she went on to *sign*—as The Company called it—high profile targets. I found it difficult to imagine the warm and caring woman I'd married was once a ruthless killer until I watched her in action. Julia no longer existed. She became J—the gray woman.

The extent of her anguish became apparent during her harsh and aggressive session. She preferred to practice alone, and I understood why. Dashing over uneven ground, J stopped, drew her .38 and emptied it into the target. After a quick reload from a speedloader on her belt, six more rounds were delivered downrange, then another refreshing of her cylinder before slamming the gun into its holster.

I held my breath when she dove forward, tumbling head over heels to come up shooting with her suppressed work pistol. Although never admitting an actual number, stories she once confided meant her kills went over fifty or seventy-five, perhaps even a hundred. Shots from the .22 Ruger were silent from where I watched. A few rounds fired then a run, dive, roll, or summersault and come up shooting again—empty magazines exchanged with others carried on her belt. More bullets went downrange while barrel-rolling without slowing her rate of fire. Blazing away from her side with her weak or strong hand, J stopped only when her gun ran dry after shooting her way back to the bench.

While a handgun was her preferred tool, next was another suppressed weapon, a Ruger semi-auto rifle in .22 rimfire. Raising it to a shoulder, she ran at the ragged paper—never slowing her trigger finger. A quick reload, and she backed away using her weak side. Right-handed, then left, J timed her retreat to reach the bench when the extended magazine locked the action open. Setting it aside and snatching her M4, reports from the significantly louder 5.56 NATO rang across the valley floor. One moment sprinting and firing—the next shooting from a knee or diving prone—J provided an insight I'd not considered. Shooting from every conceivable position, angle, and weakness. A hat-sized rock on the hillside some two-hundred yards distant became the object of her wrath. White puffs exploded from its surface with each bark of her rifle, stopping only to exchange thirty-round magazines.

To watch was mesmerizing until a voice at my shoulder shocked me. "Jesus Christ..." Automatically drawing the .44 Magnum Colt Anaconda on my belt, I turned fully prepared to kill our intruder. Scotty stood a few feet behind me but his gaze never shifted from Julia. His mouth left open, he observed slack-jawed while she switched from empty to loaded magazines. My drawn revolver got ignored, and I holstered it. "I...holy shit..." Scotty was finally at a loss for words, holding the shotgun he promised to bring.

"How long have you been watching?"

"Long enough," he whispered back.

"Buddy, you've gotta get out of here. She can't know you saw." I attempted to edge him away.

He tried more gawking over my shoulder. "What the hell, Pelletier?"

"Scotty, as God is my witness, you have to leave. Run." I pushed and turned him toward the house. I suppose he felt my panic and let himself be shoved. To be honest, I wasn't sure of Julia's reaction. My worry wasn't so much with her. It focused solely on J. Continued gunfire didn't slow as I marched him inside. "Out," I pointed through the kitchen to the front door. "Get in your truck, leave, come back another time. Now isn't good."

He didn't move. "I don't believe what I just saw. It wasn't Julia, was it? No way."

"No, it wasn't Jules," Nor did I want him to meet the gray woman.

He made the mistake of trying to push past. "Who the hell was it?"

I shouldered him rearward and doubled a fist, setting my feet. If punching him saved us all from J's reaction, I was willing. His hands came up, and for a moment I thought we would fight. "Leave. Now."

My biggest fear was Julia hearing his clattering bucket of bolts when he drove away. She wore earplugs, and gunfire continued for a bit after he disappeared. I waited at the dinner table with a fresh pot of coffee while texting Mom when the backdoor slammed. A woman filthy with dirt stalked past the kitchen and vanished into the bedroom. Not able to stand it, I followed. Guns and the box lay on our bed as she disrobed.

Her clothes were ruined. The blouse tossed aside couldn't be saved with such large tears. With jeans ripped at the knee, I wondered if she would mend them. When they were dropped into the same pile, my question was answered. Julia wasn't one to save things. Me? I'd deliver mine to Mom and let her repair the damage. My wife's dirty face didn't bother me, but a cut running crimson over an eye did. Another on her left shoulder got my attention. Other scrapes and scratches could be ignored. "Feel better?" J—I think it was her—offered a cold glance without answering and left for the bathroom. I checked the box after the shower started and the curtain closed.

A quick estimation confirmed she fired at least two-hundred rifle rounds. I couldn't imagine how many .22 rimfires. The barrel of her M4 was still hot—I moved it only enough to stop any scorching of our bedspread. These tools belonged to Julia and J and were not to be touched unless told. To be honest, I couldn't remember handling either suppressed firearm. She would spend hours scrubbing her weapons until satisfied.

Her shower ended when I was in the kitchen. Mom's pleasure over how her salsa turned out made me smile. I answered the text and asked her to save me a few pints. We continued our conversation until Jules appeared and tossed our first aid kit to the table. She nodded at my phone. "Melissa?" Blood oozed from both injuries.

"How'd you guess?"

"You don't text many people, and I recognized your *mom* smile." Good, my wife was back—J scared the hell out of me whether she knew it or not. Plenty of coffee remained in the pot. She poured a cup after refilling mine and sat across from me.

I gestured to her injuries. "Ready for a couple patches?"

"Please."

The cut on her shoulder proved easily dressed. Slightly more problematic was below her eyebrow where skin is thinnest. "I should go to college." I cleansed the area of blood with alcohol, gauze, and a Q-tip. Bringing the two sides together, I made sure the edges were even before using a dab of superglue to hold it closed. A small bandage went over a healthy dob of antibiotic ointment.

"You should," she said immediately. "What are you thinking of studying?" She'd earned her BA in education while I was happy with a high school diploma.

"After all my work on you the past year, my residency should almost be finished. I wanna be a full-fledged doctor."

Her immediate trill made my heart sing. "Doctor Pelletier! I can hear it now: 'Paging Doctor Pelletier, please prep for surgery.'"

Another text came in from Mom. *How's Julia? Bess called to say she took Mr. Windward's death hard.* I glanced to my wife before answering and kept my tone even. "Mom wants to know how you're doing."

She made a face. "Good. Okay, better. Tell her thanks for thinking of me."

After sending the message, I set my phone aside. "How are you feeling now, little dove?"

"Truth?" Her glance seemed sheepish, and I nodded. "Sore. I'll hurt for a few days." She touched the bandage above her eye. "If I can talk the administration into a pirate day, all I'll need is a sword, patch, and tricorn hat to be a swashbuckler. Bust out a few arghs. Got scars down pat."

I wasn't surprised when Julia left and returned with her firearms and cleaning kit. She lost all expression as she disassembled her old work gun to clean. The job would take much of the afternoon. I decided to leave her alone. The longer we were together, the more I realized her loneliness was self-made. Jake pointed through the screen door at a robin searching for worms before flying south for the winter. I made a quick decision. The pointer needed to hunt, and grouse season opened two weeks before. Perhaps I could guide him into a ruffed grouse. Chances were low during midday, but we could get exercise while leaving Julia to brood and work in peace. "I'm going to take Jake out along the dry creek bottom and see what he does if we run across a bird." I hitched my Anaconda and got an extra hole on my belt. The cross-draw holster was comfortable for daily wear even with the heavier handgun. Although longer barrels were available—a six-inch model resided in the safe at my log cabin—I was most comfortable with the four-inch version for everyday carry.

Her focus was on her job. "Okay..." I didn't respond to her halfhearted wave when she didn't bother looking up.

"Jake." My stern voice got his attention. "Heel." Well versed in his lessons, he stayed with me while I checked the freezer kept in the garage. We'd hit a ruffed grouse with Julia's Wagoneer earlier in the summer. Stopping and wrapping it in a paper, I left it in the freezer for just this reason. I pulled a couple feathers to let him smell. His excitement level went from curious to bouncing off the walls.

Almost too exuberant to control, I made him heel until in the creek bed. To give him permission, I called, "Hunt 'em up, boy!"

To say we had a good time would be an understatement. Jake stayed reasonably close, zigzagging and working out front, while I strolled behind. Scent from a multitude of wild fowl when we hit a wet spot caused him to go birdy. His tail went wild, wagging and spinning faster, the fresher the scent. Watching him work the trail was as exciting for me as for him. Knowing whether he would make a great hunter was impossible, but his enthusiasm was contagious. I needed my shotgun if he hunted so easily. Highway US-93 was at least a half mile distant when Jake locked on point. "Goddamn it, Jake," I whispered under my breath. A grouse seemed to be inside a thick copse of willows. I hoped to shotgun the first bird he pointed while hunting with me. "Whoa." I drew my .44 revolver and eased up on the dog. "Whoa," I repeated. There would be no shot for a handgun, but anything could happen.

The bird exploded from the brush in a blur of wings and feathers. It flew straight gaining altitude until reaching a tall cottonwood. Although a couple hundred yards away, I saw the limb where it landed. Excited about the sounds and smell, Jake searched for the grouse. Opening the cylinder and lifting out two rounds, I extracted two .44 Specials from my belt slide to replace them. Much lighter in sound, recoil, and velocity, they hit a bit higher than the heavier stuff. The pointer continued searching for sign and keeping an eye on me.

The grouse watched me as I closed. Usually jittery little birds, the darned thing waited until I figured to be in range. Maybe thirty yards away, I aimed carefully and held two inches lower than usual. I felt it best to shoot while Jake worked in the brush–Julia's pointer was frightened of rifle and pistol fire. Without earplugs, I braced myself for the noise to come. The trigger broke at three pounds without creep, and I rejoiced at the puff of feathers. "Dead bird, Jake," I called. "Hunt dead, boy."

Julia waited on the front porch with a glass of sun tea and a book. Jake's dance around me eager to smell caught her attention. "My boys return." She stood, walked to the railing, and leaned over. "Any luck?"

"Luck?" I scoffed. "Behold. The great white hunters!" I held the beautiful fall plumaged grouse high. "It's not much, but you're looking at tomorrow's supper."

Amazed, my wife straightened. "You got one."

I patted Jake's side and stroked his coat. "No, *we* got one. You should have seen him work, Julia. A thing of beauty." I didn't plan to tell her of the tears I shed while praising Jake for a job well done.

"His first bird, and I wasn't there." For a moment I thought she would cry. I held it up where she could reach and stroke its feathers. "The head's gone. Shoot it with your Colt?"

"No other choice. To be honest, I didn't think he'd find one to point." The exhilaration of the hunt flooded back. "He went birdy and didn't stop working the trail until he pointed. Such a strong one, too, and he waited for me to flush it. I'm sure he has the makings of a good hunter,"

"I need my hunting license." She frowned. "Wasn't Scotty planning to show me a shotgun?"

Although prepared for the question, my heart jumped. "Probably busy today. Might not be home yet. I'll text to see if he can stop tomorrow."

"Sounds good. Could we run in to North Fork and get my license? If he shows tomorrow, and I buy it, we could go out with Jake again before dark."

North Fork sat along the main stem of the Salmon River at the intersection of where a long road turned west and continued another fifty miles to the Middle Fork confluence. A restaurant, grocery, gas station, and post office were housed in one long building cobbled together over years. Behind was an RV park. We occasionally stopped for a meal or a quick burger yet mostly for fuel. Jake didn't have to be asked twice to go. I noted Jules again wore her .38 covered by an open blouse.

We almost always took her Wagoneer if the three of us went. She loved the old Jeep and always drove. The times I spent behind the wheel could be counted on one hand. The old rig's throaty V8 rumbled as we idled to the highway. "I'm sorry," came her quiet voice tinged with regret.

I barely heard her apology over the open windows and watching Jake drool down the side in my mirror. Like any dog, his head seldom spent any time inside. "Excuse me?" I turned my attention back to Julia.

"I'm sorry about this morning after we got home. I find dealing with the deaths of those I know...difficult. I..." She hesitated, started to say something before stopping.

"You don't have to apologize. Losing someone close is tough. All of us react in different ways." I was lucky. Other than my father when I was fairly young, I'd lost few I cared for. Men I commanded in combat certainly but not many friends since reentering civilian life.

"I shut you out. Marriage means sharing everything including bad times. It won't happen again."

"We'll work on it." Rome wasn't built in a day, nor would my wife open up overnight. I didn't go into our marriage blind and without expectation of difficulties.

We were able to quickly fill out the information needed to buy her license. Not just for forest grouse, but upland gamebirds, too. Julia also elected to buy her fishing license. She hadn't forgotten her plan to hire our friend for a long pack into the mountains. Rather than return home and fix supper, we elected to stay and eat in the restaurant.

"Hey, look!" Jules voice directed my attention outside. "Scotty's here."

Chapter II

Scotty spun a chair next to me to look at my wife over its back. I feared whatever he might inadvertently let slip. Instead, he filched one of my fries and dragged it through my ketchup. "No, it's okay..." I drew my hands back to make more room. "...go ahead. Feel free to help yourself."

"Thanks. Don't mind if I do." I lost a handful to our hungry tablemate. Scotty glanced at the bandage over Julia's eye and nodded with the brim of his Stetson. "What happened?"

"You know me. Clumsiest girl you'll find." My wife's gaze cooled at the mention of the injury. She refocused on the thick burger she held. Skinny little thing could eat an enormous amount and only gain ounces.

I noted how he looked at Jules and hoped his trap stayed shut. No way could I get lucky. "For someone I've never seen even stumble, you certainly use the clumsy excuse a lot."

My snicker redirected Scotty's attention. "Hey, look. An urban cowboy." Two men were standing outside a jacked-up one ton dually with California plates. One wore a Hollywood gunbelt and holster tied low. Must've been thirty cartridges filling the loops.

What we could see of his hogleg appeared nickel-plated and engraved. A bowie knife as long as my forearm hung against the opposite thigh. Brand-new jeans and a flannel shirt were sandwiched between a virgin Stetson and polished cowboy boots. I half expected to hear spurs jingle when he entered.

With her back to him, Julia turned to locate the object of my mirth. "Oh, my." She covered her lips with an index finger to stop from smiling. After he stepped inside, I noted he stopped to stare at my wife. She continued to look, and then when he didn't turn away, Jules pushed her plate across the table and gave a brusque command to Scotty. "Change places with me."

Prompted by her tone, our friend didn't hesitate to switch but seemed baffled. "I don't get it. What's going on?"

Although we ignored him and bent to our meal, Julia didn't take her attention away from the wannabe cowboy nor his short companion. Eventually, both men turned and strolled into the store and gift shop. My wife covered her Colt with her blouse again after exposing it for an easier draw. I couldn't blame her. If The Company took interest in her again, she likely wouldn't know it until struck by a bullet. "Got a pen?" I asked Scotty.

"Yeah." He found one in a pocket of the fishing vest he usually wore. "Is there something I should know?"

I jotted the license plate number down and noted from the frame it was purchased from a lot in Los Angeles. "Nope."

Julia directed the conversation elsewhere. "Are you planning to bring that shotgun by to let me look?" she asked. "Dawson took the first bird over Jake yesterday using his Colt. Time for me to even the score."

Scotty's life revolved around hunting. Mostly guiding, but my buddy could handle a rifle with the best. Handguns were the bane of his existence. Couldn't hit the broadside of a barn while standing inside. He whistled. "Shoot another pheasant on the wing with your .44?"

"Huh uh." I slapped his hand hard when he reached for the last of my fries. "Jake pointed a ruffed grouse. It busted and landed in a cottonwood."

He nodded sagely. "Gotcha." We hunted together enough for him to know a sitting bird usually spelled meat in the pot. Many of our camp dinners were supplemented by the grouse we killed. Some with his rifle, most by my Anaconda.

Our conversation caught Julia's attention. "You knocked a pheasant out of the sky with your Colt?" She tapped the butt of my revolver. "Keep talking. You almost impress me." Her grin removed any sting.

I shook my head. "Nope. Never happened. Shooting upland game birds with anything but a scattergun is illegal."

Julia remembered where our conversation originated. "About your shotgun..." She drummed nails kept short on the tabletop.

Scotty glanced at me as his mouth opened. "I..." If looks could kill, mine would have vaporized him. He didn't miss my hand closing into a fist. "It's in my truck."

After completing our dinner and paying, we were accosted outside when Hollywood caught us from behind. "Excuse me." We turned at his voice. "You look familiar." He focused squarely on my wife. "Ever been to California?"

"I was born in the northern part." Julia kept her tone even. "But I'm pretty sure we've never met."

He stepped closer, staring intently. "Spend much time in Los Angeles?" Up close, the man looked much older than I originally thought.

Jules laughed easily, but I recognized the danger it held. I needed to get her home before J took control. "Perhaps as a baby. Not sure I've been south of San Francisco or San Jose in the past fifteen...maybe twenty years."

The man shook his head. "I have a thing for faces. Once I've seen one, I rarely forget it." With a momentary sheepish glance to Scotty and me, he asked Julia, "I mean no disrespect, but have you ever stripped? I only ask because I bounce at a club in LA."

"Okay, buddy. We've heard enough..." The heat in Scotty's voice was evident.

My wife put a hand on his arm. "It's okay. To answer your question, no, I've never danced at a strip club. I'm a primary school teacher." I didn't miss Julia's slight turn so the man couldn't see her unsnap the safety strap on her .38 Special, tucking it inside her belt. Nor did Scotty who stood next to her.

"Guess I was mistaken. I meant no offense, miss." The man nodded and turned back to where his friend sat at a window seat, yet Jules didn't relax nor look away until we turned to her Wagoneer.

I waited until we were driving home. "Mind explaining?" My question was kept intentionally mild while I watched Scotty follow us in the mirror on my side.

Julia took in a big breath before letting it out. "I thought he looked familiar when they walked in. I remember him now. He bounced at the strip joint where I surveilled Park and Kwanza. They pimped their whores out of the place. Probably Meghan, too. He made a big joke out of checking my ID each time I stopped. Can't believe he recognized me." Her sister Meghan's death was a large part of her decision to kill those involved in the drug trade.

Scotty parked beside our garage and waited with the shotgun while the outbuilding was locked. "Here you are." He handed the over and under to Jules.

She snapped the butt to her shoulder as well as any seasoned professional. My wife said shotguns were her least favorite firearm, yet she expertly checked the fit and function multiple times. It seemed about the right length with her cheek on the stock. "I like it!" she said before passing it to me.

I could see a few blemishes on the wood but none on the blued steel. My guess was the long gun spent its life as a safe-queen. Any dings were likely made by other guns going in and out. "Nice lookin' scattergun."

"A thousand, right?" Jules asked.

"Not to you," Scotty said. "I've got seven hundred into it. I'll pass it on for what I have invested." He talked to her back as she disappeared inside and raised his voice. "I'm not making money off friends."

"Take what she gives you and don't argue," I said.

"Help me understand, Dawson." I noted the change in tone. "What I saw out there..." He pointed to the area where Jules and I target practiced. "...then the way she reacted to the dime store cowboy. Was she going to shoot him?" I wished he hadn't noticed the unsnapping of her holster.

I snorted dramatically. "Course not. A little concerned about the weirdo is all."

Scotty shook his head. "I think the world of your wife, but I worry she's gotten you into something bad, my friend."

Although he didn't know it, Scotty once gazed into the eyes of J when we switched vehicles. Circumstances he was privy to were slowly adding up. Julia's series of injuries such as broken bones and facial trauma made him suspicious. A new bandage over her eye didn't help matters. To further aggravate his growing mistrust was watching her shoot. Not even I could do things she made appear easy.

I got bailed out when the door opened, and Jules appeared with a handful of cash and gave it to our friend. "Here you are." She accepted the gun from me. "Got any shells?" she asked him.

Scotty looked up from where he counted the money. "Huh? Twenty gauge? Nope, I shoot a twelve. Hey!" he said. "I said seven hundred. You gave me a grand."

Julia shook her head as I expected. "Nope. Original offer was a thousand. We aren't taking advantage of friends."

* * *

Jake and his mistress took to hunting together like peanut butter and jelly. Chasing birds was new to Jules, and while her pointer possessed good instincts, they needed a little guidance for best results. After witnessing her instinctive shooting, I called BS on her insistence of being a poor wing shot. "Let him point a little longer," I said. "He's a German pointer, so he'll hold it until he falls from exhaustion. Don't be in such a hurry to flush the grouse or to knock it down. Leave us something to eat."

Not only did the entire shot column impact the first fowl she took, but I found the plastic wad lodged inside. Instead of a wily gamebird flitting safely away through brush and timber, Julia's incredible reflexes were on full display. The bird barely exploded from the ground before she mounted the shotgun and swung. A puff of feathers hung in the air even after it fell to the ground. While some parts were salvageable, my wife realized the shot pattern needed better dispersion before impacting game.

Jake's next point couldn't have been stronger. Rather than rush to kick the bird up, Julia sauntered—if it could be called that with every muscle taut—until slowly passing her dog. The grouse jumped from a patch of brush ten feet ahead. While the scattergun leaped to her shoulder, she took her time and followed with her swing. Although it flitted and almost disappeared into deeper brush, the roar of her twenty gauge stopped its flight. Jake disappeared in pursuit as Jules turned with a grin. "How'd I do this time?"

"A split second longer, and you wouldn't have a target." My incredulity should've spoken for itself. "If I didn't see it with my own eyes, I'd have called anyone tellin' me about it a liar." I switched my shotgun, a Ruger Red Label also in twenty gauge, to the other hand. I hoped changing our adjustable chokes to ones delivering larger patterns helped with shot dispersion.

Jake appeared with his proud trophy in his mouth and dropped it in the open. Although shorthairs preferred to point and not retrieve, his halfhearted attempt meant we didn't need to search for it. The hunt was our sixth in several weekends. Our dog would only learn with time spent in the field. "Let 'em get out far enough," she said. "But shoot quick enough it can't escape in heavy brush." My wife threw lessons I tried to impart back into my face while tucking the grouse into the rear pocket of my hunting vest.

Our hike home took an hour. We made Jake heel, and I caught the bumper of a rig parked in the drive before she did and kept my voice low. "We've got company."

Though our hunt was finished and our shotguns empty, we took time to reload. Jules released the safety snap from her .38. She tossed me Jake's leash and took the lead. I followed as we skirted next to the house to a clear view of the parking area. Once there, she turned in relief. "It's just Scotty."

"Hey, man." I rapped on the window of his pickup with my knuckles. Not until he opened his door and slid out did I notice his passenger. She exited the other side and came around to stand next to him.

"Julia...Dawson, I'd like to introduce a lady new to these parts. Honey, these are two of my best friends. Robin Dickerson, this is Julia and Dawson Pelletier." I kept my reaction to his term of endearment to a barely raised eyebrow.

Where my wife barely came to his shoulder, Robin stood as tall as Scotty, around five-ten. With broad shoulders, deep chest, and built like a farm girl, her curly carrot top caught my attention. Jules stepped forward first to shake the newcomer's hand. "Nice to meet you."

I noted a strong grip when it was my turn. "Been holding out on us, bud?" His news caused us both to wonder.

"We met when I guided a corporate party into Upper Miner Lakes last summer. Robin likes our part of the country well enough she quit her job and moved to Salmon. Surprised me as much as it will you guys when she looked me up." His arm went around her waist. "We kind of hit it off."

Jake left us and waited at the front door. I guessed he was thirsty after hunting hard since daylight. Julia gave me a minor shock with her invitation. "Would you like to come inside? I can put coffee on." While the rustic interior of our house embarrassed Jules, I loved the old place. Scotty didn't mind. He'd been a guest many times in the past.

My friend seemed eager. I reckoned he wanted to make a good impression with his new woman. My wife handed me her shotgun and filled Jake's water dish. Unloading our scatterguns, I gave each a quick wipe with an oiled cloth and stood both in the closet. I returned from our bedroom to find them seated at the old metal-framed table from the 'sixties. "Have you lived in the area long, Julia?" Robin asked.

Jules, after filling the container and setting it out for Jake, turned to our company. "About three years now."

"Scott tells me you teach?"

"Substitute. I hope to earn a classroom when another fulltime teaching position opens. How about you? What does Robin Dickerson do for a living?"

My wife's a people's person, and I took pleasure in her ease at entertaining. She loved engaging with others. It's why teaching was her calling. Nevertheless, she trusted no one except me. And Jake. Maybe my mom, too. Although my auntie was her well-liked boss, I'm not sure Vice-Principal Bess Mueller got Jules's full confidence.

Our guest appeared relaxed and in command of the room. "Corporate lawyer. My coworkers were the same ones who came up with the hairbrained scheme of a pack trip with Wannabe Rich? guide service into the backcountry of Idaho. Now they're short one partner." She didn't seem uncomfortable in our tiny worn kitchen and dining room, although Jules kept it spotless.

"Plan to hang your shingle in Salmon?" Julia asked.

"Not sure. Cost of living is certainly far less than Kansas City. I have time before I need to make a final decision."

My wife nodded. "Kansas City, huh? Beautiful place. I spent a week there a few years ago."

I didn't need to ask Jules what she did there. Her mention of a particular timeframe meant she likely assassinated someone. Perhaps more than one. She made me proud when she didn't grow cold with the memory.

Robin turned to me. "I understand you farm?"

Her question caught me off guard. Scotty knew full well I no longer raised crops. Although he didn't know exactly where my income came from, he understood my mom's land was rented by another farmer growing alfalfa. "My family's planted grain and raised beef since they moved here in the early nineteen hundreds."

Jules poured coffee and sat a centrally located plate on the table loaded with brownie squares baked the previous evening. Still moist as I preferred. Scotty helped himself without asking. "I see you're hunting with the Browning. Like it?" he asked Julia.

She smiled. "I do. Comes up easy and swings fast. Got nine birds in six hunts over Jake without a miss."

Scotty glanced at me. "No kidding? What? Blues up high?"

I understood his inference. Blue grouse were slow to flush and easy to hit. "Seven ruffed and only two slowpokes. She took a double yesterday. I think we've killed or spooked most ruffs from the area." His eyes shifted to Jules again while working to assimilate what he knew about her. Slowly but surely, she exposed her natural skills to our friend.

* * *

I'd loaded Julia's plate with a waffle and four small scrambled eggs from her bantams. "Deer season opens in a couple weeks. Interested?" She needed to leave in twenty minutes to make it to work on time.

Jules set her fork aside to taste her coffee before answering. "I watched a couple whitetail bucks along the driveway the other day." She shook her head. "No, thanks...it's too soon. I don't think I can do it, honey. Birds over Jake are one thing...he needs to work, and I love watching him. I'm not ready for more."

Jake lay next to Julia's chair after finishing his own breakfast. Although I knew him to be fond of me, a bond between mistress and hunting dog left me looking in from the outside. "I understand. Mind me doing my best to fill our freezer and Mom's, too?"

"Oh, gosh, no. I love venison." Since returning home from military service over a decade earlier, I hadn't hunted like in my younger days. "What did you think of Scotty's girlfriend?" Jules asked. Finished with breakfast, she pushed back from the table.

I could only shrug. "I dunno. He's a short-timer when it comes to women. A few weeks, one as long as eight. Don't believe he's ever lived with a gal. Hunting and his business take too much."

My wife stood and smoothed her dress to make sure she hadn't dropped food or dripped syrup on it or her jacket. Her Glock went unnoticed even to my trained eye, and I'd watched her dress. "She seems nice enough. Obviously, a lot smarter than me."

I didn't like it when she got self-critical. Not only do I find her gorgeous and incredibly athletic, but clever and skillful. Fearless, too. Oh, she'll try to have me think her a coward, but I don't know many men ready to take on a skilled fighter over three times their size armed only with a letter opener and savage ingenuity. Or confront a street gang in close quarters with only a .22 pistol and be the last one standing. Sure, I've felt her heart hammer with anxiety. But how many can overcome their dread or trepidation to willingly face down an enemy alone? Few would be my guess. "Knock it off, Jules. You're sharper than anyone I know."

"You're so sweet." She stood on tiptoes to reward me with a kiss. "Now I need a classroom of eighth graders to believe what you do."

My lips drew reluctantly from hers. "I know the vice-principal. Want me to drop by to make an impression on your charges?" Aunt Bess would have a heart attack if I scared a bunch of kids. Worst part would be Mom learning about it. Although closing in on forty, to face my mother when she's disappointed or angry with me still proved a daunting task.

Julia trilled her laughter at the door while automatically scanning through the kitchen windows for danger. Her habit seemed second nature, and I'm certain she wasn't aware of doing it. No matter—if it kept her alive. I didn't bother to tell her both Jake and I already completed an earlier perimeter search. "As much as I'd enjoy it, no, my secret weapon should stay home." She squatted to pet Jake. "I'll be back this afternoon, boy. Keep this other guy out of trouble, will you?"

Jake and I spent the day hunting through the timber and sage close to my old log house. Most of my possessions remained in it. I figured the roundtrip about eight or nine miles. We picked up a ruffed grouse on the way, and I missed one on the hike back. With two already in the refrigerator, our supper would be my favorite.

After mustering out of the army and moving back into civilian life, my interest in hunting and big-game rifles plummeted. Most of my weapons were given to my brother and his kids—a few I sold. Those remaining could be considered defensive weapons with few exceptions. They were mostly semi-auto rifles and handguns. My Anaconda and a spare, the Ruger Red Label shotgun, and another I rarely shot since its purchase was for hunting.

Knowing I enjoyed my .44 Magnum Colt, Scotty contacted me after learning of a rifle for sale in the same caliber. A throwback to the old west, the modern Marlin sported an octagon barrel and a receiver sight. I installed a leather sling and sighted in the long gun. Its accuracy potential startled and assured me any big game within its limited range didn't stand a chance.

I returned with a pack heavily laden with hunting ammunition, warm clothes, boots, and knives. Jake pointed a nervous grouse, but it flushed before I could hitch my pack and bring my shotgun to bear. I sent a Hail Mary hail of lead anyway, and was the recipient of a sour look delivered by the dog when I missed and was forced to call him off. He wasn't happy when I left him inside our home while I checked the sights on my rifle. Loaded with 240-grain soft points, five shots clustered an inch above the point of aim at a hundred yards. The soft recoil and deadly accuracy seemed to point to a good chance of a successful season.

* * *

Jules watched as I checked my gear. Deer season started the next morning. "Is Scotty guiding now?"

"Yeah." I stopped to remember the location he mentioned. "Packed a group into Falconberry Peak over a week ago. Why?"

She stared into space before answering. "I saw Robin at the grocery store after school. She was speaking to a couple I've never seen. Acted like she didn't know me. I started to say something, but she only glanced and turned her back."

"Doesn't sound like she's quite so polite without Scotty around. Want me to say something?"

"Oh, gosh, no. I don't want him mad at her. There's probably a good explanation."

"Suit yourself." I left for the spare bedroom and returned with my sleeping bag and packboard.

Julia sat straighter, plainly startled. "Are you planning on staying overnight somewhere?"

34

I stopped. "Yeah. It's deer season. I might lay out if I'm too far from the truck when it gets dark."

"But I thought you'd shoot one of the whitetails hanging around the place."

Her surprise made me chuckle. I should have been clearer about my seriousness when it came to filling our freezers. "The little bucks we see along our driveway wouldn't produce more than thirty-five, maybe forty pounds of meat. I'm looking for one yielding closer to a hundred, maybe one-twenty-five. Seventy-five or more for us, twenty-five for Mom. She doesn't eat a lot of animal protein these days but still loves venison."

"You'll be back on Sunday for sure?"

"Yep. I'll hunt my way in until dark, then ease out in the morning. Might find a nice one way back at first light."

Jules leaped to her feet, startling Jake. "Then, I'm going." she said. "It's okay, isn't it?" She pushed a stray lock of blonde hair behind an ear.

"Sure. Might get cold up around eight thousand feet, but your bag ought to keep you warm enough."

Mom was happy to look after Jake. We dropped him by before five, and already out of bed, she answered the door immediately. Still dark when we parked on Pine Creek, we shouldered our packs and started up the steep hillside. Although eager to help, I kept Julia's burden to something manageable. Mine went about forty pounds, my wife's only eighteen. Dressed in boots, heavy jeans, shirts, and coat, I worried my lean wife might struggle. Loading the Marlin with ten rounds to help with the rifle's balance, I still carried my Anaconda and six spare cartridges on my belt.

The area I planned to hunt was rough with huge cliffs, timbered ravines, and plenty of high open country filled with sage. As light footed as she was, I hardly noticed Jules behind me. Her steps barely registering to my ear. We both carried binoculars and planned to use our eyes more than our feet. She toted only her .38 Special, sulking after I said we didn't need the noise of her new shotgun. When I mentioned her suppressed .22s, she firmly refused to consider either rifle or pistol. As she put it, "both are for work, not play."

We stopped a half hour after daylight, so I could point out a bear. A color-phased bruin, the front was half cinnamon with black hindquarters. It ripped a log apart with long nails searching for grubs. Watching it through binoculars a half-mile away, we could see incredible strength as it moved on to turn boulders over.

My rifle carries easy. Narrow with flat sides and a muzzle heavy balance, I barely noticed its weight. A blue grouse flushed from a few feet overhead when we least expected it, raining pine needles on us. Jules kept her squeak to a minimum and jerked my sleeve. "I almost peed my pants," she whispered breathlessly with a giggle. I smiled and nodded, pointing to my chest with a thumb. Someday a grouse exploding from its hiding place might well give me a heart attack.

I passed on three fair bucks—much to Julia's chagrin—before we stopped for the evening. The trio were nice four-point muleys, but none with the heavy mature body I hoped for. "Need something bigger if we can," I said. We each munched on ham and cheese sandwiches packed for supper. With temperatures dropping quickly, our bags were already unrolled and zipped together providing a suitable place to sit. Our night would be spent beneath the stars instead of inside a tent to lessen my load. A great horned owl hooted behind us and another answered from the timber below.

Jules kept her voice low. "To think you spent your childhood doing what we are now, while I lived in a Californian suburb. Dad didn't often hunt, and we never camped." She sighed and leaned against me. "I love the smell of sage and the wind roaring overhead."

"Mom and Dad didn't mind if I disappeared for a week or more, long as I told them where I planned to go and when I should return. Mostly I rode a horse but hiked occasionally like we are now." Mom sold the last of our horses while I did army tours. "Once, between my junior and senior years in high school, I took my saddle horse and two pack mules and rode back into the Middle Fork of the Salmon. Spent over two months exploring."

"What?" Julia jerked her head away to look at me. "You're talking potentially a hundred miles. I've heard the kids talk at school. Who went with you?"

Her question made me chuckle. "I went alone."

"Melissa let you go by yourself?" Her voice rose when she couldn't wrap her head around a kid set adrift in the wilderness.

"Sure. She helped me get ready and decide what to pack. I needed a lot of food, so I took both mules." Memories of the trip made me smile. "Got pictures stored somewhere at Mom's. "Ate a lot of fish and more than a few rabbits toward the end."

"Oh, you were so lucky. Two months traveling and exploring on horseback...were you ever afraid?"

I remembered driving a giant black bear from my food stores one morning. My old .30-30 felt like a peashooter. "Yeah, more than once." I explained facing off with the obstinate boar bruin and firing four rounds into the dirt in front of him. Jule's face was rapt with excitement.

"A kid, all alone. I don't know what I would have done."

I knew exactly how J would have approached the situation. She would have stuck the muzzle of her suppressed .22 in his ear if he got too close and killed him. "You'd have done the same." I wrapped an arm around her shoulders against the cool breeze and pulled her to me. "He wanted my food. It was him or me."

"Did you get lost?" she asked.

"Sure, I did. Plotted my course with a map and compass, but funny ridges occasionally caused me to stray off course. Remember, I carried enough food and supplies to stay comfortable. A few days here or there while I made corrections made the trip fun. I was never really lost...just misplaced." My smile was as modest as I could make it.

"Wow. I can't imagine. To think I once considered you a farmer who knew his way around tractors and seeds and little else."

Feeling chilled, we readied ourselves for sleep, wearing our long john tops, skivvies, and socks to bed. When Jules turned to her side and faced away, I wrapped an arm around her belly and pulled her to me. Her shivering stopped quickly with our combined warmth. My hand wandered over her right shoulder, and I could feel the lesion from her last bullet wound under the fabric. Still red and angry, scar tissue occasionally pulled and hurt her. She didn't complain, but I occasionally saw the evidence of her discomfort when she winced and rotated her shoulder.

I woke when Jules tried to slip from our sleeping bag without disturbing me. Checking my watch when she disappeared through the timber, I noted the time, 5:48. We could practically set our clocks with the regularity she woke each morning. Almost always half past five. I flipped the bag open on her side when she reappeared. "Did I wake you?" she asked.

"About time to get up anyway," I whispered. "Gonna be daylight in a little while."

"Sorry. My bladder wasn't going to last much longer."

Mine lasted another forty-five minutes until daybreak neared. Looking for movement as twilight gave way to dawn, we observed a neighboring ridge five hundred yards to the west, looking for movement as the morning grew lighter. A coyote appeared at the crest and trotted at an angle to disappear below us. "My turn." I opened the bag on my side and rolled out. Slipping into jeans and tugging my boots on, I stood to belt my crossdraw holster in front of my hip. I left the rifle but took my binoculars. No telling what I might see while doing my business. "Back in a couple minutes." I bent to give her rear end a light slap before jumping out of range and chuckling to myself. Julia would find a way to even the score.

Wanting to see the east ridge as it became more visible, I cut through open pines to stop at the edge. The hillside where I stood dipped another quarter mile before rising to a steep pinnacle. Using binoculars to sweep the area from top to bottom, movement in the low swale caught my eye. A nice mule deer buck fed through sage deep enough to lose himself. He stopped to lift his head and magnificent antlers to check the wind. Seemingly satisfied, he fed up the slope.

Rather than lose sight of him if he changed directions, I waited as he climbed. After reaching the rock wall, the buck opted to skirt along the base and disappeared from sight. Keyed to the hunt as the sound of a twig broke behind me, I spun to face Julia who grinned from ear to ear, knowing she caught me unaware. I covered my lips with an index finger and waved her closer.

"What's up?" She mouthed, turning from jokester to predator in a blink.

I breathed words into her ear. "Watched a nice buck feed over the top. He disappeared a few seconds ago."

"Want me to run to camp for your rifle?" she whispered back in the same manner, then turned, ready to sprint.

"No time. Gotta go after him now."

We reached the general area where the buck disappeared in fifteen minutes. I stopped as we neared the top to catch my breath and draw my revolver. The big muley might be bedded nearby or gone over the next ridge, making it imperative to be ready. My breathing and heartbeat slowing, I caught Julia's eye and nodded.

The hillside wound farther than we were able to see from a distance. A long circular trail along the rock base disappeared. Taking short steps to be sure of my footing, a glance behind assured me Jules followed. Any noise she created was impossible to decipher. Although a double action revolver, I carried the .44 ready to cock with my thumb and squeeze the trigger single action.

Fingers plucked at my shirt. I stopped and slowly turned. Julia's eyes were big as she barely moved her head to indicate the slope beneath us. Browsing nearly a hundred yards below, he fed at an angle taking him farther away. Fishing earplugs from my pocket, I crammed them in and sat hastily. Bracing my forearms between my knees, I set the front blade on his shoulder and squeezed. It startled me when the gun went off, but I didn't miss the sound of a bullet slapping flesh. The buck leaped forward to vanish.

Julia stayed with me as I picked my way down the steep ridge, doing my best not to start a landslide and tumble. On arriving where he stood when I shot, we saw indications of a solid hit. Judging by the volume of blood, he didn't go far. Jules stood on a boulder to reconnoiter and pointed. "Right there! Dawson, he's right there!"

He didn't go far. My bullet entered behind the shoulder—perhaps a third of the way down—to exit his brisket after traversing at an extreme angle. The buck was everything we wanted and needed with plenty for Mom, too. Five points to a side—six including brow tines—I'd harvested few deer bigger with high powered rifles. "Just what we were lookin' for." I smoothed hair around the entrance wound and patted the buck.

"If you can wait before cleaning it, I'll hike back to camp and move our gear over here," Julia said. "Shouldn't be a problem. Besides, I'd like to get some pictures with my phone." She stood above me and waited.

"Think you can do it without hurting yourself?"

In her mind, no job seemed too big. "Sure, I can." She raised an arm to make a muscle. "See?" Rather than wait, she crawled a few feet to stand again and see better. "I'll be..." A rock exploded next to Julia, showering her with shards. I heard the far-off roar of a rifle as she shrieked and tumbled down the steep slope.

Chapter III

"Jules!" I left the buck and scrambled up to where my wife lay motionless. Not more than thirty yards above me, I reached where she'd crumpled and checked her neck for a pulse. It seemed strong under my fingers, and I gently rolled her to me. Her eyes were closed, and I could see a bloody mess in her hair. Red ran down her cheek and into her collar. "Jules? Julia?" Rather than move her more, I stroked her face.

Her eyes fluttered and opened. "Oh..." She squirmed and clutched her head, feeling for the source of pain. "What...what happened?"

"I think a bullet hit the rock behind you." I raised my head to look for a potential shooter. Sighting along the short scar on the boulder, I guessed it originated from the far ridge across from our camp. At not quite a second from impact to incoming boom, I judged the range to be at least eight hundred yards. Sweeping the area quickly with binoculars, I could see no movement or shapes out of the ordinary. Either a wild shot gone astray or a near miss. I preferred to think the former, but I needed to beware of the latter.

"My head is killing me." She took her hand away and saw blood. "Am I going to live, Nurse Ratched?"

Taking great care as I checked, a deep laceration above her ear seemed to be the largest wound. Not particularly long nor wide, it appeared deep. My clean kerchief combined with steady pressure stymied more blood loss. "I think so." I tried to lighten the seriousness of our situation. "It could get expensive if I'm forced to take you on as a patient again."

"I'll pay anything to be home in my own bed," Jules groaned. "My head's spinning." She rolled away and vomited.

41

"I've got you." I helped Julia to her hands and knees and braced her. Eating only a small supper and nothing since waking, very little came up. I held her in my arms after she finished, keeping pressure against her head and repeatedly checking the injury. Lids drooped until closing eyes alarmed me. "Jules?" I shook gently. "Wake up, honey."

"I'm okay. Just resting." They fluttered open, and she attempted to focus.

"Julia?" My growl sounded menacing even to me. "Open your eyes."

She struggled to sit forward, and I helped her into a comfortable position. "Give me a minute. I'll be fine."

Perhaps the toughest human I've had the privilege of knowing, she once survived on an island after suffering a beating brutal enough to kill most people and being thrown from a high balcony. Weeks of scavenging for food and water while suffering a broken arm followed with both eyes swollen almost closed through much of the ordeal.

Shifting to where I could squat next to her, I dabbed at the gouge on the left side of her skull. Blood matted her hair, making it difficult to determine its severity after my initial assessment. "We'd better hike to the truck right now. You need a doctor."

Although I could see her eyes weren't focusing properly, she turned an angry look on me. "I'm fine, but you'll have to get our gear. We're not leaving so much meat behind." Her head bobbled on her shoulders.

Arguing would do little good. Instead, I eviscerated the deer and kept close tabs on Julia. Her eyes stayed open while she watched me work. She seemed to gain strength with each passing minute. Keeping pressure on the wound for a while, she finally set my kerchief aside. "Bleeding stopped?" I asked." Her nod was slow. "Will you be okay while I hike back to camp? Should be back in less than thirty minutes if I hustle."

"I'll be fine."

"All right, keep your thirty-eight handy...just in case."

Leaving my woman behind bothered me. The shot came too close. No matter what she said, Julia needed medical help. From what I could see, the largest wound needed stitches. I took off at a shuffling jog as I worked my way down from the promontory, breaking into a run as I went up the other side. Camp was exactly as we left it with no signs of intrusion. Five minutes to pack went quickly before I hustled in and out of the swale between us to where I left her.

She gripped the revolver in her fist when I appeared over the rise. "Don't think you get extra credit for coming in ahead of time, mister. What'd you do? Sprint?" Jules broke into cautious laughter at my guilty look. "You did, didn't you?"

"Here," I answered gruffly, handing my rifle over. "Gotta skin and bone the deer. You keep any bad guys off our backs."

Julia made a crappy sentry. Instead of staying where I left her, she scooted down the hill on her rear to watch. Boning a game animal is simple to someone who's done it a hundred times. She found it fascinating as I skinned one side, removing all the flesh and dropping it into my meat sack. After performing the same ritual on the opposite side, all remaining was lashing the pouch to my pack frame. I could carry the head and antlers in one hand.

I found the load much heavier than expected when I stood. Good, the deer produced more meat than I hoped. "Sling the rifle over my shoulder." With a grip close to eye guards and Jules's pack in the other hand, a little more weight wouldn't make much difference.

"No. Give me my knapsack, Dawson." I heard the dangerous tone in her voice. "Don't worry about me...I can handle it."

"You're hurt," I said. "It's all downslope from here. Easy peasy."

"You're not going to carry everything, buster." She took a step forward as if she planned to strike me with the butt of my rifle. "Now give it."

Damned if she wasn't right. Darned woman carried her gear and my rifle without falling behind. My load of over a hundred-fifty pounds made it tough to shake her. I kept us either inside timber or with a line of trees between us and from where I figured the shot originated. While taking almost a day to hike in, we reached my truck in less than three hours. My legs shook from the effort, and Julia's complexion mirrored clouds overhead—gray as a ghost. I helped her into the truck after unloading our gear in the bed and slamming the tailgate.

Forced to drive up the narrow road another mile before turning around, we met an SUV on its way down. I took the snap off my revolver in case this turned out to be our shooter. We both let out shaky laughs when two heavyset guys chatting happily waved as they passed. Behind the pair for miles before getting bars on my phone, I finally called Mom.

"Tell Julia Jake's fine," she said before I could speak. She knew my wife worried about her pointer.

"Need your help, Mom." I shot a glance to Jules as we hit the main road leading to the highway. "Julia's been hurt. I killed a buck and need to leave it at your place on the way to the hospital. Can you keep Jake another night and take care of the meat? We boned it, so if there's room in the extra basement fridge..." I trailed off, while avoiding the largest potholes.

Her instant alarm warmed my soul. "Of course, honey. How bad is she?"

"Head's split open..." Mom's gasp was loud. "Just the scalp. Don't mean her skull."

"How bad is it?" she asked again.

"Enough to see a doc, but not so terrible I don't have time to drop the deer off. I'm worried they may keep her overnight or longer."

"I don't want a doctor," came a growl from the far side of the bench seat. "Get me home, Ratched."

My nickname came after Julia returned from a shootout with gang members dealing drugs. She killed seven but caught a bullet in the exchange, and I became a fulltime medic and houseboy, learning of her employment as an assassin. During the couple months I stayed, she took to calling me Nurse Ratched in honor of the evil head nurse in *One Flew Over the Cuckoo's Nest.*

Dropping our meat off at Mom's took only a few minutes. She took one look at Julia and told me if I didn't hustle, she'd do it herself or call an ambulance. "You need to be checked for a concussion, young lady."

44

My mother was right. The emergency room physician immediately wheeled her away for x-rays. By the time I was allowed into her room, Julia's head was bandaged, and she was resting comfortably. I recognized the doc as one who took care of my wife's broken arm after her final kill for The Company. "Doctor Wells," I said, holding out my hand. His grip was stronger than I remembered. We went to school together, although I graduated a couple years before him.

"Hey, Dawson. How's Melissa? Still as healthy as the last time we saw her?"

Mom rarely went to a clinic. She seemed healthy as the proverbial horse. "She'll outlive us all, Gary."

He was finished with niceties. "We shaved the immediate area and got a good look at what we were up against. She took a hard fall. I removed rock fragments from her scalp. Seven stitches will dissolve over time. Keep the bandage dry, and she should heal nicely. However, we'd like to keep Julia overnight as a precaution. X-rays didn't find signs of bruises or clotting in her brain, but a concussion can still be dangerous, especially since she lost consciousness."

"Whatever you think, Doc." I glanced at my bandaged wife. Her glare meant she didn't agree.

He turned to his patient. "Just for tonight, Mrs. Pelletier." She didn't answer, so he shrugged and left at my nod.

"I can't afford a night in the hospital," she grumped the moment her door closed.

"You've got good medical through the school. I'll pay any deductible." I don't know who she thought she was fooling. Julia could afford her stay even without insurance. I fished my cellphone from a pocket when I heard its muffled ring. "Hello, Aunt Bess."

"Melissa called to say Julia's been hurt, and you're at the hospital. Is she okay?" My mother's sister depended on her go-to substitute teacher.

"Slipped and banged her head on a rock. You know she's accident prone. Doctor Wells patched her but she has to spend the night. She's

45

not happy about it. You'd better find someone else to fill her spot tomorrow."

"Will she be okay for Tuesday, or shall I find someone for the week?"

I turned to Julia after reassuring my aunt and ending the call. "She expects you on Tuesday if and only if you're feeling better." I caught a nearby chair and dragged it bedside. "Are you doing all right?"

Jules reached for my hand, intertwining our fingers. "Yeah. Head feels like someone used it for a drum," she said a wan smile. "You might as well go home and get some sleep. I'm sure I have a long night ahead. They plan to wake me every hour."

"Do your best to be friendly, little dove. They have your best interests at heart." I kissed the back of her hand and stood.

"Of course." She puckered her lips and waited. "I love you," she said after I pulled away.

"I love you, too." She still smiled when I glanced back before the door closed. The hall was empty, and only one man sat at the nurse's station. I waved as I passed and ducked into a bathroom. Scrolling through the numbers on my phone, I placed a call. A familiar voice answered immediately. "Dawson?"

"Yeah, Al, it's me."

"Were you expecting more out of last quarter's profits?"

As the silent partner in his business, I never complained. If the taxes on Mom's place were paid with a few dollars left over for both of us, I was fine with my share. My problem revolved around needing advice on how to handle the money we earned. "You know me better than to whine over finances, old buddy."

When I didn't go on, he asked after a moment, "How's G-dub?" His nickname for Julia when doing wetwork.

"She's why I'm calling. I think it's starting again."

* * *

Rather than go home after our conversation, I used a rear exit for janitors. I stayed in the shadows and waited for any movement. After fifteen minutes passed, I edged along the building to where I could see the parking lot and my truck. I kept vapor in the cold night air to a minimum by taking shallow breaths through my nostrils. Nothing to give away my position.

Headlights were far and few between on a late Sunday evening. The front entry to the hospital locked, I took a position where my pickup and the emergency doors were visible. A custodian left the warmth to toss garbage in nearby dumpster. She didn't notice me, although passing within a few feet. It caused me to snicker to myself. Julia's alter ego would be proud.

A newer Dodge pickup cruised past the parking lot three times before turning in. It drove through slowly, stopping in front of my old Ford. Light from overhead lamps didn't help me see through heavily tinted windows. The muffled snap on my holster seemed loud in the chill night air.

Fifty yards away, I readied myself for a charge to the driver-side window until another car entered the lot. Without enough room to pass, the Dodge grudgingly gave up its position only after the other driver waited. Watching the truck turn north after exiting, I hurried to mine. Old glow plugs took longer to heat while I waited to start the thirty-year-old diesel. The motor coughed to life the moment the dash light went out. It bothered me to leave Jules without extra eyes watching over her, but I raced after the Dodge with the hopes of learning who was inside.

On the outskirts of town, I saw taillights ahead and slowed to barely keep them in sight. I noted the driver kept speed at the limit without going over. The occupant or occupants proceeded cautiously. Brakes applied at North Fork caused me to pull back. The pickup turned into the RV park behind the general store and restaurant. Stopping along the highway, I noted the fifth wheel it parked next to. I prefer to bivouac in a sleeping bag thrown on a flat place. This person and any companions stayed in a place nicer than our home.

To investigate further tempted me. However, my wife remained alone and defenseless. If I made a mistake following the truck to North

Fork, she might well be in danger. My return to town went much quicker. I parked in the same place, backed in as I prefer.

Doc Wells noticed me hurrying down the hall. "Dawson?" I stopped at his call and waited. "Visiting hours are over. Is there something I can help you with?"

"Dropped my wallet somewhere, Doc" I answered, slapping at my back pocket. "Hoped it was in Julia's room. Mind if I take a look?"

He winked. "Make it fast. Staff doesn't appreciate family members roaming around."

Jules lay sound asleep when I entered. Goddamn, she looked tiny— even frail—in the hospital bed. I used the same chair as before where I could see her face best, so relaxed and serene. I brushed a blonde lock back from where it fell over her eyes. She shifted and tried to wake before giving in to dreams again.

The door opened before I got fifteen minutes alone with her. A custodian entered, and we both froze after making eye contact. "Dawson?" Don't know why she framed my name as a question. We'd gone out for years before Nancy broke my heart twice, but I'd have endured the pain a thousand times if it always brought me to Julia. Since our last meeting—unexpected for her—I'd not spoken to her again. Didn't plan to start and merely nodded. "You're not supposed to be here." If she planned to be in the room, I sure as hell didn't need to stay. I replaced the chair and brushed past the woman I'd once professed my love to. Reckon if anything made me feel better, Julia made Nancy look like an old mare rode hard and put up wet.

Temperatures were in the thirties when I retreated to my pickup with a tall cup of coffee and no plans to start the engine. I kept a spare sleeping bag under the backseat. Although made for warm summer months, it felt comfortable enough to continue my vigil. I cracked both windows for fresh air. Not even an ambulance got called out overnight, and only two cars left before daylight. Nancy drove one and looked right at me when she passed. She started to wave and thought better of it.

* * *

Julia leaned forward in the narrow bed to cut into a pancake when I entered at the first minute of visiting hours. She dropped her fork and did a double-take "Holy hell, what happened to you?"

I wasn't as young as I used to be. At eighteen months until forty, I no longer pulled all-nighters with aplomb. "Pretty bad?"

"If I didn't know better, I'd say you're coming down with the flu." Her brow furrowed before grinning and chuckling. "You didn't go home last night, did you? Bet you slept in the truck."

"Half right. I didn't go home."

"Half?" Jules thought for a moment before a disgusted look. "You didn't sleep. Kept the boogeyman off my back, huh?"

"Something like it." I used a sip of her coffee for mouthwash before swallowing. "How 'bout a kiss?" Our teeth clicked together with both of us grinning.

I sprung her a few minutes after nine. Still a little lightheaded, she held my elbow with a death grip. Giving her a little boost from behind into the truck, I patted her butt before she sat. Her wink let me know I wasn't in trouble. One thing about my wife, she didn't mind me taking the occasional liberty.

I thought about stopping for a quick meal and decided against it. We turned north toward home instead of into a Salmon restaurant. A homecooked meal would taste better and give me something to do. "You're awfully quiet," Julia said after we left city limits. "You need sleep after you eat a good breakfast."

My kneejerk reaction was to keep any suspicions and fears to myself while she recovered. However, I probably wasn't the target, although I very well could be. A secondary objective for sure. I drew a deep breath and reached across to take her hand. "Jules, I don't think the shot was accidental. I'm pretty sure someone missed." There. Out in the open and let her make the big decisions.

"Yeah." She sighed and looked out the window at bottomland covered in cows. "I came to the same conclusion last night." Her sad smile displayed her love. "Couldn't stay asleep without you in bed...and nurses checking all hours of the night. Gave me plenty of time to think. I'm surprised I don't look as tired as you."

I darted a glance from the road and oncoming traffic. "What is it you want to do?"

One thing about Julia is she doesn't mince words. "I should've never trusted The Company. I'm going to kill 'em all." Her decision wasn't unexpected. What I feared for most was our future. Even a few years to enjoy married life hadn't been afforded us, and it made me angry.

"We're gonna kill 'em all," I said. North Fork and the RV park came into sight, and I slowed for the lower speed limit. "Get down," I urged. "Unbuckle and put your head in my lap." Another thing about Jules is she also doesn't argue or make a fuss when something's important. She quickly followed directions while I glanced into the RV park. The Dodge sat where it did when I left the night before. I let her sit up after accelerating. "Describe the couple Robin talked to when she ignored you."

"What was all that about?" she countered.

"Answer my question first."

"Both in their thirties...my age or a little older. The male's hair is a sandy flattop with the sides shaved. Maybe Scotty's height but rangier. Narrow shoulders with wider hips. The tail of a dragon tattoo on his neck disappears beneath his left collar. Made me think of a fighter."

No fear in her. "The woman?"

"Almost as tall as Robin and the man. Slighter build with shoulder-length brown hair and chocolate eyes. Appeared athletic with big boobs and muscular thighs."

Leave it to my modestly endowed wife to notice chest size. "Did you see what they drove?"

"Nope." She stopped and appeared to be thinking while I turned into our driveway and crossed the metal cattle guard. "They kept talking while I went in and were gone when I left."

"What about your job? Planning to continue teaching while this is going on?"

Jules stared out the side window at our property while we idled down the drive. "I'm torn. Teaching is my dream, yet whomever this is might pick me off on the routine drive to school and home, if they aren't willing to do it in my classroom." She glanced back to me. "Why'd you ask me to get down when we drove through North Fork?"

"Followed a suspicious Dodge there last night after it cruised through the hospital lot and stopped in front of my truck. Couldn't see through its windows to make an identification. Another car seemed to make the driver nervous and take off. I followed to see where they went." I parked next to the garage and drew my Anaconda. I'd stashed Julia's .38 in the glovebox while she stayed overnight in the hospital. "Your gun's in there." She nodded, and I reached across to open it. Like anyone whose life depended on a firearm, she needed to see it wasn't tampered with. All six chambers remained loaded as usual. I left her in the truck with her head down while I unlocked our front door and checked the interior. Julia waited until I returned to help her inside. We took the porch steps slowly. "Mind if I make a suggestion you may not like?"

I got her settled into her favorite recliner before she answered. "Nope. Shoot." She snickered at the double entendre.

"Take the rest of this week off. I'll call Aunt Bess to tell her you're not feeling well enough. I've already called Al to see what he can dig up. There may be a chance this is nothing. Might know for sure by next week. Keep away from windows, stay inside, and heal. I'll take care of the critters and gather eggs." Almost twenty of her Cornish bantams were ready to butcher, but I could handle the job alone.

"You're right, I don't like it." Jules tipped her head back and closed her eyes.

"Got a better idea?"

"Huh uh."

"Can I call Aunt Bess and tell her you need the week?"

"I'll do it."

"No, I think it'd sound less like hooky coming from me."

"Okay. You know your aunt better than me." She opened her eyes and focused on me. "I need you to get hold of your friend...Rich, isn't it?...and find another Tactical Mark IV. I want it threaded for a suppressor."

Her request surprised me. "If there's an issue with yours, I can take it to a gunsmith here in Salmon or in Missoula."

"No, no problem with my work gun. I want an extra. Also, another five thousand rounds of standard velocity CCI .22s." She stared into space, considering things I could only guess at. While I killed in war for my nation, the idea of her previous employment was foreign to me.

No way was I going to question her. Already, I noticed a hard edge growing. She was making the switch from an ordinary homebody who educates children to an exceptional stalker who eradicates bad people. I stared hard into her eyes knowing they'd seen terrible things from identifying her family's bodies to placing a bullet into the brain of those in the drug trade. "Okay, might take a while. Want me to check with Scotty when he returns? He might know of where to find a used model."

"No." An icy gaze swung to me. I forced a swallow into a dry throat, knowing who I locked eyes with. "Not until we get a little more idea of what's going on and who Robin Dickerson is." No thaw in her stare. "I know he's been your friend a long time, but when it comes to this woman and anyone she knows, Scotty damn well better figure out what side he's on."

* * *

Aunt Bess didn't argue, and it turned out I wasn't fabricating an excuse. Julia spent two days in bed with Jake next to her after I retrieved him. If Jules didn't feel well, her four-legged friend knew it and stayed close for the duration. I also liberated about ten pounds of fresh venison from Mom's refrigerator. She promised to cut and wrap the rest for me, grinding not only burger and canning scraps but mixing her signature breakfast sausage, too.

I was up at five on Wednesday, and Julia and her pal followed at five-thirty. Jake padded past and waited patiently for me to open the front door. He ran outside to check his markers and pee, while Julia veered to the bathroom. Both reappeared about the same time—Jake through the door left cracked—his mistress wearing a robe pulled tight. "Morning, lady." I held her coffee cup out of reach until I got my morning kiss. "Deer steak, eggs, and toast. Scale of one to ten: how hungry are you?"

"Ten," came her immediate answer. She sat at the table gripping her steaming cup and opened her laptop.

I cut our venison thick and planned to cook it medium-rare. Jules stayed quiet while I worked. Rain fell through the night, picking up in volume when I rolled out of bed. Our local radio station forecasted showers into the next week. I reckoned it fell as snow on the ridgetops and was happy with the early season buck we took. "Read anything interesting?" I freshened her coffee and set a plate nearby before sitting.

"Yeah." She hardly took her eyes away from the screen, sipping absently. "My money manager wants me to diversity further. Put more money into oil stock since the government opened the arctic reserves and placed more sanctions on Iran."

Julia feared the government. Perhaps a more apt description would be she didn't trust different administrations to always have the people's best interest at heart. A significant portion of her funds were kept in cash at our house, safely hidden in the concealed root cellar.

Two thick steaks and three bantam eggs fried sunny-side up almost wrestled my attention away. "How much is she talkin'?"

"Quarter million." Julia delivered the amount as though a normal 401K.

"What? Two-hundred-fifty thousand dollars?"

"You expected rubles?"

"Jules, it's a lot of money."

She shrugged. "Sounds like I could triple it in a year."

"Or lose it all."

"Yep." She closed the computer and doused her eggs with hot sauce. I waited for her to try the meat. She cut into it—cooked rare for just her—and dredged it through horseradish. Her face lit at the first bite. "From our deer?"

"Yep. Have you decided what you're gonna do?"

"Not yet. If it's war, we'll need every penny. If it turns out we've made a mistake, then yeah, it's not like we're dependent on it."

"Go ahead and invest, then. If we have a fight on our hands, I'll fund it." Jules and I hadn't yet gotten into my personal finances other than Mom and I were comfortable.

"Thanks, but no thanks." She crammed a bloody chunk of venison into her mouth with enough horseradish on it to make me wince and pointed a fork at me. "I brought this fight with me." She took time to finish chewing and swallowed before washing it all down with coffee. "Keep your money for more important things, like taking care of Melissa."

I stared for a moment, doing my best to keep my cool. "We can afford it. Mom hardly spends anything, besides, there's not much I need anymore."

Julia knew she offended me. "Dawson..." She looked across her cup while formulating thoughts. "...if the worst comes to pass, and this is all-out war, it's going to cost thousands. Hundreds of thousands. Granted, I will force The Company to reimburse me for costs incurred, but—"

My impromptu bray stopped her. "You intend for The Company to pay for its own destruction?"

Dangerous eyes glinted. "Absolutely. They already owe me for seven." I guess she noticed my blank look. "The man and woman behind the house. Three more at your place, then the gray man and Manny. I've thought about this a lot, Dawson. Not only will I bleed them, I plan to see their veins run green, too."

Chapter IV

We met Al on Lost Trail Pass in the Bitterroot Mountains—the border between Idaho and Montana. My longtime friend sulked when I said he needn't arrive at our home in his helicopter again and raise suspicions. He flies the damned thing like a racecar, and I preferred him to be our secret weapon. We parked on a side road out of sight of U.S. Highway 93 and waited. Jules and I finished most of one thermos of coffee and two sandwiches from our lunch before he appeared. Jake relaxed quietly in the back after letting him out earlier to wet the bushes.

Arriving in a four-door Dodge Ram 3500 long bed with four-wheel drive, nothing could have been more conspicuous than the cherry-red pickup sporting a matching canopy. We hopped out of my battered Ford and waited for him to park. Temperatures were cold at the end of October, freezing nearby mud puddles. Patches of snow from earlier in the week were still visible under the mixed pine and fir.

Pushing fifty and bearing wounds incurred under my command in Iraq, he appeared to be as tough and spry as ever. "First Sergeant Allen R. Fryxell reporting for duty, sir!"

My hurried return salute wasn't as crisp as his, but I needed him to drop his telltale hand. "Knock it off, Al. Tryin' to get me IDed and picked off by some lurking neighborhood sniper?" While not in a war-torn country, I only half kidded. If I were right, someone followed us once before.

He ignored me for Julia. "How you doing, kiddo?" Al hesitated a moment to assess her reaction before administering a bearhug. He pulled back to better see her bandage. "Hear you came close the other day."

She shrugged. "Close, but no cigar. I'm as good as can be expected. You?"

"Finer than frog hair, young lady. Now, what's this I hear you need another work gun?"

Jules looked at me in surprise. I hadn't mentioned I skipped asking Richie Shrike to find the pistol she wanted. Al was our guy when it came to locating hard-to-procure items, although a suppressed .22/45 was legal if you got the proper paperwork filed. Julia didn't; however, I did. "I'm afraid I do, Al. I suppose you can tell me better if we've gone off half-cocked, or there's nothing to a near-miss from a stray."

Al's voice and shoulders dropped with compassion. "You're worth two million, Julia."

My growl was spontaneous. If one of those responsible for putting such a price on her head stood nearby, I'd have torn the bastard's throat out with my teeth. "You got names?"

Al's vicious smile hadn't changed much since the taking of Fallujah. "I have names, addresses, ages, genders, even races. You want to start at the top and work down, or vice versa? Even their law firm is downloaded in my files."

"The one calling the shots." Al and I turned our attention to Julia. "I want the top guy, then the operational money manager. From there it's open season."

"Found a bit of interesting news since your call. Seems not everyone in The Company wants G-dub dead. Quite a bit of infighting went into naming her as a client. More than a few stepped away from the organization after the smoke cleared. Not sure it's over. I catch rumblings here and there."

I didn't miss the savageness on Julia's face. "Two million. That's a pretty good start. Let's see if I can get it bumped to at least five before I run out of targets."

Al opened the backdoor of his truck. "C'mon over here." He reached and drew out a soft long gun case for me, then a hard pistol case to Jules. "Go on...take a look."

"Oh, hell, Al. This is your gun." I remembered when he purchased the Sig Sauer MPX 9mm Carbine. Although with a short twelve-and-a-half-inch barrel, the suppressor extended it past the legal minimum if it was permanent. I'd shot it more than once and liked the little rifle. Made for close-up work, it was the perfect firearm for facing multiple opponents. No scope—iron sights only—I noted the new laser unit and flashlight mounted on fore-end picatinny rails.

"Used to be my emergency rifle when I flew. Never used it. Besides, I got a new one." While he reached inside the driver's door, I watched Jules going over a new Ruger Mark IV with a factory suppressor. "Check this out." Al handed me a 1927 A1 Thompson machinegun in .45ACP. "Figured overwhelming firepower was more important than keeping quiet. I keep a half dozen thirty-round sticks and two fifty-round drums handy."

"What do I owe you, Al?" Julia asked. "For both. I don't have cash with me, but I'll get a check in the mail when we get home." She'd already screwed the suppressor off and checked both its threads and ease of removal.

"Nothing." I didn't miss the anger in his voice or the flash in his eye.

"No, that's not—"

"I said nothing, and I mean nothing. Do me a favor, girl. Kill as many of these dirty bastards as you can, and let God sort out who goes where, okay? It'll be payment enough."

She nodded her agreement. "Where am I going first? Can you tell me where their headquarters are located?"

"Two different answers, girlie." One thing about Al—he wasn't anywhere near PC. "If you're looking for their headquarters, it's in Chicago. Should you want to cut off the snake's head to start, plan on traveling to Mobile, Alabama."

I heard disappointment in her voice. "So far apart? Is there a money manager?" A shift in the slight breeze blew hair into her face, and she pushed it behind both ears.

"These assholes are spread across the country." Al spit on a chunk of ice. "I've listened to both phone and conference calls. From LA to Miami and Seattle to Portland, Maine. Near as I can tell, thirty-four bigwigs call the shots, each with his or her area of control. Not every state is represented. I think one woman identifies targets for termination in Vermont, New Hampshire, and Maine. I've confirmed twelve in New York and D.C., with another five in California."

"Thirty-four, huh?" The idea of so many made my head hurt.

"Plus managers. Don't forget what Manny did," Al said, darting a look at Julia.

She perceived our problem differently. "I expected more." I swear I heard disappointment in her tone while she sighted down the barrel of the handgun. "How many in their Chicago office?"

"They don't have offices, *per se*. Few physical meetings, although I've ascertained it's happened in the past. Usually a conference call, such as when they made the decision to name you for termination."

Their hierarchy made me curious. "How many left The Company? Or is thirty-four those who remained?"

"Sixty-six before the big exodus."

"Thirty-two bolted over Jules." I said. "Almost half."

"Sure you want to start at the top?" he asked Julia.

"No better place as far as I'm concerned. Why?"

"Because your mark left yesterday. Flew out of the country and won't be back for six weeks while meeting with officials in China."

Jules visibly deflated over the news before brightening. "I hope he comes back flush with success. Better chance he won't notice me until he's knocking on the pearly gates."

Al hesitated and kicked at a rock protruding from the frozen ground, working to dislodge it while he thought. "Got bad news for you there, girlie. He ain't a he. She's Antoinette Benton of Benton and Associates Fragrances and the woman who made the ultimate decision to see you dead."

* * *

Our drive home couldn't have been prettier. Vegetation with the exception of conifer timber turned a beautiful fall hue. In early afternoon, we wore coats and lowered the windows to smell the wind. Julia stayed quiet and handled her gun, getting to know it more intimately. A firearm is much like any other piece of equipment with quirks we need to learn if we hope to wield it correctly.

Jules finally rolled her side up, and I followed suit after noticing her shaking. "Since I'm a long-term sub, I'm going to take a leave of absence from school." Her teeth chattered. "Bess isn't going to be happy."

I turned the heater up and directed the vents at our feet and faces. "Been giving it some thought. If you don't mind, I'm going to lie in hopes of saving your job. She's my aunt. Maybe I'll have a chance to explain the why to her in a few years."

"Bess's family, honey. I hate to see you fibbing." As a habit, Jules was honest to the bitter end.

My mind was made up. "Nope, I'm gonna to tell her your head is hurting from the fall. It'll explain why we're gone regularly, seeing specialists."

She whistled. "Not bad. Still..."

My cell chirped, telling me two things. One, we were back within service. Two, Scotty was out of the hills. I answered rather than let it go to message. "You in the big money now, Wannabe Rich?"

"Naw, although one client left a big tip. Got him a wall hanger for sure," my friend informed me.

"On Falconberry?" It'd been years since I packed in by horseback to the peak.

"Yep. A nice buck fed on an open hillside late in the day. My hunter made a nice shot. Left me five crisp Franklins."

I whistled. Scotty relied on tips as much as his fees. Upkeep for horses and mules wasn't cheap. Most years, he barely scraped by, but I knew it was the life he loved and the reason he never found the right woman. Always gone from midsummer to midwinter. Plus, he didn't clear as much yearly as a mediocre bartender. "Nice job. How big of a buck?"

"Green score of one-eighty and change. A boxy four by four. Big and fat with a lot of good meat. Hey, are you and Julia going to be home this afternoon? I have pictures and want to toss an idea out, okay?"

"Running errands, but we'll be there soon."

"She's with you?"

"Yeah."

His sigh came loud and clear over the airwaves. "You're a lucky bastard. Finding her was a stroke of luck, old buddy." His next words made me curious. "I used to envy you."

I found myself nodding. "Can't disagree, man. The good Lord smiled on both of us for sure." Although she didn't interrupt our conversation, I didn't miss Julia's satisfied smirk.

We stopped at Mom's before going home to let her see Julia's head. If we were playing show-and-tell, I wanted to narrate our story. Afterward, our friend waited alone when we arrived at our place. Jake jumped to the ground the moment Jules opened the door, eager to check his markers around our property. "How's your shotgun treating you?" Scotty asked as Julia passed him on her way to the porch with our new cased loot.

"Good." She smiled. "I hear you had a successful trip."

Scotty couldn't hide his pleasure. "Yep. Clients were pleasant, good shots, and didn't complain after they tagged their bucks. We packed a lot of meat out. Overall, a great camp."

Jules left us to compare stories and keep lies to a minimum. Scotty showed me pictures of nice mule deer. The big one he mentioned looked especially impressive. "I ranged him at three hundred yards. One shot, and it was over."

I led him to my truck where we leaned over the bed from both sides. Scotty noticed the antlers immediately. "What do you think?" My question was kept nonchalant.

"C-Christ, this buck was huge!" he sputtered. "Who killed it and where?"

"Yours truly up Pine Creek. Jules and I packed in and got him Sunday morning of opening weekend."

"Holy hell, have you measured it yet?" Scotty turned the rack to see it better from all angles. "Might go one-ninety, maybe one-ninety-five."

"Nope. I leave those calculations to the experts."

"I'll take it home and give you an official green score, if you don't mind?" He grinned when I nodded.

I knew what he was thinking. "Maybe show it off to your next group to make them think you took part?"

His grin came back before it faded again. "I know this is last minute but hear me out. Talk it over with Julia because I know she's teaching. Interested in a proposition?"

His change of subjects bewildered me. "I'm lost. What are you proposing?"

"My next group flaked on me. I keep their deposit but lose customers and seventy-five percent of my pay for eight days." He cleared his throat and picked at a rusted place on my truck. "If Julia's still interested in a pack trip into the Frank Church, I'm willing to take you in for fifty percent."

The idea sounded like a good one. Perhaps the calm before a storm of enormous proportions. Give her extra time to heal before we went on offense. "Sounds interesting. I'd have to run it past my better half to see what she thinks."

"Run what past me?" I turned to see her coming down our porch steps as the door closed. "Are you boys conspiring against a poor helpless woman?" She didn't exactly come off as a mark with a two-million-dollar bounty on her head. Nor did the Sig-Sauer rifle slung across her chest complete a picture of defenselessness. I noted the new handgun under her jacket but wasn't sure Scotty could.

I laid his offer on the table while he gaped. "You've been wanting to see the backcountry, and Scotty has an eight-day opening. He's willing to pack us in for half of his usual fee. We have some free time coming up, so I thought..." I held my hands palms up.

"How much is that?" she asked him.

I knew he wasn't comfortable with semi-auto rifles. He needed a good bolt-action for his job. Our friend struggled to wrest his attention away from the long gun delivered by Al while formulating his thoughts. "I-I charge...I charge fifty-two hundred per client for eight days. Non-hunters pay forty-five. How does forty-five for both of you sound?"

"When do we leave?" she asked sweetly.

I'm not sure who was more surprised, me or Scotty. "Day after tomorrow. We'll head out from my place at five, putting us at the trailhead about daylight," he answered.

"Dawson bought an elk tag. Can you help him fill it, or is the season open?"

"You're hunting elk this year?" He turned back to me. "I don't remember the last time you went after one."

"Got Mom and Jules to provide for now," I said. "No better meat in the world as far as I'm concerned."

"You boys go ahead make plans. I've got things to do. Just let me know what gear I need." Jules disappeared around the corner of our house in the direction of our shooting range.

Scotty tore his gaze from where she vanished. "Did she have a bandage under her hair?"

"Yeah..." I hesitated, unsure of how to proceed. Last thing I wanted was to make him even more suspicious about her "accidents." The answer came to me. "Remember the rocky ridge to the south of Pine Creek? She got excited after I killed my buck and slipped in the boulders. Took a nasty tumble and banged her head. You know how clumsy she is."

Scotty's suspicious look was warranted. He stared, about to challenge my story before obviously changing his mind. Instead, he marched to the corner of our home where Julia would be visible. I trailed along with the idea of dragging him back. Rather than follow through, I watched with him.

Julia didn't slow her walk from where she left us. Waiting until fifty yards or so from her old target, she suddenly dropped into a deep crouch and opened up with the suppressed rifle. We were barely able to hear explosions of gunfire and saw dusty impacts on the hillside beyond. I counted five puffs before she stood and charged her target, never stopping her rate of fire. At the last second, she lunged forward to skid on her stomach, roll to her back, and bridged to fire overhead. I assumed she emptied the rifle before drawing her new handgun and continuing shooting while springing to her feet. Her last bullet went into the fence post at what appeared to be pointblank range. I knew it for what it was, the finishing shot to an enemy's brain.

Scotty looked as if he'd sucked a lemon when he turned back to me and spit. "Uh huh, keep filling me full of shit. Real goddamn clumsy." He pushed past to return to his truck and slammed the door before lowering the window. "I don't know what the hell's going on or what she's gotten you into, but I hope it's worth it, Pelletier."

"Worth it?" My eyes misted when I thought of what Julia brought into my life. Her quick smile, easy laugh, and the love I saw reflected each time our eyes met were things I could no longer live without. Although once a ruthless assassin, she kept the persona bottled away for no one to see. Even those she was sent to kill rarely saw until it was too late. "I'd ride into hell with a stick of dynamite to stuff up Lucifer's ass if it kept her safe. So yeah, she's everything to me."

* * *

Julia couldn't control her exuberance the night before we left, while I spoke to Scotty to make last minute plans. Jake was already at Mom's place. My look spiked her angst after I ended our call. "What? Did he cancel our trip?" she asked anxiously.

"Worse. He still wants us to go."

She gave me an exasperated frown I was learning to expect. "Isn't that a good thing? We're packed and the alarm goes off in nine hours."

"Says he made a mistake and double-booked people who were late additions. Can't read his own writing, I guess. If the first party hadn't canceled, he would've been screwed."

Her excitement and enthusiasm died at once. "This might have been my last chance." The wistful glance she cast over our gear damned near broke my heart.

"Then let's go. We won't let others bother us. Scotty assures me three wall tents are set up and waiting. You and I will have one to ourselves. He'll sleep in the cook shack; four additional men will take the final one."

"All men?"

I understood her concerns. Notwithstanding her former employment, she would be a woman alone surrounded by six men. "Don't worry. I'll do my best to protect them from you."

She ignored my lame joke. "Should we still go?"

"I will if you will." I held my breath, hoping she agreed. I wanted Jules to experience a backcountry camp.

Words weren't needed when her smile lit the room, but she answered anyway. "Okay, let's do it!"

Scotty's personal life might be haphazard, but the work he did was his first love. We rolled to a stop in front of his singlewide mobile home to find him finishing loading horses and mules at 4:55 a.m. Although four men lined a section of the corral to watch, a woman—I assumed it was Robin—helped Scotty. His stock trailer hulked in low illumination cast by the barn light. Capable of transporting fourteen head of stock and gear, I wondered how many we would take.

Jules wanted to get closer to better see. "Is it okay to stand by the pen?"

"Corral," I said. "Yeah, you'll be safe."

"Morning, Julia." It took me a moment to realize Robin spoke to my wife. The tall woman seemed chipper enough and nodded to me. "Dawson." Scotty left the trailer after securing a mule inside and closed the back. Jules and I gave a nod to the pleasant greeting.

Scotty joined us. "You guys ready? Ain't forgot nothing? Toothbrushes? Coats? Maybe shells for your gun?"

"Pretty sure we have it all. Got your money...Jules wanted to pay before leaving." I handed a thick envelope to our guide.

He opened it and looked inside. "Oh, hell. Cash?"

The four men watched from near the truck Scotty borrowed from his dad. A one-ton with a strong-running diesel, he used it only for pulling the loaded stock trailer. Robin stepped close to hear my wife answer. "Hope you don't mind." Jules used greenbacks whenever possible. "We paid full price for Dawson, but half like you said for me." I'd watched her count $7,500 last night. More waited in her pocket for a tip if we were successful in bringing home meat.

"You didn't have to," Scotty said. "Half price is fine even if he's hunting." After Julia refused to change her mind, he went inside to leave it in a small wall safe I knew he kept. When he returned with his girlfriend looking like a model from an L.L. Bean catalog, I figured our original small group was growing ever larger. "Hope no one minds, but I asked Robin to come. She'll help with cooking and camp work."

Julia answered for both of us. "We don't, do we, honey?" I shook my head while watching the rest of our group waiting near Scotty's truck. "Are we ready?" she asked.

* * *

Although our guide provided a saddle small enough for Jules which I adjusted for her, she could barely walk when we stopped for lunch. Riding a horse took different muscles than walking. Even my thigh adductors were screaming for relief before our halt. I'd learned to hide my discomfort over the years. No way would I fess up to aches in front of my friend let alone my wife.

Scotty started coffee on a one-burner camp stove, while Robin got out fixin's for sandwiches. After taking orders, she put together enough to feed the lot of us. When Julia found a comfortable place on the ground, I sat with our four extras. We'd been briefly introduced, and I directed my question to Daniel. He stood a few inches taller than me and appeared to be the leader. At least the loudest. I hoped he kept his mouth shut while hunting. "Where you fellers hail from?"

"Alabama." I noted Julia raise her head and turn in our direction. "Little place you probably never heard of called Saraland a few miles north of Mobile. How about you? Where're you from and what do you folks do?"

"We're local. Wife's a teacher, and I farm."

"My dad farms," the shortest of their group said. "Kansas wheat. Mom died of cancer a few years back, but he doesn't know how to do anything else." Job came across as a quiet and likeable man.

I figured it was best to stay amicable. "You guys work together or just friends?" The four seemed jovial until they tired in the saddle.

"Work. All of us are number crunchers and pencil pushers."

"In offices, huh?" His nod answered my question. "Not sure I could handle your sort of employment. Outdoors and working with my hands are more up my alley."

Scotty wandered over to us after double-checking our mounts. Eight saddlehorses and six mules made up the string. "We've come about fifteen miles. Should reach camp by dark."

"Ah, shit." The swarthy one said. "I hoped we were close. My ass is killing me." I remembered his name as Michael.

I kept any chuckles to myself. Scotty said, "We're about hallway. Most of you might have to walk before the day's over. We need to reach our home away from home today."

"I may have to hike from here," the one named Adam said. "My thighs are on fire."

Scotty had heard it all before. "It's a long walk. Next mile or so we start a pretty good climb."

"Food's ready," Robin called. "Coffee will be done in a few minutes."

After eating and listening to our partners groan when they mounted again, even Julia kept her physical complaints to herself. I knew how badly she hurt, because it wasn't anything different than I felt. She didn't miss the tip of my Stetson to her steeliness and got a rueful grin in return.

Scotty stopped to let us rest another four times, each for ten minutes. After topping a ridge, he pulled up and motioned everyone around. Robin brought up the rear with the six mules and stayed back. I turned my mount to stop next to her.

Our guide pointed down the hill toward a low ridge. "Camp lies there. About another mile descending on a slant. Might want to walk our horses." I noted how dark it was below where we stopped. We would need flashlights by the time we reached our base or soon thereafter. Julia followed my lead and dismounted, holding her saddle to help with exhausted legs. Turning slightly to watch the four hunters behind us, my curiosity was piqued at the glare Robin directed at one. It seemed they made eye contact, but I couldn't be sure and wondered what they did to anger her.

Tents were a sight for sore eyes. Jules flashed an excited but fatigued smile over her shoulder. Her dream was becoming reality. As we traveled the previous twenty-five miles, I didn't miss her taking in our wondrous surroundings. More than once, she reined in to stare at a far-off expanse of mountaintops. Other times, she snapped photos with her cellphone as her horse followed Scotty's.

Upon reaching our campsite, Scotty gave directions. "I'll tend to the animals and our gear. Hunters, take any personal items to your tents. Mine is the middle doubling as a cookshack and where Robin sleeps, too. To the left will be Dawson and Julia. The right one will be where Daniel, Job, Michael, and Adam stay. Figure on dinner in ninety minutes."

Didn't take more than five to unload Jules and my gear. By then, Scotty had already lit four gas lanterns hanging in strategic locations offering the most light. He impressed me by not asking for help, treating me like any paying customer, which I was. I didn't care, and after Julia shooed me away to set up the interior of our tent, I left to assist my buddy. "Need a hand?" Robin led a gelding to the corral where a few flakes of hay awaited.

Scotty loosened the cinch of the good-looking roan he rode and set the saddle aside. "Sure, but paying customers aren't required to work, Dawson. It's been a few years since you've sat a saddle, so I imagine you're hurting as much as the others."

Robin returned for the horse before I could step in. "Course," I said. "Ain't like I got anything else to do. Besides, it'll get us to dinner quicker."

Our mounts and the mules were glad to be turned loose in the corral. Robin left us to get busy in the cook tent while I got to work unpacking the last of their supplies. An impressive amount of firewood was stacked aside. While Scotty went in to help his girlfriend, I started a fire. Julia peeked from inside the flaps and came out when she saw it was me working. "I can't believe how much room there is inside our tent," she said. "Who knew it would feel bigger than our house?"

Her confession made me grin. "Fourteen wide, seventeen long, five-foot walls and a nine-foot ridge. We should have plenty of space. I'll get a blaze goin' in our stove after I'm done here."

"'S cold." She shivered, pulling her hood up.

"Once you got a good dinner in your belly and the fire to sit around, you'll be fine," I said.

After I started wood burning in the pit outside and in our stove, I heard a voice outside our flaps. "Hello the tent."

"Come on in," I called my welcome.

Job stepped in, obviously surprised by how warm our place was. "Hey, I hope you don't mind. We haven't been able to start a fire in our stove and hate to bother Mr. Rich." I nearly snorted at his calling my friend a mister. "Do you think you could come take a look?"

Their kindling was too big. Judging by the scorched newspaper inside the stove, they burned about half their pile. "Need to start with smaller wood," I said, removing everything from the interior and piling it on the ground. "A couple pieces of paper balled pretty tight, then a handful of this tinder, followed by a few pieces of bigger stuff." Inside my coat pocket was a secret weapon, and I withdrew a cotton ball smeared with petroleum jelly tucked safely within an old Altoids tin. I lit the paper, and sixty seconds later heard the satisfying crackle of burning wood. "We'll put on more large chunks after it's hotter."

"Thanks, man." Job seemed sincere. Daniel watched from nearby without comment.

"Hey, nice rifle." I noticed an all-weather Ruger with a telescope on a cot. "What caliber?"

"Three hundred mag." Of course, the big gun would belong to Daniel. The man appeared proud of it, which he should be.

"What're the rest of you fellows hunting with?" Three more scoped rifles were brought out, two .30-06s, and a .270 Winchester. All four appeared to be free of blemishes and likely new. "You men after deer or elk?"

"Deer," Job answered. "All we have are blacktails in our area. Want something with bigger horns." His three companions nodded their agreement.

His reply gave me pause. Blacktails don't live in the south. Small whitetails were the average fare. Rather than disagree, I shrugged. "How about you? After deer or elk?" Daniel finally asked.

"Elk. Already killed a nice buck a couple weeks ago."

"I didn't notice a hunting rifle," Daniel mentioned.

"Hunting with a little .44 Magnum. Cute little thing." I held my hands about three feet apart. "Short ranged and not long on power, but it'll do the job if I can get close enough."

A call to eat stopped further conversation. "Come on and get it, you hungry hogs," Scotty yelled. I wasn't entirely sure what to expect. Scotty's attempts at making food palatable wasn't something I'd enjoyed in the past. In fact, I wasn't sure he could even boil up hotdogs. Robin toiling over the stove gave me more comfort. "Dish yourselves, then grab a chair near the campfire. We only eat inside if it rains or snows."

Pork chops, fake potatoes—I saw the empty containers in the garbage—along with fresh-baked biscuits, and creamed corn made our supper. It was a good way to needle Scotty after we gathered outside. "Mighty good cooking, Robin. I expect you elbowed Mr. Rich out of the way."

"You couldn't be more wrong, Dawson," she replied. "I added water to the potatoes and pretty much sat in a corner. Scotty does the cooking around here."

"No kidding?" I tasted another bite of a perfect steak. "Gotta hand it to you, man. Really a great dinner." Others voiced their agreement.

After finishing and throwing our paper plates into the fire to give us a momentary burst of extra light, Scotty laid out the rules. "Dawson, you'll be on your own tomorrow. I suggest taking a peek north of Falconberry. Saw a lot of elk sign there not long ago. Looked like a couple herds. Bugled in a two nice bulls end of last month. I think you'd be happy with any of 'em."

"Sounds good," I said. His idea of my hunting alone suited me. "I'll take Julia for an extra pair of eyes if she's interested." I didn't think she was enthusiastic about staying in camp and conversing with Robin. Getting cut dead while the much larger woman spoke to others had hurt my wife's feeling.

"I can't wait." Jules seemed happy with the plan.

"Our four deer hunters will go with me. I suspect a few nice bucks are still waiting in my secret honey-hole." Scotty winked at me. His comment was to give Daniel and company extra confidence. "Be up at five, breakfast at five-thirty, lunches will be ready no later than six." He wasn't shy in laying out the rules. The man knew his stuff. I'd find it difficult to make fun of him in the future.

"Honey?" Julia kept her voice low after I stoked our stove and shut off the gaslight before snuggling into my sleeping bag. Our cots were wide, long, and comfortable.

"Yeah?" She made me smile by staying awake so long after a rough day.

"Thank you for talking me into this. I think we're going to have a great time."

"I'm glad, too. Better get some sleep. The call for breakfast is gonna to come quick, and tomorrow will be a tough one, too.

Chapter V

Jules and I were on the trail before daybreak. A hearty breakfast of sausage, scrambled eggs, and fresh biscuits filled us, and a sack lunch and thermos of coffee awaited our departure. Although it'd been years since I rode and hiked the area, the trail felt familiar. I remembered certain places in the beams of our flashlights.

We broke from pine timber into the open country not long after the sun started its inexorable ascent in the east. Cold at first, working our way up steep hills warmed us and kept our pulses racing. My rifle carried twelve rounds in its twenty-four-inch tubular magazine—although I rarely loaded it with more than five when target practicing. I wanted to keep the gun filled so many miles from civilization. Strange things can happen when a hunter least expects it.

I pointed out a few elk tracks in the trail—none smoking hot. In redleafed alders and birch with bright yellow foliage among dark green Douglas and alpine firs around us, birds heralded the oncoming day. Once, we heard something below us crash through the dark brush, making my wife squeak with alarm. "See anything?" Jules whispered and angled above me to run her binoculars across the open hillside. Like mine, hers were Swarovski, the best glass known to man as far as I was concerned.

"Huh uh," I grunted my whisper. "Hold it...a big doe just stood from her bed next to the burned pine at the tree line." I pointed.

"I see it," she whispered excitedly. "There's another below...to the left of the big sage."

We stopped for lunch inside a stand of timber after hiking miles on the far side of Falconberry Peak. Open beneath the forest canopy to see a couple hundred yards, I hoped something might move through. So far, six does with one small forked horn buck didn't buoy my spirits. After pouring coffee, we demolished both meat and cheese sandwiches provided by Robin. I felt better after fueling my lowered energy reserves.

"What now?" Julia asked in hushed tones.

"Let's round the hill through the timber. Keep the opening above us," I whispered back. Another two hours of stalking through pines produced nothing. Fresher tracks were visible where we hiked in the gloomy afternoon, but no signs to make my heart leap. Julia seemed excited and having a good time, so I elected to move upslope for better views. "Look!" I pointed farther north to a tall peak with a slide running through doghair timber. A crossing elk herd was visible. My binoculars were powerful enough to make out the final animal was a bull sporting impressive antlers.

She searched through her eyecups for a bull. "I see them! Are any legal?"

"Last one for sure. Got a dandy rack."

Julia was ready to take up their trail, although the herd traveled over three miles away late in the afternoon. "Aren't we going to catch them?"

Her enthusiasm made me chuckle. "Not now. Even if we caught up, it wouldn't be until dark or very close. We don't have enough gear to spend the night comfortably. We'll come back tomorrow and hope they've moved closer. If not, we might have to consider horses and spiking out."

We arrived in camp with a half-hour to spare before dark. Scotty and his charges were already back. I saw my friend was angry and headed him toward the corrals. Julia listened to my warning to take care of her feet and left me to exchange her boots and socks for more comfortable slippers.

Scotty turned on me the moment we were out of earshot. "Bastards. I put the big one...Daniel...on a nice buck." He spit. "Would have green scored at least one-seventy, maybe one-eighty. A wall hanger to be sure. Big sumbitch with over a hundred pounds of meat."

His anger confused me. "What? He missed?"

"Worse. Refused to shoot. Wanted to hold out for one bigger. Bastard smirked like he wasn't even interested. I offered it to the

72

others, and they followed his lead. Damn near could've shot it offhand from horseback."

"It's the first day. They aren't going to kill a giant if they shoot one right off."

"Yeah." He was still riled, though my rationale seemed to appease his anger a bit. "Problem is it's the second biggest buck I've seen in here this season, and they aren't likely to see one much nicer."

We returned to the cook tent while I explained what Jules and I saw. Scotty said without snow, elk would likely stay in the area. Clouds moved in from the west, sure to dump some white stuff if they didn't change direction. Long-range forecasts before leaving said a sprinkling in the high country but little more. Julia already built a fire in our stove, and I heard her voice inside Scotty and Robin's tent. My wife turned when we entered. "Robin cooked a roast today. Baked potatoes and beans to go with it." I hoped Scotty would bake fresh biscuits again. "Best of all?" She waggled her eyebrows. "Pineapple upside down cake for dessert!"

I started a fire in the pit, while Julia and Scotty stayed inside to help. Our extra mouths didn't appear until my blaze roared. Soon after, a call for supper alerted us. Julia left the tent with her plate filled as the rest of us went in. I let the four dudes go ahead of me and didn't miss the look Daniel cast at Julia, eyes squinted while he took her measure. I couldn't really blame him. She was gorgeous by any standard. When he darted a glance my way, I let him know I didn't miss his appraisal. Cheerful when we first left the truck on horseback, the big man grew surlier each day. Other than Job, the group rarely spoke unless spoken to.

"If no one disagrees, same plan tomorrow as today," Scotty said after we ate. "Dawson and Julia spotted a big herd of elk they plan to pursue. If they can't get on them, I may need to leave you four men..." He pointed at our dudes. "...to fend for yourselves for a day while I pack them farther back. We have a couple extra tents for spiking out. I can drop them off with supplies and check on 'em in a few days."

"You mean they'll leave the rest of us here and go off on their own?" Daniel asked.

Scotty nodded. "Yep. They can hike back when they kill something, or I'll go after 'em." A glance passed between Daniel and his friends. Something about our guide's plan bothered them.

Jules and I packed better prepared rucksacks for the following day. If something happened to keep us out late, I wanted to be ready. "My cup," Julia said. "I left it on the bench in front of Scotty and Robin's tent. Back in a second."

She returned shortly before I decided to look for her. Away almost twenty minutes, I couldn't imagine what took her so long even if she stopped at the privy. "Thought you got lost." I tossed my wool coat to my cot. "I was about to send out a search party." I expected a lively retort and a brief explanation. Instead, Julia didn't reply and sat heavily in her chair. "You okay?"

A deep breath and sigh invalidated her words. "I'm fine. Piddled around and enjoyed a few flakes of snow."

"Jules?" My voice lowered with worry. Her color appeared washed out in the stark light of our lantern. She drew her .38 and checked the loads before holstering again while biting her lip. I knew she kept a speed loader in each pocket with six rounds apiece. She quietly located a belt slide holding two more of the quick reloads and threaded it around her wool pants. For some reason, Julia felt the need to gird herself for war. A knife with a razor-sharp six-inch blade adorned her side each day. "Ready for bed?" She didn't answer while undressing and sliding into her sleeping bag.

To confront her before she was ready seemed pointless. Instead, I fretted too long before falling asleep. Scotty woke us in what seemed like only minutes, and my eyes felt like they were filled with sand. Julia didn't seem any livelier during breakfast and plodded after me without comment.

An overcast sky and an inch of snow made hunting perfect. We traveled no farther than halfway of the previous day when I cut our first track. "Check this out." I'd spoken low, and when she didn't reply, I turned and found she'd lagged perhaps twenty yards and stared at our backtrail. "Psst!" I hissed to get her attention.

She hurried to my side. "Oh! Elk tracks. How many are there?" While we traveled north, its trail came from below and traveled up the hill toward open country.

"Just one. Are you up for this? Gonna to be tough. If anything happens to separate us, I'll retrace steps to find you, okay?"

The Julia I knew bubbled to the surface again. "Yeah." She grinned. "Bet you can't shake me, old man."

I led at a fast walk. My stride is comparatively long to my tiny wife's two for each of mine. A quick glance making sure she didn't lag again found her slow jogging to keep with me. After noting the elk didn't travel fast and meandered to take bites here and there, I hoped to catch up to it soon. We stood a better chance at drawing closer than if it intended to get someplace in a hurry.

We'd hiked a mile or farther before I felt a tug. "Over there," she said when I froze. I looked in the direction of her pointing finger to see a bull stopped with his head down to browse in the brush. Branched antlers protruded above. I sank to one knee.

Julia crawled to my side after I motioned. "He's legal but too far to risk a shot." I figured him over two hundred yards, perhaps a bit more. My cartridge's performance was best if kept inside a hundred. "Looks like he's feeding toward the opening above. Let's ease on up if he disappears and take a chance we'll be in position if he shows."

We moved the moment he entered thicker timber. A deeper layer of fresh snow muffled our steps and those of the elk. Breaking out of jack pines into the opening, I eased us in the direction of where he disappeared. Closing the distance was important but not so fast to spook him. Five minutes went by and then ten. At fifteen, I feared it was time to return to where we last saw the bull and find his trail again. Almost ready to backtrack, movement caught my attention. An insistent tug at my coat's hem indicated Julia saw him, too.

He fed into the opening unconcerned and unaware of our presence. The elk had six long points to one side and seven on the other. I enjoyed watching the majestic animal during what I hoped were the final moments of his life. Estimating the range at twenty yards past my goal of one hundred, I waited for his head to turn away before cocking the external hammer and shouldering my rifle. Centering the front sight in the rear peep and placing it on his neck, I patiently bided time until he turned broadside. The muzzle was steady when I squeezed the trigger the moment he shifted, aiming at the crease behind his shoulder about halfway below the top of his back and brisket.

Rather than sprint downhill with a mortal wound as I expected, he dropped to the ground with his nose braced against the snow and all four legs under him. I levered out the empty which jacked a fresh cartridge in. Ready to fire if he rose, I waited with any slack taken out of the trigger. With no movement from him, we approached cautiously. Not until I pushed him to his side did I realize he was dead. Winter meat for us and Mom was secured.

"My God, Dawson," Julia whispered as she petted the mane. "It's beautiful! And huge. The size of a horse."

I squatted next to our kill to admire wide and weighty antlers, his strong male musk heavy in the air. Not only did I take the largest bull of my life by far, Julia got to be a part of it. Our trip could not have been more successful. "It is. This little rifle is quite the powerhouse." I propped it against the tines. "Tough to argue against the caliber." Looking up at the gray sky while sweating in the cold temperatures, I thought how conditions couldn't have been more perfect. "At least three hundred pounds of meat if not more."

Our combined muscles strained to turn the animal to its back where I could start the gutting process. Julia watched with fascination as I went through a routine I'd performed many times. She asked me to name the parts as I went from the bladder to the diaphragm and on up to its heart, lungs, and windpipe. She accepted the liver and heart when I passed them to her, stowing them safely in plastic bags we brought for just such an occasion. Finding not only an entry hole but an exit, too, made me happy with the heavy slug's performance.

Jules grew quieter as we neared camp. With our kill less than three miles from the tents, I elected to pack the head and antlers. Julia carried my rifle at port arms as if she expected to use it at any moment.

Although we'd heard the distant howls of wolves, I hoped to return with pack animals to recover the hide and quarters undisturbed. Not yet noon when we arrived, Scotty and his four charges still were on the hunt.

"Wow!" Robin stepped from her tent at our arrival and admired our success. "What a bull!"

"I hope Scotty won't mind if we take a couple mules to pack the carcass out." My statement was to ask his assistant's permission.

She looked startled. "Oh, no, he wouldn't care. Scotty's said many times you've taught him everything he knows about horses and trail riding." She wasn't wrong. I guided Scotty to his first bull when I was home on leave from the military while he'd recently graduated from high school.

I readied two mules. Julia accompanied me, still carrying my rifle. After I suggested it was no longer needed and best left at camp, she said, "Never know when we'll need it. Varmints and such." Julia withdrew a cartridge from my belt slide and punched it into the magazine, slinging it across her back. I figured the lever would dig into her but thought it best to let her learn. I hung a rifle from my shoulder only when I needed to use my binoculars. Otherwise, it was always in my hand. But something ate at her, and I decided to let it work itself out.

The only scavengers bothering our meat supply were a couple jays. I spooked them away and with Jules's help, got each quarter loaded on either side of both mules. Our return would be quick, but I lashed them tightly against the frame. No sense in making the mules nervous or sore.

Back at camp, with our kill hanging high on a meat pole and the antlers nearby, I settled in to start the campfire. Still a couple hours before dark, we'd have time to rest. Not until it blazed high and put out significant heat against the afternoon drop in temperatures did I find a comfortable seat.

"I hear horses." Julia's voice came from inside our tent. I noticed she didn't come out, but she'd complained about wearing sweat-soaked long underwear.

Returning early meant they likely connected on a buck. Already three days into an eight-day hunt meant one or more of the men needed to make a kill. Rather than skirt camp and walk their horses to the corral, the group surprised me by riding into the center without their guide. "Where's Scotty?" I asked. Michael led my friend's roan on a line. Blood streaked down its side.

"We need help." Daniel dismounted along with the others, including Michael, who left Scotty's horse to fend for itself.

Robin swished from the cook tent behind me, her tone distressed. "What happened? Is he hurt?"

"Where's Julia?" Michael asked. "She in camp?"

Instead of answering our questions, his demand pissed me off. "Goddamn it, I won't ask again. Where's Scotty?" I took a step only to be confronted by a semi-auto pistol held by Daniel—its steady muzzle trained on my chest. "What the hell?"

"Check to see if she's in their tent," Daniel told one of the others. Job raced up the short rise to our quarters brandishing his own handgun. Adam approached Daniel with his sidearm aimed at Robin standing a few feet from me. Job disappeared into where Jules and I slept, only to holler, "She's not here, but there's a big slit in the back."

My wife's attitude was suddenly crystal clear—she'd suspected something enough to be on alert. Before anyone could react, Job charged out only to have J—I recognized her look for a split second and knew Julia disappeared—step from behind the corner of our tent only a few feet behind the young man. She didn't bother to announce herself except with the .38. A red mist appeared from Job's skull at the bark of her revolver, and he collapsed. Immediately turning her handgun on those facing me, she shot Michael three times in the chest.

Robin fell backward to land on her butt on the frozen ground. I drew the Anaconda as Daniel and Adam turned to face J. My muzzle cleared leather and my first round hit Adam low in the back. He grunted when two more from J punched into his chest. Firing wildly as he went down, I felt a bullet impact my lower leg, jerking it from beneath me. Falling hard, I saw J open her cylinder, eject the empties, and inject six more from her speedloader. Her reload performed in record time, I didn't have a chance to fire before noticing Daniel kneeling with a hand against his stomach. I realized a stray bullet from Adam caught him in the guts. Confronted with my grim-faced wife, Daniel tossed his gun aside and waited for J to make a decision, although my urge was to put him out of his misery with a *coup de grâce.*

J stared down the sights of her revolver as she strode forward. "Where is he?" Daniel fell and tried crawling from her to seek sanctuary next to Robin. Putting the bottom of her boot against his upper back, J shoved his face against the ground. "Where?" she asked again.

"I don't know," Daniel gasped, writhing against pain. "Somewhere on the trail."

"Is he dead?" J holstered her revolver and drew the hunting knife she carried at all times.

"I don't know. I shot him from four...maybe five hundred yards. After he fell from the saddle, we caught his horse and rode back."

Robin broke into tears at the news. "Oh, God, no...you killed Scotty."

"You didn't check? You bastards just left Scotty where you shot him?" J said. My eyes grew when she dropped to a knee on his upper back and gripped his hair.

"Yes..." he choked in terror after feeling the sharp blade against his throat.

"On the main trail?" she said over his shoulder, pulling harder.

"Yes!"

"J," I could only whisper. "Don't..."

It was the alter ego of my wife in control. Her grip didn't relax until Daniel's struggles ceased. She released his hair to let his face splash into a pool of his own gore. Only then did she rise to step lazily in my direction. "How bad are you hit?" she asked.

"Dunno." Her crimson blade parted the leg of my jeans to the knee as if by sharp scissors. Entrance and exit holes seeped blood into the sides of my boot. I watched while she unlaced and opened the top to pull it off. It hurt like a bastard.

Robin drew away, scuttling backward on her butt before J—not Julia—redirected her attention with the point of her knife. "You stay. I want answers...or this is your future, too." She pointed to the corpse behind her. "I'm not stupid and want to know what role you're playing in this. You'll tell me, by God, or lose every finger on both hands to start." Robin could only moan her terror. J turned her cold attention to me. "Can you ride if I catch their horses?"

"Course I can." I wrapped my kerchief around my calf, tying it tightly, but it took both of us to pull my boot on again and lace it to hold the makeshift bandage.

True to her word, J retrieved two horses and helped me mount. Daylight waned, and we needed to ride hard to find our friend's body before wolves or other critters got there first. We armed ourselves with handguns and strong flashlights, and I caught Scotty's blood-soaked roan before we left. J again pointed to Robin. "Make your decision. Answers...or run for your life. If you elect to stay, keep the fire blazing high."

*　*　*

My guts cringed when we heard the first howl. With J leading and already what I guessed four miles from camp, their constant barking and yelping worried me. No fear for us. Our concern was for Scotty's body. My leg killing me and darkness falling, J was the first to see him ahead, stumbling toward us on the trail. "Scotty?" We urged tired mounts to a gallop when I hollered. Dark crimson covered the side of his head when I reined in for a hard stop.

He halted in the middle of the trail, obviously confused. "What the hell?"

I was shocked to see him alive after what we'd been told. "You okay, man?"

My right leg wouldn't hold me when I dismounted, but J was there and caught me. "Easy." Her voice came low.

With J's help, I limped to his side. Using my flashlight, I saw where something hit his head. "What happened? Are you shot?"

"Damned if I know." He sat on a high spot next to our horses. "One minute I'm riding...the next I'm waking up on the ground and walking out. Wait until I catch those bastards after leaving me to fend for myself." Scotty must have seen me trying to walk while supported because he questioned, "What the hell? Are you hurt, too?" I could find no bullet wound, but hair matted with blood made it obvious he'd sustained a serious injury. I hoped it was only from landing hard on the frozen ground. "Holy shit! What happened to you?" he shouted at J. Like me, my wife's face was spattered with red along with her hands and coat.

"She—"

"Wait until we're back at camp."

"You guys poach something after dark?" Scotty said. J didn't respond while we completed our examination of his head, finding a big knot with a gash. I stood with her help, and we both aided our wounded comrade into the saddle. "Goddamn it. What happened to Sun?" He pointed to more gore covering his mount.

"It's not yours?" His question startled me because I'd assumed all the blood was Scotty's.

"I don't think so. Too far forward in the crest under his mane." He found the injury. "Here it is. Either a gouge or bullet."

"Mount up." J directed me toward my horse and followed to help me into the saddle after my right calf was unable to push me from the ground. Making sure neither Scotty nor I would fall, J leaped into her own saddle. "Back to camp. I'll follow."

Although he navigated with a head injury, I had confidence when Scotty left the trail to cut cross county, saving valuable time. Ahead, a bright light led us directly to camp. Nothing changed when we dropped from the crest and into base camp. Scotty drew to a halt. "Holy hell, what's happened?" Robin stood from where she waited next to the fire and ran to his horse's side. All four lanterns hung nearby. None of the bodies were moved from where we left them.

"You." J materialized next to Robin, her .38 aimed at the much larger woman. "On your knees with fingers laced behind your head until I say differently. Stand or say a word until you're told, and I'll cap your ass."

"Julia?" Scotty stared in surprise when Robin followed her directions without complaint.

I supported my wife with a unified front whether she wanted it or not. "Just wait, Scotty. Please."

J helped me dismount and catch my balance before we both aided our guide. I wanted to lead the horses to their corral, but didn't dare leave J alone with our friends. Whatever she learned to be ready for the attack, I hoped to hear. Instead, I tied the three horses nearby.

"Who did this? What the hell happened here?" Scotty repeated a third or fourth time as he waited beside Robin. The woman seemed to know enough about my wife to follow her every direction. "Julia..." Scotty watched J draw her bloody knife and stalk toward them.

"Sit." She directed him to the seats next to the fire with her blade tip.

He glanced at Robin before stepping forward and protesting. "I don't think—"

J's hand swept down for her revolver as she shifted back. It came up pointed at his face. "I don't give two shits about you think. I said sit."

"Dawson?" Scotty edged away from her and to the fire.

I love Julia and harbor a healthy respect for J, although she now was scaring me. I'd been around her only once when she killed, although many times after the fact. The killing machine I saw now was horrifying. "Do what you're told, bud. It'll go a lot smoother if you do." I feared him saying or doing the wrong thing. I stayed between J and Scotty, hoping to save both from themselves. I held my breath until she holstered her gun and held only the knife.

"Stand up," J's tone was harsh when she directed Robin and pointed at Daniel's body with her blade. "You witnessed when someone who plots against me and mine refuses to answer. Now it's your turn."

We heard Robin's bowels relax as she broke into tears. "Anything, I'll tell you everything." She sobbed.

"Damn it, Julia," Scotty said.

J turned to glare, and for a second, I wondered what I'd gotten myself into when she entered my life. Each moment took us farther from Julia and moved us closer to the gray woman making a terrible decision. Panic for my friend's life made me draw my Anaconda and point its muzzle in his general direction. "Shut up, Scott. Not another word." My unfamiliar use of his name caught his attention as much as my gun.

J started frisking Robin. Quickly and with no gentleness, my wife pushed her toward the fire. "Back on your knees." Robin assumed the same position and waited. J's gaze flicked to me. "Sit." She nodded toward Scotty. I didn't hesitate to join him. The more we fulfilled her every request the better chance we'd all survive.

Scotty could better see the dark red covering J and me in the stark light of our fire and lanterns. He exhibited a healthy fear when my wife stopped behind Robin and rested her knife on the bigger woman's shoulder. Blood dried on the back of J's hands and knuckles could be seen to stretch and break, some falling off in flakes.

J let the flat surface of cold steel touch the side of Robin's neck. "The floor's yours. Your life depends on the story you tell."

Robin struggled to quell terror-filled sobs and hysteria. "I-I-I…" She stopped, trying to catch her breath.

"I'm about tired of you," J said. "Clock's ticking." She ran the knife tip along the back of Robin's neck. Scotty's mouth opened in protest, but I caught his attention before he could say anything and shook my head.

"O-okay," Robin panted. "I'll tell you what I know and everything you need to hear."

Chapter VI

Robin harbored information vital to our survival, and little patience was shown while waiting for her to spill it. J's expression was cold rage as she stalked to and fro. Scotty seemed bewildered, but how could he know anything? Robin broke the silence. "I worked for CJ Crowley and Associates. Over the past decade, we've been employed exclusively by The Company and entities making it up." She stopped to gather her thoughts. "My job was liaison between Mr. Crowley and Toni Benton as our firm provided the best legal advice possible."

J bristled at the name. "Antoinette Benton?"

Robin cringed at my wife's reaction. "Y-yes..."

"I'll punch her ticket. Keep talking."

Watching her pant with terror, I feared Scotty's girlfriend might faint. She changed to slower and deeper breaths to regain control. "I gave up everything for you, my job, my home, everything for a woman I knew only by reputation."

A wild thought came to me. "J? Could she be the one...?" I left my question open.

I saw a flicker of my wife return to the frightening woman. "You were a voting member of The Company?"

"No-y-yes-no..." Robin stuttered. All of us waited. Scotty sat back in his chair and stared as if at a stranger. "Not me," she tried to explain. "Mr. Crowley, my boss. We worked closely...I was privy to decisions he made and offered my input. He often listened, but I think he was...is...more frightened of Toni than any other voting member. For good reason," she added. The fire shifted, and sparks shot into a cold night sky twinkling with stars.

We listened as she spun a story of deceit and deception—of assassination and extermination. Benton ran a campaign more sweeping than Julia had confided to me, one using execution against political foes and business competition. "Although still in contact, Mr. Crowley could no longer be a part of The Company after Toni twisted it from dealing only with drug dealers and importers. The last straw came when she designated you as a client to be signed without a vote. Members rebelled, and it opened a contentious fracture. Almost half left the group, affording Toni an even stronger grip." Her admission corroborated what Al had said.

I noticed J no longer paced or brandished the knife to threatened Robin. Rather, J appeared to seriously consider the fantastic story. "You knew Manny, didn't you?" I asked, fully expecting Robin's nod. While Jules hadn't told me everything, I understood much of her job, although the tale Robin wove was much more intricate than I imagined. "Did you or someone under your direction hack his phone to warn Jules of the gray man?" Again, I was positive of an affirmative answer.

"After I got moved to work as Mr. Crowley's personal assistant, I transferred money to her account each time J signed a client," she said. "Manny would contact us with verification. Unlike most, she did her job without complaint, accepted each one, and figured a way to fill the contract." Robin twisted her position to speak directly to J. "I pointed out your successes to my boss and Toni, and they quickly offered you more lucrative assignments. Even after being wounded in Washington state, you never complained. The doctor got scared and discharged you too soon. Rather than lodge a formal protest as you should have, we learned Dawson moved in to care for you. I didn't know how to make contact when they forced you into signing Tyree Wiggins. Toni obviously sent you to die. Because of the dedication you practiced and everything I learned about you, I couldn't allow Manny to later set you up for assassination without somehow giving a warning. You wouldn't have listened to a faceless unknown, so I hacked into his phone." She closed her eyes, tears finally gone. "It was easy enough."

I breathed a sigh of relief after noticing J's knife was sheathed. She pointed to the four bodies. "These were under contract to sign me?"

"Of course. You're worth two million. They contacted me weeks before arriving in Salmon. Daniel threatened to expose me to both

Scotty and you if I attempted to warn anyone." No longer menaced, Robin licked her lips nervously and lowered her arms. "If they weren't called off after I contacted Mr. Crowley, my greatest hope was what you accomplished." She shifted uncomfortably. "May I sit?"

J fingered the hilt of her knife. "One more question. The couple I saw you speaking with at the market in Salmon when you ignored me. Where do they fit?"

"I'm so sorry," Robin said. "Your feelings were hurt. I saw it immediately. They also work for The Company and are likely responsible for your headwound. If it helps, I hoped any attempt on your life would awaken justified paranoia toward any operative The Company sent after you. You're J, a survivor against all odds and able to do what few others could."

J's intense gaze swung to me. "I'll take care of them after we return home."

Scotty finally made his presence known during the lull by breaking the silence. "I don't understand." His teeth clicked when fierce eyes turned on him in warning before she gave her consent to continue with a tip of her chin when he didn't continue. "What company are we talking about? I remember the name Wiggins from your dream when I stayed at your place last winter. What sort of work would make someone want you dead?"

He posed a question Julia would never answer, and I waited to see if J was any different. She looked away, and Robin replied for her. "He's got to find out eventually." She gestured toward the corpses. "Especially if we're to get through this with law enforcement." She waited for J's response. An indifferent shrug gave tacit permission. Robin stood and moved next to the fire. I figured she was cold wearing only a light hooded sweatshirt. After warming her backside for a moment, she turned to the flames and extended her hands, briskly rubbing them together. "Julia worked as an assassin for an organization known as The Company." The shivering woman paused a moment to let the concept sink in. "We never met her, nor did she know who we were."

"Julia a...a killer? She murdered people?" Scotty fought to wrap his mind around the idea. I hazarded a guess none of the suspicions he harbored after watching her shoot approached the reality he now heard. J turned her back to us and stared into the darkness. "Who'd she whack?" I almost laughed out loud at his TV terminology.

"Drug dealers and importers. She wasn't simply a killer-for-hire. J is arguably the best The Company fielded." Her smile seemed real, perhaps tinged with envy. "We all thought one other to be better, but J killed him with Dawson's help." My wife turned back to the fire with night temperatures dropping rapidly. "Where did the gray man fit in your body count?" Robin asked. "Was he number Forty? Maybe forty-five?"

I didn't think Julia would respond, but her alter ego surprised me. "Seventy-one."

"Now seventy-five," Robin pointed out.

"I don't care how many," my wife said harshly through clenched teeth. "The Company owes me. All those sent to sign me are on The Company's dime. I plan to collect on eleven extra scalps."

"Interesting concept." Robin grimaced at J's declaration. "I'll forward your request to Mr. Crowley. Do you have a price in mind?"

"Not a request...a demand," J answered. "I'll offer a one-time fee of a hundred per head. If they wait too long, they'll find the new price to be a killer." Any grin was merely exposing her teeth.

"God," Scotty whispered under his breath. I supposed he no longer saw the Julia who still owed him a dance and kiss. A parted curtain revealed a monster staring at us.

"One-point-one million for eleven?" Robin mused. "Sounds like a deal to me. I'd love to see Toni's face when Mr. Crowley passes this on."

"How deep are their coffers?" I said.

Robin still wasn't comfortable and licked her lips again. "Don't think millions or even hundreds of millions. Imagine billions."

The thought of so much money didn't surprise me. Some corporations approached worths of nearly a trillion. "Even after half the members left?" I asked.

Robin shook her head. "Those who fled offered the least monetarily."

J couldn't resist. "Will there be contracts issued for them?" She stood stoically without a cap or heavy coat, unaffected by a cold wind rising.

After snorting, Robin explained. "Toni and the remaining members know where all the skeletons are buried. 'If one goes down, we all go down.' That's the mantra they repeat at the beginning of any joint session."

"I can't believe you were a part of this, Robin." Scotty sounded beat. I guessed some of it was normal after a serious head injury. "All this time I thought you came back because we hit it off. Not part of a job."

"Oh, no!" she bleated and left the warmth of our fire to rush to his side. "I returned because I fell in love with a man who felt the same about this country. Losing my job when they discovered I hacked Manny's phone and warned J only caused me to move here quicker." She looked over her shoulder at my wife. "I knew being discovered was a possibility, but someone needed to have this woman's back."

"You didn't know me," J said. "I don't need anyone's help."

"Oh?" I cleared my throat for the obvious reason, only to have her stalk into the darkness. I heard a nicker and remembered the horses. "Scotty? Can you and Robin take care of our animals?" My calf hurt worse than the time I took shrapnel in combat. Robin left with him, I think as much to make amends as to help. My old buddy was fed a lot of information he needed to digest.

They wandered back after thirty minutes. The fire burned down, but J hadn't yet returned. I wasn't worried about her; I worried for her. What we planned as a relaxing vacation before the coming storm turned out to be anything but. "Other two horses were waiting at the corral," Scotty said. Although faced with a terrible situation, the hunter in him surfaced. "How come you didn't mention killing a nice bull?"

My glare seemed answer enough. He mumbled something under his breath to Robin. "It's late." He pointed to the bodies still littering the ground. "These guys ought to keep where they are through the night. We're hitting the sack."

I noticed he didn't throw off Robin's helping hand, making me hopeful they might work through his hurt feelings. Figured I'd get an earful from him at some point, too. With our tent cold and lifeless, I planned a fire before enjoying the comforts of my sleeping bag. Taking the last burning lantern with me, I retreated to our shelter nursing a painful limp. Not until I hung the light overhead did I notice the long slice in the rear canvas wall where J sneaked out. Although the huge tent was aging—perhaps as much as a dozen years—I made up my mind to reimburse Scotty for its cost.

I built a hot fire in our stove while I marked time for J's return. A first aid kit was provided for each shelter, and I used ours to tend to my calf. Stripping to my long underwear, I cleansed the area using antiseptic, wrapping the wound with gauze after packing it with a healing balm. A hole straight in and out with no fragments meant a full metal jacket was the likely culprit.

After stoking the fire with larger wood, I resolved to stall no longer before turning the lamp off. Already in bed as it hissed out, throwing our quarters into pitch blackness, I tried to make myself comfortable while I waited. A rustle in the direction of Julia's cot caught my attention. I cursed myself after realizing she'd been deep inside her rumpled bag the entire time. While I didn't hear her feet on the carpeted floor, I felt her hand searching for the zipper. Once it opened, she crawled in with me, although neither the cot nor bag were made for two.

Soft lips found my ear as her body wrapped around mine. "I'm so sorry. I didn't mean it. I'll always need you, my love. Always..."

I have to admit she cut me to the quick, and I wasn't so easily won over. "Who are you?"

"Julia," she said. "Your Jules."

I spent the night holding her while she clung to me. The shoulder and chest of my long john top was soaked with tears when she finally slept. Jules jerked and twitched in her sleep with an occasional whimper. As her husband and protector, I could do nothing less than be the shield she desperately needed.

* * *

The following seventy-two hours were exhausting. I worried for my friend when he appeared in the morning. If I were to guess, he didn't sleep. Robin looked almost as bad, yet the pair rode away to get help.

Julia looked refreshed and ready to face the day. After my murmurs of love and adoration put her to sleep, I spent much of the night making sure she stayed comfortable. Scotty and Robin returned late in the afternoon by helicopter, one of three landing nearby. Police and forensics accompanied my friend. For a few hours, I feared Jules might be read her rights and taken to jail.

We'd rehearsed our story carefully before Scotty and Robin rode out. The gist was events led us to believe Daniel or one of his men accidently shot Scotty horse from afar, thought they'd killed their guide, and planned to murder the rest of us to hide their crime. Only an accident mistaking the horse and rider for game made sense because there was no apparent motive for harming the man they'd already paid to lead them. Insane as it sounded, the pact of the four men to cover-up the more minor crime could have been as simple as fear of being sued. Removing the spotlight from Julia seemed to work as officers reconstructed what played out. It seemed cut and dried since the four men coordinated an attack in panic after thinking they'd killed Scotty. Thankfully, the would-be killers missed Julia, and she was able to retrieve a gun to save us all. Three officers—two of whom were females—privately thanked Jules for her quick thinking and action. When officials finished with us at camp, we left our firearms in police custody and were flown out for more questions. We didn't return home until daylight the following morning after a lengthy stop at the clinic. Doc Wells took care of Julia's head and my leg. "Scotty Rich just left," he mentioned with a grin. "Bastard wouldn't stay. Does your wound have anything to do with him? The two of you were always thick as thieves."

I could only shrug. The news would come out sooner than later. "I didn't see everything with my own eyes, Gary. Law enforcement is still putting facts together. I'll have to wait with you to read it in the funny papers."

He glanced over the glasses he wore to examine my gunshot. "Curiouser and curiouser," he said and went back to work after my nod.

* * *

Julia marched past me straight to the bathroom as I hung my Stetson on a nearby hook. Her shower seemed lengthy before appearing wrapped in a towel. She stopped at the threshold to our bedroom. "I'm beat, honey. Why don't you clean off some grime, and we'll catch a few hours of sleep before going to your mom's?" She needed her young pointer as badly as she needed me. The bedsprings squeaked even with her light weight.

Fearing what might come, I unlaced and kicked my boots off and retrieved a decorative gallon bucket made of steel from the kitchen. Jules kept odd utensils in it unable to fit elsewhere. I slid them onto the counter and hurried for our bedroom. The light was still on, and I peeked within to see her resting on her side. She seemed relaxed until a deep belch escaped as she twisted in a desperate attempt to roll clear of our bed. "Dawson..." I heard her panic. Another burp brought up vomit she tried to hold back with her mouth closed. Instead, it exploded, drenching my shirt until I got her face over the container. Dragging more than leading her flailing body, I helped Julia to the toilet where she desperately clung. I knew the lack of control over her bodily functions embarrassed her. Only when she waved me away did I leave her alone and closed the door.

I waited until the shower stopped again before entering. "I'm so sorry." She said, weeping and wiping her face free of tears with a washcloth. My wad of putrid clothing was impossible to conceal. I stuffed them into the washer and handed Julia a bath towel.

"Stop apologizing." Although not entirely used to her purging, diarrhea, and violent tremors, I knew from her rare revelations it was inevitable following a kill once she felt safe.

"I'm sorry..." she repeated while stepping out. I reached behind her and started the water again. "I mean, it's awful, and I'm really sorry."

I kissed the tip of her nose. "Don't give it a second thought, little dove. You know it doesn't bother me."

Waking before she did around noon, I lay and considered our future. The idea of fleeing to another country crossed my mind, quickly tossed aside as futile. The Company could reach us in other parts of the world easier than our own.

My long sigh woke Jules. "Sometimes I wish I'd never involved you in my life," she said.

I lifted my arm to make room, and she scooted against my side. "Bite your tongue, young lady. There's nowhere I'd rather be."

"I should've never gone to work for The Company."

"Then you'd still be in Astoria teaching...probably married to a commercial fisherman. Half dozen rug rats runnin' around."

"But you'd be safe...along with Melissa, Bess, her family, and your brother's. I would rather give you life than a short time with me."

"Let me worry about my folks and me. You decide how you want to deal with The Company." I kissed her forehead.

"First, we have to let this attack at Falconberry Peak blow over. Once it's cleared...time for a road trip." Her voice turned monotone.

A thought came to me. "Got an idea. Let's buy another truck. We can keep your Jeep and my pickup for around home, especially with Jake. If we're planning to knock The Company off one-by-one, it's best to have something more reliable."

Her head bobbed against my chest. "You're right. We should probably drive rather than fly. Use cash and not provide a paper trail."

"I'll talk to Scotty and see if he's willin' to use my credit card to buy diesel from time to time. Anywhere there isn't a camera. He could even use my truck while we're gone. His work Stetson looks similar to mine." The plan slowly wove itself together. "Make it look as if we're still in Salmon."

Mom appeared on her porch when we drove in. I swear she was mad enough to have Dad's old shotgun handy. Jake came running from behind the house at the sound of our engine while Mom folded her arms and waited. I couldn't help my limp, worse after Doc Wells rummaged around in the hole before patching me. Wasn't easy ascending the steps to where she stood. "I don't know whether to slap or hug you," she cried while engaging in the latter. "How bad are you hurt?"

"Just a scratch." However, it felt much worse and was more serious than I said. A tiny hole six inches above my heel barely missed my Achilles. "Who've you been talkin' to?" I asked in scolding tones. "Someone at the police department?" The daughter of one of her friends worked as a dispatcher.

"Never you mind, young man," she said and turned to Jules. "Are you okay?"

"I'm fine, Melissa." Julia fought for air through a tight hug.

Mom marched us to her kitchen breakfast bar. "Have you eaten? Are you hungry?" she asked after getting out bread and poking around in the fridge. "How does a meatloaf sandwich sound?"

Jules grinned while I tried to muffle any sigh. "You know how much I enjoy your cookin'." She cut her homemade bread thicker than usual. The slab of meat between two slices felt like a pound or more, making it difficult to cram into my mouth. Julia's appeared far smaller. Mom treated us like kids—even serving glasses of milk. I waited until we said grace before broaching a subject I hadn't yet spoken aloud. "What you need, Mother, is a vacation. Cold weather's here for the next six months. You should think about spending some time enjoying the sun closer to the equator."

"I'm fine, honey. I wouldn't know what to do away from home."

I noticed Julia's growing smile. She approved of my idea. "Ma, you haven't taken a vacation since Dad died." Fishing my rarely used cellphone from a side pocket of my jeans, I punched in the most common number after my wife and my mom and after switching it to speaker, set it on the counter.

"Yo, Dawson. G-dub ready to move?" The excitement in his voice came through loud and clear. "I've been doing my homework and have some ideas."

"Hello, Allen." My mom's prim voice was familiar to my partner. "Who is G-dub?"

"Oh, hell...I mean, hello, Mrs. Pelletier." Al's normally orotund speech cleaned up quickly.

"Sorry, Al," I said. "Need a big favor."

"It's yours if it's possible." he returned without taking time to consider.

"You still got your little villa down in Belize?"

"Yeah, been thinking of selling because I don't go often enough. You're part-owner, you know."

"Would you mind if Mom spent a little vacation time down there? A few months or even the winter?"

"Hell, no!" A long pause. "I mean, you're welcome to stay as long as you'd like, Mrs. Pelletier."

"Dawson...Allen," Mom said. "I don't think..."

"It'd do you good, ma'am," Al said. "You're within walking distance of the beach, a private pool if you don't feel like hoofing it a few hundred yards, plenty of fresh fruit growing nearby, and a farmer's market you'll want to partake in every day. The villa consists of a couple acres."

Al stood the best chance of talking Mom into a stay. By the time I ended the call, she was seriously considering it. I finished my glass of milk and stared into its cloudy dregs. Mom was studying me when I looked up. "I don't have a say in this, do I?" she asked quietly.

The shake of my head was as serious as her question. "We're really sorry, but you gotta go. I'd prefer to see you pack tonight and be gone tomorrow. Plan on staying away a while."

"Julia?" At first, Mom seemed angry before changing to sad. "Take care of my boy, will you?" She sniffed and dug an ever-ready tissue from an apron pocket. "I need grandkids from him...from both of you, before I leave this world."

"Yes, ma'am." Julia could have mentioned she'd taken care of me since entering my life.

* * *

We saw Mom off the following morning. After a much lengthier phone call with Al, he helicoptered in to escort my mother to her plane in Missoula. He'd already called ahead and made reservations. First-class to Dallas, then on to Central America. My brother William, his wife Susan, and their kids had recently moved to the Texas city for his job. Mom wanted to stop, not knowing when they would return to Salmon. Al promised to remain at her side until the plane door closed and it was airborne, removing a huge weight from my shoulders. Now, all we needed to worry about was my Aunt Bess and her family.

It felt odd knowing Mom wasn't handy only a few miles away. The old farmhouse looked sad and empty when we left. "She'll be fine, honey." I reckoned Jules felt the same way I did—scared for my family.

We hired Frenchy Bowman to fly us from Salmon to Kellogg, Idaho, for a new truck. Acquaintances had bought pickups at a big dealership known for reasonable deals. We called ahead, and a salesman waited at the airport. Frenchy refueled and flew home. I wished he would have charged more after saving us the headache of driving, but he accepted the hundred-dollar bill Jules gave as a tip.

Our salesman was a go-getter named Zack. "Let's get right to it, shall we?" About our age, the guy obviously loved his job selling trucks. "What're you looking for, and what budget are we talking about?"

Jules didn't allow me to speak. "My husband hasn't bought a vehicle in this century. The one he drives was old by the time we flipped from 2000 to 2001. I plan to buy him one with all the bells and whistles. Money isn't an object." I groaned when Zack's eyes lit with dollar signs, knowing she'd tossed away any chance to make my best deal.

We chose a new F250 with six miles on the speedometer. Four-door, four-wheel-drive with a longbed, and the diesel engine sounded quieter than I would have believed. I liked red, but got overruled by the boss when it came to colors. We went with a slate gray and matching canopy. Power everything with a damned backup camera. Jules laughed when I said I'd never learn to drive it. Zack helped until I was pretty sure we could get home. My wife and I nearly came to blows after I realized she meant what she said earlier. She planned to pay for the truck and hauled out enough hundred-dollar bills until it's almost sixty-thousand-dollar cost was covered. The dealership didn't bat an eye at the cash, making me think it wasn't their first rodeo.

We drove home through Missoula on highway 93, eating a late supper in a casino before continuing south. We were through Hamilton and were driving toward Darby when I switched the radio off. "If you want to hit this Toni woman first, I suggest we wait until we know about any police reports over the Falconberry attack. Once we're in the clear, we pack our shit and drive for Alabama to start the ball rolling."

"Live out of the pickup?"

"Yep. Used to do it a lot after buyin' my first truck about a thousand years ago."

"I want the two staying in North Fork first if they're still around."

Leave it to J to not leave any strings unraveled. Kinda wanted them for myself after they tried—in their cutsie lingo—to "sign" my wife. I reckoned it easier for her to cap a female than me. Trained as a soldier in the US Army, we paid a terrible price in combat, and one plaguing my conscious was killing women trying to destroy my men. Almost as bad as terminating a youngster wired to blow.

We passed our driveway to continue to North Fork. Only a few minutes away, I slowed before turning around to see if the fifth wheel belonging to our targets remained. Parked next to it was the same Dodge Ram. I couldn't help but notice Julia's unforgiving features when she looked to where I pointed and nodded.

* * *

The temperature dropped to only twenty by the time we returned home. Nothing seemed changed, but we waited with the high beams on while I considered. Julia already held her Glock. With my trusty Anaconda in police custody while they worked out particulars of our attack, I'd picked through my safe for a proper handgun to get through what we faced. While I preferred a big-bore, choosing a Springfield Armory XD9 was more for using the same ammunition as Julia's Glock. Her weapon of choice carried seventeen plus one in the chamber—mine held sixteen plus one. "Wait here and give me backup while I check things out."

Although no one lurked nearby or inside, we couldn't be considered paranoid after what happened. We knew the North Fork couple were in Salmon to assassinate Jules but didn't seem to be in any hurry. I waved her in as Jake ran out. He'd suffered through a long day cooped up while we truck shopped. The pointer returned before we were ready for bed. After sleeping all day waiting for our return, he was ready to put in a long night.

Julia clattered pots and pans in the kitchen when I woke. Yesterday behind the wheel and on alert had worn me. A glance at the clock indicated five-forty-five, meaning she'd been up for fifteen minutes or more. I could adjust the minute hand by when she woke each morning. "There you are, sleepy head," she greeted me happily as I went by on a mission to reach the toilet. I grunted in return and waved a careless gesture. Leave me alone when I first wake up, and we'll get along fine. Jules always hit the floor cheerful before the day got a chance to drag her down.

"Toast and scrambled eggs." She handed me a full coffee cup on my way to the table.

On my third refill of jo after finishing breakfast, a distant clatter caught my attention. "Got company." Odd before seven. I pulled the curtain aside to see Scotty park and both doors open. It appeared Robin possessed the intestinal fortitude to beard a lioness in her den. A thick sheaf of frost made the yard appear it snowed overnight. Jake stayed next to Julia as I waited at the entrance and greeted our guests while both stomped their boots free of ice. "C'mon in." I stood aside and held the door wide.

"We don't plan on staying long," Scotty said. "Just wanted to let you know your elk is at old Joe's in town." Joe Snyder served as one of the town butchers since before I was born. "Got the rack in my truck."

"Thanks for takin' care of it." During the last thirty-plus hours, I'd rarely thought about the beautiful animal.

"Got a new pot of coffee going. Have a seat," Jules said, finding the two least chipped cups in our cupboard. Her tone held a hint of command.

"Good morning, Julia." While not meek, Robin wasn't the assertive woman we originally met. "How are you, Dawson?"

"Morning." My wife's response sounded friendly enough.

"Good," I replied to Robin's greeting. "How's your head?" I asked Scotty.

Rather than sit on the end where he normally did before Robin entered his life, Scotty sat next to her. He acted as skittish as a long-tailed cat in a room filled with rocking chairs. Jules's M4 propped in the corner and my AR10 next to the couch probably didn't comfort him much. "Got some headaches," Scotty said. "Doc Wells took X-rays. Seems I got a concussion when I smacked the ground. Nothing serious outside of a few stitches."

"What about clients? Surely you're booked to the end of November." Self-employed, he didn't have any choice but to work.

He shook his head. "Gonna lose business. Forced to contact my deer and elk hunters and cancel. Cops said no backcountry trips until the case is closed, so I'm sending back deposits to unhappy groups I don't have the money from any longer. Duck and goose hunters are still a go through January." I didn't have to study his face and posture to understand his dejection.

Julia filled cups. "I don't want to sound nosy, but how much do you generally net each year? I understand it fluctuates but an average over the past three years?" She replaced the pot and sat again.

"Uh…" Scotty mumbled under his breath. Wheels turned while he did mental math. "Probably thirty-eight…maybe forty thousand. Horses cost a lot to maintain," he rationalized. "This lull and bad publicity's probably gonna break me."

"I'm going to put on more coffee," Julia said, finding our carafe beneath the sink. "Dawson, why don't you take our guests out back and show them our chickens and rabbits? I'll have it ready in about ten minutes." Her tone left no argument.

Scotty led Robin and me outside to his truck. "Sorry I missed out helping with your bull," he said while we admired its rack. "We didn't get a chance to compare before the shitstorm, did we?"

"Your excuse is pretty solid. I took it with one shot on the eastside of Falconberry. We cut his tracks in the overnight snow and stayed with him. Jules had a great time. I imagine she'll want to do it again."

"Jesus." Scotty kept his eyes on the antlers. "Not sure I'm the guy, Dawson." His sniff caught me by surprise. "She scared me, man. I got to camp only to find bodies everywhere. Thought for sure I was going to watch her murder Robin." He knuckled his cheeks while she put an arm over his shoulder. "She…" He darted a look to his girlfriend. "…told me how it went down. How Julia appeared and killed the first without warning, right down to the way she cut Daniel's throat and why." His speech thickened with emotion. "I might have been forced to watch her do the same to the woman I love." Scotty started sobbing. There's nothing more painful to me than watching a man cry, and seeing my friend's pain was agonizing.

"Then you understand better now, don't you?" I looked from him to Robin who nodded.

"Never would have believed sweet little Julia Hampton is a freakin' killer. She seemed so introverted when we first met. But yeah, Robin hasn't stopped talking since we got home." He dug out a kerchief to wipe his cheeks.

With my back to the house, I heard the door open before Julia's voice. "Coffee's done." Whatever reason she wanted us out of the house would soon be revealed. Our guests followed me in, only to stop short.

"What the hell?" Scotty said.

Jules gestured to the table. "Would you sit, please?" A large stack of cash waited in front of her. She hesitated until we sat, then filled our cups again. "As with Dawson and his family, I've brought my problems to your door. The bad people are those who twisted the worthwhile mission of The Company, but none of this would have happened if we'd never met." Jules blew across her mug and sipped before setting it aside. She lifted a bundle and tossed it to land in front of Scotty. "There's ten thousand." She slid another nine over. "This should reimburse you for this season and next year, too, in case you get poor online reviews." While Scotty had eyes only for the hundred thousand, I wondered about the money remaining on her side of the table.

Scotty licked lips dried by surprise. "I-I don't know what to say. Hell, I don't know if I can accept it."

"You'll break my heart if you don't, my friend." Julia said simply. "We *are* still friends, aren't we?"

He didn't look up. "I don't know. You scared me. I thought I was going to lose everything. Not just my life...but Robin's, too." His waterworks switched on again. To see his pain a second time was powerful. I'd never known him to shed a tear in front of others. To unburden himself before all of us showed me the depths of his anguish.

My wife nodded. "I get it. Believe me, no one could understand better." She hesitated, waiting for him to regain control with Robin's head against his shoulder.

Five minutes passed. I went to the bathroom and returned to see Scotty wiping his face. "Okay," he broke the silence. "I accept, and understand you aren't the evildoer," he said with a wan smile and shrug. "I think. Any strings attached?"

"Of course not." Julia's quick smile changed to delight. "Can I make another offer?" Scotty nodded. "I'd like to buy into your business." She slid the remainder to the center of our table. "This is another hundred. I'd like to purchase ten percent of Wannabe Rich?"

Scotty glanced at me with a frown and back to her. "It's not worth it. You'll be centuries old before you recouped your money."

Julia smiled. "Let me worry about that. Sometimes investments are about the person, not his business."

Robin no longer smiled when Jules provided a shoebox to carry their loot. "You have to think about this, honey. How you can use it to improve and grow your services." I hoped he listened to his girlfriend.

"Now you." Jules turned to Robin after sliding the carafe to her. "I want everything you know about the two living in the North Fork RV Park...the ones who tried to kill me and missed."

Chapter VII

I stomped the snow from my boots against the steps of the back porch after feeding Julia's rabbits and remaining dozen hens. Home four days from Falconberry and two weeks into November, we'd finished butchering and freezing two dozen of her dark Cornish bantams. About the size of a store-bought game hen, they doubled as a meat and small egg bird. Jules loved them, and I could see why. They were relentless during late summer when grasshoppers appeared. Anything they could catch—including field mice—were fair game to the voracious fowl. The house smelled of fried chicken when I entered with an armload of wood.

Jules looked up from the cookstove. She normally used the kitchen gas range but occasionally liked to press the old woodstove into service. "Should be ready in a few minutes." She moved out of the way so I could toss in a couple pieces of kindling before she checked her damned purple potatoes baking in the oven. I liked 'em, they tasted good, but hated to dig the blamed things because of the way they blended in with our dirt. "I'll make gravy, and then we're ready."

"Sounds good," I told her.

There's something about food cooked over pine and fir. It simply tastes better. Mom used her pioneer range far less than when I was young, simply because we could afford the extra propane. Yet gassed meals never seemed as good. "Could you grab the rolls in the warming oven and beans on top?" Julia came into the kitchen where I set the table with a cast iron frying pan in one hand and a basket of baked potatoes in the other.

I like dark meat while Julia prefers white. Works out perfectly for us. After she took the breast, and I helped myself to the rest, only a little oil remained on the plate. Her efforts at homemade gravy were paying off, and I ladled enough to cover my potato. Most of our meal was raised or grown on our little homestead except for the rolls, which were mixed, raised, and baked by Julia. Although it wouldn't go on much longer, we were living the dream she always wished for. I wanted to provide whatever made her happy. Our lives would be filled with more bloodshed and death soon enough. Anything might happen no matter how carefully we planned. "Perfect," I praised the cook.

"Whasht?" Hungry Jules tried to talk through a mouthful of potatoes, gravy, and hot sourdough roll.

"The chicken." I raised the little bone after I cleaned a drumstick of meat. "You couldn't have done better."

Her eyes sparkled. "Thank you."

"You've done good, girl," I compliment her a second time. "Took this old place and made it into a home again. Now we're eatin' the fruits of our labor and dreams. What a great life."

Jules wiped her mouth with a napkin. "This's what I always hoped for. Dad wanted to live this way. Mom humored him, but even I knew they would never change or move. Too easy to get caught up in the rat race. All I've ever wanted was a place to stay warm, produce my own food, and a job to make it happen." She glanced around the worn kitchen. "I've got everything here, right down to the perfect man to share it with." Both of us avoided the elephant in the room. Soon we would leave to wage war. Two against...how many?

"Mom called while you napped this afternoon. She spent a week with William and Susan before flyin' on to Belize. I swear she loves the place. She mentioned we should buy a home there until I explained we owned thirty-three percent of where she stayed. Sounds like she spends most of her time in the water, whether the ocean or pool."

"Do you think..." Julia said. "I mean...when this is over...do you suppose..."

I guess she couldn't say the words. If she didn't want to articulate them, I wouldn't either. "Yep. We'll stay as long as you want. A week, a month, a year, as long as it takes, okay?"

I thought her smile looked sad. Maybe because of the lighting. "Yeah, it'd be nice to spend time in my bathing suit again." She glanced outside and shivered. "Maybe celebrate Christmas there?"

"Sure. There's five bedrooms and three baths, a separate apartment over the garage, and a private swimming pool with a sauna. Should be plenty of room for Aunt Bess and her family and William and his. Might even be room for Scotty and Robin."

I paused after mentioning them. The two women spent lots of time talking or texting. Julia claimed they mostly compared notes about The Company, but even though she needed a trusted female friend, I wasn't convinced Robin was everything she seemed.

* * *

I handed my fuel card to Scotty along with the keys to my pickup. "Make sure you purchase diesel for our truck to make it seem like we're still here. I'm leaving my everyday Stetson on the seat."

"How long until you leave?" He glanced where Julia waited next to her Jeep, talking seriously to Robin.

"Don't know. We'll call when the time comes. Then start using my truck and buying fuel. Not till then, okay?"

"Gotcha." He looked back from our women. "She needs to take care of the two in North Fork first, huh?"

"Gotta do somethin' about 'em. It's weird knowing people who tried to kill her are still in the area biding their time." Jules and I talked about how to handle them. I wanted to storm their RV and kill them inside. True to her usual stalk and stealth, she held out for a way to do it without drawing unneeded attention. I deferred, knowing assassinations were her *forte* not mine. Killing to me meant employing brute force with overwhelming odds. The thought occurred to call in an airstrike by Al if we could mount a rocket launcher on his helicopter.

Scotty walked me to the Jeep. Jules saw us coming and gave Robin a cursory hug. Even after what J nearly did, my wife was building a friendship I hoped she got to continue. "Ready?" she asked.

"I think so. Scotty promises to wait until we call, then use my truck to take care of your critters." He and Robin needed only to look after the bunnies and chickens. Without Mom around, we'd leave Jake with Aunt Bess and her kids.

Jules turned. "Thank you, my friend." I noted Scotty hesitated for a moment when she stepped close to hug him. I knew she'd spooked the big-game guide when he realized she might cut Robin's throat.

"Shouldn't be hard to take care of your animals." His arms finally went around her. "Stay safe, okay?"

Jules waited until a few miles outside of town before breaking the silence. "Robin talked to Bobby Joe and Kennedy this morning." We'd finally learned the names of the two rats living in North Fork, but I still wasn't sure which was which. "They're tired of the snow and cold. Robin told them to go home while they still had a chance."

"And...?" I figured there was more.

"They seem to think my contract is almost inked."

"Jules..." I trailed off, wondering what we'd missed. Reconnoiters around our place relieved me with an absence of human footprints in the snow. A thousand—even two-thousand—yard shots were possible for the right shooter. They already proved it by coming close during hunting season. If they got inside such long ranges, I couldn't figure out where. Julia slowed for a long look at the truck and fifth wheel still parked before turning into the village store and gas pump. I thought it was foolish. We could have topped off for less in Salmon. Knowing her, she was probably two steps ahead of me.

"Be a dear and fill the tank, would you?" She retrieved three twenties from her wallet. "I'll pay when it's done."

Even in heavy boots, jeans, thick coat, and a hat, I couldn't imagine anything sexier than my wife walking away. She didn't need to sway to cause her gait to be more alluring. After putting in only four gallons, I noticed Jules sitting inside next to the *café* window. She waved me to enter. Rather than leave the Jeep, I moved it from the pumps to a parking lane. "Planning on lunch?" I slid across from her to find a waiting glass of water and cup of coffee.

"Maybe." Although I think she planned to smile, her attempt could only be described as ferocious. Her voice dropped. "We have company." Rather than keep my back to the store opening, I switched to sit next to her. Movement through the entrance to the store and post office caught my attention. "Don't you trust me to keep you safe, honey?" Her tone dripped with the term of affection she used. I glanced down to see her Glock on her lap.

Our server came to take our order. "Hey, Dawson. You and Julia make a decision?"

I'd known Mrs. Peters since she went by her maiden name, Suzy Long. About ten years older than me and already a grandmother of at least six. She was hard of hearing after driving gravel trucks until her kids were born. Perhaps she suffered other problems, but her voice carried just under a shout, and customers needed to speak up. Julia answered for me with a voice almost as loud. "We'd like a couple turkey sandwiches to go, Mrs. Peters. We plan to spend today beating the Salmon into a bubbly froth. I'd like to catch a nice fat steelhead for our Thanksgiving dinner." Suzy topped our cups and left to fill our order.

I noticed two pairs of big ears in the store section and kept my voice low. "We're going fishin' now, huh?"

Julia ignored my question. "I don't know," she said with a voice loud enough to carry. "Why not downstream past Shoup? We could hike into the Day hole and be drowning worms in less than an hour. I'd like to spend the day concentrating on catching a nice big hen." She'd listened to Scotty and I describe the popular hole where steelhead took bait above and below a bend in the river—salmon in the deepest cut.

"Sounds good. Maybe put money on who scores first?"

She giggled, getting into the macabre joke. "I'll bet a hundred I bag two before you even get a hit."

* * *

Julia watched her rearview mirror carefully after she turned down the river road. "Anything yet?" I asked.

"No, I don't expect to see them following. I hope they know where the fishing spot is." Thirty miles of driving as fast as conditions allowed got us to the trailhead in forty minutes. Elk season closed a week earlier, while anglers were few and far between on the picturesque waterway. Not planning on a fishing expedition, we didn't have any gear. Jules held the steering wheel at ten and two after we stopped and stared into the timber ahead. "Ready?" Her voice flattened—she didn't approach tapping her marks lightly.

I wasn't, but we didn't have much time. "We'd better hurry. Take your M4 and hustle to the river bar. I'll be fine handling this with my XD."

"What?" J reappeared. "You're not doing this. I am."

I adore everything about Julia, yet J troubled me nearly as much as she did Scotty. "Okay. What's the plan?"

"You take the lead. I'll follow until I see a good spot to leave the trail. Keep going, but get out of sight after you reach the river."

J flipped the scope covers up and switched on its electronics. The red dot needed to be adjusted smaller in the lower light conditions. I didn't expect her to set up for a long shot—probably inside ten yards. Activating her laser didn't surprise me, either. It worked perfectly for a close first shot. She chambered a cartridge from the thirty-round magazine and checked the safety. I waited silently until she glanced at me, then headed down a trail I'd hiked hundreds of times.

Walking a path little more than a quarter mile long, we didn't go two hundred yards before J spoke. "Here." Rather than turn my body and make extra steps in the melting snow, I waited. We'd passed a sharp bend, and the white stuff was almost gone inside the warmer cover. I heard her leave the trail. "Be careful, Dawson," she said softly as Julia departed. "Don't come back. I'll find you," J's tone sounded harsher. Rather than respond, I hurried toward the river.

Thick brush grew along the timber's edge. I left the beaten path ten feet from where forest met sandy soil and doubled back. Not far enough to disrupt the ambush, but they wouldn't see my tracks disappearing if something went bad, because I'd have already killed them. Hunkered next to the rootwad of a downed pine, I shielded most of my body behind it and a dislodged boulder. Only waiting was left to me as I gripped the XD9 in hopes of not using it. The river's roar blocked out all other sounds including melting clots of snow falling from branches overhead. Nothing to do but standby for Julia—more likely J—to come for me.

Whoever said patience is the capacity to accept or tolerate delay, never bided time while the fate of the love of his life hung in the balance. I strained my ears to decipher even the slightest hint of a diesel engine, a door closing, or the running of footsteps. Seconds felt like minutes, and minutes turned to hours. Checks of my wristwatch happened twice each sixty seconds. Three minutes, then five, another ten went by without a sound but the river. I made up my mind to go back after fifteen but still waited and stood cautiously at twenty. My eyes strained to catch any movement. Not wanting to face the wrath of J, I soaked sweat with a sleeve before it dripped into my eyes and stayed. At twenty-two minutes, I knelt and begged God for Julia's life.

Two shots sounded almost as one. My grip on the XD tightened as I raised its sights to eye level in anticipation. The noise was much louder under the pine and fir canopy than I expected. I recalled the gunfire. For a moment, I thought it was two before my brain attempted to trick me into believing it to be a single report. Whether one or two, it sounded like a rifle. A bottle-necked case in a long gun produces a far different report than a short, straight-wall handgun cartridge.

My heart pounded. Ready to squeeze the trigger if anyone but J appeared, my blood pressure soared at a slight movement. Her steps soundless under the noise of the river, I shook with relief when I recognized my wife. No doubt which form she took with her teeth exposed and features drawn. I worried she wasn't entirely successful with the rifle still at her shoulder and searching through the scope with both eyes open. Even months away from her old job, it was no contest; J stood alone at the top of her field.

She caught the movement of me standing. The barrel swung in my direction, and I raised hands in surrender. No way did I want her to make an error. She dropped the rifle to hang from its sling. Twenty feet from the trail, I reached her in six long strides. "I worried another assassin was a part of this," J whispered. "One we didn't know anything about. They seemed too sure of themselves according to Robin." She gave me a sharp look. "Ready?" My nod was her answer, and this time I followed her lead.

The bodies lay as they fell. The male face down, the female in the same position but lying partially on his lower legs. I guessed they never knew what hit them. No wonder two shots sounded almost as one. The man carried a rifle, and the woman a handgun. Both were headshots leaving their features unrecognizable messes. Blood stained the little snow left on the trail. Grasping the woman by the back of her coat, I dragged her to the water's edge before returning for him. Fast water started where the deep hole ended, and I left them on the steep bank. I checked my watch and turned to J. "About an hour until dark. I suggest we delay until we can't see to push 'em in. I'd sincerely hate for any fisherman downstream to notice a couple floaters. Agreed?" My wife nodded and made herself comfortable against a chunk of driftwood. I attempted conversation. "No problems?" She barely shook her head and looked away.

The splat of a big raindrop hit my Stetson. Soon, the swirling surface of the back eddy was alive with splashes. Until then, I didn't see a way of cleansing our bloody mess from the trail. If we were extremely lucky, their bodies would never be found. No matter, nothing tied us to them if no one witnessed the killings. Too many fishers parked at the trailhead for us to be identified as the culprits.

Hopes of continuing rain were dashed on our way home. It fell just long enough for J to run the Jeep's wipers, then stopped. Lost in our own thoughts, neither of us spoke during our short journey. My mind turned and twisted with a number. Seventy-seven. Each so much more personal than combat. Assassins got to know their targets if only in a small way. In war, you kill anyone on the opposing side.

Jake met us at the door. When my wife knelt to hug her boy, I knew J was no longer present. I prepared for what was to come by taking down a towel hanging from the shower curtain and moving the dog's favorite toy from the middle of the floor. She disappeared into our bedroom to lay her guns on the bed. Returning wearing a bathrobe and her cute bunny slippers, she sat next to me and accepted the bottle of beer I offered. "Thanks." She melted against me and pulled Jake into her other side. Sandwiched between those she called her two favorite boys, my wife's sigh signaled the world's weight sliding from her shoulders.

She got less than five minutes of relaxation before I felt it. First a barely perceptible tremor. Then she jerked to lunge from the couch. I followed her into the bathroom where she shed the garment and fell to her knees before the toilet. Her purging was always extremely personal, I wasn't surprised when she pointed to the door as everything in her stomach made its way up. I'd made it clear—if she needed me for anything during her time of extreme vulnerability, all she had to do was call. Her heaving and other noises were audible in the poorly insulated interior. They dissipated while I heated soup and warmed fresh buns. The shower started, letting me know she reached the end. Chicken noodle with a glass of milk, rolls, and butter waited on the table. I kept my back to the living room for when she sneaked past me on the way to our bedroom. Although we'd married a few months before, we were still in the shy stage. Her far more than me.

"For me?" Julia asked after entering the kitchen and winding a little arm around my waist.

"To start. I'll cook more if you want."

She sat and smelled her meal. "No, I probably can't finish this." Her sad smile didn't reach her eyes. "Thank you, Dawson."

After her customary sickness and loss of appetite, I knew Jules would rise the next day famished. Old Fred Howell needed help rebuilding his fence's during the last of summer and first week of school. I put in six long days before we finished and took any wages in trade. Our freezer wasn't small, but the quarter of beef he sent home with me filled a significant portion. He wanted to give me a half until I begged off, citing not enough room. While Jules ate, I retrieved a couple packages of round steak and our cubing machine from the storeroom. Although her weight occasionally crept up to 108, our hunting trip and resulting crisis caused it to plummet. Perhaps I could help increase her body mass before we left to take the war to our enemy's door.

* * *

I realized the depths of Julia's exhaustion when she left me for bed before eight. Her normal time was closer to nine. Slipping out a few minutes before five the following morning, I hustled into the kitchen to cook. I smiled at the continuing sounds of hard rain begun not long before I retired last evening.

Four steaks were draining on paper towels when her tousled head appeared in the living room. To avoid grinning back at her sleepy smile was impossible. She disappeared into the bathroom while I heated gravy, broke eggs, and turned the hash browns. "Good morning, milady." I pointed with my spatula. "There's your coffee. Breakfast should be ready in five. Hungry?"

"Famished." I swear her eyeballs rolled back at the first sip of java. "Smells good," she said. "Whatcha cooking?"

"Chicken fried steak." Toast popped up, and I buttered it before loading the toaster with another two pieces. "Want your eggs scrambled or sunny side up?"

"Make 'em stare at me."

We finished everything I cooked. As petite as she was, Julia could eat as much and sometimes more than me. With dishes from two meals stacked on the counter, I filled both sides of our sink with hot water. She wanted to help, but I declined. "Sit. Relax and enjoy your coffee while breakfast settles."

Dishes were done, and I was putting them away when she broke the silence. Comfortable to go hours without it, our time together wasn't always filled with nonstop talking. "Let's buy a trailer," she said.

"Huh?" I stopped scrubbing the counter and stared in surprise. Old or not, wasn't our home better than a tin can?

"Not to live in, silly. To tow behind the truck. Leave even less of a paper trail while I hunt." I detected a harsh tone in her final three words and wondered who spoke them? "Well?" An eyebrow went up, and she cocked her head while waiting for an answer. Yep, still Jules. J would have dictated terms.

"Got anything planned for today?"

"Clean my rifle and go through my work guns. Why?"

"We could drive south with the new truck and shop in either Idaho Falls or Pocatello. If we can't find anything there, go west to Twin Falls. Install the seat cover first, so Jake can come."

"You mean look for a trailer?"

"No time like the present."

Jules started her laptop. "Let me check online for the best deals. I'm thinking something small."

"Self-contained?" I asked. A nod, and her attention focused elsewhere told me I was excused. I took Jake outside to run while I fitted the backseat cover inside the garage where prying eyes couldn't see.

"Found five new," Jules said when I returned to the house. "Two in Idaho Falls, one in Blackfoot, and two in Pocatello."

"What manufactures and what length were you considering?" It meant little to me. I was comfortable sleeping in the back of our truck.

"I'm kind of sold on this twenty-one-foot Winnebago. A queen bed, couch, nice kitchen, and it's self-contained. Probably get it for less than twenty-five thousand."

The pictures she provided sold me. Fifteen minutes later, we were southbound. Shopping didn't last long when units in Idaho Falls weren't quite right, and the one in Blackfoot was exactly what we wanted. Travel trailers didn't sell well during an Idaho winter, and the dealer sold it at what Jules felt was a rock bottom price. We returned home with only enough light left in the day to back it next to the garage.

Jules spent two days outfitting our home away from home. Since her biggest worry seemed to be leaving it behind if we were identified, she spent half a day at a local thrift shop buying items she didn't mind losing. I purchased a small Honda generator to produce extra power and charge the batteries if needed.

"Where're you going?" Julia looked from the trailer door. We'd worked most of the morning hauling groceries from the house to trailer. With little storage available in the cramped quarters, she worked at being creative. We were almost ready to leave.

"Gotta make a few phone calls." I waved my cell in the air. "Stretch my legs a little." Mollified, she disappeared inside. Waiting until I was behind the house, I punched a number and waited.

"What's up?" Scotty never answered any other way.

"We're leavin' early in the morning. Wondered if you could bring Robin out for a few last-minute questions?"

"Oh." Our connection grew quiet. "I guess you're saying you, I mean she..."

"We'll discuss it later. Can you show up with a couple pizzas 'bout suppertime?"

"See you then." He ended our call.

I keyed in another number while wandering far enough on the wet ground to barely see the trailer. Movement inside relieved me as a boisterous voice boomed into my ear. "Ready to leave yet?"

"Planning to be on the road at oh-four-hundred, Al. Got anything for me?"

"Yeah. Antoinette Benton isn't happy after losing six of her soldiers."

No bulletin there, although the last two could only be listed as MIA rather than KIA. I hoped they were already in the Colombia River floating toward the ocean. We'd heard their pickup got towed from where they parked it next to ours. However, without any indication of a crime, it still sat impounded. We'd contacted police to see if we could take a couple days away to gamble in Missoula. With their investigation winding down as a simple accident escalating into a planned murder, we were told to have fun and try to forget. "The Company will lose significantly more very soon. She's next. Any news on our assets?"

I loved the satisfaction in his tone. "Yeah. In place before she got off the plane and was driven home. Helluva limo. We've got eyes on her twenty-four seven. I get a report if she even farts."

"Can you have a printout of her grounds ready for me when we get there?" Although Toni Benton lived in a mansion fit for a billionaire, there was always a weakness no matter how well targets were hardened. I was sure J could exploit it.

"Sure. I'll have one waiting."

"Guards?" I waved after noticing Jules look outside.

"A shit ton. Four within arm's length always, except when she's working at her office in Mobile. Another three are drivers with three more as doormen. Don't have an accurate count as to those patrolling her property. Figure another four or five."

"Paranoia? Or does she have a good reason?"

"Her net worth is around three billion. I suppose with her kind of money, one doesn't need cause."

"Significant other?" According to reports Julia provided, her target went through a difficult divorce about a decade before. She swore to never remarry.

His answer was dry. "How many do you want to know about? Only one to make G-dub worry. One of her guards never leaves her side. It's rumored they have something going. Don't mess with him, sir. Sounds like a tough son of a bitch. Worked for Blackwater for a dozen years or more."

His report concerned me. I got to know a few of the Blackwater folks while overseas. Most were great and hard-working guys noted for doing their jobs to return home with a good paycheck. Yet a few enjoyed the lawlessness of war-torn regions and took full advantage. These gave the rest a bad name. We ended our call with Al promising to make contact should he learn anything new while we traveled.

I'd let Jules know company was coming, and they arrived at six. No way did I want her surprised or angry around Scotty. I feared he was half a fart from crapping his pants when near my wife. She seemed sure our trailer was road-ready, and I couldn't disagree. Our guests knocked with two cooling pizzas. "C'mon in, guys." I held the door wide to make sure Scotty didn't drop our meal.

"One with everything on it, including anchovies," he said, setting both boxes on the table. "The other is sausage and pepperoni."

"Hi, Dawson...Julia," Robin took the beer I held out, and sat next to Scotty who didn't wait.

Jules understood how he felt toward her and sat farthest away after handing out paper plates and napkins. She and Scotty enjoyed the supreme with hot peppers and the works, where Robin joined me in eating the other. I broached the subject first. "We're leavin' in the morning. Check our critters every third day until it gets really cold. Then they'll need the ice broken."

Scotty eyed the dog lying closest to Jules. "Jake's going with you, right?"

"Nope. Aunt Bess is keeping him. The kids will wear him out or vice versa."

"We need to do anything inside the house?"

"Huh uh. Should be fine."

I wish Jules could have been more delicate, but she asked Robin in a harsh tone. "Did you pass my message to your Mr. Crowley?"

Robin made a barely perceptible flinch. "I did. He choked a bit before asking if you were serious."

"Dead...serious," my wife answered.

"He promised to pass it on, but I could tell Mr. Crowley didn't understand the gravity."

"Contact him again. If the answer is still no, the price doubles and my list widens."

"He's a good man," Robin said. "I would hope..."

"He's a dead man if he thinks I'm bluffing." Julia's voice dropped to a whisper.

"Do your best to make him grasp the seriousness, could you?" I asked the other woman, hoping to diffuse growing tension. She nodded with a frown. I wondered if her friendship was as strong with Julia as with a boss who ultimately fired Robin?

Chapter VIII

Since our new truck towed the light trailer with ease, we'd planned to arrive in Mobile under 72 hours, but a call from Al slowed us. Toni Benton wanted to stay an extra four days at New York fashion shows before returning home, so we took a full week to travel over 2,100 miles, and I swear Julia welcomed each one with the eagerness of a schoolgirl until we entered the state of Alabama.

My wife stretched her legs and met me back at the truck after I used a rest areas facilities. "Got an idea of where we should set up home base?"

I nodded. "Our quarry lives near Ashley Oaks west of town. Her place borders a small lake. She doesn't spend every day at her office. According to Al, her compound takes in about four-point-four acres. We're setting up in a small wooded lot a few miles south of her. It's rented for a month."

"Can we drive past her place on the way?"

I thought about it and shrugged. "Sure. Make it easier to learn the roads."

Jules never took her eyes from Benton's estate as we cruised by. A large fence blocked much of our view of the mansion, although dual massive gates allowed us a peek inside. A guardhouse outside the compound stopped visitors and checked them. Finding a way in could prove difficult.

Our lot was easily located after passing Benton's. Straight south until we reached a T, then east a half mile. Without much room for our truck, we were forced to back in. I put the trailer to one side to allow for parking. Cinder blocks awaited us, and we were quickly leveled and disconnected from the towbar. "No power," I said. "We might have to run the generator every few days to charge the batteries."

She took it in stride. "No problem. We'll rough it for as long as it takes. Interested in lunch?" Barely noon, we'd been driving since six after only a small breakfast. I followed her inside and watched her decide. "Soup and a sandwich?"

According to Julia, she rarely cooked before moving to Salmon. Eat out or heat something in a microwave. After living in a rural area where driving to the store took much longer, she learned to love making dishes. Instead of a warmed can of soup, she started with chicken broth and moved on to dicing leftover thigh meat from yesterday. I watched as she added butter, chopped onion, celery, and carrots, then pasta shells, basil, oregano, and finally ground pepper. I'd cooked the same before, using recipes from a book, but Jules never seemed to follow any sort of written formula. She might read one, then change it to suit us. Plenty was left for supper. Her obvious intent was minimum food until filled. Meals were simply to provide energy.

While I decided whether or not to have seconds, an engine stopped outside. Jules froze for a moment, staring at me in surprise. Neither of us recognized the lime green Dodge Charger with heavily tinted windows, so she retrieved her work gun from under a dishtowel on the countertop. The Glock on her hip would prove noisy. She worked the action, chambering a round and leaving the safety off while retreating to near the bathroom.

I opened our door at the knock. "How are you, sir?" Mandy Bradford entered with her husband Mark. I got a hug from the best army medic my unit fielded.

"Mandy!" Jules hurried to meet our friends after engaging the safety and sliding the suppressed pistol inside her waistband.

"Hey, girl!" The much larger woman gave my wife a tight hug. "The gulf coast is a lot warmer than Idaho, isn't it?"

"Snowing when we left. Does that answer your question?" Julia seemed happy. "Hey, Mark," she greeted our second guest and got a peck on the cheek in return. "Why are the two of you here?"

"Reconnaissance," Mark said. "We're part of a four-member team observing Antoinette Benton."

"Dawson?" Jules turned on me with a frown.

"We're not in this to die, honey. This fight is to liberate you and me from some very bad people. We won't win this war alone."

"I don't want anyone else involved who could be killed." Jules backed against the counter and gestured for our company to seat themselves on the couch. She drew her .22 and set it on the counter behind her. Not even those who saved her life once before were allowed access to her work gun.

"Our job is to watch Benton and report to Al." Mark tried to set Julia's mind at ease. "We're not here to engage in gun battles. Besides..." He grinned. "...we're three and half months pregnant."

"Congratulations! Another reason to be home relaxing. Not here." I said, "What can you tell us?"

He grinned and produced a rolled map from a small tube. "Al said you wanted an aerial view of the compound. He forwarded this, and I printed it. Foliage makes identification difficult, but you can see where a trail leads to the lake. We've observed her take this route twice and think it's the weakest link." He pointed. "You can discern bench seating set back from the shoreline. It's public, but her guards drive interlopers away. I think most locals get the message. Kids are another matter. We watched three teenage boys with fishing poles escorted away three days ago."

"Escorted from her property and released?" Jules asked.

Mandy shook her head. "Huh uh. Armed men forced them to lie face-down with their arms to the side before Benton's thugs called police who responded in approximately four minutes. They seem to be on speed dial."

Julia squinted as she considered. "How many men for three boys? Were weapons drawn?"

"Three. None actually pulled, but all carried sidearms and submachineguns," Mark said.

His news surprised me. "Uzis?"

Both snickered. "You got it, Cap. Not out in the open but visible even to us. The boys certainly saw them. Probably fifteen...sixteen years old, and one was crying. Scared shitless, just the way Benton's bastards wanted it. They were still laughing when the cops left with the kids."

"Jules?" I looked to where my wife rested against the counter. No doubt the story made an impact. The frightening orbs of J glared back.

"Signing a client isn't supposed to be personal. But this woman and her hirelings are exceptions. You'd better contact Robin. The bill is going up in a big way."

"Robin?" Mark and Mandy asked simultaneously.

I spent the better part of an hour explaining Scotty's girlfriend and how she fit. Neither were aware The Company split over Julia being designated as a target nor the price on her head. Yet they relished the story of J's killing the four men in camp. Obviously, both wanted to question further, but each seemed fascinated by the emergence of the gray woman. I changed the subject. "What's the plan for tomorrow?"

"Hunt," J said. I avoided an annoyed look.

"I'll have a drone in the air periodically throughout the day," Mark said. "We learn almost as much flying it as we do with eyes on the ground."

His revelation surprised me. "A drone? Wouldn't've thought of it, man."

Judging by Mandy's beam of pleasure, the idea was hers. She didn't try to take credit. "If you want to lay low here, we can make contact if and when we detect something interesting."

"Seems like a good idea," I responded before J could. "Give us a chance to get a better idea of the area. Explore the surrounding routes best for infil and exfil."

Neither Mark nor Mandy let my wife's cold reaction to their leaving bother them. They'd listened to enough of my stories to know her attitude wasn't personal. She withdrew into herself to plot and plan. I'd watched it before, the last time in camp when she suddenly shut down and stopped talking. Now, she again strategized—deciphering the best way to kill Antoinette Benton.

* * *

119

We spent two days resting from our drive. Although we hadn't pushed hard, a couple thousand miles towing a trailer wore on me. While J didn't completely relinquish control of my wife, Jules interacted enough to have conversation and enjoy our meals together. On the third evening, we were visited again. An old blue Dodge pickup idled to a stop near our truck, disturbing my study of the map, layout of the mansion, and trails. Julia played a video game on her cellphone and looked out at the interruption of her fun. "Company," she said abruptly, swinging her legs down and slipping the Ruger inside the waistband of her jeans.

A glance from the big kitchen window set my mind at ease. I threw the door open before they reached it. "Jose," I greeted the first warmly and shook his strong grip. The second—a bear of a man—didn't bother. Instead, I damned near disappeared inside arms bigger than I remembered. "Ox...Donny...I'm breakable."

"Sir." The mountain released me and limped back a step before executing a perfect salute, eyes brimming.

"None of that, man." Voice gruff with memories, I noted they both focused behind me.

"Dawson?" Jules stood in the doorway.

"Julia..." I stepped aside. "...these are two of the men I served with. Jose Ramirez...Donald Dean...my wife Julia Pelletier. She's the reason for huntin' season." Both smiled at an old joke.

Suave Jose hadn't lost a step. "Mrs. Pelletier..." He accepted her hand and kissed the back instead of shaking it. "...stories of your beauty precede you." I reined in a chuckle. Even with large scars on her cheek and jaw, he wasn't wrong about her looks.

"Careful." I said. "This beauty's bite is much worse than her bark."

"Ma'am..." The way her tiny hand disappeared inside Ox's worried me. "...I couldn't be prouder to meet you." For a moment, I thought the tender-hearted son of a bitch would shed more tears. Jules looked confused.

"Both did duty with Mark, Mandy, and me. Two tours in Iraq for Ox—three for Jose."

She nodded graciously. "I'm pleased to meet you. Any friend of Dawson's will always be one of mine." The prim and proper schoolteacher meant every word.

Jose snickered. "Never thought double-D would ever tie the knot...or turn into a damned hippie." He grinned at my hair left to grow after discharge.

"Double-D?" Jules left eyebrow rose. I knew she thought it meant breast size.

"Down and dead, ma'am," Ox said. "The enemy didn't stand a chance when your husband pulled the trigger."

Julia took my measure. "He *is* a pretty fair shot," she said, giving me a gentle elbow to the ribs.

"Ma'am?" With a look of displeasure, Ox squared himself on the prosthetic he wore below his right hip. It's why he didn't accompany our unit's third deployment.

"At ease, big fella," I said gently. "You don't want to be on the bad side of the fastest and finest shot I've had the pleasure to watch." I would never forget my wife in Scotty's camp. Nor her brutality. The speed at which both men's heads swiveled to Julia was no great shock. "You have to see it to believe." Although I worried about the bulk of Ox in our camp trailer, I invited them inside. The big man sat on the end of our bed while Jules stood. Jose noticed the map I studied when they appeared.

He stabbed a finger to indicate a location. "Our objective walks this route every third or fourth day." He pointed to the trail leading to one where the kids were arrested.

Julia tensed. "When will that be?"

"Last time was..." He looked to Ox for validation. "...three days ago?" He continued after a nod. "She didn't show today, so I'd guess tomorrow or the next day."

J made her appearance. "Time?" Her change in tone, cadence, and focus was instantaneous and fascinating.

Jose said, "Morning. Always before noon. Less than an hour before Mark and Mandy take over."

"Bodyguards?"

"Yes, ma'am," Jose answered.

"How many? How do they travel?" J asked. "In tight formation?"

"Two within reach behind her, another pair farther back," Ox said. "Gives her the feeling of walking alone, I suppose."

"How long is this jaunt in the woods?" I inquired.

"Not long." Jose stared at my wife. "Fifteen minutes, sometimes a half hour. She likes to sit along the water, too."

"Have any of you been compromised while surveilling?" I noted J's voice dropped to a whisper.

"No, ma'am," Ox said. "Ain't none of these city dudes gonna spot a country boy."

"Mm..." she mused, poring over the map. "Can we get eyes overhead about the time she normally goes for a breath of fresh air?"

"Sure," Jose answered. "I'll call Mark to come early. He'll want to set up beforehand. Needs to fuel his drone and do pre-flight inspection. He's a fanatic when it comes to his equipment."

I barely heard her whisper while she stared at the map. "Perfect."

* * *

J seemed satisfied with our newfound knowledge. She brooded and plotted while Jose, Ox, and I caught up. "How's the leg, Donny?" I asked.

"Good, sir." He lifted his right pant leg and exposed the prosthetic. "Can't sprint with this one, but it gets the job done."

"Shit." Jose drew out the invective and grinned at our friend. "You never did more than a slow shuffle before Cap saved your ass."

Ox glanced at me. "Never got a chance to thank you in person, Captain."

I wasn't going to blow him off and say it was nothing. To Ox, it was everything. "You'd do the same for me...hell, for any of us. Could I do less?"

J turned her intense gaze to Ox. "Thank my husband for what?"

"House-to-house fighting in Fallujah, ma'am. Nasty stuff. Insurgents hiding behind women and children used as human shields. We were ordered to set up in empty quarters already cleared to target a block. We found ISIS utilized tunnels too late, and a hell of a lot more of them than us sprung up all around. I took a hit in the thigh right off. Cap and crew turned the tide while I hobbled to our fallback, but fresh rats boiled out of the sewer to catch us in a crossfire."

More of an awestruck schoolteacher's curiosity emerged than a killer's thirst for details when Julia asked, "How did you escape?"

"The others neutralized opposition inside, while I put down the guy outside trying to get an RPG through a window. Damned rocket collapsed a stone wall on me." Ox slapped his prosthetic. "I was left exposed with my leg crushed and pinned under the rubble. While our side kept the bad guys on defense, your husband belly-crawled to my location. Took him a lifetime to dig me out enough to drag me to cover."

I remembered the fight as if it just happened. Automatic gunfire, the smell of burned powder, and screams of the dying. It didn't take a lifetime to dig Ox's leg from beneath the crumbled ruins. It merely seemed like it. Pulling my giant friend across the inner garden to comparative safety while prostrate took even longer. Set my heels, drag him a few inches, then repeat. We knew the instant Mandy cut his fatigues back he'd lose the leg. Only her medical assessment and training kept Ox with us. "You're short a leg, but you're alive, man."

Donny nodded. "Yes, sir." He glanced at Jules before looking back. "I owe you, sir. We all do. "This..." He pointed at my wife. "...is just a small way of repaying. I'm with you for as long as I'm needed."

"I thought you were married with a young'un?" I said.

"Cap." Jose shook his head.

The trailer fell silent. Although always the tenderhearted one, Donny surprised me with his tears. "No, sir. Some asshat jacked up on smack and booze hit my girls head on. Supposed to be a quick run to the laundromat, but my wife and baby were gone."

"Oh, hell." I sighed. "I didn't know."

"Nobody did." Jose said. "Bastard kept it to himself."

123

Julia moved to stand beside Ox, resting a hand on his shoulder. Even sitting on our mattress, his head towered above her. "I'm so sorry, Donny."

"It's why I had to come after Al tracked me down. Said you helped take people like the creep who killed my family off the streets. I don't understand why this woman we're watching wants to stop you. Doesn't matter to me. When the old man told me Cap and his wife needed help, I saw it as a way to give Tammy and Kimmie an opportunity to rest easier." He sobbed. "Pay Cap back the best way I could."

* * *

"Jesus." I returned inside after seeing the boys off to find Jules on the bed, her eyes red-rimmed with grief. "Talk about a tough one."

"I don't understand why he's here," she said. "Your friend needs help."

I shook my head. "This is help. Ox needs to be needed. This is his way to heal." I sat at the table and poured a jigger of whiskey. "His is a fragile soul, Jules. We can't lose sight of his loss and pain." Our trailer never seemed so silent while we brooded.

Up late with thoughts of my fellow soldier, I woke in the morning to a different woman. Similar to Julia, the stranger gave me a start. She turned to me, and I recognized J's cold visage staring back. Instead of a shorthaired blonde, she wore a wig of black reaching six-inches below her shoulders. Darkened eyebrows and lashes completed her transformation. "Who are you, and what have you done with my wife?" I said, hoping to converse before we left.

"It's already seven." J didn't budge an inch. "We leave in thirty."

If she decided on a plan, I wasn't aware of it. "Are you gonna clue me in on what you're thinking?" I asked, while finding clean clothes in a drawer beneath our bed.

Her voice stayed flat. "I want you to drop me off and come back later."

My depth of anger surprised me but didn't ruffle a hair on J's head. "Like hell." I snorted to show my displeasure. "We didn't drive all this way for me to let you—"

"To let me what? Do what I do best? There's a big difference between what you did in the army and what I'm good at. Power versus..." She glanced down before meeting my eyes from under her brows. "...finesse."

My cell rang before I could answer her. I hoped my irritated look got my point across. "Hey, Al." I said.

"Today or tomorrow," he informed me without fanfare. "Your person of interest leaves for London in three days."

J and I continued with our staring contest. "I understand."

"I've learned something else you need to know."

"Okay?"

"I listened in on a video conference last night. Eight of the thirty-four remaining partners agreed. Price on G-dub's head went up a half mil. They plan to increase it again if needed."

Although not surprising, his news made my stomach jump and left me feeling sick. "Roger that." I pressed end when the call went dead.

Js question came before I was the first to blink. "Al's found something?"

I lost when it came time to look down and lace my boots. "*Our...*" I emphasized the word. "...quarry leaves for another overseas trip in three days. We tap her today or tomorrow. Otherwise, we wait.

"Is that all?"

Her question caused me to hesitate. "You're worth two-point-five million." J gave a dark and fearless smile, and the hair on the back of my neck stood at her response.

She didn't say anything when I slid my handgun on my belt. Two spare magazines in their leather pouch went on the other side. With the day appearing cool and windy, I opted for a light jacket to cover my hardware. My Stetson was left behind as I faced the day bareheaded, my hair pulled back in a tight braid.

For the first time since we met, I was witness to the alter-ego girding herself for work. Wearing jeans torn at the knee and simple tennis shoes with a heavy blouse, she checked how tightly the suppressor fit on her Ruger. She pressed firmly until the ten-round magazine locked in place. She drew the slide back and let it run forward, checking a final time to assure herself the chamber was loaded. Tucked in the front of her pants, it was well-concealed by a short jacket. Two extra magazines went into a back pocket. A razor-sharp Mini Tanto found in my gun safe hung from her belt. No identification was carried on her person, but she stuffed a wad of bills in a front pocket. A burner phone went into an inside pouch of her jacket.

"Have you eaten yet?" I asked.

"Huh uh. A thermos of coffee right there." She pointed.

"Shall we stop and pick something up?"

"No."

While J pored over the map, I made two meat and cheese sandwiches. One I dropped in a sealable bag. The other I ate. A little coffee remained in the pot. I wiped my cup rim from the night before on the front of my coat. Only two lukewarm swallows but enough to get us to wherever she planned. "Ready? My question was meant as a challenge.

She stood without a hint of fear. "Let's go."

We stayed only a few miles from our target, so the ride took a quick couple minutes. I parked where she pointed, a lake visible through the trees. A check of my watch showed seven-thirty. "Now what?"

"We wait."

J barely touched our coffee while we watched. I gave up hope when noon passed. The second sandwich I didn't offer to her tasted good. While I searched hard, neither of us noticed Mark or Mandy nor Jose or Ox. I even looked for a drone without any luck. Shadows grew long before she called it quits. "Damn," I remarked, "only one more day."

"Yeah," she said with a thoughtful look. "Stay here."

J leaped out to close her door and disappear over the high fence into the timber before I could react. I cursed myself for not being prepared for her lateral move. Following crossed my mind—except I worried she might call with a need for extraction from a different location. Nothing to do but remain where I was and try to not show my anger when she returned. If one of my men behaved similarly in battle, he would have faced court-martial or a bullet. Yet as she mentioned, the life of an assassin was nothing like a soldier.

A police cruiser passed after dark, its light sweeping in my direction. I made a show of texting and waved my thanks for checking. After a brief hesitation, the officer drove on without delving further. If Benton or one of her guards made us, the hunt was over. The area where we parked wasn't illuminated by street lamps. My heart almost stopped when the passenger side opened and J slid in again. I started the engine and pulled away without taking time for instruction. We needed to talk.

Mark and Mandy were waiting when we arrived at the trailer. J didn't acknowledge them and entered without me. Our visitors stopped next to my rig. "Sorry, man," Mark said. "Burned six tanks of gas in the drone without seeing a thing. No movement outside the home."

"Dawson? You okay?" Mandy stared at me in the poor light of our front porch bulb.

"Not really. You might want to stay outside for a few minutes." I stomped away to jerk the trailer door open and shut it hard behind me. "Don't you desert me again," I told J where she sat at the table going over the map again.

"Do what?" She seemed mystified.

"A soldier who abandons a post or team in wartime gets shot." My voice rose with bubbling anger. "You left me without warning."

J pushed back and regarded me coolly. "This isn't that kind of war. These people are bugs, and I'm the exterminator." My skin crawled when I recalled a story of the gray man telling Julia much the same thing when he recruited her for The Company.

My frustration elevated at a smirk. "Is this some sort of game to you? Others rely on you now. Do something stupid, and people I fought with who only want to help are gonna die." I forced myself to relax when I noticed my clenched fist.

"Did I ask for help?" No doubt J was in complete control when she whispered.

"Hey." Mandy somehow opened our door without a sound and stepped inside. "Sir? She's right. This isn't a war, and she didn't ask for assistance. Since when did we do summary executions? I suggest we take time to cool down and sooth frayed nerves."

Mark peeked around the corner. "If anyone's interested, we have a family-sized pizza in the car. Still warm."

Mandy didn't give us a chance to accept or reject the offer. "Bring it in."

We stuffed four around the table using two small folding chairs. Mark ate like I remembered—as if he'd never see food again. Mandy took her time with two slices, while J picked at one. Me? I tore into our dinner like it done me wrong. "I'm betting tomorrow's the day," Mark said. "If not, we can drive to our place until Benton returns. Lots to do in Baton Rouge."

I said, "If we don't have an opportunity, J and I will wait. You and Mandy need to get back to your jobs."

"Took a leave of absence, sir," Mandy said. "Needed a mental break from working the emergency section of a trauma ward. Mark can do his job with a computer or his phone, so this is a vacation. Kind of like when we flew to the Bahamas." She laughed.

"You mind if we stay, J?" Mark's use of her alias sounded odd. It's like calling Diana Prince "Wonder Woman" when she's not wearing the outfit. "We'll keep out of your way. Won't even know we're here."

She shrugged without looking. "Don't care."

Unable to sleep, I got up the following morning at five. If Julia—or J—was awake, she did a good job of faking it. I dressed and slipped from our trailer for a walk. Temperatures were relatively cool as I hiked east toward town, then north. A road forked, and I wasn't sure which one to take. Choosing southwest, I hoped it led me to where I would cut due south and to our place faster. A check of my watch showed the time already seven-fifteen. I cursed myself for being gone so long. J would be justifiably infuriated at my absence.

I recognized my location after passing Benton's mansion at the end of a lake. Heading south on the next street, I broke into a jog. Used to putting miles on my feet, I pushed harder, needing to cover the distance quickly. When I got to where we parked the evening before, the empty spot made me breathe a sigh of relief—except twenty seconds later, I noted our truck sitting on a side road in front of an abandoned single-wide trailer. Shit. I turned to look more carefully under the trees. Unless she planned to take a chance and enter the house, my wife lurked somewhere close.

My cell rang. Instead of Julia, the number was Mark's. "Yeah?"

He spoke without pleasantries. "She's seated on a bench near the south end of the lake. Very close to where we saw the boys arrested. About four hundred yards northeast from your present location." Such exact data could only come from a team running at least one drone. I couldn't help but look overhead, though the tiny vehicle flew high enough to be invisible and impossible to hear.

I left the asphalt and ducked under low hanging limbs, to see better. "How long's she been there?"

"Already in place when we got eyes in the air." Without a doubt, Mark referred to Jose, Donnie, or most likely both, and foreboding jabbed me—J hadn't been informed of a spy-in-the-sky cam. "Double-time, sir. We've got early movement at the south end of the residence." No time to second guess my team. I jumped the fence to break into an opening and saw her ahead.

Antoinette Benton and five instead of four goons walked in the direction of my wife—again wearing her wig—when I first caught sight of the group. I ended the call and picked up the pace while dropping the phone into my coat pocket. It didn't seem as if they saw J as my long strides took me closer. A fork in the trail moved them our way. J didn't bother to look when I sat on the bench next to her. Three men advanced in front of Benton, while two more got closer from behind to box her in as they neared us.

"Stay here," J whispered while twisting toward me. I noted she wore eyeglasses. "Don't move," she continued before breaking into screams. "No more! I'm done with you!" J yelled. She seized the front of my coat and jerked. From twenty feet, they probably couldn't tell I wasn't holding her. Jumping away to face me with her back to the group, J nearly pulled me from my seat before releasing my jacket and wheeled for their safety. "Help! Help me," she howled in realistic fright.

"Hey." One of Benton's men left them to situate himself between my wife and me, one hand going to a holstered gun without drawing. J ducked behind him and hid, backing toward the larger group. "Right there, buddy," the youngish man said. "Ass on the bench."

"Oh, thank you!" I barely heard J when she reached Toni Benton's side, who instinctively held out a protective arm.

Although I found watching her in action on Falconberry Peak illuminating, nothing could have prepared me for the instant ferocity of J's attack. One moment, she seemingly reached safety—the next, her suppressed barrel rose, and a bullet went into Benton's face near her eye. J followed it with two more at the goons behind as Toni collapsed and exposed them. Rather than wait to see their bodies fall, my wife pirouetted, her muzzle beneath the chin of the nearest guard. He dropped at the shot, giving her an opening at the two remaining. Only the one nearest me had a chance but didn't have time to raise his gun—although a hand rested on it. J engaged the final target at less than ten feet.

I knew her signature. Yet watching her administer the *coup de grâces* turned my stomach. Two of Benton's goons squirmed where they lay, and J drove four more slugs into each of their skulls. Although motionless, Benton and the remaining three men received the same treatment. The soldier in me wanted to assess and make sure the threat was neutralized. Yet my humanity didn't want to witness the act. J allowed me no chance when she stalked past. "Let's go." Her tone was no different than if Julia planned a grocery run to Salmon.

I'd hitched our trailer and was securing outside storage compartments when a car slowed and turned in. J—Julia hadn't reappeared—stepped outside without her wig or makeup. Her work gun got left inside, while on her hip rode the trusty Glock inherited from her father. Mark and Mandy stood next to their car as if unsure how to proceed. Hell, even I wasn't certain how to treat my wife. "Everything inside stowed away?" I asked. She nodded before leaning against the truck.

Mark spoke hesitantly. "Pulling out?"

I nodded. "Yep. North to Chicago."

"Come to our place," Mandy said, edging toward J with care to not pose a threat. "We're less than four hours west of here. Jose lives north of us about sixty minutes, but Ox has a small apartment in Baton Rouge. Please...come spend a few days or longer recuperating before Chicago." Her offer was directed at J.

Mark and I moved closer. "Well...J?" I said. She might find me calling her J embarrassing in front of our friends, but I sure as hell wasn't going to call her Julia.

Her question surprised me. "Where do you live?" she asked Mandy.

"A few minutes outside of a little town called Baker...north of Baton Rouge. We can be there before suppertime."

J turned a cold stare to me. "What do you think?

"A little R and R would be good. Give us a chance to decompress and contact Al. Reckon it'll take a few days before there's blowback."

J made eye contact with each of us in turn. When her gaze fell on me, Jules briefly emerged only to be controlled and pushed aside. "Okay. Let's go."

Mandy gave me their physical address to program into the truck's GPS system. "You going to be all right?" she whispered.

"Yeah...you know how she is. It's just going to take time." I glanced to where J waited on the passenger side after closing the door and shutting Mark out. "We'll see you later this afternoon.

Chapter IX

J mimicked a statue until we reached Interstate 10, then fidgeted while I increased our speed to sixty in the slow lane. Twitchy at first, we didn't travel a dozen miles before she stripped her belt from her pant loops and stored the Glock and spare magazines inside the glove box. She didn't say anything—no words were needed. I was still her husband, and Jules resided within the woman next to me. After releasing her restraint, she lay on her right side and squirmed until her head rested on my lap with her face pressed into my shirt against my abdomen.

Rather than lie still, her legs writhed slowly as if riding a bike. A black SUV caught us and swung behind—my attention diverting from J when it sidled in to tailgate. The aggressive driver took an upcoming offramp only a moment before I alerted my passenger. I breathed a sigh of relief before a hand slid between my back and the seat. She squeezed hard as if to lose herself in the flannel of my shirt. I could do nothing except caress her shoulder. By then, tears soaked through to my skin. We traveled almost forty miles after I noticed a sign pointing the way to Moss Point before realizing she slept. My belly rumbled, making me think about food too late. I'd stay hungry if it gave Jules a fighting chance to rest.

Leaving The Dime when it dipped south, I continued west on I-12. Driving slower with the trailer made the trek much longer than the three and a half hours Mark said. The woman using my lap for a pillow stirred and stretched before sitting up. She looked out sleepily while trying to get her bearings. Rather than slide across to the door, she fastened her seatbelt next to me. "Where are we?"

"Who are you?" My challenge was unneeded, but it made a point for me.

"Julia. Your little dove," she said, her voice breaking. If I thought to gain an unfair advantage, her answer destroyed it. My little dove. I gave her the nickname when she seemed most broken. Finally mended to fly free, she again fell to earth as a tiny fractured bird.

I glanced away to regroup and gather my thoughts. My reply didn't want to come out. Napkins in the storage area of my door came in handy. I used them to dab at misty eyes and a runny nose. "We passed...ahem..." I cleared my throat. "...we passed the John C. Stennis Space Center about twenty miles back. Probably ninety minutes or longer to Mark and Mandy's."

"Oh...I would've like to have seen the space center." A catch in her breath damned near choked me. Her tone came off as dreamy.

A growl from her stomach prompted, "Hungry?" It came out gruffer than planned, but it didn't seem to bother her.

"Yeah, I should probably eat."

"Did you have breakfast this morning?" She barely touched food the day before.

"No..."

I located a fast food restaurant with easy in and out and parked. I hogged too much room, but we hurried inside to use its facilities before ordering. She took longer than usual and returned looking fresher with a damp face. We carried a large bag of various items from the menu when we left.

I nibbled at a sandwich after noticing Julia's hunger. She needed to refuel and prepare for what was to come. After she ate three burgers and a large order of fries, I suggested she either slow or stop. "I know you're hungry, but don't gorge yourself and get sick." Her response was to learn her head against my shoulder and suck up a large chocolate shake from a straw.

We drove directly to Mark and Mandy's home with the help of GPS. Rather than a closed-in suburban area, their neighbors were barely in sight. Mark heard us and hurried outside to guide me to park near a fence next to their backyard. "Christ, you make me envious at how easily you back trailers," he said.

I shook the hand he offered. "Did it all my life. Hell, I was towing a manure spreader with a John Deere before I got out of junior high." Jules clambered down heavily and leaned against me.

"You guys hungry?" He glanced from one of us to the other. "Mandy's making spaghetti and garlic bread. Should be ready in an hour or so."

"Ate a while ago, but we could probably put away a little of your wife's good cooking," I said.

Mandy bustled about as if preparing to feed an army, and the place smelled like a gourmet restaurant. Even Jules perked up when sliced garlic released the scent of her favorite herb to us. I hoped she would stay and talk to Mandy, but she pressed against me like a beaten dog. Mandy shook her head at me and gave a smile for Julia. My one-time medic understood signs of PTSD.

Mark gave us the tour and offered us any one of three spare bedrooms. I begged off, explaining how comfortable our trailer mattress was. His house was to be used as our own, he said, and they would accept nothing less. Mandy came in to set the dining room table about the time we heard an engine stop. She peered through a window and hollered to come in at the knock. "You're just in time," she told Ox and Jose. "We were about to sit."

Julia and I waited on a loveseat, while Mark made himself comfortable in what looked like his normal spot. The worn easy chair looked out of place with the other furniture. It appeared like Jose had to drag Donny inside. They sat across from us on a full-sized couch. I felt guilty, having given no thought to them after the morning slaughter. "How you doin', men?" Jose sat back with a curt nod without taking his eyes from Julia. Ox sat forward without pretense of hiding his stare.

"Freaked out, Cap." Ox's intense gaze flicked to me from Jules and back to her. Mandy appeared with a spoon still in her hand.

I trusted my life to those in the room dozens of times in the past. Yet something about Ox and Jose disturbed me. "What's the problem?"

134

"We were fifty yards from you this morning." Donny's eyes never left Jules even when she shifted away from me. "We ain't in the sandbox, Cap. Rules of engagement are different in civilian life than a warzone. No one warned us we were taking part in an operation with so much...collateral damage. A goddamn heads-up was warranted, don't you think? We could be looking at a long stint in prison."

My attention immediately shifted to Mark. "You brought them in without an explanation?" I feared the growing tension would cause J to make her presence known.

"My mistake, sir. Didn't know we'd all get a front row seat." I'd forgotten about their drone after what could only be described by civilians as a savage execution. "Al's plan was to keep eyes and ears on Benton twenty-four-seven. We put Jose and Ox in as recon only, not present when J terminated her quarry."

"When and where did I lose your trust, Donald?" I used Ox's given name on purpose to make our discussion formal as if on the record. "I haven't changed since the last time you saw me." I wanted him to remember the circumstances facing us in Fallujah. Even Jose's eyes narrowed at the reminder.

"You haven't, sir," Ox said. "It just... well...sir, I watched your wife do what Jose said . . . commit way too much collateral damage today. This ain't Iraq."

"Collateral damage? I'll show you collateral damage," the woman at my side said. She tried to rise, but my arm around her shoulders didn't relent. With her seated to my left, I made reaching her gun wedged between us difficult. She grunted during the tussle, but her strength was no match for mine.

"Easy..." I held a palm out to Jose and Ox while she struggled against my grip. "You, too, Julia." Since I'd never raised my voice to her, she immediately ceased struggling. "All of you...stop...now."

Quiet until Jose said, "We trust you, so make Ox and me understand."

Mandy stepped farther into the room and pointed her wooden spoon. "Do either of you seriously think I'd jeopardize my career and life with something I didn't believe in? I don't know everything, but enough to give all I have for Dawson...and now Julia." Her voice shook with suppressed anger and emotion when she gestured. "I watched her struggle after suffering a beating you can't imagine. Mark and I have been privy to stories of more attacks on her and Cap over the past weeks. If either of you think so little of us that we'd involve you in something not worth giving our lives over, leave my house now." She wiped tears away in anger.

Jose wasn't backing down. "You're up, sir. Make us believers."

* * *

I guess I did a good job. Mandy and sometimes Mark prompted me about something left out of the narrative from the time Julia lost her family to narcotics traffickers and was hired by The Company to our latest attacks because she wanted out. Some details were new to our hosts; all were unfamiliar to Ox and Jose. The former eventually slid back to sit more comfortably, while the latter never moved. Both watched the subject of my tale far more than me.

Jose was the first to break the silence after I finished our story. "The heads of all thirty-odd companies have to die?" I frowned at his low tone, and he pointed to Jules. To find her asleep at my side astonished me. While I knew her stress level shot off the charts while planning and following through on an assassination—exhaustion after completion extracted a heavy toll. To allow herself to fall unconscious around strangers flabbergasted me. Then it hit me. No longer was my wife alone without anyone offering help to bear her responsibilities. Trust in me was complete. Perhaps my little dove wasn't as broken as I feared.

Help me, I mouthed to Mandy. She leaned Julia away and assisted me in positioning her supine. A throw pillow went under her head, and a decorative afghan tossed over the back of the couch provided cover. With her right side facing out, the Glock wouldn't dig into her hip.

"Dinner's ready," Mandy whispered to the room. "We might as well eat."

At first, I supposed she put me where I could keep an eye on Julia. Then, I realized none sat with their back to her. I couldn't blame them.

J's struggle to draw her gun was a real threat. Seated across from us on the couch, both men had briefly gazed into orbs promising eternity. Julia later voiced horror at her actions. "I don't know," I said in response to Jose's question. "Maybe the loss of Benton will be enough to end to it."

Ox finally got what was bothering him off his chest in a loud whisper. "We watched it, Cap. Didn't take but a couple seconds...maybe less." The big man shook his head. "Like a goddamn whirlwind. It was beautiful. She went through professional guards whose job it is to keep rich people safe like a hot knife through butter. Never seen the like. If I didn't know better, I'd've thought she was dancing to steps practiced a thousand times. Like butter, hard to believe."

"We didn't see it from ground level, sir," Mark said quietly. "Have to admit it didn't appear differently at seven hundred feet than what Ox described. A few heartbeats before five men and a woman were down."

I glanced at Julia lying so still and quiet, her chest barely moving. Eighty-three. The number seemed impossible, but I knew it to be true. Julia hated to lie, where J refused to. How could such a demure little woman be responsible for so many dark souls sent to their maker? The concept seemed out of place knowing firsthand the joy she got from teaching. For her, it was much more than a paycheck—money she didn't need. She loved children and witnessing their excitement while learning. "She's tiny, but a word of warning. There's no backdown nor reverse in her when she's on a job. Her mind is always busy planning and making sure she's one step ahead of everyone else. Don't make the mistake of standing between her and her objective."

Mandy gave me a gentle backhand. "She's not as bad as you make her out, Dawson. "I've seldom met another with as big of heart. Julia is so...so..." Mandy stopped and thought a moment. "...so sweet and innocent. As if a young girl unsure of herself."

I tried a forkful of spaghetti before setting it aside. "You're right about Julia," I looked to where she napped. "You won't meet a sweeter or more naïve woman. She's a great teacher, but her alter ego J—well, J's in a league of her own when it comes to killing."

137

We kept our conversation low. No need to wake the sleeper. Quiet laughter was kept in the dining area while we reminisced over time served together. It helped rebuild a bond never truly broken. Even with Ox helping, we hardly put a dent in the feast Mandy provided. She returned from the kitchen with another loaf of garlic bread. It called my name with the ancient staff of life as one of my weaknesses, but stirring from the couch caught my attention. Jules sat up and pushed her hair back before rubbing her eyes. Those with me at the table stilled, waiting to see her reaction. Was it Julia or J?

We shouldn't've worried. A tremulous smile crossed her features as she stumbled to us. "I'm so sorry," she said as she faced Ox and Jose. "Can you ever forgive me?" Julia sniffed and ran a sleeve under her nose. Her shoulders slumped and wringing her hands, the picture of despair.

She stood closer to Ox than me. "Like it never happened, little one." Ox battled his own tears. Big as a bear and twice as mean in combat, the man wore his heart on his sleeve without embarrassment. He held out an arm, and Jules stepped into it, waist disappearing as beefy muscles encircled it. Although he sat in a low chair, she barely stood taller. He whispered in her ear, getting a little nod in return. Jose got his apology next along with a warm embrace.

"I've set you a plate, Julia." Mandy pointed across the table from where we sat. "Plenty of spaghetti and garlic bread left. The boys weren't as hungry as I thought."

Jose didn't wait for an elbow from me. "Let me trade places, Mrs. Pelletier. You should sit next to your husband."

"Thank you," she said. "Please, call me Julia."

We continued with war stories. Not those of combat but of daily living and the characters we served with. To see Jules follow the tales of our exploits and even smile made me give a silent sigh of relief. I hoped it would be a long time before J made a reappearance. Julia picked at her food, eating very little. She knew, I knew, and our hosts knew. Getting comfortable with my comrades set an easy mood and allowed her to relax.

While Ox roared after regaling us with a story about his nurse, I saw Jules' first tremor when her empty fork shook. "Mandy," I said, needing a clear path to the bathroom. Julia dropped her utensil only a moment before she convulsed. Mandy led the way when I scooped Jules from her seat and into my arms. She belched as we hurried, spurring me to greater speeds.

Mandy gave me a gentle push toward the door after I got Jules in front of the toilet. The smell of spaghetti-tinged stomach contents assailed my senses. "Go on, Dawson. I've got this." My final look before closing the door was of Mandy holding Julia's hair from hanging and rubbing her back. Yes, it was a blessing to have friends like these.

* * *

I woke to unfamiliar sounds. Alone in bed meant Julia'd got up at her regular time. The clock read six-fifteen. I'd been alone forty-five minutes. We slept in one of our hosts' bedrooms connected to a bathroom after Jules soiled her clothes. I'd joined her after Mandy got her situated. My one-time medic was nice enough to launder my garments along with Jules's while we slept. Slipping into clean duds started my day right.

Low voices caught my attention. Rounding the corner from the hallway, I damned near had a heart attack. Not only were Ox and Jules seated at the dining room table drinking coffee, she scrubbed her work pistol while Donny watched. "Good morning, honey," she whispered, then continued her talk with Ox. "Only after I've swabbed all the lead particulates out and run a dry patch through the bore will I replace the bolt assembly." I wasn't going to tell her he already knew.

"Coffee, sunshine?" Mandy caught me flat-footed and gaping at post-use gun scrubbing in front of another.

I followed Mandy into the kitchen, pointing a thumb over my shoulder. "What the hell?"

She filled a cup for me and smiled. "Your guess is as good as mine...maybe better," she said. "Almost crapped my pants after walking in to see them talking and her gun lying near her hand. The way they chattered, each barely noticed me." A loud giggle made my eyes grow larger. Ox chuckled in return at whatever tales they told.

The entryway darkened when Ox appeared with two empty cups in hand. "Your wife is a hoot." He guffawed while refilling them. "Forgot what it was like back in middle school. She's got a million stories." I could forgive his hyperbole. Julia often regaled me with narratives of her day after she returned home from work.

The croaking of a bullfrog in my pocket alerted me to an incoming text. A knock from the dining room meant Jules got one, too. Messages from Al. *Watch the national news.* "Mandy? Can you turn on the TV?"

Choppers hovered overhead while reporters recorded and took photos of a familiar scene. Police cordoned off the area, keeping gawkers at bay. "Although police haven't yet released the identity of those killed, sources close to authorities have reason to believe one of the bodies is that of Antoinette Benton, founder and CEO of Benton and Associates Fragrances," said the talking head. "Those at the scene believe at least six bodies have been recovered at this time. It is far too early in the investigation to know whether this was an accident or deliberate. Toni Benton was beloved by her employees, customers, and friends from around the globe..." I stopped listening the moment Jules turned her attention to me. Devoid of expression, the bleakness of J threatened to break through.

"Am I late for something?" Mark appeared, wearing pajamas bottoms and a T-shirt.

Mandy switched the television off. "Not really. Police are working the Benton estate in Mobile.

Mark shrugged. "It's not like this comes as a surprise. We might as well get used to it." He couldn't have acted less interested.

"Biscuits and gravy and scrambled eggs sound good to everyone?" Mandy asked. She seemed satisfied when most of us nodded. "Julia?" Cold eyes swung to Mandy. "Would it be asking too much to give me a hand?"

I'm not sure what they talked about, but the two women occasionally chuckled in the kitchen, other times breaking into outright laughter. For a while, I thought about checking until my phone rang. Jose, Ox, and Mark stilled their conversation at my gesture. "Hey, Al." I kept my voice low.

He didn't bother with fanfare. "You've watched it?"

"Only a few minutes. Anything we need to be worried about?"

"Not yet. Give 'em time. I know she exports to China. Perhaps an anonymous tip to point in the direction of their mafia?"

"Whatever you think best. I know very little about her dealings."

"Are you at Mark and Mandy's?"

"Yep. They brought in Ox and Jose."

"My idea. Figured Donald could use some positive direction in his life. Jose was between jobs, and I knew you liked him."

I stood and walked to my bedroom while he talked. "Both were a little freaked out after J's hit. Turns out they were pretty close to us when it went down. Almost got themselves in a world of hurt questioning her."

Al loved Julia like a daughter. "Early reports say six dead. How in hell did G-dub manage to smoke a half-dozen? They wrong...or did you help?"

"Goddamn, Al. I wouldn't have believed it if I hadn't watched." I went on to explain how easily she made the take-downs look.

The air went dead long enough for me to think we'd lost our connection. Then I heard a sigh. "She's a scary one. No two ways about it. You need to keep tighter control, sir. We don't want a repeat of Mobile if she's to win this war." He sighed a second time. "Wish I'd been there to see her in action."

"No. You don't. I worry the gray man was right...she enjoys it." I shook my head at the memory.

"Yeah, kinda figured. It's why I mentioned keeping her on a short leash. Sometimes the taste of blood is difficult to forget. You might have to jerk her back. No sense in winning if she's too damaged to take home."

Until my jaw popped, I was unaware of gritting my teeth. "She'll be fine."

141

"Don't lose her to G-dub, Dawson. Hate like hell when this is over to find Julia isn't in there any longer."

Despite raising my hackles, Al's comments fueled my worry. What if the gray man proved right, or worse—Al's suggestion I might lose Julia to her alter ego came true? "I won't let it happen," I said. "I can't lose her. Not to The Company and certainly not to herself."

"Do your best, sir. It's all any of us can ask. Even Julia."

"We still heading for Chicago next?" I wasn't ready to leave before Jules broke the shackles of J for a longer time.

"Depends."

His statement caught me off guard. "On what?"

"Does she still want the financier, or would she settle for number two?"

I considered his question. "Why?"

"The money-man is the head of a meatpackers association in the windy city."

"And the number two?"

"Joel Simon of Simon and Sons. They're an oil fracking company based in Texas but drills in Oklahoma and North Dakota."

His revelation made me grunt. Everyone knew their name since hitting it big, pumping millions of barrels. OPEC hated the corporation and vowed to— I broke off the thought when an idea came to me. "We'll go with number two, Al. Find out what you can about his whereabouts and let us know."

"You sure?"

"Yep. Jules needs a few days of decompression, so call only me with what you find."

"You got it."

The others had waited on me like one pig waits on another. Julia noticed my appearance first, her eyes full of both laughter and questions. Mandy was next. "Plenty of breakfast left. Dig in, Cap."

Ox scooted his chair aside to let me squeeze in next to Julia. "Al?" she asked.

"Yeah. Keeping me informed of what he's hearing," My casual answer seemed enough, and she went back to bantering with Jose. She seemed to hit it off with all my former army grunts.

Mandy caught my eye with a curious look—Mark watched me, too. Each nodded when I gave a lazy shrug, one small enough not even Jules noticed. We would accept rest and recreation wherever it found us.

* * *

The six of us enjoyed our time together on the gulf coast, eating too much fresh seafood—and in my case, drinking too much Tequila. I suppose I made a fool of myself more than once, but if so, it was overlooked. Julia rarely touched alcohol, and I'd only witnessed her tipsy once. Ever the careful assassin, she almost always refused to relinquish control to booze. She held me upright more than once and helped me to bed twice. For her to see me surrender to fun and drink relaxed Jules as much as me.

Ox and Jose left without fanfare in the early hours of the fifth morning. They were gone when we got out of bed—me with a headache and Jules laughing at my discomfort. We spent the day cleaning our trailer, emptying black and graywater reservoirs, and filling freshwater tanks again. A trip to the nearest supermarket helped stock our cabinets, fridge, freezer again. I topped off the propane cannister and made sure our batteries stood at a hundred percent. Although we didn't talk about it, Jules and I knew the time to leave neared.

Our call came not long after we finished dinner. Mark's specialty was a seafood boil, treating us to every kind of meat from the gulf waters. When Julia 'fessed to never tasting lobster, he made it his mission to pack our meal with the delicious crustacean. I feared our pocketbooks would quickly grow lighter after her positive reaction to the expensive flavor.

The bullfrog ringtone I used for Allen's number sounded in my pocket. "I need to take this, ladies and gentleman."

Mark waved me from their patio. "Go wan...waisht valuable drinkie time," he tried to say. I complied, wandering toward our trailer.

"Hey, Al," I answered.

143

"Joel Simon plans to be in Brownsville, Texas, next week. Figure about five days from now. Apparently, they have new oil and gas wells coming online. Gonna be a big whoop-de-do attended by the rich and powerful."

"In downtown Brownsville?"

"No, it's actually a bit closer to Laredo than Brownsville. Northwest of a place called McAllen."

"Will the party be held onsite or at a more formal location?"

"Don't know. Let me work on it while you drive west."

"What's the fallout over Toni Benton?" Neither Jules nor I watched television, and our hosts didn't bother to turn theirs on. If anyone used a phone to access the internet, no one bothered to tell me.

"Seems to be a mystery only to authorities." Allen chuckled. "The Company has no doubt who the real culprit is. G-dub's head is worth a cool three mil. Something about her calling card tipped them. Any idea of what they know?"

"Yeah..." Jules came from behind me and put her arms around my waist. "...thanks for the info, Allen. We'll be in contact."

No doubt he knew I could no longer talk. "Sure thing." I switched my phone off after sensing dead air and turned to my wife.

"Is it time?" she asked, holding her mouth up to be kissed.

I complied. "We leave in the morning if it's okay."

I felt a tremor in her slight frame, gone before I knew it. "No time like the present." I wondered if the eagerness I heard in her tone was real or imagined.

We said our goodbyes before retiring for the night in our trailer. Mark and Mandy's home lay dark when we pulled away a few minutes after four. A Beaumont rest area gave us a place to cook a meal. As our trip from Salmon to Mobile proved, Julia loved the open road and chattered constantly. At half past eight, she slid a cup of java across the table, while I studied a map of West Texas. I glanced up to an expectant look on her face. "What?"

"I asked if eggs and toast sounded okay, or if you'd rather eat something else?"

"Oh." I'd been more engrossed in our route and destination than I realized. "Sounds good with a couple tiny adjustments." I held my index finger and thumb about an inch apart.

"Like what?"

"Change the eggs to fried, warm a little of the sliced ham, melt cheese over it, and slide it all between two pieces of toast slathered with mayonnaise." I batted my eyelashes while stroking a beard in need of a trim. "Pretty please?"

Jules made a sound of delight and licked her lips. "Oh, I like the sound of that! Want onion on yours? I'm going to slice a thick piece and *sauté* it for mine."

Rather than the sandwich I envisioned, she put one together to keep me until supper. Stacked with a half-inch of meat, fried egg, pepperjack cheese, and enough mayo to drip all over the paper towel she served it on, half would have been enough. In place of wrapping it for later, when I saw how quickly she ate the twin to mine, I couldn't help but man-up and finish. "Good. Really good," I said, while leaning back to enjoy the last of my coffee.

Jules finished the few dishes and stacked them away before sitting next to me. "You've spoken to Al at least twice I know of. What's the plan?"

I made a face before breaking the news. "We're going after their number two instead of the numbers cruncher."

I didn't get the protests I expected. She only wanted an explanation. "Why? Both of you knew I counted on signing the money manager next."

"Because Joel Simon will be north of McAllen in a few days to celebrate a newly discovered oil reserve coming online." Her confused look made me give further details. "Simon and Sons?" A shake of her head meant she didn't know. "Simon and Sons are finding so much oil across the country OPEC considers them a threat. I think if we do this right, it's possible to make it look as if one of the member-states made the hit. We need Al to send an anonymous but credible tip."

"Take the chance of starting an international war?" Jules shook her head. "Huh uh. Not on my watch. We let the chips fall where they may. No way will we be responsible for something so terrible."

I threw my hands up in the face of her certainty. "Okay. We'll do it your way."

"It's the only way, honey," she said. "In and out. Sign the client, then walk away and never look back."

To argue was difficult. J's results spoke for themselves. She closed in on a hundred kills, and something told me her final tally would be well over the century mark.

Chapter X

Directions to a space in an old RV park were texted to my phone before we reached McAllen. A tall man wearing scuffed cowboy boots and a Stetson in far worse shape than my daily wear pointed the way. We drove through once before turning around and backing into our spot. Plenty of room existed on both sides for parking and sitting outside. In front was enough area to leave a couple more vehicles. We unhitched and connected to water, sewer, and power.

We were among travelers in giant motorhomes over forty feet long worth a half-million dollars to tent trailers pulled by small crossover SUVs. My best guess was out of ninety-five available, about thirty lots were full. The closest to us was an old man and his wife of at least eighty a half-dozen berths away.

At five-thirty and almost time to eat, a knock on our door surprised us. Jules was cooking venison tacos while I texted with Al. Damned burner phone didn't behave like my old one waiting at home on the counter next to Julia's. I spent more time correcting mistakes than sending messages. A series of quiet taps made me lunge from the bed where I lay close to the door. Making sure my shirt covered my XD9, I unlocked the entry and pushed it open.

I guessed the caretaker's age to be around forty or forty-five. Although I hung onto thirty-nine with a tenacity I didn't know I possessed, the big four-oh crawled in its hideous and inevitable manner to overtake me. "Wanted to welcome you folks to Whisperin' Pines Trailer Park. Smell your cookin', so I don't wanna keep you."

"Thanks," I said, doing my best not to glance toward Julia on my right. A hand rested on her work gun—both covered by a kitchen towel. "Got something I need to sign? We shouldn't be here more than a few weeks at most." I sure as hell wouldn't be inking my name or handing over photo ID.

He was quick to set my mind at ease. "No, sir. Already been taken care of by an old buddy of mine. Knowed Al since I was a young'un. He done handled everything on his end."

I tried to keep the eye-opener to myself. "You know Al?"

"Yes, sir. His ma is second cousin to mine. Him and me used to raise holy hell together up in Laredo once he got his license or down in Brownsville when we were flush with cash. 'Fore then, we spent our time on the Rio Grande shootin' turtles and frogs for the pot with our slingshots or .22s." Sounded as if the man was older than I originally thought.

Although we were partners, guess I didn't know as much about Al as I thought. "I'll be damned. Only time I noticed an accent was when he got excited. Didn't know he was from Texas."

"Yes, sir." The man said with a solemn nod. "Texan through and through by God."

"Your cousin's a good man. We served together. One hell of a guy."

Our visitor nodded. "Said the same thing about you. Told me to stay the hell out of the way while you and a woman were here. Maybe others. Just wanted you to know ain't no one gonna bother you none." He offered a curt dip of his hat and disappeared into the darkness.

I closed the door and turned to Jules. "Son of a bit...gun," I amended, remembering how much she despised the word originally meaning a female dog. "Never knew Al was from this neck of the woods. No wonder he wanted us to tap Simon next. Knows this area like the back of his hand."

"Ready for dinner?" Julia left her gun covered on the counter and handed me a plate. Our lean deer burger from home would soon run out from such a small freezer. She filled three soft shells with meat, hot sauce, refried beans, grated cheese, lettuce, most of an onion, tomato, and topped it with a handful of lettuce.

I'd already been working on two fingers of whiskey and finished it before eating. "A great dinner." While hard to mess up a taco, she could cook anything and make it taste good.

She chewed a small bite and washed it down with milk. "Lots more if you're still hungry when you polish off that." She gestured to my plate.

I noticed she made only one for herself—not very big, and she only nibbled. I guessed her appetite waned as it did when she planned to hunt. Three were more than enough for me.

Cleanup afterward took little time with both of us pitching in. I washed. She dried and put our dishes away. She sat at the other end of the couch, surprising the heck out of me when she poured a half-ounce of whiskey in a shot glass. Raising the amber liquid for a sample, she ran it around her palate before swallowing without a grimace. "Hey, we both messed up in Mobile," I said. "Mandy offered us a way to better communicate. I'd like you to consider it." I pushed a box across the table to Julia. "Two shortrange radios with whisper mikes. They pick up voices easily and transmit with the press of a button. As long as we're working line-of-sight, we shouldn't have to deploy an antenna. Press the earpiece to speak, press it again to cut your mike. Sound okay?"

She glanced at the box. "Looks similar to the Bluetooth unit I used with Al."

"Kind of. Only these are transmitters, not cellular, so no lag time. We'll better know what the other is doing or seeing."

"Hey." She read more of the instructions. "We can set them up to take voice command. A keyword to activate the microphone, another to deactivate."

"What words are you thinking of?" Her genuine smile gladdened my heart.

She thought for a moment, then shook her head. "Can't use *on* or *off.* Probably say those in normal conversation too often."

"If you're serious about using them, let's figure it out over the next day or two." I didn't want us to make the mistake of separating again before...well...before. Although I should never have left her while stretching my legs, I knew in my heart J wanted to handle the job herself. She worked best as a lone mountain lion than a wolf within a pack.

We were early in bed with Julia showing all the signs of needing physical love. Afterward, she clung to me with a desperation she seldom exhibited. For a tough woman so sure of herself, I noticed she tended to cry easily. Holding her was easy—showing how much I cared easier yet. I enjoyed the tight bond we shared, one often strained when J reared her head.

My chest and shoulder were wet when she reached for a tissue and blew her nose before drying her face with the sheet. Julia lay back with our covers pulled above her chest. "I love you, Dawson. You know that, don't you?" Her voice was low, though not whispering.

I rolled toward her and kissed more tears from her cheek. "Of course, I do, little dove."

Her cries exploded. She rolled into a fetal position facing away, using her pillow to stifle what sounded like overwhelming anguish. I couldn't do much but cushion her body against mine. Finally, she twisted to face me, putting distance between us. "Y-y-your little dove is m-more b-b-broken than you can imagine." She continued sobbing.

"I'm here, sweetie. I'll always be here. If you feel like you're drowning, you only have to reach out. I'm your lifesaver, no matter how choppy the seas."

"I-I-I know." She hiccupped. Rubbing her back seemed to calm her. She seemed to regain at least partial control. "It's not you...it's me."

"Let me help. Talk to me. Tell me what you're feeling. I can't read your mind."

She took a deep breath, allowing it to escape slowly while she relaxed. "I'd almost forgotten what it feels like. I love teaching, but hunting and signing clients is what I'm best at." Her terminology caught my attention, although I wasn't surprised. Sign a client rather than kill her target. Even now she couldn't articulate the end result. "The chase is exciting. It's a necessary part. But the endgame..." The noise she generated was one of content—almost a purr. "...is what I'm good at."

I couldn't disagree after watching her in action. A maestro conducting a great orchestra—or as Ox noted—an acclaimed dancer performing the same steps she did a thousand times. I liked to think of her as a middle linebacker who sidestepped three linemen and bore down on an unprotected quarterback waiting for a receiver to come open. An unstoppable force. "What can I do to help?"

Her answer came so quietly I could barely hear it. "Nothing. I want to be turned loose. Show them what they've created...demonstrate my potential...and in the end, kill them all."

* * *

I almost lost her to Joel Simon. Turns out the bastard was more prepared than any of us anticipated. To our surprise, Ox and Jose appeared the next morning to guide us to the place Mark and Mandy already watched with their drone. Where Julia got in our truck to follow our friends, J stepped out to coldly ignore them. Rather than ask questions while we looked on from fifteen hundred feet above the ground, she simply watched, paced, and listened. The ceremony was planned for the following day with large open-sided tents erected to keep the weather off. A storm moving north from the gulf threatened to drench the festivities and us.

Mark pointed to his screen. "We think the biggest tents are for guests and food. Loudspeakers are set up in these." He used the tip of a pen to indicate their whereabouts. "Kinda figure Simon and any of his allies will be here." Again, he aimed his ballpoint at the smallest enclosure.

My phone burped to indicate Al's incoming message. *Call me ASAP.* I saw where I'd missed his voice call with my phone pocketed. He answered on the first ring. "Simon's there."

"Where? In McAllen? Brownsville?"

His voice raised with impatience. "Are you with Mandy and the rest?"

"Yeah. We're watching them erect a series of enclosures near a wellhead."

"Then he's not far from where you're standing. He's talking on the phone to one of his boys sitting in a meeting, and I can hear wind. Do you feel it?"

151

"Yep." It buffeted the six of us while we tried to keep tabs. Mark's drone threatened to leave us without eyes overhead.

"Don't stop looking, but keep G-dub on a short leash like we talked, okay? I'd like to see the body count stay a bit lower." Rather than wait for an answer, he ended our call.

"Al?" Mandy asked.

"You need to zoom in," I instructed Mark. "Al swears Simon is here."

"What?" Jose straightened and gazed across the mostly flat ground to where the party was to be held some half-mile away over a low rise. "I thought tomorrow was the big day."

"Looks like he's early," I answered dryly, absently noticing J meandering to our truck. She seated herself inside and poured a cup of java, seemingly lost in thought. Turning my attention to the screen while scouring the grounds for our quarry, we lost ourselves in the search. Mark moved his drone and camera while we scrutinized the few cars, trucks, and people moving around. We'd soon need to bring it in for a refueling.

"Hey!" Mark's voice rose when he jabbed a finger at the screen. "Isn't that Julia?" A lone figure could be seen crossing an empty field in the direction of the tents.

"Jules?" I sprinted to the truck. The doors were closed and the cab empty. She was nowhere to be seen. I hustled back to where everyone huddled around the monitor. "She's gone," I told our team.

Tapping my earpiece to talk, I attempted to initiate contact using our new headsets. "Jules? J?" I hoped she wasn't out of range. "Julia, respond if you hear me." After trying more taps, I turned the mike off. "She's not answering."

"She's almost reached ground zero, Cap," Ox said.

"Wait here." Leaving them in place to guard my six, I raced away in the truck. Barreling toward where we saw her last, I reached into the backseat for Al's rifle. We'd attached the suppressor and left the rifle loaded with a twenty-round magazine. Although driving too fast for road conditions, I took time to work the action and put one directly into the chamber.

My burner phone rang. "Yeah?" I answered, hoping against all odds Jules called for an extraction. "She's been made, Cap," Mandy calmly relayed from Mark. "Not sure if it's a guard or Simon. Looks like they're about to tap her."

"Goddamn," I yelled, throwing the phone on the seat next to me. The truck almost went airborne as I came over the rise to see J ahead, hands held above her head. Lowering the passenger window, I slowed and departed gravel to parallel the encampment. Closing on them, I measured the distance in my mind. Two hundred yards, one-eighty, I drummed fingertips on my earpiece in the event hers was activated. "I'm here, honey. Tap to talk if possible." She lowered her hands slowly, to interlock fingers behind her head. On the way, she keyed her mike with a thumb.

"...can't believe it. Of anyone in the world, I get to sign the legend." The voice chuckled. "Three point five million as of this morning. Think I'll take the family to Tahiti." A huge enclosure and stacked gear blocked them from the main gathering area.

I slowed my roll, trying to appear to drive toward the tents and a few more trucks parked nearby. One-fifty, one-twenty-five, I eased to a stop with the passenger side facing the pair at a hair over a hundred. "I need you to move six inches to your left," I whispered. "Just shift your weight."

Simon probably couldn't see inside the truck even with the window down and his attention on J. Exactly as I asked, she leaned enough to expose part of his chest. "I've never killed anyone before," he said. "Didn't think my first would be a beautiful little bitch worth..." Taking a huge risk, I held tight against J's right shoulder, and the bullet took him on the inside edge of his shirt pocket. Another three subsonic 124 grain hollow points thudded home as quickly as I could squeeze the trigger and still keep the front sight lined center mass.

Like the killer she is, J didn't turn and run toward me. Instead, she drew the work gun still in her waistband and shot Simon after he collapsed. Unable to hear the sound or see recoil, I could only assume she put another four into his brain. Turning abruptly, she strolled nonchalantly toward me. We were moving the moment her butt touched the seat. Not racing across the landscape, simply driving steadily. I hoped no one noticed his body until we vacated the area.

Ox and Jose were nowhere to be seen when we arrived. Mark was closing their trunk, and Mandy hurried to the passenger side of our truck. "I'm so glad you're okay," she said while stepping onto our running board. "Oh, you're hurt," she said to Julia. "Any other wounds?"

J jerked away. "I'm fine."

"Sir?" Mandy looked across the cab to me. "We'll follow you to your place. I need to take a closer look at Julia's shoulder."

Too angry to answer, I merely nodded. She didn't appear wounded to me. Mark stayed behind at a safe distance until we arrived at our trailer. He went inside with me, while Mandy stopped at J's side of the truck. "Shit." Mark tossed his baseball cap to the counter and sat on our couch. "Close...way too close." He noticed my ill temper when the two women entered. "Sir?"

Mandy carried a bag as she came in with J. "She needs stitches. Your bullet opened the skin covering her lateral deltoid. No muscle fibers appear severed...should be an easy fix." Mandy sat her patient at the table for a closer look and grimaced. "I didn't bring any pain medication...it's gonna hurt like a bastard."

With J still in full control, Mark and I watched Mandy clean and prep the area for sutures. While Mark flinched when the hook broke through J's skin, neither she nor I winced. As far as I was concerned, she earned the pain. Julia would likely have been reduced to tears, while J embraced it stoically. Five stitches went in, then a pair of neatly applied butterfly bandages.

Mandy stepped back and leaned against the counter beside me. "You cut it awfully close unless this was a miss, double-D," she said gently.

"You should know by now I don't." I said. J didn't look my way nor change her expression.

Mark ignored her. "What now, Cap?" It'd been ages since I'd been given either nickname. Ox probably never thought of me as anything else. "Any idea of who the next target is?"

We'd overstayed our welcome. "I think we'd better get the hell out of Dodge and regroup elsewhere."

Mark and I needed ten minutes before the trailer was tow ready. Mandy got J changed into another blouse and a hooded sweatshirt. "Baton Rouge?" Mandy asked.

I shook my head. "I was thinking south to Brownsville or west toward Rio Grande City. Not sure if we're leaving for Chicago or if another target is closer. I'll call Al later."

A Chevy truck—I'd guess late 'seventies—arrived to block us from departing. The park manager stepped out. "Figured you might be leaving."

"Yeah," I shook his hand and stepped back. "Think we might vacation south of the border for a change. Better exchange on our dollars."

Al's cousin shook his head. "I'd advise against it. Gonna be police stops between here and Mexico. Seems some big-ass muckity-muck went and got himself killed. Heard on my scanner cops are doing random searches at blockades. My suggestion is to take Six-niner Charlie north to Edinburg. Turns to Two-eighty-one after about five miles. Stay on it until Falfurrias, then Two-eighty-five to Laredo if you're on your way home."

Damned if we don't meet the oddest people at the strangest times. Allen's cousin proved to be right. The area crawled with police. I drove sixty and not a tick over. Mark and Mandy dogged us until reaching 285, then left us in the dust. We planned to meet again at a Walmart on San Bernardo Avenue. With J retreating further into herself, I didn't mind when my cell croaked. "Hey, Al."

"I guess you didn't listen to my suggestion." He didn't sound happy.

"About what?" J didn't appear to pay any attention to my call.

155

"You gotta choke up on G-dub's leash."

I couldn't argue. I'd taken my eye off her for only a few minutes but long enough for her to almost get herself killed. "Might be worse than you think. Significantly more than I imagined."

"She with you?"

"Yep." I couldn't say more without her getting wind of our conversation.

"Which direction are you driving?"

"First, I love your cousin. He's helped us more than we can repay. He said go to Laredo. We plan to spend the night in a Walmart parking lot."

Al chuckled. "Steve-O? Got in too much trouble with that one. Salt of the earth. Might be a third or fourth cousin, but I love him like a brother."

"Where are we going next?" I knew very well Julia wanted the Chicago moneyman.

"Too soon. Take a night to rest and relax. I'll contact you after I gather more intel. Should be a hell of a lot of communication over the next twenty-four hours."

We spoke about Mom and how much she enjoyed the villa in Belize. Al stayed in contact with her almost daily. Made me feel bad to know he spoke to her significantly more often than me. With another hour before reaching our destination, I ended our call and rang my mother. She answered before I was ready. "About time I heard from my prodigal son."

"Hey, Mom. How's the weather? Word on the street is you turn a lot of heads wearing a two-piece bikini."

Her laugh slipped spontaneously. "Oh, you. I've bought a couple of one-pieces that look like they were designed in the 'fifties."

"Do you like it there? You're in Belize swimming in the ocean, while Salmon is under a foot of snow."

"Go ahead..." Her chuckle sounded forced. "...make me feel guilty for having so much fun."

"Enjoy yourself. You deserve it. I was only kidding."

"How's Julia? Bess tells me she isn't back to school yet. Headaches still a problem? Don't let her slip and fall in the snow. You know how clumsy she is."

If only she knew. "She's better and being tested." I'm glad Mom didn't know of the trials her daughter-in-law was going through.

"Oh, good. Tell her I love and pray for her daily." One thing about Mom—she cared deeply for my wife almost before they met. Figured if a dog as sweet as Jake was her boy, Julia must be a good woman.

My next call was to Aunt Bess at her school. "Bess Mueller's office. How may I direct your call?"

"Hi, Mary. Could I talk to Aunt Bess?" Mary Calhoun graduated about the time I mustered out of the army. She was a really nice woman with young four daughters and a hard-working logger of a husband.

"Sure, Dawson. Let me put you through."

Aunt Bess answered immediately. "Dawson? How's Julia? You should have never taken her into the backcountry. Now it's going to be longer before she's ready to return to work. What a horrible mess."

"What have you heard, Auntie?" Scotty never contacted me to let us know what came out in public. I think with the lady who scared him out of the area, he didn't want to poke a bear and wake it.

"Four men were murdered while hunting with Scotty Rich. You and Julia were listed as witnesses."

"Have they named any suspects?"

"No, not that I've heard. There's been a terrible rumor floating around though. Some seem to think Julia was involved."

"What an awful thing to say. Anyone in particular?" If someone spread the news of Julia defending herself and the rest of us—whether true or not—I'd take care of it.

"Now, Dawson, I recognize your tone from when you walked these same halls almost thirty years ago. Don't worry. Truth always comes out in the end."

In a way, I feared she might be right. I loved my hometown of Salmon. The idea of living elsewhere scared me. To be without Julia was a future I couldn't and wouldn't contemplate. "I hope so, Auntie,"

I said ominously, if for no other reason than to ease any suspicions she might have.

"Are you back in Salmon yet? Jake misses his mistress terribly. The kids play with him, but he watches the driveway for her return."

I glanced to where J stared out the side window. "No, we're out of state for the time being."

We ended with Aunt Bess asking me to impress upon Jules how badly she was needed. Not to hurry though—health was far more important than work. I almost laughed my slow boil away while she expressed her terrible need for her teacher, yet not to come back too soon. "Sounds like Jake misses you," I said after ending my call. J gave a curt nod, but I heard a wet sniff a few minutes later.

* * *

I found Mark and Mandy's car at the outer edges of the Walmart parking lot and set up camp nearby. Mark waited outside his car while I shut off our engine. "Mandy's inside finding a few things for dinner, and I got us a room a few miles away." He waved his cellphone as if I didn't understand its multitude of uses. "Got a text from Al telling us to sit tight."

"We talked." I turned after hearing the trailer door close. "He hopes to intercept more communications before committing us to a new target."

Mark saw his wife striding toward us. "How about if we eat before Mandy and I leave for the night?"

Their idea sounded good. "Sure, bring her in."

I went inside first, not sure of what I'd find. I flicked lights on in the darkened place to locate Jules in bed. "Hey, we've got company, and they brought dinner."

"Don't want any," came the muffled reply. I couldn't see anything but her crown above the covers. Her work gun wasn't in sight, but the Glock lay on the shelf near her hand.

"I brought sandwich supplies," Mandy said. "How about if I make two, then we'll get out of your hair." Always the pragmatic one, she quickly fulfilled her suggestion. They left, promising to be in touch.

Although still early, I wrapped our meal and stowed it in the refrigerator. The day's events and terror coming from almost losing my partner taxed my energy. Julia was already snoring softly when I slipped between the sheets next to her.

I woke to the gray light of morning feeling almost as exhausted as when I fell asleep. Julia lay with an arm draped across my chest and a leg over mine. A kiss was administered to my bare shoulder. "I love you," she whispered.

"Good morning." I said, unwilling to totally release simmering anger since her stupid move the previous day.

"You don't love me?" She didn't seem willing to lift her head to meet my eyes.

I kept my sigh to a minimum. "Of course, I do, little dove. Nothing can ever make me stop."

"Promise you will forever, no matter what."

"Cross my heart and hope to die."

"No, never die as long as I'm alive."

"Jules, as the sun will always rise in the east, I'll never stop loving you."

I felt lips against my shoulder and then neck. "Remember your pledge no matter what stupid things I do, okay?"

"I can still be angry, right? As long as I still love you?"

"Uh huh." She squirmed upward toward my ear when I heard a gasp. "Oh, my shoulder." Jules groaned for a moment. "You could have held at least a half inch to the right, couldn't you?"

Her question was worth consideration. "No, I wanted him dead instantly, but it was too chancy for a headshot. Center mass was the best option hoping to catch his heart. Even then he could have gotten a round off."

"Thank you, my love." Julia seemed in full control. "I owe you my life."

"You gotta talk to me, girl. I don't know what to do after I've been shut out."

"I'll try to do better." In my heart I knew she wouldn't or couldn't.

159

I wasn't particularly hungry and chose cereal for breakfast. Jules ate her sandwich from the night before. Parked so close to Walmart, we wandered in to use their facilities. Mark and Mandy were waiting at our door when we returned, and he hurried to meet us. "Bad news, sir." Even from a distance I saw Mandy in tears. "Mandy's mother died in a car wreck a few minutes ago. T-boned at an intersection in Baton Rouge. Mandy's dad was driving her mom to work. He's alive, but hanging on by a thread." Jules sprinted toward the distraught woman. "We hate to leave you on short notice, but these are her parents."

"Say no more, my man. Blood is everything. You shouldn't have waited...a text would have been enough." I put a hand on his shoulder after seeing how dangerously close to the breaking point he teetered. We hurried to where Jules lent her strength and arms to the much larger woman.

"I'm sorry." Mandy fell into my embrace next. "We hate to leave you in the lurch."

"Family is everything, hon. Besides, you have a pregnancy to take care of now. Jules and I got this."

"T-take care of her, Cap," she whispered through hiccups. "Julia may seem tough on the outside. She's nothing of the sort within. Cut her slack where you can. Rejoice every minute in her being alive."

Mandy's sage advice couldn't have come at a better time. Anger at my wife dissipated as our friends drove away. Life can be taken in an instant when we least expect it. With Jules in retaliatory mode, another mistake like the one made with Simon was all it would take. I followed her inside. We collapsed—her on the bed, me on the couch. After a few minutes, I moved to lie next to her. My phone's ring made me wince. "Morning, Al," I said.

"I heard about Mandy's mom. Nice lady. Met her at their wedding."

"You went?" The news surprised me, although it shouldn't've.

"Yeah, an older version of her daughter. The world has dimmed with her loss."

I needed to talk about anything else. "Any news from the media after Simon's death? Or Benton's?"

He chuckled. "Turns out Benton's company was infiltrated by competitors. Officials are examining corporate espionage. Too soon to say about Simon."

"And The Company? Any rumblings?" Jules arm tightened around my torso.

"Almost waited to call because not a peep. Like Simon wasn't a part of them."

I tamped down sudden alarm. "He was, right?"

Al chuckled. "His company donated over fifteen million last year. Yeah, he was a big cog in their machine. I understand you tapped him, sir. Good shooting as always, but your conscience should be clear. I'll be interested to learn whether his sons fill his place or if they even knew."

"What do you recommend? Stay or relocate?"

"I suggest you rest another day. Let me find out what I can. If you'd like, I can work G-dub from Texas to Chicago. Sir, a dozen or more of The Company lie between you and the windy city."

Chapter XI

Our free time was spent with Julia showering me with far more attention than usual. We didn't leave the trailer except to use the superstore bathroom. We made love at her insistence while a pork loin baked along with potatoes. Wonderful aromas filled our place long before dinner was served. Jules made a cake and offered to buy ice cream to go with it. Whatever the occasion, she went all-out to make our evening memorable.

"I love you," she repeated after we retired for the evening without word from Al.

We read in bed using twelve-volt lights—hers a romance novel—mine a hunting magazine. "I know you do, honey. Right back atcha."

We still hadn't heard from Al after finishing breakfast the following morning. "Dawson, could you run inside the store and pick up sliced ham from their deli and any bread you like?" Jules asked in her sweetest voice. "Sliced cheese, too. Colby jack unless you prefer something else." She removed my phone from the charger and dropped it in my side pocket with a kiss to my cheek as I went by. No real reason than she might remember something while I was inside, I surmised.

The deli wasn't yet open. With twenty minutes to go before I could purchase Julia's order, I waffled on whether to wait or return. After deciding to stay, I used the time to peruse Walmart's sporting goods section. Ten minutes tardy when I returned to buy sliced meat, a line forced me to be even later when I left the store. A hard wind caused me to draw my sweatshirt hood over my head as I trudged to the trailer.

Our home was no longer parked where I left it. Both the truck and trailer vanished. Scanning the lot, I didn't see our outfit anywhere. My heart jumped into my throat with my worst nightmare come true. I couldn't imagine Jules leaving for fuel without calling first. Besides, she professed to be uncomfortable towing and felt navigating a gas station would be too much. I could only think The Company snatched her. Except, wouldn't they sign her and leave the body for me or others to find?

Stifling growing alarm, a call would be the smartest place to start. I checked my cellphone only to find it shut off. Restarting the damned devise, I found a voice mail from Al. "G-dub's got all the info, Dawson. Remember to keep her leash snubbed tight, or we're likely to have a bloodbath. I've provided the names and coordinates for her next eleven targets." My shouted curse came when his message ended. I punched his number in a panic. Al picked up on the second ring. "On the road already?"

"We've been hit, Al. Julia's gone."

He stammered while organizing his thoughts. "G-g-gone? You mean The Company has her? Or did they..." He didn't say the terrible word.

"I don't know." Frantic images crowded my mind. Was Jules already dead? "She asked me to pick up a few things inside the store. Took me close to forty-five minutes before I got out. She's missing, along with our truck and trailer." I spun in circles while I talked, searching in every direction.

"Oh, shit. No, no, no..." Dread filled me as I absorbed Al's panic. "I don't think it's The Company, sir."

"Who, then?" I shouted. "Who else is there? Police would be here waiting."

"Dawson..." I knew what he was going to say. "She's cut the strings and gone rogue. No wonder she texted to ask if I'd call her back and leave the info she wanted as a message. Shit. She's in possession of enough details to make it possible to extract further knowledge from any of her marks who may know where the rest are. J doesn't need us any longer, sir."

I was certain Al was right. Sure, Jules loved me, but then there was J, and J could no longer tolerate a drag on doing what she did best—hunt and kill quickly and efficiently. As an old army man, I wanted to recon and map out the best way forward. J simply located her prey and performed a simple assassination. To make matters worse, a drop of wind driven rain quickly turned into many. I hustled back to the superstore through the growing rainstorm while we spoke. "You're right, man. Damned little terminator felt it best to deal me out and handle it herself." My jaw tightened as I accepted the realization. Once inside, I hurried to the restroom parents used to change children's diapers and locked the door.

Al didn't stop planning. "Shall I can contact Jose or Donny? I'm sure one can give you a lift home. It'd look bad if you rent wheels so close to the site of the latest hit."

"Al..." A worry gnawed its way into my subconscious over the last few days and grew each hour. "...I'm worried about Mom."

He stopped me. "Don't be. Her location's the safest place she could stay."

"She's alone. The Company knows who's picking them off one at a time. If my name is connected in any way to where she is..." I didn't want to reveal the spot over a cellphone call. "...it wouldn't be difficult for someone to find a way to hurt us. Attacking me is a way of getting to Jules."

"What do you want to do?"

"I'd like Jose and Ox there. Hell, move them in with her and tell her they're groundskeepers. Al..." My panic bubbled over. "...I'm worried, really worried." The thought of losing both my wife and mother was too much.

"Say no more, sir. Keep your phone handy. I'll contact you the moment I know if they're willing to take the job. We'll look into your extraction later today."

Alone almost two thousand miles from home, I took inventory of my belongings. First was my Springfield loaded with seventeen rounds—along with an extra magazine, a short stout belt knife, small flashlight, my phone, and wallet. Although carrying debit cards, we relied on cash rather than leave a technological trail. Even our cells were burners. Most of our money lay hidden in multiple locations in the truck and trailer. A quick count added up to almost twelve hundred dollars in my pocket—enough for a week or longer unless an avenue home arose.

I wandered outside after the rain stopped. It poured for only a brief period, and clouds looked as if they could produce more. After finding a place to sit, I took the time to make two dry sandwiches from the sack of groceries J—I couldn't think of her as Jules any longer—ordered.

The idea she left me behind infuriated me as I ate. We were supposed to be a team. One second angry enough to strangle her, the next left me shaken to consider I might never see her again except to identify a body or perhaps only to view her through a prison window. While the latter frightened me, at least she would be alive.

I wandered the lot and around the building while keeping a sharp eye to locate our outfit. My phone's battery dropped precipitously as I called Jules repeatedly, then worried enough power might not remain to converse with Al and paced calls. I ran hot and cold each time her number went to voicemail. Although I didn't shout my displeasure nor threaten her, I left J with no doubt as to my level of unhappiness. Eleven percent remained in the battery when Al phoned again. My feet hurt from walking on asphalt, and my head ached from worry. "Tell me good things, Al."

"Can you be at the far end of aisle nine in ten minutes?"

"I'm looking at it now." From where I stood at the entrance, both eight and nine were straight in front and led out to a main thoroughfare.

Al grunted. "Good. A car will pick you up in nine. You'll be transported to a small airport outside of town. A jet is fueling now."

I started my trek into a stiff oncoming wind. "Mom?"

"Good thinking. I'm glad you brought it up. Ox and Jose are packing their gear as we speak. Melissa is expecting a grounds crew to move into the garage apartment." Who except Al and now Mom knew we owned something so nice?

"Make sure they're paid handsomely, my friend. I'll make it up to you after I'm back and able to transfer money."

"No worries. I can use a portion of your profits this quarter if you'd like." Al made automatic deposits into my account four times each year. Some were large and others small, but even the least provided enough money for Mom and me for a year. With the farm paid off and few other bills, our savings seemed to grow out of control.

"Sounds great. Whatever they need...don't scrimp. Nor do I want Mom to know the reason they're there."

Al's wry chuckle told me he understood. "Have no fear. I know Melissa well enough to understand I'd hate to be on her bad side." His assessment was indeed correct. Mom spent much of her life as a housewife and mother of two boys. She could come down hard when she felt it was warranted. "Four minutes," he said. "Do you see a black Mercedes AMC G-65? It should look something like an older Land Rover."

I scanned the lot and primary highway feeding it. "Not yet." Although I wasn't familiar with Mercedes, Land Rovers were a vehicle I'd considered interesting, even if I wouldn't own one. My old Ford F250 got the job done. A large black SUV exiting the highway captured my attention. "Hold on. I think I see it."

"Your benefactor's name is Vasily Sokolov. I do a bit of business for him with imports and exports. Not sure if he'll accompany his driver—Vasily is Russian and difficult to understand. Play nice, Dawson."

I ended the call as the SUV stopped with the passenger window not more than a few feet away. Al knew how little I appreciated Russians after we faced them in Iraq across the Syrian border. Their shelling of my men was admitted as a mistake only after I called for an airstrike on their coordinates. We suffered two wounded, and more could have easily been killed or injured. Hell, our entire unit might have been wiped out. They lost one man in our retaliation with another six casualties.

The window lowered, and I looked in to face an obvious Russian. "Name?" His voice was thick with accent.

"Dawson Pelletier."

The passenger stepped out to open the rear door and gestured. "Get in, please." He closed it after I found the restraint, and he seated himself in the front again.

I waited in silence rather than start a conversation. "You need a ride to Idaho?" the driver asked.

"I do. I've somehow found myself without transportation." I wasn't going to tell them jack-shit.

Not sure what to expect, twenty minutes of silence brought us to a private airstrip. Rather than stop at the gate, the Mercedes angled toward a single Leerjet 75. Small and sleek, I wondered if it was in my immediate future.

My ride stopped only yards away from the plane. My door was opened again, leaving me no option but to exit the vehicle. "Your way home." The Russian pointed to another person standing at the top of the stairs.

"Mr. Pelletier?" A pretty American woman of perhaps twenty-five awaited and motioned me inside after my nod. "If you would make yourself comfortable..."

Other than our pilot, copilot, and stewardess, I was the only one onboard. Not only would I arrive home much sooner than I anticipated, it would be without an electronic trail. After making a quick phone call, then ordering and finishing two Tequila Sunrises, I settled in for the ride.

* * *

Scotty dog-eyed me in his peripheral vision on the drive. He waited my arrival in a nice but used F350 purchased with the money Julia provided. I knew what he wanted to ask, but I took a different route. "Police clear you yet?"

He expelled an explosive breath of relief. "Yeah. Looks like those bastards were in the wrong line of business. Cops figure they wanted to cover up killing me."

"They still got our guns?" I figured my .44s would be returned, but wasn't sure about Julia's .38.

"They gave mine back. I suppose yours are available now, too. Before I forget, the meat from your elk is cut, wrapped, and waiting at the butcher's. Might want to pick it up...he's contacted me a few times."

Angry and sick with fear and dread, I wasn't much of a riding partner. Scotty drove me to his place where my truck was parked next to his barn. I caught the keys he threw. "Thanks, buddy."

He stopped me when I turned to leave. "Sure you don't want to come in?" I'm sure he hoped to learn why I arrived in a Leer without Jules.

"Mind if I take a raincheck?" His front door opened, and Robin stepped onto the porch to wave. I pivoted to my truck after returning her greeting. All I could wish for was getting home and closing the world out.

"Sure, man." Scotty followed me to my Ford. For a truck made in the 'nineties with almost three hundred thousand miles, the engine barely cranked over before starting. Rather than exchange more meaningless niceties, I left for home.

Jake was on my mind as I drove north. I felt bad not stopping at Aunt Bess's and getting him. Temperatures were cold with over twelve inches of packed snow along the roads. Pheasants and grouse would be likely targets if I wished to hunt the sleek pointer.

I parked my truck inside the garage, a place I'd never left it. However, I didn't wish any visitors. Without any gear to pack in, I hurried to the house to build a fire. Snow in front where old tracks were clustered looked odd. Remembering Scotty taking care of our animals, I realized he couldn't do it without leaving signs. Retrieving a key hidden on the top of a porch rafter, I unlocked the door and almost stepped inside when something caught my eye.

The glint from a wire so thin as to be invisible showed as the sun descended. Hunkering close, I saw where someone strung it three inches above the threshold—perfect to catch a toe or heel. On all fours, I followed the strand to where it hung over tiny finishing nails on either side of the entry. From there they disappeared between porch slats.

Hustling back to my truck, I retrieved a flashlight and multipurpose tool from the glovebox. Climbing beneath the porch decking, the trap was plain to see. I played my beam on two US fragmentation grenades beneath either side of the threshold. Even if I walked inside the house after triggering the bombs, the resulting detonation would have torn the front of our house away and likely killed or wounded me and anyone else nearby. With a fifty-foot range of destruction, someone planned for Julia's and likely my death, too. I took great care and used the pliers on my tool to cut the grenades loose. Their pins were barely holding the spoons. I expanded their tips to keep the striker from moving and render the powerful devices safe.

I spent two hours searching in and outside of the house for other booby traps. Someone planned to take the fight to us, and I needed to know who. After assuring myself of no other ambushes, I locked the door, pulled the shades, and built a fire. The small house warmed quickly while I took stock of my situation.

Most of our guns were in the truck and trailer with J. Other than the Springfield on my belt, the only firearms available to me were our hunting shotguns. Perhaps my .44s if the police agreed to release them. Taking the quickest shower of my life—worried I could be caught naked and defenseless—I changed into clean clothes. By then, my course was set. Gathering items I might need, I opened the trapdoor and the bomb shelter beneath. Blankets, clothing, my sleeping bag, canned and packaged food, a lantern, most of our ammunition, and my camping stove—I stored enough to get by if needed. With plenty of room for my cot, I set up a place to sleep in the shelter rather than on the main floor. Satisfied I could live comfortably for a week or two, I took time to fix dinner.

After the dishes were washed and laid out to dry, I turned to our laptop. Time taken to read articles of our first two targets were minutes well spent. Police looked elsewhere without the mention of a tiny woman and her tall partner. Unable to find more high-profile deaths on the internet, I took my cellphone and computer with me into the shelter. Lowering the hinged piece of flooring first, I closed off my hidey-hole to the world. My fear of no service inside proved correct. Instead of reading further or calling Al, I played solitaire until I could no longer keep my eyes open.

* * *

Jake was glad to see me. With no one home, I left a note on Aunt Bess's table and another on her cell. She didn't use it during work hours, and I counted her habit to my advantage. I left a quick message explaining Julia was staying at a hospital treating headwounds, and I'd taken our boy off her hands. A call to the police station alerted them to my pending arrival. As Scotty indicated, my .44s and Julia's .38 were remanded to my custody. I breathed a sigh of relief after belting on my trusty Anaconda. I wasn't much of a fan of semi-autos. A stop by the store replenished our dwindling supply of food. Some was bought with the basement hide in mind.

Jake appeared beside himself with joy. He loved riding in my old Ford with his head hanging from the window in the freezing air. After we returned home, he searched the house and surrounding area for his mistress. Rather than sulk—once satisfied we were a duo instead of a trio—the pointer was happy to be home with me as his company. Watching carefully as the dog made his normal rounds, I didn't see anything to indicate he found a cause to make me worry. On the couch with my Marlin loaded with twelve rounds in its tubular magazine and a thirteenth in the chamber close to hand, I settled in to see what I could learn on the worldwide web.

Two hours of searching was wasted when I didn't find anything new. Sick with fear and anger and no way of contacting Julia, I pushed my chair back from the table in time to hear my phone ring. Hoping for the best but fearing the worst, I answered. "Got anything for me, Al?"

His sigh warned me there would be no good news. "Yes and no. I just got off the phone with G-dub—"

I broke into his report. "Is she okay? Did she indicate where she was or planned to go next? I could intercept her, Al."

"Easy, Dawson." His tone became businesslike. "No, I didn't learn where she was or her plans. Only she was safe and asked me to tell you how sorry she was." I didn't have to see his shudder—it was clear over the phone. "Her voice...goddamn, sir. I don't want to ever hear anything so cold from someone I know. Liked to have frozen my ear."

I forced myself not to shout. "Anything else?"

"Not much. She thanked me for my help and said she'd be in touch. Likely ended our gabfest early to keep me from downloading a tracker to ping her phone." He chuckled. "Almost got her."

His news didn't surprise me. J was a killer. Without feelings or remorse, she made an appearance to only take life. Neither warmth nor tenderness existed when she emerged. "No indication of what direction she took?"

"No, sir. I heard road noise, so she's obviously moving. I thought you said she didn't care to handle your rig?"

I remembered well Julia's response to my offer of letting her drive. It was too big, she said, making sure I understood she would probably wreck it while trying to access a gas station. Yet J was nothing if not resourceful. No job was too big or slowed her. Single-minded in her focus, nothing could stop her retaliation. "Jules, no. But J? Nothing gets in her way."

"She hasn't contacted you?"

"Not a goddamned peep."

"She loves you, sir...Dawson." Al never forgot where we came from or how we met. Especially with me as his superior officer.

He wasn't particularly surprised when I explained about the booby trap awaiting my return. Al offered to pick me up in his helicopter and let me stay with him. Even get me another ride on the Russian Leer to Butch Prayde's place in Boca Raton or south with Mom. One bit of good news was Mandy's dad was expected to survive. Her mom would be buried over the weekend. Beyond those items, Mandy would need time to heal and have her baby.

"The Russian Leer. Should I even ask?" I assumed Al dealt with sketchy individuals—he provided IT work to those who...those inclined to move within the shadows. Knowing the man as I did—a patriot through and through—nothing he did would prove to harm our country in any way. Some folks preferred to work beneath governmental radar.

His chuckle tickled me. "No, I'd feel better if you didn't. However, rest easy knowing Vasily Sokolov loves the US far more than his former country. He simply wants to keep the largest portion of his billions to himself."

"Allen..." I knew many millionaires over my lifetime, but no billionaires. "...could he be involved with The Company?"

"No, and no. If anything, I could very well elicit his help. He's aware of our partnership...yours and mine. After hearing you needed immediate help and knowing he was closest, Vasily offered money, a car, or his jet. He asked we not reimburse him for even the fuel used or the flight crew."

"Thank him for me."

"Already done. Said he still owes us for all we've provided. Say, how are things on the home front?"

"No problems but the grenades. A few minutes later without enough light or if I'd been more tired and not paying attention, Jules would be short a husband." I snorted. "Hell, at this rate, she might be anyway."

The urgency in Allen's tone was plain. "Don't go off half-cocked and do anything stupid, sir." He'd gone through a marital split, and it damned near killed him. He mustered out a few weeks before me and arrived home to find divorce papers waiting. Our partnership gave him something to live for.

"No worries. Jules is my life."

"Very good. From here on I'll change my algorithms to learn anything I can about a counteroffensive against you and Julia. There's a chance it was a one-time attempt, rather than a long-term concerted effort. They know for sure she's away from home. Perhaps this was to injure someone checking on your house and bring you back."

We ended our conversation after he promised to keep me updated no matter how small the news. Jake wanted out and nosed me until I followed him to the door. The coast appeared clear, and he scooted through like his hair was on fire. I thought about going back online and searching for more info, but figured it was a waste of time. Instead, I watched the pointer searching for birds and decided to hunt instead. Not necessarily only wild fowl but signs of anyone lurking.

Jake was thrilled to see me outside with my old twenty gauge. I might not be as quick a shot as his mistress but swore I'd hit anything he found. "Hunt 'em up, Jake!"

We bagged two pheasant roosters and a ruffed grouse before hiking back. Any tracks I searched for were covered by drifting snow. It was useless to continue looking. Whomever set the booby trap likely drove to our house or walked in from the highway. Other than glad I wasn't killed or maimed, I was relieved Scotty didn't surprise them while performing their dirty work. The people Julia dealt with allowed no witnesses to live.

With the doors locked and every shade and blind drawn, I settled into the kitchen to prepare supper. Not particularly hungry, I went with a porkchop sandwich and provided a dish of dogfood for Jake. All my scraps went onto his dried meal. Julia was right—he really did appreciate it and tried to thank me. Afterward, I spent a few hours attempting to learn her whereabouts by searching for a body count. The trail came up zeros, and I decided to retire early. With Jake over one shoulder and braced by my arm, I retreated into the bomb shelter one rung at a time.

* * *

I spent the next day putting together a bug-out bag. Just my old knapsack filled with anything I could think of to survive a few days on my own. Worst case scenario, I'd toss it in the back of my truck and drive north to Missoula or south to Pocatello and beyond. The Ford sat with a filled diesel tank capable of five hundred miles before needing more. I tossed a couple boxes of supplies on the passenger side floorboards, too. No telling if or when I'd be forced to flee for my life.

Given three days alone surprised me. Oh, Aunt Bess called to check on me and Jake, but no one stopped at our house. Even Al offered nothing but radio silence. I knew it was coming, just not when. Scotty's new truck surprised me when it stopped in the yard. His old Chevy could be heard coming for a mile and a half. I checked from behind a shade after hearing a door close to find my buddy and his girlfriend halfway to the porch. "Hey." I stepped outside to Scotty mounting the stairs and Robin hanging back. Did I imagine her staring under the front porch, or did my natural skepticism rear its head? I couldn't forget she once dealt cards for the other side.

"Ho!" My friend stopped startled as he reached the decking. "Cripes, farmer. You 'bout took a decade off my life."

"Oh, hell. Stop being such a scaredy-cat," I said before stepping aside. "C'mon in. It's too damned cold to stand out here." Peeking from the cracked door, Jake jumped back to let us in. "Can I get you anything? Coffee, tea, beer..."

"Beer me," Scotty said.

"Is the coffee hot?" Robin asked. "I'll take a cup...black if you don't mind," she said after my nod.

"What brings you all the way out here?" I asked after we sat.

"A couple things." Scotty nodded his go ahead to Robin.

"I got a call from Julia yesterday."

"What?" I half stood at her announcement.

"Yeah." Robin waited until my sputters stopped. "I need to restate that. J called."

"And?" I spread my hands wide.

"She asked if I passed her demand to Mr. Crowley." I guess she noticed my frown. "She plans to charge The Company for the kills she's racking up. I had to tell her he laughed at me...or rather at her suggestion."

"Didn't go over well, eh?"

Scotty couldn't help himself. "Crowley's dead, killed this morning."

"Shush," Robin told him. "Let me explain." She turned back to me. "Mr. Crowley was found dead outside his home early this morning. Passenger side window of his car was down, the engine still running, and a series of small caliber bullet holes in his skull suggesting he either knew his assailant, or this person didn't appear threatening." We all knew how benign Julia normally looked. Who knows how she changed her appearance for tapping her chosen mark? Boxes of wigs and make-up once stored in our closet were in the trailer.

"Was he the only fatality?"

"Yeah. Thankfully, Chelsea, his wife, and their kids were inside when it happened. No one heard or saw anything."

Looked like J struck again. "Police come up with any leads?"

"Huh uh. No one seems to know anything."

"Dawson," Scotty asked, "why aren't you with her? We heard about Benton and her men, then this Simon character a few days ago. I assume you were together then?"

I shook my head. "Can't say anything."

Robin reached across the table to put her hand on mine. "They're going to kill her, Dawson. The price on her head was increased to five million. Can you understand what that kind of money means to the average gun working for The Company? Most are sent for the low-level offenders...those rarely paying more than five-grand. Some only twenty-five hundred. Very few sign those at the top. Five million will have every employee tracking her."

"How many? How many of those like J work for The Company? A dozen? Twenty? More?"

"About two hundred. Used to be a couple over until your wife thinned their ranks." She shrugged apologetically. "Who knows? They may have hired more after I left."

God. With so many, how could they not locate J? "Call whoever'll take control of Crowley's company. Tell, no...*demand* they pay Julia and drop their bounty and vendetta against her. No more need to die."

Robin nodded. "I planned to after speaking with you. If I talk The Company into standing down, can you get J to do the same? Can I?"

"You bet, even if we have to hogtie her. Between you, me, and a friend of mine, one of us should be in contact with her to pass on the message." If The Company listens, I could finally see light at the tunnel's end. At last they understood what they did—now they needed to swallow their pride and let bygones be bygones.

I couldn't get a nagging thought out of my head. Would J relinquish control of Julia?

Chapter XII

Staying in the bomb shelter wasn't for Jake. He accepted it stoically, seldom taking his gaze from me while we did anything but sleep. Two days passed without a word from Robin, Al, and certainly not J. Already mid-December, fallen snow melted back to higher elevations before temperatures dropped again. Daytime highs under a clear sky rose into the high teens and sometimes low twenties. After the sun went down, the bottom fell out of the thermometer. I worked at filling a couple boxes with mementos to pack away with the cash Julia stored in our bomb shelter.

Our break came on the third day while I serviced my truck. Changing the oil, filters, and greasing any Zerk fitting I could find gave me something to do. Pulling axles to replace or repack wheel bearings was next on the agenda. The number appearing on my cell belonged to Robin. I tried to keep my voice casual. "Hello?"

Worry tinged Robin's voice. "They're willing to pay what Julia's asking if she agrees to stop now."

A shaky breath left my lungs. "You're saying if one of us is able to make contact and plead with her to stand down, it's over?"

"It's never that easy, Dawson. They wanted you to know teams are scouring the country for her. Most are in information blackout. They'll be recalled if and when individuals check in with The Company. Same as the way J worked. She contacted Manny after she was in place and didn't call again until the mission was completed."

"You're sure we can trust them? They let us down once before."

"Antoinette Benton let us down."

"What if no one can be stopped? I'm talking about both J and those searching for her."

"I'm not sure. Play it by ear, I guess."

"Okay, let me know if anything changes...or J calls."

On one hand, my spirits were uplifted, and I was pleased. On the other, I knew in my gut many of the assassins would never get the message. I called Al to pass the information on and stressed he contact J if possible. He promised to let no stone go unturned.

Jake seemed pleased to go for a ride. With little room between my Ford and Julia's Wagoneer, I made him stay outside while I backed from the garage, careful not to hit my favorite bird hunting partner. The cold weather was perfect for transporting frozen meat, so I paid the butcher for my elk and stored it in Mom's freezer with our beef. Julia's deep freeze was filled with chickens, rabbit fryers, and our mule deer. Mom loved venison and preferred elk over all others. She'd turn her nose up at whitetails, reluctantly accept a fat high country muley, but would fight over wapiti chops. Tenderloin I took home for breakfast—plus backstraps for dinner. Venison breakfast sausage was something I looked forward to sampling. Although nothing like Mom's, our butcher seemed to hit the sweet spot between too spicy and bland.

Another four Company leaders met their untimely demise over the next two weeks. Somehow, J stayed under radar while evading those searching for her. I cringed each time the phone rang, sure an official needed me to identify a body. I guessed Al and Robin likely pissed her off by leaving so many messages. Probably removed the battery from her cell as I'd watched her do in the past.

Christmas neared. I spoke with Mom—she sorely wished to return home. Although I couldn't tell her the reason coming back was impossible, I think she recognized the fear in my tone. I loved how she enjoyed the two men living above the garage, even wondering aloud if they were in a relationship. Her musings caused me to howl with laughter after our call ended. Ox and Jose would be horrified at her questions. I could badger them with it for the rest of our lives, but I decided to keep it to myself and hoped Mom did the same.

No other attempts were made against me—any I was aware of. Checking for bombs or traps took too much time each day. Going online soon after returning from Texas, I ordered a wireless driveway alert. If a vehicle turned onto our road and drove a hundred yards, an alert sounded in the house. Still not satisfied, I stationed sensors all around. A professional could've made the job much simpler. I figured how I set them was best for me and Jake.

My driveway alert sounded for the second time since I put them in. The first turned out to be a small whitetail buck. I almost brought him home to put in the freezer, but my tag was already filled, and the season ended. However, keyed up searching for an intruder almost made me forget game laws.

I carried Jake into the bomb shelter and closed it. He didn't like being in it with me, and I assumed he liked it even less alone. I waited for his bark or howls while I dressed for the cold and snuck out the backdoor when they weren't forthcoming. A dead sprint along the tree line brought me to a thicket of willows next to the gravel road. Waiting until the vehicle was almost on me, I stepped out with the .44 Marlin cocked and leveled. The pickup brakes locked, and the truck slid to a stop. Scotty and I stared through the windshield at one another for a moment. Lowering my rifle and the hammer, I sent him a look of disgust. His window came down, and I walked to the driver's side. "You bastard," he said, "took a decade off my life."

I wasn't particularly friendly. Frightened for Julia and without any news, my nerves were frayed and left bare. "Whatcha need, Scotty?" I gritted. "Ain't safe for you out here. Don't you have duck and goose hunters to guide?"

My friend did his best to act offended. "Clients limited out on geese this morning. I put 'em in blinds I built at the edge of old man Barlow's wheat field. Got nothing else scheduled until after the first of the year. Anymore hurtful questions?" He grinned, removing any question of wounded feelings.

"Yeah. What in the hell are you doing here?"

"Robin thought you should spend Christmas Eve with us. Next day, too, if you don't mind coming to Dad's place."

I planned to stay put and ride herd on our home. "Thanks, man." My tone softened automatically. Scotty always came to Mom's place for holidays. We'd missed Thanksgiving while Jules was busy killing

Benton. "Think I'll sit this one out. I'm not in the mood for celebrating."

Scotty did his best to change my mind, but I held fast. "Okay, how about lunch in town instead? I'm buying."

When I almost said Julia was buying, I knew my frustrations were taking over. Jake was alone in the shelter—he couldn't get in too much mischief lying in the dark. The doors were secured; besides, he'd hunted hard yesterday and needed rest. "You're on." I grinned. "Hope like hell a big-ass steak is the special." I slid in after he unlocked the passenger side. Scotty barely glanced at the rifle resting along my leg after I got situated.

I enjoyed the restaurant where Julia and I ate our first meal together. The ambiance was great in The Jumping Salmon, prices were okay, and the place usually bustled. Steaks weren't cheap, but you got what you paid for. "How are you, Allison?" We followed the wife of Julia's coworker to our seat. We'd known her since she was a little girl. Mr. Edwards taught for my Aunt Bess, and how he landed a beauty like Allison was a headscratcher. Always figured the girl would leave Salmon to become a runway model or famous actress. Yeah, she's that gorgeous.

"Good," she said over her shoulder. Hulls crunched underfoot when we crossed sawdust-scattered floor planks and stopped at a far table adorned with a full bucket of peanuts. "This okay?" At least thirty feet from other patrons, I nodded.

She left us with menus—as if we needed them—promising to return with coffee and water. I didn't bother to open mine and noted Scotty didn't, either. I let my attention wander across others I could see and nodded at a few. My old girlfriend—Nancy—smiled from across the floor when my gaze passed. I ignored her and looked to others.

Allison returned to our table with our drinks. "Coffee and water. You boys ready to order?" Scotty didn't blink when I asked for their twenty-four-ounce fillet, and he followed suit. Allison gathered our menus and shuffled her feet instead of leaving. "Dawson, folks at school are getting worried. How's Julia? My husband said the kids miss her."

I figured the question would come up when I least expected it. My explanation was the same as I gave Aunt Bess. "She's better. Headaches aren't as bad, and she's getting treatment at a clinic out of state."

"It sounds as if her fall was terrible. No long-term damage?" Allison stood behind Scotty with one hand resting on the back of his chair. She couldn't see the way he rolled his eyes.

"Doesn't seem like it. She's healing slowly but surely."

Allison left with our order, and I turned my attention back to the room. Most were people I'd known for years, but some were from out of the area. I identified two tables—each with four strangers—and another two with a single individual at each. None looked in our direction except for a middle-aged woman perhaps a few years older than me. Not tall and a little overweight, I ruled her out as a killer. Housewife, yes. She reminded me of a shorter version of Mom at the same age.

Scotty kicked me under the table. "Robin's worried," he whispered. "Another three down without any contact with Julia. Robin's afraid . . ." He looked around before mouthing the name. *"The Company* won't stand by their agreement if Julia waxes more."

I could only shake my head. "I don't know what to do, man. There's no way to contact her. She keeps up this radio silence horseshit much longer, and we won't have to worry about any agreements." A couple sips from my cup allowed me to scrutinize the room again. The older woman no longer looked my way, but two of the men at a table of four did.

We went silent for a bit, both lost in our thoughts. "Robin talks about it quite a bit, you know," Scotty whispered. "Up in the hills after my horse got shot. How Julia handled the bunch. Freaked Robin out to see people die, but she did better than me. I think what troubled her most was the way it didn't bother Julia. Made her job real, I guess."

His revelation caused me to go back in time. All I could think of was the same blank face I saw when she killed Toni Benton and her men.

Savage toward Robin in camp on Falconberry, but not while she ended someone's life. Her expression wasn't any different than if she were reading a recipe, sometimes with a slight smile. "You can't imagine, my friend, until you've seen her in action; it's nothing you can picture."

"Were you there when she took care of the rich woman and her bodyguards?"

"Yeah..." I trailed off, lost in the memory. J fooled me as much as them when I got used without a second thought. I'm sure she didn't plan for me to arrive when I did but quickly improvised. She thinks fast on her feet.

"Was it a long gun battle? How'd you escape?"

I closed my eyes and remembered the dance analogy Ox offered. Steps seemed rehearsed, each taken surely without wasted movement. A shot, a light footfall, two more dead, a twist of the body, and the gun went off again. She made killing look so natural. Me? As I'd said before, I'd want a machinegun for cover, mortars with heavy artillery on standby, and my unit prepared to unleash hell before I would consider attacking. "It only lasted a couple seconds. Then she walked away, stone cold."

"I...I don't understand?" Scotty struggled to make sense of what I said. "For Benton? Or two for each man?"

"All in less than a few heartbeats." I remembered the way she went from a scheming assassin to a scared little girl and then a blank-faced monster before leaving the scene as if nothing happened.

We were nearly finished with our meal when my phone vibrated inside my pocket, I almost didn't answer. Only two would interest me, Al or J. The number was the former. I took it in hopes of good news. "Are you near a television or computer?" he said.

Two sports channels blared. "No, I'm in town. You got something for me, Al?"

My heart almost stopped at his revelation. "It's G-dub, sir."

"Did you hear from her? Is she okay?"

181

"No, and I don't think so. You'd better try to catch the news. They've got her trapped. Reports say three are confirmed dead, likely more. She's cornered in an office building in downtown Chicago."

* * *

Robin already watched the live televised events before we arrived at Scotty's ranch. Cameras showed a high-rise with smoke billowing from windows on one side. She turned at our entrance. "Looks like Julia hit The Company again."

I sat next to them on an old couch I'd given Scotty ten years ago. "You're sure it's her?"

Robin shook her head. "No, but it's a good assumption. The Company owns this building and most of the surrounding block. The meatpackers guild offices are on the first ten floors. Those above are leased to other businesses. Reports say the shooting is taking place on the ninth."

Police cordoned off the area with ambulances on standby. Gawkers looked on from behind police tape with officers keeping civilians at a safe distance. We held our collective breaths when media discussed the FBI joining any investigations. Feds were the last thing Julia needed. She feared them in every way. We could only witness events unfold.

"Look." Robin pointed out people running from behind the building. Apparently, some of those hiding in their offices were either escaping or allowed to leave. Police hadn't yet been in contact with the shooter and were trying desperately to make connections to learn of any demands. No one seemed to know if hostages were taken by terrorists or if a random act of workplace violence took place. Those inside continued dribbling out, sprinting in pairs and trios—sometimes up to a half dozen—to the safety of officials. Cameras panned to show a safe zone where employees could be interviewed by officials.

I identified J before Robin or Scotty. They knew her only as a fragile-appearing blonde. The long, dark wig didn't hide her from me. I'd seen her don it carefully before a hunt. She rushed to safety with four other women. All wore heavy coats except my wife. She had on a thick sweatshirt with the hood down. I knew it to be her before she glanced in the direction of the camera for only an instant. "There!" I leaped to my feet and pointed to the television. "There she is."

Neither Scotty nor Robin noticed her. "Where?" Scotty asked as he held the remote.

"Back it up." I waited impatiently as he rewound the few seconds I needed. "There. Pause it!" I said. Creeping closer to the television, I put a finger on the image of the third in a line of five running women. She wasn't in the center by accident. "Her." I couldn't believe she was so brazen, yet J possessed the internal fortitude of a wounded cape buffalo charging a hunter. "Go forward one frame at a time."

We followed as the women moved slowly, and J twisted her neck to identify possible escape routes. "Oh, my God." I turned to see Robin covering her mouth with a hand. "It's her. It's Julia." The evidence lay plain before us. Although the wig changed her appearance with darkly stenciled eyebrows matching it, she couldn't change the shape of her features and slender neck.

"Are you sure?" Scotty strained to identify what Robin and I stared at. "Let me back it up again," he said. I fixed on the woman moving backward, then forward. Scotty and Robin stepped to my side, viewing from only a few feet away as we struggled to find a frame with her more easily identified. He eventually froze the picture after going beyond where we originally stopped. J and the others were diverted by a plain clothes officer who pointed to another official. The camera panned away to more making their escape but not before she glanced toward the news crew a last time with a contrived look of terror. "Shit." Scotty froze the picture, and we could only stare. "It's over," he whispered in the silence. "She'll be arrested, and we'll never see her again."

Robin's sudden burst of laughter caught her boyfriend and me by surprise. "Are you kidding?" She cackled again. "Police likely won't storm the building for hours. I'll bet you supper at The Jumping Salmon J's already escaped."

Scotty turned to me. "Dawson, think she stands a chance?"

"Julia? Probably not. But J? Never underestimate her."

I stayed until late in the afternoon before remembering Jake. Although they asked me to stay longer, Julia's poor pointer needed time outside. I hoped no messes were made in the shelter. Scotty drove me home while Robin promised to continue monitoring news reports. So far, we'd not identified J again as survivors were being interviewed. If she still remained, the tiny killer stayed hidden in plain sight.

Jake whined the moment I opened the shelter entrance. A thick, heavy section of concrete and rebar on a pivot pin, it allowed me to access the opening with one hand. Once inside, I fastened a nylon strap to a link protruding from the concrete wall. To open it from topside would take machinery or explosives. I hurried down the ladder and lifted him to a shoulder. We'd worked together until finding a way to help him in and out without frightening the poor dog or making it too difficult for me. I got him onto the main floor with a minimum of fuss and crawled out to follow him to the door. Letting him run from the back, Jake barely made it to frozen ground to relieve his bladder. I grinned with envy when he disappeared into the darkness at a run. To have natural night vision would alleviate anxiety growing each day until those who tried to kill me were recalled.

Al was the first to make contact when I arose the next morning. My phone beeped with a missed call and a text message. *Good news. J escaped unseen. Four were found inside dead of gunshot wounds. Police are still searching for a female described as dark haired and unassuming. Of those who saw her, no two can settle on a description. Police are expanding their search.*

I breathed a sigh of relief. At least she wasn't caught red-handed by authorities. *The Company?* I typed back. *Hear any rumblings?*

No. I've got radio silence. I'm worried they're too afraid to talk. Everything okay on your side of the mountains? No other attempts?

Huh uh. Maybe The Company recalled them in good faith.

We can only hope. Take care, my friend. I have work to do, but I'll make sure to learn anything I can. You'll get a call or text the minute I do.

"Momma's still alive," I told Jake while he gulped his breakfast. J escaped, but she wasn't safe. While I cooked my morning meal, she could be dying or dead. I collapsed into my regular chair at the table to bury my face in my arms. It's been a long time since I cried. Damned if it didn't feel like the right time. Jake and I were alone, maybe forever. He stopped me after a couple minutes of feeling sorry for myself with a nudge of his muzzle. "Hey!" I dug my kerchief from a rear pocket and wiped my face. "Guess we boys better act a bit manlier, shouldn't we?"

We spent the morning of Christmas Eve alone. Scotty and Robin wanted me there—Jake, too—but I would make poor company. Instead, after a hearty meal of elk steak, eggs, and toast washed down with a pot of coffee, I backed my truck from the garage. Two vehicles parked in a space made for one left no room to work. It'd been years since I packed the front wheel bearings. Should one run out of grease and freeze, I could find myself alongside the highway with a ruined axle if I needed to drive a long distance.

My cell beeped with a text message from Scotty. *Supper tonight, breakfast in the morning, and dinner on Christmas. Will we see you?*

Thanks, but I don't think so, I texted back. *Tell Robin and your dad I appreciate the offer. I'll stop by in a week or two if we don't hear anything about Julia.*

All right. No pressure. Be safe, my friend. Merry Christmas.

Merry Christmas to you, Robin, and your family.

With Jake inside the house enjoying the hot stove and out of my way, I returned to the garage for my floor jack and tools. Took three trips before I was ready to tackle the job. Lifting the driver's side high enough, I pulled the tire and checked the brake pads. Wouldn't be many more miles before they needed replaced. I wished I'd purchased a set before starting. Rolling the big truck tire aside, I broke chunks of mud away to check the rotor. A noise caught my attention, and I stood to see better. I didn't notice anything unusual and passed it off to the wind until hearing the distinct sound of metal. Walking past the cab of my truck allowed me to see three men within four hundred yards. One held a long cylinder and swung it over his shoulder. Two others stepped away and plugged their ears as the first pointed the tube in my direction.

I turned and ran. It'd been over a decade since I'd faced an RPG, a fearsome weapon I hoped to never see again. The rocket propelled grenade left the launcher. I made the porch steps before it impacted the front end of my truck, the explosion lifting it from the ground. Although stunned by the concussion, I regained my senses and fled. Few things were impervious against a shoulder-fired, non-guided light anti-tank weapon.

Whether they missed the house or aimed at my pickup made no difference. I hit the front door at a sprint, barely turning the knob before the impact of my shoulder. A hasty glance rearward let me see they were getting ready to fire a second round. "Jake!" I shouted, running for our shelter. "Come, Jake." I swept up my rifle by the barrel as I passed.

A second explosion in the sage behind the house gave me the extra moments we needed. My guess was they used cheap imports from China or Russia. Not accurate nor dependable—yet plenty powerful. In the extra seconds allowed to us, Jake and I were in our shelter with the entrance secured. "Hang on, boy." I hunkered in a corner on the floor with him in my arms and a blanket covering us.

The third explosion rocked our world. The house shook above us only an instant before we lost power. I smelled dust, and Jake howled in my arms. My attempts to comfort him were as much for me as for the dog. I petted him and spoke gently while we listened and felt the house collapsing overhead. "Easy, my friend," I whispered and rubbed his face like he preferred. "Man, Momma's going to be pissed if she makes it home." We waited together, Jake for his master to make things better, me hoping the explosion was high explosive. White phosphorous meant we wouldn't be long for this world.

Jake stayed in my arms until most sounds above us died out. A glance at my illuminated watch showed us three hours post explosion. I strained to hear voices, but outside our sanctuary seemed silent. No sounds of hammering or searching. Our place felt silent as a tomb. I hoped it wouldn't prove to be our final resting place. If so, and Julia lived, I guessed anyone even remotely connected to The Company would pay a high price. With Al working with her as I knew he would, J would teach them the meaning of scorched earth. I guessed it would go much further than merely killing the leaders. No one dear to them would ever be safe for however long as J survived.

"Okay, boy." I moved Jake gently away. Feeling blindly, I found the twelve-volt lantern on a shelf and switched it to low. The stark white light cast an eerie pall on our quarters. Our oxygen supply seemed adequate—with four-inch entrance and exhaust pipes leading to a rockpile—capped against rain and moisture. I could pump more with a hand cranked blower if needed, but no sense in making more noise than needed. Whomever attacked likely searched the building and surrounding area. They needed to think I perished and lay buried by debris. A check of my phone assured me a call out was impossible. Thick concrete barred any hope of connecting with a cell tower or the internet. "Well, hell, Jake." I sat in my steel folding chair and pulled him against me. "Looks like it's just me and you, my friend. Nobody around to help even if they could get past the bad guys."

Nothing to do but take inventory. My pack still waited in the corner. I'd planned to throw it in the truck if needed, never suspecting we'd need to hump it to safety. Inside was almost everything I could think of, all while keeping it from becoming impossibly heavy. Weighing sixty-five pounds—one-third my mass—each step would seem like it grew in weight. I'd tied my sleeping bag on top without room left for a tent. No matter, I'd cross that bridge when I came to it. In the meantime, with enough food and water for a few weeks or more, Jake and I would bide our time until an avenue of escape arose. Although our attackers likely left, I planned to behave as if they waited beyond the ruined structure above for us to appear.

We ate when hungry, slept when tired, and played dead. With a commode and sink fed by spring water, I needed only to hand pump it to the sewer line. Jake proved a more difficult problem—solved by letting him urinate and defecate in the small shower. His mess was easily cleaned, keeping our living quarters free of stink. My single burner stove got pressed into use during mealtimes. I almost laughed aloud before finishing my coffee while reading a paperback. Nearly forty-eight hours post attack, I hoped they were freezing their asses outside while we were warm and comfortable. I hated doing it even while we slept, but I switched our light off to save power. It threw our quarters into such darkness I could imagine never seeing the light of day again.

I tried to open a route out on the fourth day by first releasing the strap tension and pushing our entryway upward. The horizontal door pivoted easily at first before pressing hard against a stop. Only a crack of light appeared around the opening. Getting my head close enough to see out was impossible. Retreating down the ladder, I sat and tried to control my first real panic. For a short time, I felt like battering my body against the barrier until something gave. I stifled that urge.

Most items stored in our shelter were to keep us alive. Food, water, and blankets. Much of Julia's fortune—in cash—was secreted away in cases at the base of the ladder. I'd built a stout landing big enough to step from. Only a professional would give it a second thought. But three-quarters of a million dollars in fifties and hundreds hidden inside wouldn't help my escape.

I finally tore a rung from the wooden ladder. Using the short-axe lashed to my pack, I split the two-by-four. Its crooked grain didn't separate like I hoped, and I quickly whittled it thinner on one end. Using the flat side of the single-bit, I hammered my crude wedge into the narrow opening with hopes of forcing it upward.

Jake watched while I worked through the night. I finally lifted the hatch enough to see with a flashlight and reach out with my hand. Our house both exploded and partially burned and left an interior wall to settle on our only way out. I used all but two rungs to finally lift the heavy concrete to where I thought I might squirm through. I left the pointer to watch while I wormed my way out with the rifle. Coming up beneath the main floor, I crawled from under the front porch.

I let my vision adjust to the low light before I moved. No one seemed to be lying in wait when I stood and turned to look. My heart fell when the damage surrounding me became apparent. Very little of the house remained intact and none of it salvageable. My faithful truck was nothing but a burned-out hulk lying on its side. At least the garage remained intact.

I found my undamaged tire jack before picking my way through the house. Our possessions were gone. Even our shotguns were ruined. Clothes, household items—nothing was left to salvage. Julia's beloved wood cookstove got reduced to twisted iron and steel. Forcing the destruction from my mind, I set it to rescuing Jake.

Morning sun chased away early shadows before I finished. With the pointer, my pack, and guns out, I quickly erased any signs of our exit. Our concrete chamber was locked again. If located and someone wanted in, the job would be long and arduous. Even then, Julia's money would stay hidden away.

Any escape was planned around my truck. Now without wheels, I needed a backup. Julia's Jeep was still inside the garage. Racking my brain, I could only remember her extra set inside in a cookie jar on the counter of a twisted and destroyed kitchen.

Movement caught my eye. A sedan I didn't recognize negotiated the driveway. I noticed a second one following after I changed positions to get a better view. I lifted the pack and slung it to my back, putting my arms through the straps. "Let's go, Jake. We'd better get the hell out of here if we plan to live long enough to see the sun go down." I tightened either side and jumped a couple times to secure my load and latch the belt. It felt light as a feather with my sudden burst of energy. Fight or flight, and I chose running like hell.

I might have stayed to pick them off when they came within range, but the memory of facing an RPG nearly made me piss my pants. Outside temperatures were cool—certainly below freezing. I rushed from the garage with Jake on my heels but not quick enough to avoid detection. I heard engines gun the moment they saw me.

We stood a chance only if we sprinted north toward my old place. Any other direction, and they could run or shoot us down. It lay about four miles through the timber and sage. I figured we could get there and come up with a secondary plan. With Mom still in Belize and Julia playing psycho killer on her own, our necks were mine to save. Jake and I entered the timber with sporadic gunfire following. Using a long stride, fear driving a well-rested body, only a sprinter could catch me even while I humped a rucksack. I raced through the trees with Jake on my heels.

I have to give them their kudos for planning well. After my initial burst of speed before slowing to a more moderate pace, we stopped twice to catch our breath and survey our surroundings. With the opening not far ahead, and my cabin lying some three hundred yards distant, we were almost home free.

The woman was the same harmless-appearing middle-aged one I noticed looking at us in The Jumping Salmon. She stepped from behind a copse of brush and a big pine. "Gotcha." The semi-auto in her hands was aimed at me, and I'm not sure why she didn't squeeze the trigger. Maybe they wanted me alive. Carrying my .44 rifle in both hands, I cocked the hammer, lifted my barrel a few inches, and squeezed the trigger as one movement. The heavy slug took her dead center in the chest. Classic guerilla tactics dictate taking or disabling her weapon, but neither of us risked slowing as we passed her body.

With another group materializing near my cabin and shouts behind me, I took our only way out. Up the steep hill to the west leading Jake into the far reaches of the Frank Church Wilderness.

Chapter XIII

Jake didn't hesitate to follow. Generating speed inspired by certain death if caught, I took the upslope as if never planning to slow. Without snow to track us, I hoped my pursuers might miss our change of direction. We stopped once to hunker behind some brush, watch our backtrail, and catch our breath. Four men met another group who'd waited at my cabin. I faced at least nine and fed one round from my belt slide into the side port of my rifle to make up for the fired case. I wished I carried my AR10 still in the trailer with Julia. Thirteen rounds from my short-range lever action hunting rifle didn't stand up well against high capacity semi-auto rifles with three times its range.

I noted one pointing in my direction after they finished milling about. Two knelt beside the body I left behind. The finger aimed at us was plain enough; they must have a tracker. I turned away and continued up the steep hillside with Jake close by. A high promontory beckoned, and I set my sights on reaching it. Chances were they would see me before I could travel from my hiding place to the narrow band of pine forest above. "Jake, you heel," I said when a small bird caught his attention. "I can't have you screwing up, dog. Not if you want to live long enough to see Momma." His ears perked at her mention. "Bastards won't think twice about killing you, either."

Fishing my cell from a pocket when we stopped to rest, I called Al with only one bar on my phone and my battery at less than seven percent. He always answers unless on a job. For one of the few times since becoming partners, I got his recording. "On the run, Al." I panted. "Julia's place burned after it got hit by an RPG. Assholes blew up my truck, too. Me and Jake are working our way into the Frank Church—River of No Return Wilderness. We've got a few supplies. Our pursuers so far number nine." I chuckled. "They used to be ten." Made no difference to me if the woman I killed looked like a dowdy housewife. Aim a gun at me, and I'm going to end you. "Not sure about our route, but I plan to work our way north into the Bitterroots." An alarm from my low battery indicator beeped in my ear. "Out of power, Al. Hope to see you after..." I thought about it for a moment. "...after the shit storm blows over."

I reckoned they spotted me when a flurry of shots was sent in my direction with small chance of hitting us. After ending the call and locating my binoculars inside the knapsack, I focused the powerful lenses to observe my foes. Only one seemed to have fired with another doing his best to stop him. They argued before the group split. Four hiked back to an SUV I could see from my higher vantage, while the other five started in my direction. I called Scotty with only a few seconds of battery left. "Scotty?" Our connection sounded tenuous.

I could barely make him out. "Hey m...change yo...ind?"

"Not sure if you can hear me. Stay away from my place, Scotty. Hear me? Stay away. *Do not* come out here. I'm hiking into the Bitterroots..." My phone died mid-sentence. I could only hope he received the gist of what I tried to tell him. I'd hate like hell to learn he got tagged after deciding to check on me.

Four men and one woman trailed me. A burst of anger washed over me as I watched them moving up the hill. They'd closed the distance to a half-mile or less. Sons of bitches thought they could take me on my home ground? If they wanted my hide, I'd teach 'em the meaning of earning it.

Taking time to rehydrate and rest while I watched them come, I tightened my shoulder straps and stood. I assumed some or most of them were tough fighters, but likely none knew these Idaho mountains as well as me. They probably figured to run me down while I was loaded with a pack. Carrying light rifles and no gear wouldn't slow their chase. I stepped out where they could see me best and launched a bullet down the slope at what I guesstimated over five hundred yards. I held thirty feet above their heads and squeezed the trigger. When I didn't get a reaction, I held a little lower and fired a second round. It got me a response when they scattered and alarmed shouts drifted to me. Holding about the same spot, I sent a volley of five more before turning and taking long strides up the steep slope. "Come, Jake." The poor dog hated the crack of gunfire and waited some fifty yards away.

Clearcuts and the roads to reach them crisscrossed the mountains until we reached wilderness. We would have to avoid long stretches of truck thoroughfares and denuded hillsides. Snow lay above us, making me hopeful even four-wheel drive vehicles were unable to navigate at the higher altitude. Air temperature hovered in the teens or low twenties. With wind chill making it dangerous, Jake and I would do whatever it took to survive.

We waited at the top of the next knob surrounded by patches of snow. Soon we would fight through some much deeper, but first I wanted our pursuers to see me rather than lose them. Three eventually stopped to spot me from below after we'd waited too long. Sweat soaking through my shirt cooled and chilled my skin. I wasn't shaking when they appeared, but cold mountain air was finding its way inside my wool coat. Where we sat was at least a thousand feet higher than our foes and three quarters of a mile distant. I feared they might quit if my trail proved difficult to find. My plans didn't revolve around their surviving our game of cat and mouse.

They let me stand and wave my arms, performing brisk exercises to warm my body before noticing. One eventually pointed me out to the others. A pair left a single man behind before coming after me. My binoculars showed them each armed with semi autos with much longer reach than my .44. Didn't matter. No bullet of theirs would even come close if I didn't get stupid.

Leaving a man behind after appearing with only three finally made sense as I worked my way to the ridgetop. Those left along the way were likely bringing equipment for the chase. By stringing out on my trail, they could more easily guide their compatriots to the fight. I hoped their gear was cold weather approved. Otherwise, they might die from exposure before I could kill them. I planned for each and every one to die by my hand.

The first road I encountered could barely be called one. I crossed it without care of tracks left behind. Wintery landscape surrounding us seemed frozen and lifeless, yet nine more souls would soon traipse through. A brisk wind increased as I hurried across a half-mile flat to enter the tree line on the far side. Snow lay deep enough to cover most stumps with a frozen crust to make travel easy. Rather than wait in the open and allow my enemy to observe me before disappearing, I didn't slow until Jake and I were under the forest canopy. From there, I made a wide loop, stopping at the west edge where I could plainly see my tracks enter from the south. I removed my pack while we waited, finding a bottle of water and splitting it with Jake. I hadn't forgotten him when packing my knapsack. To Julia and me, no other life was more important. My watch showed almost two o'clock, two and a half hours before darkness would catch us.

We needed to press on if they didn't show by two-thirty. Snow under the timber wasn't as deep or frozen hard as in the open. I kicked through it until reaching dirt to provide a place for Jake to rest. Counting down the minutes, they appeared as I prepared to leave. Three crested carefully, reading my tracks disappearing north. My plan didn't account for three. Two would be a handful. I turned ready to flee until one got left behind again while a pair trailed me. I couldn't believe they would follow me to the woods where my ambush lay ready.

Already, we'd traveled six or more miles from my cabin. They couldn't easily retreat with twilight not far away. My plan couldn't be simpler as they stayed on my tracks. I moved Jake while I waited, whispering a stern warning. "Stay. Jake, stay." I couldn't risk him running and eventually finding himself on a wolf's menu.

The two men followed too quickly on my trail to understand its basic tactics. They'd likely become lazy after pursuing so long in hopes of running me down. Other than stopping once to lob a few warning shots to catch their attention, as far as they were knew, I'd only fled. Their rifles were slung while I tracked their progress. Two hundred yards, then one-fifty—I needed them much closer. A hundred, seventy-five, they were within twenty-five yards of entering the pines—about sixty from me—when I squeezed the trigger.

I took careful aim and shot the closest man through the ribs. He collapsed at the report. Working the lever briskly, I looked at the second through my sights. Unslinging his rifle, the man seemed indecisive whether to hit the ground or stand and return fire. My second round hit center mass, and as his partner before, his legs gave way to let him crumple.

Their rifles were important, and I sprinted to the bodies. The gun from the second kill appeared intact. I stripped the sling from around his shoulder and searched his coat for extra magazines. He carried two which went into my pocket while I kept an eye on the third combatant on the hill above. I could see damage from my bullet to the long gun of the first kill. Didn't matter, neither the magazines nor ammunition from the AK would work in the AR15. I threw what I could find of the 7.62x39 shells far back into the snowy brush. Both men appeared in their twenties and were dressed for a cold climate. Already my opponents' numbers plummeted by almost thirty percent. They wouldn't be taken so easily in the future. I lashed the spare rifle to my pack and the extra ammunition went inside. Jake waited patiently seventy-five yards through the brush. I slung my knapsack on again and hurried to where he stood. "Good job, Jake. You're learning, boy. The easy stuff's done. Now our real work starts."

* * *

Jake trotted to keep up. With less than two hours before absolute darkness, I wanted to be far away from here, yet not too distant from pursuers. Without dense cover, the night would be colder than a witch's tit. We crossed a deep ravine and followed the lip into a larger patch of pine and fir. I found some areas with overhangs thick enough for bare ground to show. Not wanting to leave easy tracks to follow, we kept to open spots until I selected a place to stop. A dozen trees blew over to make a canopy with its underside suspended three to five feet from the ground. I figured we'd hiked two miles from my last ambush.

No way could anyone track me through the brush and timber in the dark. We were as safe as possible with seven killers on our trail.

Where I planned to hole up was more than adequate. With the ground relatively bare, Jake nosed about while I used the last few minutes of light to make camp. First, I picked up and broke boughs and leaned limbs over the tree trunks to form an enclosure before laying out my sleeping bag to regain its loft. Its manmade fiber rated to thirty degrees below zero, I'd used it in conditions of nearly fifteen below. I figured we'd be safe enough even with the wind chill. Bushy branches would help keep any breeze to a minimum. While Jake shivered, I didn't think the air temperature was colder than zero. He followed me inside through the narrow opening I left where I could sit and fix supper.

Although too salty for my tastes, Ramen noodles carried light and made a quick meal. I brought only six water bottles, but snow and ice could be melted to refill them later. With time of the essence before we chilled too long, I brought some to a boil on my single-burner butane pack stove. Jake wasn't forgotten, and I dug the small bag of dry dogfood from the bottom of my pack. He wasn't going to have enough—hell, there wouldn't be for me, either. His first meal on the trail was his normal amount, about two cups softened by warm water. Once the pot boiled—taking less than three minutes with the powerful gas—I dumped the Ramen in to absorb the hot liquid. The pointer watched without blinking while I ate, not hesitating when I gave him the last few warm bites. I used my shirt to clean any germs he left behind, hoping I hadn't missed him licking his butt before he ate.

We drank the third bottle, and I hoped it was sufficient to stave off thirst. "Well, Jakie, looks like it's time we figure out sleeping arrangements." I didn't think my bag was big enough for both of us. With his short hair and penchant for chilling easily, I needed to keep my boy warm. Removing my Stetson, coat, boots, and handgun, I slid into my bag while he contemplated my actions. I preferred rectangular to mummy style, with room as the tradeoff for extra weight. Zipping it to my sternum, I loaned him my wool coat for his bed. His shivering worried me, so I opened my bag enough to cover some of the dog. Tired and knowing I'd feel the chase when I woke, I drifted to sleep with Jake groaning in my ear.

I didn't freeze and neither did my campmate. He squirmed his way farther inside as the night wore on until he pushed his way toward my feet. Giving up and opening the zipper far enough so he got plenty of oxygen, I used my abandoned coat as a pillow. Dawn broke with my feet warmer than they'd been since we lit out. "Jake?" I opened my bag, letting in far too much cold air to coax him out. "You gotta get up, man. Time to hit the trail." His muzzle lifted while he peered at me before moaning his early morning distress and curling into a ball again. "C'mon, boy," I whispered.

I kept movements to a minimum. Tugging on clean socks and then my boots, my Anaconda slid onto my belt next. Seven rounds were gone from my cartridge slide, and I broke open a box of .44s to fill it. Another five went into each front pocket before I stored the rest in my knapsack. "Ready for breakfast, mister?" I cajoled the dog still warm burrowed in my sleeping bag. When he didn't respond, I unzipped it and rolled him out. He saw breakfast and wolfed it down. I uncapped a fourth water bottle to drink and boil water for dehydrated potatoes. I loved those purchased from any supermarket in different flavors. The one I opened was cheesy bacon. With only enough hot water for part of a packet, I made do and stored the rest. I cracked a thick-shelled brown egg carried in a plastic crate into the water first, followed thirty seconds later by the potato flakes. After mixing, I ate and scraped the pot clean while wishing for more.

I left Jake with our gear to scout for signs of pursuit. Smoke rose from the trees where the ravine turned into a canyon. Good, they hadn't quit on me. I hoped to see six men and one woman after they stirred and sniffed after my trail. Shouldn't be hard. A blind man could see the path I left.

The purloined AR was loaded with a twenty-round magazine. Spares held the same, except one with only six, missing fourteen cartridges. I guessed he was the one who first fired in my direction. The rifle

197

seemed nice, if basic. With only an Eotech one-power scope mounted, he lacked the extras some shooters enjoyed, such as a flashlight, laser, or vertical foregrip. I felt a distant kinsman to the poor bastard who carried it before—we preferred the same simple weapons.

Jake seemed keen for the trail, except I couldn't catch our pursuer's attention. Not even melting snow and ice into water bottles while sitting in the open got their attention when they struck camp like dudes-in-the-woods and left their fire still burning. Only after crossing the canyon did they suddenly fan out to come our way. "Looks like they woke up. Reckon we can move on."

Rather than plan another ambush they'd likely expect, I headed north for Allen Mountain. A tall and rugged peak, I'd ridden horses through the area many times as a teenager and later. Killed my first buck not far from the open country at the tender age of twelve under the watchful eye of my father. Jake strayed farther as we traveled but not out of my line of sight. Just a wave or low whistle brought him back. I figured my destination a three-day hike. During those miles, I'd work hard to leave enough signs, but never let them close enough for us to catch a bullet.

I left the semi-auto lashed to my pack and carried the .44 in my hands. Although having great familiarity with both AR15s and M16s, I trusted the lever action. We stopped on a low hill to scan our backtrail with my binoculars and eventually located them following our tracks next to a frozen pond. Four carried packs and long guns—three more traveled with only rifles.

Clouds gathered from the west as we hiked. Snow meant two things to me. Air temperatures would warm—if only a little—and we could hide easier. Yet to leave an adequate trail would become increasingly difficult. Jake suddenly swung wide to stop and point a moment before a blue grouse flew from brush to a low pine limb. I thought about it for a moment before taking aim from less than ten yards and killing the bird, aiming for the head to save meat. Yes, I created noise, but I wanted to worry our enemies while giving them direction to ease after us. Jake retrieved the bird and left my side to find others. Cleaning supper quickly, I saved the guts thick with yellow fat to feed him much-needed calories. He returned after determining no other grouse remained and didn't hesitate to gulp his warm meal before hoping for more.

We hunkered on the low rise where I cleaned the bird while waiting for our pursuers to appear. I sipped water during our halt and shared it with Jake. In such an expansive backcountry, they were required to track me. In no way could they decipher a direction other than vaguely north. More than once I purposely turned due west—both to take us farther from civilization and to make them struggle to determine my route or planned destination. The group appeared and gathered around the skinned pile of grouse feathers, wings, and feet. One seemed the leader and pointed to where I shot the bird and what I left. Whether they understood I harvested food or not, I couldn't tell.

The first flakes fell not long after I looked for a place to camp. Another day, and we'd be in true wilderness, far from logging roads and clearcuts. Jake and I crossed an enormous hillside recently harvested of pines—the sharply rising mountain beyond it my intended goal. Deeper snow made hiking difficult as the crust occasionally broke to let me sink knee-deep. Although Jake didn't suffer the same problem, he sometimes struggled for purchase on the icy surface. We stopped to watch our backtrail before swinging around the steep slope.

"Son of a gun, Jake. Not sure if these turkeys are quittin' on us or not. Easier to kill 'em and sort it out up here than closer to town." I spotted movement not more than a few seconds after speaking. All seven grouped tight enough for one grenade to take 'em all out halted halfway across the hillside, apparently in discussion. I guessed their conversation revolved around rapidly approaching darkness. Through my binoculars, one gestured back the way they came and another pointed in our general direction. Seemed they couldn't make up their mind where to stop. Figured I give 'em a helping hand in making a decision.

From over eight hundred yards when they appeared, the group stopped at what I estimated to be four hundred. Using the recently liberated AR, I took careful aim after inserting earplugs and walked my fire to them. The final ten rounds struck very close judging by how quickly they fled. "Don't want 'em forgettin' why they're here, little fella," I said, after Jake and I were ready to resume our march. The empty magazine was left jammed deep into the snowy hillside.

With extra batteries available for my mini mag flashlight, I didn't hesitate to press it into service after we didn't find a place to hole up when darkness fell. We pushed on in hopes of locating a shelter or a place to fashion one. I wanted somewhere out of the growing storm where we could stay relatively warm and dry.

We stumbled into the perfect spot. The top of a wind-fell pine larger than my waist rested on a pile of boulders. Five feet from the ground, the surrounding blowdown provided all we needed. Dragging broken limbs and splintered tree trunk, I leaned them against the top to form an A-frame. More debris went to block off one end and leave the other open. Saving the densest branches for last, I used them to barricade the last opening after crawling inside. Snow fell heavier each time I checked with only a few flakes drifting through the roof of our shelter.

Jake was ready for dinner. I again fed him dry food softened with warm water and filled his collapsible travel pan with more. We couldn't drink enough to stay well hydrated in such dry conditions and exposed to the elements. I prepared my own meal while he made himself comfortable on my sleeping bag and watched. Fried grouse, more potato flakes, and an egg got washed down with a single cup of cowboy coffee. I stripped any remaining meat from the bones with my knife and fed it to the grateful dog. Although I'd grown used to the cold, Jake suffered enough so we made our bed. He wormed his way inside to stretch from my feet to chest. It didn't matter to me as long as we survived the night and got some sleep. Jake shivered and pressed closer when the howl of a wolf drifted to us on the growing wind.

* * *

Three days later not far from the Montana border, I was squatting above my pursuers' new camp, although I'm not certain they fully understood who hunted whom. The chase slowed as they ran out of food—and with it, energy. Unless they possessed a good compass, I figured it unlikely any knew which direction Salmon lay. With an extra eight inches of snow falling overnight, they were slow to rise. Seven bodies stuffed into a pair of two-man tents likely provided poor sleep. I wasn't even sure if they brought enough sleeping bags. We spent the night on the north side of Allen Mountain with the border of Montana not far in the distance.

I hunkered little more than a hundred yards above them on a narrow flat. They bivouacked among sage as tall as their tents. Following a comfortable night due east, Jake and I rose early to backtrack and watch. Though we ate two more grouse and one stringy rabbit mixed in with our staples, Jake's food stores couldn't be stretched much further. Even sharing mine and what I could kill along the trail, we couldn't make it more than another seventy-two hours. Already, my belt tightened two holes.

Tent sides moved before I heard voices. "Goddamn it, my leg's cramping, and I don't have enough room to stretch," a male said. More mumbled curses drifted to us before bitching and moaning dried up.

"No!" A deep voice rose. "We aren't stopping now. Two million beats the hell out of nothing."

I'll be damned. No wonder they blew our house up and chased me into the backcountry. I'd never been worth so much. Julia? Her head could make someone fabulously wealthy—only if they could find and earn it.

"I can't do it, Anderson. No food for two days. I don't have the energy," another said.

"Fine," the deep voice answered. "Go back if you know which direction."

I couldn't help but bare my teeth in a smile while listening to the bickering. Didn't matter to me. They were going to die tired and hungry in the end. We all drew cards from the same deck. Seemed my hands got better as the game moved along.

Two decided they were finished. Five elected to continue. If they stayed on my trail, they'd pass to the east of where I waited. Eventually they'd locate my camp and to where I watched. While they made plans to catch me, one struggled to build a fire. They'd carried a heavy pot and filled it with snow. Once flames grew hot, they melted it for drinking water.

It took another forty-five minutes before each drank enough and got their poorly equipped camp packed. Five passed within fifty yards of me, winding around the hillside on my trail. As I hoped, they walked in my tracks made last night. The remaining two squatted near the fire, obviously unsure what to do without shelter or which direction to take. Neither spoke while I eased around to appear from less than seventy yards. Busy feeding the fire and speaking in low tones, I wasn't noticed until one stood. He jumped when he saw me looking through the peep sight of my .44. Rather than allow him to surrender, I shot him in the chest, levering the empty out and a live one in. His compatriot didn't get a chance to stand before he caught the next slug through the lungs. I didn't wait for movement before retreating. The cold would kill them if they somehow survived heavy bullets through the briskets. Jake waited next to my knapsack and spare rifle when I returned, thumbing two cartridges from my pocket into the loading port.

We struck due east. According to overheard comments, none of my enemies knew what to do beyond following me. They certainly heard my gunshots and would return to learn their fellow bounty hunters' fate. I hoped to be out of the area and into another I knew fairly well. Instead of ranging out to hunt and inspect our surroundings, Jake plodded at my heels. With my antagonists softened by the elements, the hour to finish it drew nigh. Another day—two at the most—and the fight would be over. Once ten against one, the fight narrowed to half. We damned near had the bastards surrounded.

The next day, instead of hiking in a group, they strung out almost a quarter mile, one straggling farthest. I doubled back and put a bullet in his armpit when he passed below. Before those remaining could return fire, I'd retreated into the thicker timber above.

Did I feel sorry or guilty for the way I took their lives? Not even a little. They had to lose theirs for me to keep mine. I remembered reading a story when growing up about an old trapper around the turn of the twentieth century. A reporter came from back east and asked if he ever killed anyone in a gunfight. *I killed plenty, the trapper replied, but never in a dime novel duel. I wasn't stupid and shot every last bastard in the back at the longest distance I could hit 'em with a rifle,* much to the reporter's horror.

I kind of looked at my predicament the same way. Style points weren't given if I faced them in a stand-up fight. Hell, they started it with a surprise RPG through my front door. Using a rocket sure as hell wasn't fair. They were led into the mountains, so I could settle our differences with the least amount of fuss.

What started as a planned simple murder of me and Jake ended with a whimper. In the end, I left them to die of starvation and exposure. The howl of wolves filled not only each night, but most of the day, too. Forty-eight hours later, I left three men and one woman in their tents at almost nine thousand feet in thirty inches of snow. Without a way to contact help or know where I was, they retreated to the only refuge they knew. I left the AR15 leaned against a nearby stump, and not even a fire burned outside their tents when I turned my back for the long hike to civilization.

Chapter XIV

Jake and I reached Lost Trail Pass after two days of difficult hiking. Minimal travel on snowpacked roadways at this altitude made finding a ride difficult. An older gentleman stopped to offer a seat in his SUV with all four tires chained, not worried about a tired wet dog wrapped in my coat. He made available his cord and the opportunity to charge my phone. I waited only long enough to reach cell service before calling Scotty. "Pelletier?" He sounded surprised and relieved.

I dispensed with trivialities. "Are you home?"

"Yeah, but what the hell happened? Julia's house burned. Fire marshal and cops have been combing it for your body. We thought you were dead."

"I'll explain after I get there. Should be less than an hour. Can you have some wet and dry dogfood waiting? Maybe something for me to eat?"

My ride didn't balk at taking me to my friend's place. Our good Samaritan routinely traveled from Missoula to Pocatello selling farm equipment, and my stop wasn't more than a couple miles out of his way. Scotty and Robin hurried outside when we pulled in. I took his business card for better thanks later and tipped my hat to my benefactor before making sure Jake stayed out of the way. Hate like hell to have him survive everything we went through only to be run over at the end.

"What in God's name happened? To both of you?" Scotty nodded at Jake's protruding ribs.

Ignoring the beginning of his interrogation, I asked Robin. "Got anything to eat?" She nodded and led us inside. I stopped her with my next question. "Julia...is she alive?" I held my breath waiting to hear the answer, able to think of little else since starting my trek home.

Her answer nearly folded my legs like a newborn colt. "Yes, alive and well. It's over, according to my old firm. The Company has shut down and disbanded."

"Have you talked to her? Have you seen her?"

"We spoke once. Scotty, get his pack, will you?" She was right. I took a step and grasped the bannister before stumbling and nearly falling on the first tread. I caught myself using the rail and butt of my rifle.

Scotty took my arm to help steady me. "Hey, man. You okay?"

I stopped to consider his question. "Yeah, I think I am. We haven't eaten much in the past few days and hiked from my place past Allen Mountain to the Montana border close to Lost Trail summit." I scratched Jake's ears when he leaned against me—I supposed just as tired. "But yeah, we're both okay."

Robin dished me a hearty homemade stew and fresh buns as I limped in. My mouth salivated at the odor. Rather than sit and eat, I noticed a case of canned dogfood and a small bag of dry. Knowing they didn't have pets or food bowls, I mixed the two in a nearby sauce pan and placed it on the floor for Jake.

Food beckoned, and I didn't take the time to wash my hands. Grouse and rabbit guts and blood staining my digits and palms didn't hinder my attack. Scotty and Robin sat across from me and waited. Rather than combine an explanation with eating, I focused on filling my stomach first. Robin passed a bun after I finished the first two. Jake nuzzled my elbow after finishing his meal with the obvious hope I'd share mine. I gave him a chunk of the warm bread.

Scotty broke the silence. "We thought you were dead. Hell, everyone figures you were murdered. A woman was found shot dead not far from your cabin."

I gave him a sharp look. "You didn't go out there, did you?"

"Huh uh. Not for a few days. Maybe seventy-two hours after your call. Couldn't hardly hear it, but pretty sure you said to stay the hell away. Called the cops after I saw the mess." His eyes watered. "I thought you were dead."

"Anyone contact Mom?"

"Huh uh. I asked them to wait until we located your body. Robin and I have been worried about how we'd break the news."

I nodded and didn't pull any punches. "They would've killed you without thinkin' twice if you showed up at my place." My attention turned to Robin while she filled my bowl again. "Where's Julia?"

Robin shook her head. "I'm not sure. We got the call from her the day after Christmas. Someone you both know called her to say The Company surrendered. I checked with my old firm, and they confirmed what she told me."

Scotty filled Jake's empty pan with tap water and set it on a dishtowel. He knew how messy Jake could be. I nodded my thanks. "How'd she sound?" I asked anxiously, fumbling for my phone to see if she'd left a message. She didn't. "Was it Jules or J?"

"A little of J but mostly Julia." Robin smiled. "I got tears after explaining you were becoming a hermit and staying away with Jake. Still, the coldness when she spoke of The Company made me shiver."

"She didn't say when she planned to return?"

"No. I got the feeling she might spend some time in California near where she grew up. Said she needed to reconnect with her roots." Robin shrugged apologetically when she didn't have anything to add. "Want me to find her parents' address?"

My heart steeled against what I knew was coming. "No, I don't think so. Gotta call the cops and see if we can straighten out any problems with the dead woman at my place." But first a few hours of solid sleep on their couch, and then I'll look toward the future.

* * *

Local police demanded a series of lengthy conversations. By lengthy, I mean every day for nearly two weeks. We made numerous trips to the remains of the house Julia and I once shared. I think they were impressed after I pointed out how Jake and I survived in the bomb shelter so long before I finally squirmed out. They held me twenty-four hours before the district attorney cut me loose on my own recognizance. Scotty loaned me his beat-up Chevy so I could stay at my cabin. Only sixteen by twenty with a loft on one end, the log house served my needs. Julia could decide what she wanted done with her old place.

Maybe it was a mistake, but I didn't tell the authorities about my flight through the mountains. Armchair environmental "experts" back east were fond of claiming there's never been a confirmed modern case of wolves killing humans. I can understand the reason as a pack won't leave a scrap of evidence. Wolves closed in as Jake and I left the area. I figured they'd take care of business as usual. None of the .44 slugs I killed with would fail to exit, and any examination would be performed on scat and gnawed bones strewn throughout the mountains. If their tent filled with semi-auto rifles and equipment scattered about were ever discovered, investigators could frame their own findings without my help.

After playing phone tag for a week, Al and I eventually made contact. I'd dug into my enormous box of paperbacks and worked my way through three of Max Brand's novels before my cell rang. Hoping for Julia's call, I didn't check the number or answer until almost too late. Damned phone was under a pile of books. "Hey, Al."

He apologized immediately. "I'm sorry, sir. Your call was so broken I couldn't make out your message. When I couldn't contact you again, I used a computer program to rebuild it. Too little, too late, I guess." I gave him the short version of what the police knew. One thing I'd learned during my time with Julia, we never knew who might be listening. "Goddamn, you've been in the bomb shelter the entire time? Hell, Dawson. You could've died if you didn't pry the entrance open."

I ignored the obvious. "Where's Julia?"

"Don't blame her, man. She's scared to death."

His statement floored and alarmed me. "It isn't over? Robin swore The Company disbanded."

"She's terrified to face *you*. Hell, The Company isn't half as intimidating. I don't know what you're thinking but go easy."

I repeated my initial question with all the calmness I could muster. "Where is she?"

"I suspect California."

"It's a big damned state. Where and when did you last speak to her?" Al cleared his throat, before hemming and hawing. "Answer me, damn it."

"This morning. She was leaving Sacramento. We've spoken four times since I learned the news of The Company."

I was silent for a minute while I digested his news. She could phone Al four times and ignore me? "Fine." Be a cold day in hell before I took her call. "You can talk to her all she wants—"

"Now you know why Julia's avoiding a confrontation. You're a scary man if I may say so, sir. Thought for sure she tamed you. Reckon not."

I didn't give two shits about what he thought. Julia was my wife. "Gotta go. We'll talk another time."

Jules called three days later—I reckoned after contacting Al or Robin—perhaps both. Maybe her conscience got the best of her. I tossed my cell aside rather than answer. Perhaps I was being an asshole, but I figured to let her stew.

* * *

Mom came home the last day of February. We'd talked a few times before she arrived. I learned quickly she and Julia often spoke at length. Mom didn't mention the day she planned to fly back, and I didn't think to ask. My first inkling something was afoot came when Al's 'copter swooped low above my cabin. Jake howled his fright, and I rushed outside with my rifle. I didn't trust J's old employers as far as I could throw them. Al peered out from his vantage before twisting hard on the stick and pulling the collective bar. Rather than land, he disappeared toward the main highway.

Mom and Al ferried most of her belongings from his whirlybird to her house before I arrived in Scotty's truck. He said I could keep it as long as needed, and I intended to hold him to his word. Mom walked straight into my arms. "I hardly recognize you, old lady. You're brown as a berry."

She stepped back, her grip holding strong on my shoulders. "Fit as a fiddle, too. I haven't been in this fine shape since you were a boy."

"Belize looks good on you, Mom. Sorry you had to go, but I'm glad you enjoyed yourself."

Al followed us inside with the last load. She suggested I build a fire, a recommendation said with a firm tone. Since I filled her woodshed each year, it wasn't difficult to locate kindling and ignite it. She started coffee brewing before making herself comfortable in the living room. "Have you patched things up with Julia?" Mom could be as subtle as a freight train.

I sighed. "Ain't seen nor heard from her. Not sure I want to."

She ignored the last part. "Then drive over and talk to her."

I sat upright in shock. "She's back? Where's she staying?"

"Not only is Julia home, she's working for your Aunt Bess again. I wanted to put her up here, but she preferred to live in the travel trailer at her place. You'd know if you took her calls."

Mom was right. Jules called six times, and I ignored them all including text messages. She contacted everyone else but me until the end. Me, her husband, the one she promised to love and cleave to. Eventually, she stopped trying.

"Can't believe she's been so close and hasn't stopped for Jake. He misses her." The idea Julia would penalize her poor dog bothered me.

"She's worked four weeks as a substitute, son. I'm sure she's exhausted by the weekends. She doesn't have anyone to help her, you know." The old woman made sure to get her digs in.

Al's big voice boomed in the living room. "Isn't like she's got anyone to give her a hand around the place."

I wasn't in the mood for more abuse and left without answering. Not sure if either followed me to the porch—I didn't bother to look. Scotty's rattletrap eventually started after turning over for at least ten seconds. The tires didn't spin from a lack of effort on my part. The damned clutch and pressure plate needed replacing. Goddamned embarrassing exit is what it was.

Rather than go home to Jake, I headed for town and The Jumping Salmon. The joint was packed, and I chose a table against the wall. My waitress was new to me, probably another goddamned do-gooder from out of state. Rather than order dinner after eating little throughout the day, I asked for a Wild Turkey, neat. Three were gone before I slowed enough to glare at my fellow patrons. Six cowboys I couldn't place but looked familiar grinned and tipped their Stetsons. Molly and Chet Irwin ate quietly without speaking, even to each other. They were never the same after their boy—a kid in my class throughout school—was killed by a drunk driver while crossing a street in Twin Falls.

I knew some of those in the band warming up. A couple were in their twenties, but a few were my age. They played gigs from Yakima in eastern Washington to Billings in the middle of Montana. I thought they sounded great but figured they'd never make it big. Not because they weren't good—they were—but unlikely to get their lucky break.

My fourth whiskey lasted much longer. First three were kicking my ass. The house filled with regulars mostly to support the band. I guess to completely ruin my evening, Nancy appeared on the arm of Thomas Howell. Throwing down my drink and getting my server's attention for another, I sat back to nurse it.

No doubt about it, I was gunning for a fight. I wasn't given a chance to look for one, it came to me. Steve Owens and Fred Hutchinson took the closest table.

No love was lost between my family and the Owenses. Steve's old man tried to buy our farm when I was a boy. Dad was French and Shoshone, the Indian half from an almost extinct branch called the Sheep Eaters. Mom came from a line of pure Italians. Our land got passed down through the years—I was a fourth-generation owner with my brother until I bought him out. Once he learned my old man wouldn't let it go for any price, Steve senior figured he'd liquor Dad up to get him to make a shitty deal and sign it over. Strong drink was something he typically avoided, but not that night. He died from alcohol poisoning after drinking pure grain spirits. Always figured to collect the hair from the man who did my Dad in, but the bastard died of a stroke before I returned home from military service.

Both Steve and Fred put away several mixed drinks before taking to the dance floor with a couple regulars. I squinted and pulled my brim low when my old girlfriend and Howell joined them. Always surprised me the way the pain of Nancy's second betrayal dissipated so quickly. Probably because I half expected it after the first time. It bugged me, but I was forced to admit they looked good together.

"Your woman still around?" The voice brought me from memories of the old days—Dad's excitement when I killed my first pheasant. I shot it after Duke, our black Lab, flushed it near the creek.

"Huh?" I glanced around before I realized Steve spoke.

"Heard she went wild for no reason and murdered a group of men paying Scotty Rich to guide them. Bitch oughta be in jail instead of working with kids." He glanced at and got a nod from Fred. "Heard you killed some woman, too. You ain't nothing but a drunken Injun, same as your old man."

Rather than retaliate, I tipped my chair back against the wall and grinned. Pushing my brim up with an index finger to see better, I could only smile my disgust. Nothing to do but play up a portion of my roots. "Too bad the old shyster you called a parent croaked. Figured I'd take his scalp and tack it to my lodgepole." I stared at Steve's bald pate. "No sense in wastin' my time with your polished dome."

Steve stood to tower over me. At least six-five, I guessed he went over three hundred. A short-haul truck driver, much of his weight hung over his belt. Didn't too much matter, his arms and shoulders were massive from pure genetics. Me? I rarely broke two hundred after a big meal. "I'm going to kick your ass one of these days, Pelletier."

I chuckled and made sure all four legs of my chair were on the floor with the back against the wall. "Don't let nothin' but the fear of God stop you."

He sounded incredulous. "You think I can't take you?"

"You're a big, fat, soft slob." Christ, what was I thinking? Thankfully, a burst of sanity crept in. Wouldn't be long before I left my thirties behind. A sip of my whiskey drove the brief clarity aside. "Only way you stand a chance is if I get between you and a buffet, porky."

I didn't have time to add a couple pig snorts. He leaned over to grasp my jacket lapels with one hand, drawing back the other in a fist the size of a ham to beat my ass. This wasn't my first rodeo—my left bootheel and instep impacted his right knee with a sickening crunch. Steve went down clutching the torn joint with both hands. I calmly lifted my drink again and tasted it while enjoying his discomfort—surgery likely his only option. No matter how big a fellow is, take his legs away to cut him to size.

Fred knelt beside his friend. I didn't mind the man. Only a few years younger than me, he excelled in most sports. Organized athletics didn't interest me but certainly made him popular with the girls. "It's pretty messed up," he said. "Better let me get you to the emergency room."

"Hey, Steve," I called as Fred supported most of his buddy's weight. "Don't worry. I've got your tab." My solemn nod didn't win either of them to my side before I noticed my empty glass. A wave made sure another was coming.

* * *

"Ohh..." I rolled to my back on the narrow bunk. Bright light streaming through a window caused my pupils to contract wildly when I attempted to open my lids. "Shit." Turning back and facing the wall, I covered my head with the blanket. If I held deathly still, I could hear blood pumping through every vein and artery. Most of it seemed to have migrated to my brain, creating far too much pressure. A stirring in my kitchen alarmed me when the faucet sounded. I should have rightly been in jail, not home with another inside, too.

"Drink this," a familiar voice said.

"What the hell are you doing here?" I said—rolling slowly to face Julia.

"Got a call last night from your old girlfriend offering three alternatives. One, wait until you needed bailed out of the county jail. Two, wait until you were in the hospital. Or three, save your dumb butt before things got more serious." I noted she didn't smile. "I chose the last." Julia continued holding a water glass and a handful of pain reliever. "Sounds like you weren't a pleasant diner at The Jumping Salmon last night."

I sat upright and swung my feet to the floor wincing at the stabbing pain in my skull. My eyes closed as I tossed her choice of hangover remedies in my mouth and washed them down with water. I chugged until the glass was empty and handed it back. "Where's Jake?" By all rights he should have been all over his mistress.

"At the trailer. He wanted to follow me last night, so I let him come. If you'd rather, I can bring him back, or you can come live with me...us." Her intense gaze burned its way through me.

My retort sounded harsh even to me. "Who's us?"

My question caught her by surprise, although I'm not sure why. "Us...me and Jake." Her frown lingered after she answered.

I guess I didn't realize the depth of my pain until my lips pulled back in unconstrained anger. "Who...is...me?" My voice thundered each word.

Julia shrank from my growing fury, a portion of which came from an uncomfortable hangover. "Jake and me," she said in a soft voice. "Julia. Your Jules." Her eyes filled to appear glassy. She sniffed and glanced down, rivulets of tears escaping to her cheeks.

"Sure, ...for now. How about in five minutes?" My heart broke with each word but I bulled ahead. "Or when I'm expecting you home after work, you don't show, and I find your work gun gone? What name do I call you then?"

I stopped with Julia bawling, choking in her anguish. "I'm sorry," she lamented between sobs. "It seemed like a dream...like I watched a movie on television."

"Must have been a little more real than you let on. You left me marooned in Laredo. Sent me on a wild goose chase and disappeared. You planned it beforehand, then carried it out after I left to do your bidding." I pulled on dirty socks I supposed she stripped from me last night. "No calls, nothing to even let me know you were alive. Hell, I thought The Company hijacked you while I was inside." Her shocked response told me she hadn't considered my initial reaction. I laced my boots before retrieving my revolver. "You didn't have the decency to call your husband and let him know you weren't dead. I wasn't sure you

213

were still kickin' until watching you on TV in Chicago after your killing spree."

My anger drove me outside. Rather than do more harm and cause further anguish for my wife, I snatched a coat and my Stetson from their pegs inside the door and stalked north. Nothing but logging roads, timber, and deep mountains stood between me and the Montana border. With temperatures hovering in the forties, my angry hike took me farther than I planned. I could see nothing to be gained by continuing to rage at Julia. It hurt to remember watching her collapse inward and silently accept the abuse I dealt.

A frigid wind blowing from snow-covered mountains brought me to a halt. I was suddenly tired of the cold and exhausted from my anger and hangover. Stopping along a feeder creek running low but providing water to the North Fork, I searched the ground for dry twigs. After building a small stone ring, I used matches always carried inside a zipped inner pocket for emergencies. I kept the fire as small as my father's ancestors did so long ago. Feeding it limbs broken short, it provided enough heat to warm me. A rotten stump gave me a place to recline and ponder my life and future.

I didn't expect Julia to await my return. Although gone when I arrived, she left me the gift of a smudge build in my stove. Unlike her place—before it got blown to smithereens—my cabin's only heat came in the form of a fire. A surprise awaited me on the back corner of the wood burner, a pot of proper homemade chili made without beans but plenty of hot peppers. I'd filled my small freezer with elk meat stored at Mom's. Steaks left out for a couple breakfasts and supper went into making the meal. I guess I was wrong when figuring my wife left soon after me. She'd remained for hours to get it just right. A spoon dug to the bottom found a small scorched area, but man did her cooking taste good.

Julia didn't call again. Al did, Mom, too, conversations I steered away from my erstwhile spouse. Mom tried to make each one about Jules until I abruptly ended our conversations. For once, I wished we still used the old rotatory phones so I could slam the receiver. Didn't matter. Even then, all they heard was a click and dial tone.

William Daugherty headed the investigation into the attack on me and subsequent loss of our home—along with my killing of the woman. I heard his engine stop while in my generator room checking and filling any low cell of the battery bank powering my place. The closing of his door and a knock on mine came as I filled the final chamber with distilled water. My guts clenched when I stepped out to see the sheriff's SUV. "Hey, Will." I offered my hand to a man I'd known most of my life. "Here to haul me in again?"

His grip met mine, bearing down with all he could muster. I met it with my own strength, grinning at his attempt to overpower me. "Damn." He released my hand and worked his digits to regain feeling. "Not sure I've felt a grip like yours, Pelletier." I got a shake of his head. "No, I'm not here to arrest you."

"Coffee's on if you got time. No donuts though..." I pointed to his growing paunch and led him inside. "How's the case moving?" I asked, after we sat at my small table. No fire—March provided enough radiant heat through my windows. Besides, I found cooler temperatures easier to sleep in.

Will removed his hat and set it aside. I figured something big was coming after he rubbed his forehead while gathering his thoughts. "Learned who the woman was." He jabbed a thumb in the direction where I'd killed her and the body was found. "Anita Munier. Some kind of heavy-hitter from Chicago. A well-known killer. Why she was in Salmon to murder you may never be answered."

"Oh?" I waited to hear more.

"Ever hear the name?"

I didn't hesitate. "Nope."

"Damnedest thing," he muttered. Sipping at his coffee for a bit, he eventually sat back to regard me with a sharp look. "We got word from the feds. State and county were ordered to stand down. Your case was to be dropped ASAP. No reason given...we were told to back away."

His news didn't make sense, and he'd have to be a blind man not to see my surprise. "I don't get it. Why the feds? Because this Munier came from Chicago? Crossing state lines and all?"

"Uh huh. At least, I think so. We entered her prints into the national data base for a positive ID. FBI took their own damned time getting back to us before explaining who she was. They promised to dispatch an agent to help with the case, except later we got word he wasn't coming. State and county were to forget what we knew."

Even though we were friends, I wondered if his story was only a ploy. Make me comfortable enough to get a confession and then drop the hammer. I might not be the sharpest tack in the box, but I wasn't falling for an easy lie. "You're full of shit." His story didn't pass the smell test. "Now tell me how the case is really looking."

Will answered by opening his briefcase and removing a folder. From there he withdrew a handful of papers and pointed to the signature at the bottom. "This John Henry exonerates you. It's the DA dropping all charges. The case is closed. Included is a copy of the letter we received ordering us to cease and desist signed by the attorney general. Not sure who you know, Dawson. Whoever it is has more pull than I ever imagined."

Who, indeed? Al didn't have strong contacts I knew of within the federal government. I read through the thin sheaf and noted an extra name, Julia. Why would she be named when she wasn't here, only to be cleared of charges—what charges? Like Will, the actions of the United States government baffled me. Nevertheless, he was right. Not only was everything dropped but our slate wiped clean. "Not me, man. I don't know anyone to have contacts this big."

Will pushed his cup closer when I offered to fill it again. "There's something you're not telling me. Dawson, I've known you since before you snuck Nancy off to Challis after junior prom and got a motel room." His remembrance made me cringe. I thought Mom was spending the night at Aunt Bess's and wouldn't know I didn't return home. Nancy's folks thought she spent the night at a friend's place. All three were waiting when we arrived at my date's house. Mom's cool disapproval hurt worse than being grounded for a month.

They would learn soon enough. Even wolves wouldn't consume the bones, although they'd be cracked open for the rich marrow they could provide. I gestured up the hill behind my place. "You'll find a trail of bodies come spring thaw. Critters will've scattered what's left, because another nine were dumb enough to follow me. I s'pose you'll be able to backtrail 'em to Chicago, too."

Will stared hard. "You took on ten hitters from back east?"

"Nope. I ran from 'em. Big difference. I fled what was left of my home to avoid them...they made the error of catching me." My return gaze didn't waver.

"Christ almighty." Will heaved himself from his chair to look from my south window toward Julia's place. "What have you gotten yourself into, Dawson?" He turned to lean a shoulder against the wall where he could keep an eye on me and still view the area where they found the body.

What indeed? "Will..." I scratched through my beard and made a mental note to trim it. "...you ever break the law?" I brushed away his quick attempt to answer. "I don't mean stealing candy as a boy or even going over the speed limit by fifty. You're a marine hardened by combat. Did you ever break the laws of God and man?" I kept my tone low, even, and measured. He looked away, staring outside while I watched the muscles in his jaw work. No sense in pushing—the man tried to decide how to respond. He finally returned to his seat, angered by my question. "Well?" I asked.

His palm struck my table with enough force to slosh coffee from our cups. I didn't blink at his dynamic reaction. "We all do things we're not proud of and wish we could take back. Is that what you're asking?"

"Nope. I'm wondering if you've done something wrong you were proud of?"

He blinked twice and frowned. "Yeah..." I noted an almost imperceptible nod. "...yeah, I have."

"Me, too. The last nine times are scattered throughout the hills." I didn't blink first while we stared at the other.

He nodded to the papers I'd moved to the counter. "You know more than your letting on, don't you?"

"Some. Part of it has me in the dark as much as you."

"I've been your friend longer than I've worn this badge, Pelletier. Are you going to tell me what you're hiding?"

I shook my head slowly. "Can't. You know the old adage if I told you I'd have to kill you?" He nodded without comment. "In this case, it's true, because even if I didn't, someone else would."

Will's countenance grayed while he gnawed at a spot on his bottom lip. "You aren't kidding, are you?"

"Nope. This I can say for sure. I don't know what the feds have to do with my case. To be honest, their involvement shocks me."

My guest stood abruptly. "I guess if anyone can take care of himself, it's you, Pelletier." He extended a hand I met with my own. "Can't say I'm not relieved this case is closed. I'd hate like hell to have cuffed you if the DA ordered me."

I clapped his shoulder as we made our way outside. "Anytime you gotta zip-tie my wrists, Will, just do it. You'll never find me resisting arrest."

His news decided for me. Dragging my phone from a side pocket in my jeans, I used speed dial.

It rang once, twice, before a surly voice answered. "Yeah?"

"Can you call in another favor from your Russian friend? I'd like to spend some time in Belize."

Chapter XV

Al and his Russian friend came through to provide my getaway to Central America. Not as a favor, however—I bought the fuel and paid handsomely for the crew. Jose and Ox met me at the grass runway where my hopper flight brought me from Belize City. My sudden departure came without announcement to anyone, although I left a brief and vague note on my counter should anyone appear to check on me. Exoneration papers delivered by Sherriff Will Daugherty were in the open for Julia to read if she stopped.

Al's news I wouldn't be alone surprised me. I figured when Mom left, the boys would, too. Seemed they enjoyed the tropical climate as much as her and didn't see a reason to go. Not when the place cost them nothing but the food they ate. Ox grinned. "Goddamn, double-D, sure as hell good to see you." If Will couldn't imagine a grip stronger than mine, I needed to introduce him to Donny.

"Goes both ways, man. Jose," I nodded at my other old buddy.

"Great to see you, sir. Will Julia be joining us?"

Ox took my bags before I could. "Not this time. Maybe another."

Jose drove their beat-up Jeep exactly as the locals: Fast with the horn sounding and without regard for other drivers or pedestrians. Our place was close to the beach and only a few miles from where the Beechcraft landed me. I sat in the back with my seatbelt tightened enough to nearly cut me in half, and I gripped the overhead rollbar for dear life. "You ain't never been here before?" Ox shouted past his shoulder.

"Nope." I hollered back. "Didn't know I was part owner until Mom needed a place to get away from it all."

"You're gonna love it."

The villa was imposing from the outside. I knew the living quarters ran over two-thousand square feet with a detached garage and mother-in-law apartment above. A thick stone wall two feet taller than me encircled much of the place. After Al revealed Ox and Jose stayed behind, I naturally figured they moved into the main house. Judging by the interior cleanliness, they still lived in the smaller apartment.

"Your mom is awesome," Ox said as he and Jose led me inside. "Her cooking was incredible. Mrs. Pelletier insisted she fix most of our meals while she was here."

"Any reason in particular you stayed?" The living room was open to a rear patio by way of sliding glass doors. My bags were deposited in an adjoining room.

Jose pointed to a chair and motioned. "Living the dream, sir." He continued into the kitchen, where I heard rummaging before he returned with three cold beers. "We offered to pay rent, but Al blew us off. Said the place could use someone to keep it from running down. We're cleaning and repairing whatever we find." A sneaky smile turned into a grin. "Besides, we traded into a small cabin cruiser to fish from. Can't let it go to waste." His flash of teeth didn't falter, nor did I miss the wink from Ox.

"Guess I got a couple of Belizars on my hands then." All of us snickered at the butchered way of saying *dos Beliceños.*

Donny changed the subject. "Al tells us The Company is done for, and Julia's in the clear. Is he right?"

I grunted an affirmative and stared at the pounding surf through the glass door. "It's what they tell me." He cleared his throat and I turned to see him look to Jose for what I guessed was support. "What's going on?"

"Al should've got us here sooner." Ox's roommate nodded his agreement. "Jose noticed a couple guys nosing around 'bout six weeks ago...not long after we arrived. Seemed to be keeping an eye on Melissa...Mrs. Pelletier. We're just the help and paid 'em no mind. I reckon it's what they thought, anyway."

Always in a hurry, Jose took the story over. "We made it look as if we were heading into Belize City for the weekend, then doubled back to keep an eye on your mom. Damned if we weren't right. Bastards moved on her less than three hours after we pulled out."

"She didn't know?" I'd hoped Mom would never think she was in danger.

Jose's grimace was ugly. "She never heard a thing. We used fish knives and hosed the area pretty well." He gestured to where the scuffle must have taken place. "Moved our cleaning station over it and we aren't careful with fish guts and messes. Been plenty of slime and blood to mask the spots."

"Identification?" I asked. Both shook their heads. "Their bodies?"

My friends knew enough not to articulate a location. Jose gave a slight head tip and cut his eyes in the direction of the ocean. "Thirty miles, give or take five or ten." His grin remained ferocious.

I drained my bottle and set it aside. "Can't thank you boys enough. Truly I can't." I gave both a solemn nod. "We're blood now. You ever need anything...no matter what...it's yours." They accepted my hard stare—a curt return bob from them was enough. We'd been through battle together, but this was different. They killed to protect—not only one of ours—but my mother. Made no difference if they were on my payroll or not. We'd take this bond to the grave.

Donny battled tears at my strong reaction and looked for a way out. "Hate to ask..." He stopped to blow his nose and wipe his cheeks. "...why ain't Julia with you, Cap? If it's over and everything...?"

How to explain your wife isn't always the same person? Yes, I knew both Julia and J before we married. Yet I was ill prepared to see J take over and her bloodlust embraced by my wife. Jules loved to teach, and as far as Aunt Bess was concerned, good at her job. Yet J took control far too easily, undermining something else at which Julia proved a master. J'd worked to become a hunter and killer—an assassin at the top of her game. I couldn't imagine another as accomplished and proficient, and she slid into the role quicker than I ever anticipated. Accepting Jose and Ox as family, I didn't withhold our story starting after Jules and I separated from them nor the resulting fallout.

"Never saw anything like it when she capped the rich chick and her goons," Jose said. "Difference between a professional killer and a soldier are night and day. One's an intricate ballet, and the other's native steps around a bonfire preparing for war."

Could have a point. I'd watched Julia practice hard out back—not all of it running, jumping, rolling, and diving. Much of her time got spent taking deliberate steps, firing, then more careful placement of her feet before shooting again. "Yeah, her calmness freaks me out. One second she's Jules, and the next J is blank-faced on a killing spree. Not a sound...she never says a word. You'd never know people are dying except by the clacking of her gun's bolt."

"Hell, man. They hit your house with RPGs?" Ox was incredulous over my surviving a true weapon of war. Both men knew what I encountered after having experienced firing LAWs and facing rocket propelled grenade attacks many times.

"Yeah, my truck with the first shot, missed the house on the second, and smoked it the third. Jake and I were buried alive a few days while parts of the place burned."

"I'm glad it's over, Cap." Donny said. "Make up with your woman when you get back and fill your home with little ones." He swallowed hard, and we knew who he saw in his mind's eye. I couldn't imagine the pain of losing Julia, let alone family. If Jose and Ox hadn't been doing their job, Mom would likely be dead. Although it was my idea, I needed to thank Al once again.

* * *

We spent the week fishing. I didn't do it often enough, considering I lived on a well-known river—one Scotty guided on. Snook, snapper, grouper, and jacks were new to me. My southern guides seemed well-versed and comfortable with their boat. Bigger than what I envisioned at twenty-two feet, its twin seventy-five-horse Mercs provided all the power we needed. Our meals each day were what we caught from the ocean.

Jose brought the boat in very close to an outer island. Not big, I'd guess less than a half-acre, and he pointed out a spot fifty feet from the water's edge. Ox tossed the anchor after Jose cut the motors. "Right there, Cap." He stood close so I could look down his arm and finger to where he pointed. "You wanted to know where we buried 'em. Five, maybe six feet deep, right there."

"I can't thank you boys enough." Acid rose from my stomach to make me swallow to push it down again. "Mom never knows, right?" I wanted her to fly back here on a regular basis.

Ox's disgusted glance was enough. "Melissa's family." He went silent a moment before a grin started. "If I were twenty-five years older, I'd be chasing your mom and making you call me Dad!" His howls of laughter were contagious. We baited our hooks and cast them away, while I observed the burial site of men stopped from killing my mother. Far as I was concerned, they deserved their lonely resting place.

I spent two weeks with my new family before flying home. Al didn't help on the return flight, making me go commercial. Reckon he was still pissed over the gulf existing between me and Julia. A layover in Dallas with a connection the following day meant I got a chance to see William and his family. They were hoping for another little one and planned for at least three if not four kids to carry our family name. Susan made a great wife for my brother—I enjoyed watching their level of comfort with the other. Julia and I worked to build a similar bond before it got waylaid—a marriage I looked forward to rebuilding if possible.

* * *

Scotty gave me a ride home from the Salmon airport. "You want me to what?" he asked.

"Do what you're told and make yourself useful by holdin' the dumb end of the tape," I said. "Ain't like you got anything else to keep you busy. You'll get five, maybe six weeks of work at a time you're usually twiddling your thumbs." Other than a little fishing on the Salmon River, February through June were his leanest months.

"I can't pound a nail to save my life," he said. "Not sure I've ever drove one without bending it."

His protests made me laugh. "When I was a kid, Dad always told me when I bent a nail, it meant my pecker was still growing. Come work for me, and you still stand a chance to make the ladies happy...at least Robin. Apparently, it's never too late."

Scotty glanced my way. "It's nice to hear you laugh again, Dawson. Been a long time."

His observation caused me to reflect. Yes, it'd been a while since I'd been given the opportunity to relax and consider the future. My time in Belize helped. "I thought it was over, my friend." I stared out at the familiar scenery. "Figured we fought until one or both of us were killed. End of story."

"Hope you don't mind, but Julia's spent quite a bit of time at our house the last few weeks. Where in the hell have you been?"

"Naw, she needs friends...people she can talk to. I'm sure Robin's been good for her." He didn't press after I ignored the rest of his question.

"Who'd have thought it," he said. "My girlfriend, a bigtime lawyer, is best friends with your wife, a doggoned..."

"Schoolteacher," I said loudly, drowning out anything else he might say. "It's all she ever wanted. To teach and complain about district functions she's required to attend." I raised eyebrows at my friend. "You okay with her now? I know she messed your head up for a while."

Scotty mulled, driving a mile or more before replying. "Yeah," he finally answered. "You ain't wrong. I wasn't right upstairs for a few months. Never been around people being killed. There's a hell of a difference between shooting an elk you're going to eat and someone trying to murder you. Robin helped, having personally dealt with scary people like Julia. Things feel strangely normal since she's been back. Almost like old times with the woman I first met. Shy, soft spoken, wouldn't say shit if she swallowed a mouthful..." He trailed off while preparing to turn into my driveway, waiting for an oncoming car.

He didn't expand his thought on the gravel leading to my cabin. We broke out of the timber and into the meadow where it stood. "Hey, did Jules move our truck to my place?"

"Said she drove it over and hiked home through the woods. Figured you needed it, and she'd rather drive her old Wagoneer." The shake of his head explained his level of disgust. Julia loved her rig, which was good enough for me.

I almost called for Jake when I went inside. Julia's pointer and I bonded while she was away. Scotty left with the plan of meeting me the following morning. While I was sure Robin helped him invest the money Julia provided, making a little more on my payroll wouldn't hurt his bank account.

It felt good to be home. I started a pot of coffee before sitting in my beat-up recliner and tipped it back to rest my eyes. Absolute silence consumed me, a reminder of how good life could be in the Idaho backcountry. I'd felt it before after returning from military service. Now it was time to let it settle into my core.

* * *

Damned if Scotty wasn't waiting when I arrived on my John Deere backhoe with its frontend loader at the remains of the burned-out house. Outside of police tape, it looked about how I remembered. Jules parked the trailer on the roadside of the garage—easiest place to put it—as far from the house as she could get. I noticed a garden hose and heavy extension cord leading to her living quarters. She'd hired someone to put in a temporary electrical service. Swinging around Scotty's new truck and avoiding the garage's eave with my backhoe boom, I parked and throttled down next to the burned-out hulk where I once lived with my wife.

Scotty left his truck with White-ox gloves in one hand, and a coffee cup in the other. I looked over our job while he sauntered. "What's the plan?" he asked.

"We'll use a chain and the bucket for big stuff I can't handle with the backhoe. Make sure you stay back while I tear it down." Part of the destroyed structure leaned precariously.

We got most of the building flattened and dragged to a burn pile. Wanting to avoid nails after the heap turned to ashes, I built the fire a hundred yards back. Jules lost her rabbits and most of her chicken flock to cold and starvation while Jake and I were buried and then running for our lives. I noted she'd cleaned the coop and scoured the bunny cages. Five of her Dark Cornish hens survived, along with one mean little rooster. Blamed thing was convinced he was the cock of the walk, attacking me anytime I cared for them. Knowing Julia as I did, she likely planned to let any broody hens set. Five would turn into forty by summer's end.

We used the backhoe to keep the fire going. Anything combustible went on. Roof structure, walls, flooring, furniture, even foundational timbers were incinerated after I found rot. As I feared, her beloved wood cookstove lay damaged beyond repair—a victim of our war—and one I planned to replace. Appliances were chained and moved aside. Later, I'd bring my flatbed in for a run to the garbage dump.

Noticing Scotty waving, I throttled down to hear him. "Time, man." He motioned to a wristwatch he didn't wear. Almost four in the afternoon on my Seiko, I gave him a thumbs-up. I meant to be long gone when Julia arrived home from work. He and I made a good start in about eight hours. Scotty gave me a ride home after I parked my machine out of the way.

I didn't expect Julia to contact me and wasn't surprised when my phone didn't ring. After taking measurements before leaving, I made a call to Salmon lumber outside of town. Jules always planned to either rebuild or update the old house—my goal was to provide it for her. The order would take less than a week, and they could deliver it onsite.

Took us three days before there was nothing left to burn. We heaped the pile as it shrank, then used the bucket to haul away metal left behind. Nails mostly but also cabinet pulls, knobs, and hinges—things I didn't want littering the ground. Scotty and I spent more hours with rakes and shovels picking up what the John Deere missed.

I didn't see where anyone entered our bomb shelter since the police investigation before starting the job. Using a piece of matching colored thread, I secured it across the hinged opening to see if Julia or anyone else might poke around. I checked each morning only to find it unbroken. Near as I could tell without crawling inside, her money was secure within the landing at the ladder's base. She knew where it was hidden and how to access the opening to slide it clear.

My intention wasn't to do the complete rebuild myself. I put in a subfloor with Scotty's help before starting up with the walls using two-by-sixes for a cathedral ceiling. A two-bedroom one-bath home got expanded to a loft above for extra sleeping quarters, a second small bathroom, and space for a good-sized office or a place for privacy but open to below. Its previous eleven hundred square feet increased to almost sixteen hundred. Once the structure was framed in, I contacted contractors to do what I couldn't or would rather not handle. Siding, roofing, wiring, plumbing, insulation, and sheetrock—I would much rather pay for expertise rather than have our county inspector tell me to do it over.

Mom didn't drive. Never learned and didn't plan to. If she needed a ride, she called me or Aunt Bess. Occasionally friends she knew, but it needed damned near to be an emergency. When she called me not long after I left the worksite, I figured it was time for another grocery run. "Hey, Mom," I answered. I'd not been back since feeling like she and Al ran me off.

"How long before my second favorite son might stop to see me?"

"I could give him a call. But I'm not sure how long it would take him to get a flight out of Dallas."

"It isn't William I wanted to see." Mom sounded less than happy. Damn, her firstborn demoted to number two.

She waited in the recliner closest to the woodstove with her needlepoint. Mom ran cold the older she got, burning a fire if temperatures dropped below seventy. I tossed my coat aside and popped the top two buttons of my shirt. "What's up, old lady? Need a ride to town?"

Cold eyes lifted from whatever she worked on. "Have a seat, boy." She nodded at the closest couch, an old loveseat.

Mostly I worried she might find out about the men Ox and Jose stopped. Only way she could learn would likely be through Al, and he wouldn't make such a costly error. "Should I cut a willow switch, or would you rather use a piece of kindling?" I asked. Where Dad never spanked us boys, Mom made up for him.

"I'm too damned angry to think of tanning your hide. I hoped to have more grandkids soon, except you're too proud to make it happen."

My brow furrowed. "What're you talking about?"

"I'm talking about your wife, Einstein." She berated. "She and I speak almost every night. Her heart is breaking, Dawson."

"I've been busy rebuilding her house." As always, my voice deepened as my anger grew.

"And leave before she comes home from work. I didn't raise any son of mine to behave that way. So, she did something to make you angry. Get over it. It's part of life. She's your wife, for God's sake."

I breathed a silent sigh of relief. Mom didn't know what happened between us. Only two could let it out of the bag—Jules or Al. Neither would be so foolish. I guessed Scotty could, too, but even he was smart enough to keep it to himself. "Meant to when I got back. Whole idea got shoved aside when I started the house."

"Got back? From where?"

I mentally cringed at my error, having hoped no one learned I'd left the country for a few weeks. "Went on a looky-loo. Clear my head and get my bearings." My attempt to stare her down failed. "It's none of your damn business where I went." I fought to keep my growing anger under control, and Mom knew it.

"Dawson, that girl loves you." Her tone softened as we reached the breaking point. "Maybe what happened on your elk hunt has affected you more than either of you kids realize. Don't let it drive a wedge between you that can't be knocked loose. Tomorrow's her last day of school before summer break. She's chosen interior colors for sheet rocked walls, and the painter should be finished in a couple. Go back and move in with her, okay?"

The days somehow got past me. "School's out?" Mom nodded. Damn, her news changed everything. I needed to do my best to make amends and be there when her new wood cookstove got delivered and installed. The one I ordered appeared identical to her old one, only much more modern and controllable. Weighing over four hundred pounds, the crew I hired would have it moved in and set up in a few hours.

* * *

School usually let out at ten forty-five on its final day. Figuring Jules would need a few minutes to tidy whatever room she worked in, I waited until eleven before arriving with a dozen roses. Kids with their excited screams were mostly gone. After stomping the halls and finding the place empty, I double-timed to Aunt Bess's office. When I didn't see her secretary, I figured even Auntie was gone but tapped on the door anyway. "Come in," came her cheery call. I opened it enough to poke my head inside. "Dawson! What a nice surprise." Aunt Bess greeted and waved me in. "Are the roses for me?" she said.

I shook my head. "Sorry, Auntie. Did I miss Jules?"

"I don't know. Is she gone? She stood in for Mrs. Velasquez today. Fourth grade."

I'd passed the primary school classrooms without seeing anyone. Somehow, I'd missed her. "No lights were on."

"Probably at The Jumping Salmon for their year-end party. Might want to check there if she doesn't answer her cell."

I could use a sandwich and hoped to catch Julia before she ordered food. My call went to message, dashing any hopes. I tossed it to the passenger side and drove the short distance to the restaurant.

Seemed as if a lot of folks wanted lunch. I spotted Jules's Wagoneer in front and drove around back to find a parking spot. With the days warming and wearing only a flannel shirt with sleeves rolled to my elbows, I left my Anaconda under the front seat. I walked halfway to the door before remembering the flowers. Returning to the truck, I made sure the roses looked good by pulling the paper back.

Although no live band, a radio played in the background as I entered, and a few couples were on the dancefloor. I stepped to where I could best see most of the tables—searching for my wife. Not spotting her anywhere, I assumed she visited the bathroom and took a seat at

229

the bar to wait. "Morning, Pelletier. Get you something?" I turned to find Glenn Fowler ready to serve a drink. Other than an occasional bloody Mary the morning after, I rarely touched alcohol early in the day.

"Hey, Glenn. Coffee, please." I didn't need to tell him black. He'd served me for years. He finished what he was doing before getting a cup. A decade older than me at almost fifty, I wasn't prepared when his hand shook, splashing coffee outside my cup. "You all right, man?"

His gaze flickered over my shoulder. "I don't want any trouble, Dawson," he warned. I spun on my stool to see what flustered him. The object of his fear slow danced thirty feet away—Thomas Howell and my wife.

Julia saw me at the same time I noticed her. She was pulling back from his arms to push him away. He wasn't having any part of it and drew her in again. She struggled against his greater strength—her eyes locked on mine as her face drained. Rage colored my vision for a moment until I felt a calm. Although keeping it to myself, I'd promised I'd kill him if he entered my life again. Tossing the flowers to the floor— the glass vase shattering—I bolted for my truck and gun. I supposed Julia understood and shrieked as I charged out the front entrance. "No!" I heard her fear-tinged yell. "Dawson, no..." I didn't hear more after the door closed. Around the corner, I was at my truck in an instant. Fishing the gun from under the seat and tossing the leather scabbard aside, my plan was clear. End Howell's days on earth.

Watching through the windows for the object of my rage as I returned, the front banged open and Thomas sprinted toward the highway. I heard the shriek of rubber and came around the corner in time to see him cross the asphalt, barely avoiding highway traffic. He didn't slow and disappeared into an alley. I knew where it came out and turned back for my truck.

Julia almost caught me. Almost. I avoided her hand and locked the door as I started the diesel. While she screamed and banged on the window—rather than back out and lose time I engaged four-wheel-drive, crossing the concrete curb to gun the engine through manicured vegetation, crawling up a short hillside to the road. I turned toward the street where Howell would appear. I ignored my chirping phone, sure it was Julia.

Thomas appeared from the alley to cut across a lawn when I was struck with an epiphany. He wasn't worth it. Twice he interfered in my private life—the man obviously possessed something I didn't. If he wanted Julia, he could damned well have her. I turned toward home and swore off women and perhaps Salmon. Al could find work for me in whatever field he dabbled, although I preferred something legal. Punching Scotty's number, he answered on the second ring. "Too late to make me sweat in the hot sun, man. I'm on the road." Although he swore helping me build the house was brutal employment, we enjoyed working together.

"Where are you?"

"On our way to Challis and into Falconberry with a load of horses and mules. Robin and I are riding in to clear trail. Get my camp ready for fall hunters. What's up?"

"Wait for me, will you? I'll get my saddle and gear if you got an extra horse?"

"Well...yeah. I can shift supplies and tools between the mules." Damned if he didn't mind me tagging along. "Can you meet us at the trailhead? Hustle, we'll be loaded and waiting."

I hurried, spending less than twenty minutes packing my shit. Mom's place was my second stop. Reckon she didn't see me drive around the house to park behind the barn. No other saddle fit my butt like one I'd used most of my life. Sitting in one of Scotty's on our elk hunt tried to wear the skin off my ass and inner thighs.

Back on the highway without any sign of Julia, I slowed after noticing a rig turn onto my driveway. Her Jeep was easily recognizable as it disappeared into the timber. I guessed she'd not contacted Robin if she looked for me at my cabin.

A little after one when I arrived at the trailhead, eight hours of light remained. Two saddle horses were ready, while six mules were packed with supplies. A third gelding standing seventeen hands and wearing

231

only a bridle stood at a hitching post. Scotty couldn't wait for me to get out and took long steps to my door with a grin. "Plan on earning back the money I got from you? Ain't gonna happen. I don't pay even minimum wage."

"Should be fine then. I don't intend to work hard enough to be worth five bucks a day." I forced a smile. "How are you, Robin?"

"Good. I'm looking forward to spending time in the backcountry. Is Julia coming? I tried calling after you contacted us, but it was busy and put me straight to voicemail. I didn't get a chance to leave a message and don't have service now."

My shrug was lazy and nonchalant. "Probably yakking at Mom. They talk regularly."

Didn't take long to saddle the gelding and load my gear. Fishing pole, clothes, sleeping bag, air mattress, and my guns. I even brought elk meat to go in a cooler. With the Anaconda on my belt—the Marlin went into the scabbard under my stirrup. I waited for Scotty to start his pack train, holding back to ride drag. No way did I want conversation. Too much to think about and consider. Because other than the actual divorce, my life would be lived on my terms.

Chapter XVI

I lost myself in the hard work of our first week. Blowdowns crossing the trail had to be sawed or chopped out by hand, as motors weren't allowed in a wilderness area, Scotty put me to work manning a pulaski, axe, shovel, or crosscut saw, sometimes all four within a few minutes. He and Robin worked equally hard, earning a degree of respect I didn't realize I withheld from Scotty. No wonder his arms, chest, and back were so muscular. Sawing and rolling logs, splitting most into planks, and rebuilding trail erosions with a shovel and those roughhewn boards required physical strength.

Only one wall tent came with us. Scotty apologized, offering me a place inside with them. Other than socializing in camp and at meals, three's pretty much a crowd at bedtime, so I decided to make do with two canvas tarps for a reasonable facsimile of a Baker tent. Not nearly as secure to the outside as Scotty's deluxe version, few mosquitos troubled me with a smudge burning outside my shelter. If any critters with teeth and claws got too close, I'd wear their fur as a coat.

Wolves often howled day and night. While it got the livestock's attention, none seemed to find it frightening. Left on a picket line where browse grew thickest, they ate anytime we didn't ride. Scotty brought a bag of oats as feed and nothing else. Our steeds relished green vegetation.

With Scotty scouting trail conditions, Robin and I worked to produce planks from a white fir fallen across the path. We fashioned manageable lengths with the crosscut saw—allowing the boss to pass with the stock—then used a maul and wedges to split them lengthwise. None of the resulting boards were uniform, and many twisted after released from the trunk, but we pressed them into service to repair a washout by burying the ends.

I'd relented after Robin's constant bombardment over Julia and our plans for the future—finally breaking down and telling them the truth. Scotty and his girlfriend were to be in the mountains six weeks or longer. No way could I avoid personal and painful questions about my homelife for a month and a half. She'd barely returned from savaging The Company brass before going back to work for my aunt. After she spent most of her time at our friends' place without me, they were bound to figure it out. Robin took time from digging. "Even if the two of you were having problems, I'm still surprised at Julia." She wiped sweat from her brow with a kerchief tied around her neck.

The log was about to give up its third and final plank to my wedges. I applied light blows with the flat side of my maul before stopping to rest. Three four-by-eighteens six feet long would cover much of the washout when we braced beneath before working them into place. "I reckon it's my fault as much as hers. Just couldn't get over being pissed after she talked to you and Al but never me. Should've swallowed my pride sooner, I guess."

"Bullshit," Robin said. "A spouse should speak to their partner before moving on. Julia shouldn't have waited for you to catch her in the act, so to speak. I ought to paddle her ass the next time I see her. Problem is, she'd probably kill me."

"Naw, she thinks the world of you. You're kindred spirits sharing a familiar past...at least working for a common employer. What surprises me most is she didn't mention anything about Howell to you."

"Nary a peep. That's why I'm so puzzled. If we were as good of friends as you seem to think, hos before bros, right?"

"Oh, hell, I don't know." I lifted the maul to continue making lumber. Rather than tap the wedge to coax the crack to elongate, my anger drove it deep to stick inside. We listened to the pops and cracks of the wood relaxing. "Jules wasn't the same after Laredo. Don't know if it's because she messed up, and I bailed her out...or some other reason. This felt like something more, like she didn't have any control." The clink of iron on rock alerted us Scotty neared. "Don't see how J would be pissed because I save her life."

234

"Can't leave you guys alone for a second, can I?" Scotty said. "The way oughta be opened by now, but you're standing around talking. Should I demonstrate again?"

He didn't make an empty boast. My friend didn't waste a move while working in the wilderness. I'd taken him up earlier on what I assumed was no more than bragging. To prove a point, he braced a fir bole and split two planks far faster than I could've cut one with a chainsaw. "You're a tough man to work for, Scotty Rich." I mimed breaking rock on a chain gang.

Winter storms left trails damaged by blowdowns and runoff, worse than in recent years. Ten days passed before we accessed his basecamp from where we hunted the previous fall. Riding into the clearing, I wasn't surprised when he reined in to look. Streamers of weathered police tape waved in the breeze where his tents were normally erected. I followed him, Robin, and the pack train farther up the slope to where he stopped again.

Rather than dismount, Scotty stared at the area where four bodies once lay. "Wondered how I'd feel after getting back." His musing was for himself as much as for Robin and me.

Tickling my horse's ribs with my heels, I rode forward to stop next to his. "Time to make new and better memories," I said. Weather worked to scour away signs of any chalk if police even marked around their bodies so far from civilization. "Got a lot of trail left to open along with firewood to saw, split, and stack. Last year'll barely be a memory by the time season opens."

Robin was first to dismount. "Come on, Scotty. Daylight's burning, and we still have a tent to erect and supper to cook before it gets too late." Her remark nearly caused me to burst into laughter. Not long from being a city girl, she became the voice of reason while predators howled and yipped in the distance.

I got my camping area ready while they put up their wall version. Rather than pack a metal frame in, Robin and Scotty left together with an axe and saw to cut poles to brace their shelter. Busy as I was making my spot comfortable, I didn't miss them for an hour. Knowing which direction they took, at first I thought to become a one-man search party. Then their tardiness dawned on me. With a third unplanned body in camp, they needed to get any of their noisier loving in the privacy of the outdoors.

My grin widened when they appeared with five long poles. One to act as the ridge, the others to work as an X in front and back, holding the top pole high. Stakes and ropes would keep the tent walls stretched wide and tight. "You two look relaxed. Figured wolves were dining on your carcasses, or you fell asleep...you know...afterward."

Scotty blushed, whereas Robin simply laughed. "Told you he'd figure it out, Romeo." Thrusting a thumb over her shoulder, she giggled to me at his embarrassment. "He acts like a high school girl caught necking by her dad."

After we got the tent up and gear inside, I left them to situate their place while I started a fire in the pit. Some of the wood left over from the previous season was rotted and too wet for building a smudge. After I got the driest of it burning, the old stuff and wet branches went on to produce extra smoke. Already, mosquitos made themselves known even with a breeze and the sun shining. Livestock seemed happy in their corral with their feedbags filled with oats. After grass in their corral got beat down, the animals would be allowed time on a picket line where they could browse. My blaze was growing when Scotty stuck his head out. "Hey, mind getting a couple buckets of water?" He left two on the ground before disappearing inside.

His supply consisted of a pipe dug into a wet spot on the hillside below camp. It ran a substantial flow even during the driest of summers. Cold and sweet, I couldn't help but take time to drink straight from the source before washing my face, neck, hands, and forearms. I'd save the rest of me for another day with a washcloth and soap. Returning with the filled containers, I took them inside where my fellow campers worked. "What smells so good?"

"The last of your elk steak in gravy with quartered potatoes." Robin stirred it before adding more water. "Another hour, and the meat should fall apart."

Her assessment proved correct. The three of us demolished everything she cooked, plus an apple each. After cleaning the kitchen, we retired to the firepit with a whiskey bottle and three shot glasses. A stack of branches thrown on caught and blazed high providing plenty of light. Scotty filled each of our tumblers before sitting back with a sigh. "Damn. Every year I forget how good this is until I'm back. This's the life."

His girlfriend rested a hand on his forearm. "Now you know why I quit my job and moved here. I'll never forget how this country affected me. Almost as if it were calling me home. Hated leaving J in the lurch while she worked for The Company, but after getting my ass fired, I needed to be here." She glanced to me. "Sorry. Didn't mean to say anything."

I threw the alcohol back and held my glass out for more. "No problem." Bracing the drink against my chest, I closed my eyes to absorb the smells of high-country sage on a warm wind moaning through camp.

"Forgot to ask," Scotty said. "Is it my imagination, or did I see a little solar panel in front of your shelter?"

"You didn't dream it," I returned without offering more than a smirk.

"Well?"

"I bought a tablet from the computer place in town. Downloaded a couple hundred books. An app lets me read them without the internet. Coolest thing is how the solar array generates enough power in a couple hours to keep me reading all night if I wanted to stay up."

"No shit?" Scotty said. I'd assumed him my technological superior but reckoned I could thank Julia it wasn't true in this case. Although she didn't consider herself savvy, she knew far more about computers than I was interested in knowing. "All this time I could have watched movies in camp?"

"I reckon." My friend rarely read—other than magazines, preferably with pictures. "Learn to sound out words. You might be surprised at what you can grasp without centerfolds."

Scotty grinned. "Funny. You ain't seen Miss June yet, have you?" I closed my eyes and sipped my whiskey while listening to the sound of Robin backhanding her boyfriend.

* * *

I spent a week in camp sawing wood for a hunting season filled with nights around the fire. Finding dead or downed trees, I used a mule trained to drag logs back to camp. There, I used a single-man crosscut saw for bucking them into manageable lengths. Splitting each chunk into halves or quarters, I stacked six cords before Scotty stopped me. "Only need enough for one autumn, man."

Of course, I explored while on Falconberry. Burned a day and rode my tall gelding to look at the area where Julia and I took the bull. Seated high on an open ridge with Tonto grazing nearby, my binoculars picked up a doe and fawn exploding from the timber on a far hillside. Imagine my astonishment when a pack of wolves sped behind the pair. I adjusted my glass in time to see a lobo pull the young deer down. In moments, they tore its belly open and guts out, eating while the poor thing died. I wondered if those who insisted reintroducing wolves would feel the same way after watching life play out up close and personal. I'd spent most of my years witnessing things I killed die and knew intimately the savagery involved. Even Julia—once a sheltered schoolteacher from California—understood barbarism and the finality of extinguishing a life. The doe fleeing from the sounds of her young perishing didn't surprise me, although I knew many times they were killed trying to protect their offspring.

Most of the wolves lay sated afterward, cleaning their muzzles and paws of blood, fat, and particles of meat. One cracked bones in an effort to get at the nutritional marrow. I touched the .44 in front of my hip, knowing it would keep me safe if I ran afoul of the huge beasts. Although a half-mile distant with a shallow canyon between us, their heads raised when Tonto lifted his head to nicker. If I wanted a way to test their hearing, it was no longer needed. Two stared longer than made me comfortable. Stowing my binoculars in the saddlebags, I mounted to return for dinner before Scotty and Robin gave up waiting.

"Hate to say it," Scotty mentioned over breakfast weeks later. "We're pulling out day after tomorrow."

His news wasn't unexpected, but I wasn't ready. "So soon?"

"'Bout outta food. Besides, I'm sure messages of last-minute bookings and cancellations are adding up. Gotta take care of business, my friend." We tossed our paper plates into the fire and handed the silverware to Robin.

"Yeah..." I stared at a far ridge and wondered about traveling rather than personal problems. "How far do you think it is to Indian Creek?"

"Indian?" Early settlers in Idaho named many of its creeks long before the term "Native American" for some of my ancestors was coined. "Are you talking about the one lying between Pistol and Thomas? Just upstream from Marble Creek?"

"Yup. On the Middle Fork." I'd ridden through much of the mountains we were camped in but never from Falconberry to the Middle Fork of the Salmon.

Scotty scratched his head. "I'd have to dig my maps out. At least five...maybe six days on horseback. More than a week of hard miles on foot. "Why?"

"Mind if I borrow Tonto and a mule? Thinkin' of staying in here most of the summer."

"Running from your problems won't help anything." Robin came from behind me while Scotty and I talked to lay a friendly and calloused hand on my shoulder. Most of her once long, beautiful, and professionally manicured nails were clipped back to the quick.

I couldn't help but agree. "Nope, but I ain't ready to face 'em. Still getting over the idea I've lost her. Gotta rebuild my self-confidence before I'm prepared to sign divorce papers."

"I'm thinking of hiring another guide and an extra cook to help Robin," Scotty said. "If you're interested in either, you'd be number one on my list."

I sniffed and looked away before poking the fire with my stick. "Thanks, man...means a lot." His from-the-heart offer caused a lump in my throat. Scotty always had my back when I needed him. Always. "Not sure what the future holds. A few years ago, I'd have reenlisted. Pushing forty is a mite old for the battlefield. Ain't going back to be a damn paper-pusher."

The hope in Scotty's voice was clear. "You're interested in the job?"

"Thanks for thinking of me but probably not. Go ahead and hire someone else. Push comes to shove and nothing comes up, I'll ride in to volunteer my time. Deal?"

Scotty was right when we scavenged the last of our food and loaded a pair of panniers on my mule. Only a box of brown rice, an unopened carton of potato flakes, powdered milk, pancake mix, and freeze-dried eggs, along with salt, pepper, oil, and a couple pounds of flour remained. Enough food to last me a few weeks at most. Already my belt tightened a hole from the physical labor. I wondered if the two remaining would be enough to hold my jeans and Colt from sagging. "How long do I wait before contacting search and rescue?" Scotty asked.

"Don't worry about me. Either I make it, or I don't. My plan is to eventually come out and give you a call from Stanley or the Lower Loon trailhead. There's a hell of a trail system west of Big Baldy. Got my fishing pole...maybe I'll test some of the lakes up there."

"Damn." Scotty scratched a face usually free of whiskers. "I've been there. Wild country on the other side of the river. It'll probably take a fly-in hunter or another guide to locate your carcass if anything happens."

"Tell you what. Send a box of supplies in with Salmon Air to Indian Creek around two weeks from now. Leave 'em with the Forest Service guys addressed to me. Should be a few fellows in there keeping the cabins shipshape.

Scotty frowned. "Two weeks?"

"Yeah, planning on takin' my time. Hit the river and fish my way down. Should go a long way in supplementin' my vittles."

"What should we tell Julia? We're bound to see her, and she'll have questions." Scotty shivered. "I don't want her mad at me again."

Yes, what to do with Jules. After all we'd been through—much of it life and death—our end was heartrending. "Don't much care. Tell her I said it's over. She leaves with her shit...me with mine. Make out the papers anyway she wants. I'll sign 'em when I get home."

We broke camp early after Scotty tightened Tonto's shoes. Besides me, the big gelding carried only my rifle and saddlebags. Erlene took the rest of my freight. The mule wasn't overloaded—her burden more bulk than weight.

Robin came to me first while Scotty lined their animals for the trip out. "You take care, Dawson. I don't know what got into that woman of yours, but I may go ahead and slap it out of her when we meet." As tall as I am, her crown reached my nose during her powerful hug.

"Whatever you think best. Keep a close eye on Scotty, will you? I saw a side of him up here I didn't know existed."

She chuckled. "The man's growing up and becoming a bit more adult, but he's a work in progress for sure."

I mounted Tonto and rode to Scotty with Erlene in tow. We leaned closer and shook. "You take good care of Robin. You've definitely found a keeper, man." I watched as she mounted her mare as if she'd done it her whole life instead of less than two years. Rather than wait for his answer, I turned Tonto's head west.

* * *

The terrain could be described in no other way than steep. I oftentimes dismounted to lead my animals rather than put added pressure on Tonto's shoulders. I searched for long ridges sloping north or west to avoid the worst. Many were rocky and to be avoided, causing us to occasionally backtrack and find another way. Water wasn't easy to find up high, making me glad I'd packed plenty. I dug out the few wet places we encountered to parch the thirst of my animals. We stopped to make camp wherever darkness found us.

Got hit by one hell of a thunderstorm on the fourth day. We only went a few miles after packing and leaving before I saw it moving in from the southwest. Black clouds with a curtain of rain leading the way—I took shelter in a stand of small timber. Using a single-bit short-axe, I cleared away low limbs for a place to string a tarp. Building a Baker tent would likely be for naught—instead, I opted for a simple inverted L by draping an oiled canvas over a rope strung six feet from the ground. One end was tacked against the soil with stakes, while I pulled the other taut with more rope. My gear fit nicely with plenty of room left for me, and a pile of dry wood for a fire afterward.

Wind struck first with limb cracking ferocity. Tops blew out of nearby trees much larger than where I hunkered. With the back of my shelter aimed at the oncoming storm, the exposed sides whipped hard enough to loosen grommets. A rain squall followed, settling into a strong downpour without signs of letting up. I peeked out to check on my animals and found both pointed their rears toward the tempest, weathering it without signs of distress. Rather than worry about our situation, I made myself comfortable on my sleeping bag and started another novel I'd read more than once. Mom kept her Zane Greys in her bedroom library and let us boys into them if we took great care with each hardback. After finishing *Riders of the Purple Sage* the evening before, I moved on to *The Rainbow Trail* as the follow-up to the popular story of years past.

Plenty of power in my tablet got me through the day. The squall let up in late afternoon, but I chose to enjoy the comfort of my hideaway. Water dripped from limbs surrounding me, and already I could smell fresh air cleansed of summer dust. Limbs stacked hastily under my shelter before the rain hit made a cheery blaze. An early dinner of hotcakes, rehydrated potato flakes, and eggs seemed enough.

Wolves howled nonstop beginning my seventh day away from Falconberry. We broke out of a nice stand of pine in late morning to a feeding pack. A well-used elk trail kept our noise to a minimum. Tonto snorted and refused to continue with Erlene tugging hard on the lead. Both animals dug in to protest. Retreating inside the timber, I tied each securely. I slid the Marlin from its scabbard and left them behind.

A pack of nine glutted themselves on a young bull elk. They started with the guts first, feeding on the more nutritious fat-rich organs and intestines. Meat was the last to be consumed—protein I badly needed.

After I'd crept within a hundred yards, eighteen eyes turned to stare when I levered a cartridge into the chamber. The giant canines came to their feet gracefully after I fired a round into the air, retreating a dozen yards before stopping. Two more shots into the ground nearby warned of my intentions—give me room or die. The pack glided into the forest without a sound.

Not sure if they'd return, I hurried to the elk to check its condition. Everything inside was gone—from its heart and lungs to anus—except the dense material inside its paunch. Flipping the hide back, I found they hadn't started on either loin or bottom hindquarter. I skinned the animal to remove first the backstraps, then a large portion of the haunch. Slinging my rifle over a shoulder, I retreated to my horse and mule with bloody hands and thirty or more pounds of prime venison.

Two days were spent smoking a portion of my newly acquired protein. Nearly three pounds of fresh steaks were eaten the first night. Rolled in flour, tossed in a hot pain of oil, then garlic salted and peppered, my taste buds went wild with the familiar flavor. Another panful the next morning tasted just as good. Both Tonto and Erlene seemed happy enough with the feed around camp, so I decided to stay an extra couple of days.

Noise from the river nearly a week later caught my ear long before I saw it. Cessnas loaded with whitewater rafters and their gear flew overhead. Stopping at the shore of the North Fork to let my animals drink their fill, I waved to three passing boats loaded with tourists. A few lifted cameras for pictures of a man wearing a Stetson, belt gun, soiled clothing, chaps, and worn boots. Another two were offered the same greeting when they passed minutes later. One, a shorthaired blonde wearing only a bikini and life vest caught my attention. I stared hard until realizing it wasn't Jules.

Tired of being dirty, I set Tonto and Erlene on a short line. Divesting myself of clothing, I stepped into water cold enough to question my sanity. Hot springs could be found downstream, but I needed cleaned now. I slow-walked into a back eddy reaching my chin after I sat to soak. Nature's bathtub felt worth any initial discomfort after acclimating to the temperature. My body was cleaner and my hair washed best I could before retreating to the warm shore.

I rode downstream in late afternoon with the idea of reaching a small suspension bridge and crossing to the far side. Camping areas and the trail were substantially better on the northwest shore. I heard chatter as dusk crept into the canyon bottom and rounded a corner to find rafters making camp with a couple of young guides helping tourists as much as possible. While I loved Idaho and wished to keep it pristine, it didn't hurt to let others see why we lived in our beautiful state.

"Here's our cowboy." I drew up when a seductive female voice caught my attention. It sounded distinctly Brit or Aussy. A woman in her forties rose from a comfortable-appearing seat. "What brings a man's man to ride the banks of this wild river and country?" she asked. I noticed her fascination with the revolver in front of my hipbone. Even the rifle secured in its scabbard under my stirrup wasn't missed by her keen eye.

I leaned forward, resting my forearms and weight on the saddle horn. "Runnin' from my problems like everyone else." I gave her my best drawl and puppy eyes.

"Interested in filling your belly, Pelletier?" A man attached to a familiar voice was one I'd known for years. Rob Dotson and his brother Chuck ran a rafting business for almost as long as I'd been alive. Hell, I'd given them rides when I found their original work bus broken down along the river back in the old days.

"Jesus Christ." My saddle creaked when I dismounted. "If it ain't Robbie Dotson. Figured you'd have drowned by now, seeing you can't swim a lick," I said. He was my dad's age if I remembered correctly. Now probably in his mid-sixties.

"Nope. I make sure at least one of my clients can swim and another can perform CPR." The long-bearded man came from behind the stove and firepit he cooked over and thrust out a gnarled hand. "How've you been doing, boy? Ain't seen you in what seems like years."

"Pretty good...takin' care of Mom when she'll let me. You know how she can be." I dropped the reins and followed him to the kitchen.

Tonto was trained to ground tie. Lazy Erlene wouldn't run except to a feed sack. Looked to be about fifteen, maybe sixteen paying customers. Some—the woman first accosting me, the once bikini-clad blonde now wearing more included—gathered to pet my horse and mule.

"We miss Melissa," Robbie said. Mom went to school with his wife, Jackie. "Need to make time after season's done and spend an evening with her." He turned big sirloin steaks over the fire and stirred an enormous pot of beans.

I kept one eye on those surrounding my horse. Not long before I'd been running from The Company assassins in mountains not so far away. Getting over the suspicion someone wanted to kill me proved difficult, especially with a whole lot of folks I didn't know. Tough to forget the four sent to cap Julia in camp until she turned the tables on them. Most of the city dudes petted both animals or stood close to admire them. One, a man in his late twenties or early thirties grasped the butt of my Marlin and began to slide it from the scabbard. "You..." I hollered. "...take your hand off my rifle." Somehow, I found myself looking over the sights of my Anaconda. If he continued and swung it around, I'd have no alternative but to shoot.

"Shit!" The man released it and backpedaled away. He fell to his rear on the sandy soil. "Sorry, man. Didn't mean anything...I was just looking."

"Here, now." Robbie left his kitchen again. "Awful jumpy for a man long home from the war, aren't you?" I holstered my revolver before he rested a big paw on my shoulder. "Hell, didn't I read something about you and some woman attacked not far from here?"

My rifle caught by the barrel in the scabbard. I retrieved and shucked it free of cartridges before replacing the Marlin in its sheath. Robbie's tourists backed away. "Yeah, up on Falconberry."

"No problem, folks." Robbie raised his voice to reassure his wards. "Ask before you play with a man's guns. Dinner in fifteen. Steaks, taters, and all the beans you can eat. Clean your plates and keep your forks, should be enough pie for everyone afterward." He motioned me to follow him back to the kitchen area. "Wasn't Scotty Rich mixed up in it somehow?"

I kept an eye on the English lady edging closer. "They shot and left Scotty for dead before hustling back to camp with plans of finishing the rest of us."

"Christ!" He said. I noticed him running an eye over his charges. "What happened? How the hell did you stop 'em?"

"My wife overhead the four making plans. She was out of sight when they returned. Sons of bitches drew down on me and the cook, planning to kill us. Julia snuck up from behind and capped 'em all."

He whistled. "Whew, my kinda woman."

"Yeah," I said not wanting to think about her. "She's a tough cookie."

I helped dish and serve Robbie's customers. Even spoke to the bastard who touched my rifle. Afterward, me and my old buddy sat at a table to the side. My steak tasted pretty damned good, the potato even better with all the fixin's. I couldn't eat enough beans. To hell with consequences later.

I'd given up finishing the bowl when the English woman brought a stool over. Her frank stare made me nervous. "Where the hell did you come from...and where you heading?" Robbie asked.

"Been cleaning trail into Falconberry with Scotty and his girlfriend. Lots of blowdown...winter left its mark for sure. Plumb wore my ass out with his damn crosscut saw. I headed this way once we finished, and he got ready to pull out."

Robbie stared. "No shit? You cut cross country?" He likely knew the ground better than me. "Rough territory between there and here."

The English lady was ready to have her questions answered. "You are a woodsman rather than a western cowboy?"

"Not much cowboyin' left these days, ma'am. I ain't much of nothing but a vagabond."

"Don't let him fool you, *Mrs.* Thurman." He emphasized her title and stared hard at me. "Bastard owns a thousand acres of prime bottomland. Been in his family for generations."

She appeared startled. "So much? I can't imagine having a deed to such a large estate." Her delicate fingers traced the pattern on my shirtsleeve.

Robbie's eyebrows raised when he saw the attention she gave. Got no idea why she looked more than once. My clothes were not only dirty, like me they stank of horsehair and body odor. "Hey, you hear something?" Robbie asked. His group growing ever more raucous quieted.

I listened hard until the clink of metal sounded above the river. Holding a finger up to ask for silence, we heard it again. Horses were coming up the trail and would pass only yards away. Tonto nickered where he fed with only halters on him and Erlene. Horse's ears and the brim of a hat appeared as the first rider came over the rise.

"Scotty?" I stood to see better. He led a short string with first Robin and then Julia, riding to where I could see them better.

Robbie came to my side. "You're right. Scotty Rich. Don't know the women. Do you?"

Scotty noticed Tonto after seeing our group and guided his horse and mules in our direction, stopping a few feet away. "Hey, Robbie, how you doing?" My friend asked.

"Good," the riverman answered. "Busy as hell."

"Yeah, I know 'em," I answered. "The tall one's Robin, Scotty's girlfriend." She bobbed her head at the introduction. I could only stare at Jules.

"Who's the last one?" Robbie asked.

My teeth clamped tight—my jaw refusing to open. Julia gave up waiting to be introduced and dismounted like one sore from riding. Rather than stand for a bit, she wobbled to us and gave me her best glare. The girl who almost always attacked with a gun caught me by surprise. A series of gasps from onlookers came when she launched a looping right into my guts followed by a slap across the cheek. I could tell by the way it popped and stung her blow would leave a mark. My eyes watered from the force.

"I'll tell you who I am since he won't. My name is Julia Pelletier. Dawson's my husband."

Chapter XVII

I pointedly ignored Julia and turned to Scotty and Robin waiting in their saddles. "Hungry?"

Robbie held back from the line of fire. "Don't have any steaks thawed, but we got baked potatoes...and beans if Pelletier left any."

"I got meat." I left Julia to steam and hurried to my saddlebags, removing a bloody shirt from one side. Unwrapping it, I held my final chunk of wapiti loin. "Robbie's probably got herbs and spices." I shot him a glance and got a nod. I noticed a couple elk hairs in the fading light and carefully plucked them away.

"I could eat." Scotty looked to Robin who gave a matching nod. Both dismounted and led their horses and pack mules near Tonto and Erlene. A grim Julia followed me and Robbie to his kitchen area. Mrs. Thurman hovered nearby.

Julia jerked at my sleeve. "Are you going to talk to me?"

I focused on slicing the meat into thick steaks as a way to avoid her seething anger. When I refused to engage, she took a seat in the nearby chair I vacated. "May I help?" Mrs. Thurman asked.

Apparently, Jules didn't mind making a spectacle of herself. "No, you may not help him. Stay away from my husband."

I smiled to set the older woman at ease. "Thanks, but I've got this." Glancing around the silent camp, our interaction seemed to have captivated the attention of the rafters.

"How in the hell did I miss you, Pelletier?" Scotty demanded after loosening the belly strap of his mount and leaving the string of animals in Robin's hands.

"You didn't. This is as far downstream as I've traveled." I tossed four steaks into a reasonably clean pan to start them frying.

"You left camp near three weeks ago. Where've you been?"

I shrugged and poked the cooking meat with a fork, adding Johnny's Seasoning Salt and a healthy dose of course-ground pepper. "Between here and Falconberry. Spent my time camping, reading, sleeping..." I shrugged a second time. "Got caught by a hell of a storm."

Robbie braved Julia's unyielding glare and came to watch. "Fresh elk meat?" he asked.

I'd already given it a smell test. "Yep."

I got a raised eyebrow from him. "Dare I question?"

I figured he thought I poached it. In a way I did. "Fought a wolf pack off a young bull. Took some haunch and what was left of the backstraps."

The young man who made the mistake of touching my rifle said, "You fought wolves?"

His breathless anticipation of my answer made me chuckle. "Wasn't much of a battle. Their bellies were full after eating the guts, and I carried a gun. Get away from the river, and you'll hear them howl just about every night."

Scotty went back to picket his string near Tonto and Erlene. I enjoyed watching him and Robin work together. He taught by example unless she didn't understand. Then his patience as he explained to her seemed endless. My friend was certainly in love. They finished in time to enjoy a freshly-plated dinner with Julia.

"Venison's good," Scotty said. Robin's smile showed she agreed, while my wife scowled between bites. "We left supplies at Indian Creek Ranger Station. Told 'em you'd stop by if you weren't dead."

"Thanks for the vote of confidence. You were supposed to fly 'em in. Why waste time doing it yourself?"

He poked his fork at Julia. "We weren't a mile out from Falconberry when we met her. Doggone woman hiked twenty-five miles in the dark hoping to catch us in camp." Jules didn't look up from her plate. "She squirted past us after I told her trailing you would be near impossible." He snorted. "Didn't have anything but a gun and flashlight with her, no gear at all. Would've died of exposure if Robin didn't go after her and explain."

Sounded about like my wife when she was mad. Shoot first and ask questions later. "Explain what?"

"We were flying supplies to you at Indian Creek," Robin said. "We figured to keep you from starving to death." She held up a chunk of medium rare venison on the tines of her fork. "Never dreamed you'd be eating this good. Julia asked if we would pack them instead...with her as extra cargo. We've been on the trail after a grocery run, which we left at Indian Creek and went searching for you." Robin's gaze flicked to Jules and back to me. "You were a sight for sore eyes just as we were getting worried."

I wasn't accepting excuses. Like my old flame Nancy with the wandering ways, I planned to have nothing to do with Jules again. Now here she was where I least expected or wanted her.

Julia surprised me by keeping to herself. I caught her dog-eyeing Mrs. Thurman a couple times and considered it a minor victory that J didn't draw her little Colt. I pitched in to help Robbie clean his kitchen rather than deal with an angry and unreasonable woman. Conversation and laughter picked up again when the rafters didn't have anything exciting to watch. A fire in the largest pit was doing a good job of keeping mosquitos away when I yawned. "Guess I'll hit the hay," I said to Robbie in a low tone. "See you in the morning, but I'd like to apologize first."

"Ain't nothing to be sorry about, son. You'll find married life can be...stressful at times. Me'n the old lady been having spats since we got hitched forty years ago this last June." He grinned. "Just a part of spending your life with a woman, I reckon."

I left to get my gear from where I picketed Tonto and Erlene to graze. Only taking the smaller tarp, my sleeping bag, pillow, and air mattress, I disappeared into the timber behind camp and headed upcanyon. It didn't take long before finding the perfect spot to sleep on a forest floor atop deep pine needles. With a small penlight held in my mouth, I strung a rope between two jack pines to drape the tarp over and pushed my gear inside. After damned near passing out filling my mattress with air and tossing my bag on it, I undressed to my skivvies and slid in. Raucous laughter in the distance floated to me, and I wondered if they made fun at my plight. Tired from the long day, sleep came quicker than I anticipated.

Something woke me from a deep slumber. A light shone on my shelter, and I felt someone crawl in next to me. I grasped the butt of my gun hidden under the pillow, but a knee came down hard, pinning and coming close to breaking my fingers. Jules didn't bother to whisper. "It's just me, dumbass." Her weight lifted from my trapped hand when I stopped struggling.

"Get the hell out of here." Making my anger clear, I turned my back and fluffed my pillow. A mosquito buzzed in my ear, forcing me deeper into the bag. "You're not wanted." I hoped my voice wasn't so muffled she couldn't understand.

"Not ready to hear me out yet, you big ol' baby?" I didn't answer and took another knee in the spine while she apparently undressed. The zipper of her bag alerted me to her getting inside. A sharp elbow barely cushioned by flannel caught me on the ear when she didn't get the response she hoped for. I knew then neither were accidents.

* * *

I slept like the infant Julia claimed me to be throughout the night. I got no idea how long she lay awake after my snores started. Kind of hoped it was for hours. Sliding carefully from the mouth of my bag without using the zipper, I squeezed out into the cool gray dawn. Something woke me, but I didn't know what it was. My wife lay snuggled deep inside her cocoon from where I could barely hear her quiet snores escaping. Dressing silently but quickly, I slid my bag and air mattress out. Carefully pulling the tarp back from the rope, I folded the covering and coiled the line.

What woke me became evident the moment I reached Tonto and Erlene. An extra pack mule and a second horse were tied nearby along with Julia's saddle, blanket, bridle, and panniers, yet I could see no sign of Scotty and Robin nor the rest of their animals. Bastards were long gone, probably laughing at how they pawned Julia off. My plan for escape stymied, I tossed my gear aside and hurried to see if Robbie was awake. He was kneeling and blowing on coals to start the campfire.

He sat back on his heels when the smoke grew thick. Startled when he noticed me standing so close, Robbie grabbed at his chest—I hoped in jest. "Damn near gave me a heart attack, Dawson." A tendril of flame licked up between the pine chips and twigs he dropped on the coals.

"How long since Scotty and Robin pulled out?" I said quietly. Not so much for the rafters, but for Julia still sleeping. Sound carried well in the cool morning air.

The old bastard was grinning after adding larger chunks and then glancing at his wristwatch. "Caught sight of their south end just as I got up about thirty minutes ago. Looks like they planned an early start. Coffee's done, and I'll start biscuits in the oven if you're interested."

I wanted to pack and ride in the worst way. Yet Robbie would soon be heading out with his customers, and to leave Julia behind in such wild country was unpardonable. I decided to pack her out, then return for the remainder of summer. Already well into July, I could spend another six to eight weeks alone. Me and thousands of tourists if I wished to stay near the river. Fresh trout sounded good after a week of elk cuts and jerky. "Yeah, if it's not too much bother."

Mosquitos honed in on us before the blaze grew enough to put off smoke. After delivering a filled cup, Robbie retreated to his kitchen to develop whatever gourmet delicacies he prepared for his customers. Left in command as the head fire tender, I coaxed the blaze large enough for airborne insect relief. Tiny feet doing their best to stomp angrily alerted me to an impending crisis. "You're plotting to leave me here, aren't you?" A quietly-raging Julia threw herself into a nearby chair. At least she possessed enough decorum to keep her voice down. I sipped at the hot brew while using a poking stick to keep the fire burning. Being ignored infuriated her further. "You bastard. I wanted to explain this morning. Changed my mind after finding you gone. You deserve the torture of not knowing anything but what your vivid imagination can produce."

Robbie's voice came over my shoulder. "Mornin', ma'am. Got coffee if you drink it."

Her attitude changed in an instant. "Thank you, sir. Yes, I do. Black."

We ignored each other as campers awoke and stumbled their way to the fire. Julia didn't miss Mrs. Thurman's nails running behind my flannel collar when she passed. If the older but gorgeous woman knew my wife, she would have run screaming into the cold river. Julia's gaze hardened and didn't leave the woman while she waited for her cup of java. The giant pot Robbie used for coffee quickly emptied.

He made sure I understood we were welcome to breakfast. Still, Jules and I waited until the paying customers were served with their choice of hotcakes, bacon, and eggs, or a cheese omelet. I chose the former, while Julia decided on the latter. Boating enthusiasm rose as rafters emptied their plates. A wild and scenic river awaited them with the unknown lying around every bend. After they loaded, and her boat floated out, Mrs. Thurman drew a growl from shore when she blew me a kiss. Leaving me alone to face the ire of my wife, the Englishwoman got only a lift of my hand in return.

Although we snubbed the other, Julia and I helped Robbie and a hired man load his gear in the largest raft. I offered my hand and a steady shoulder when he was ready. "Thanks, man. Appreciate the meals. Sorry about scaring the dude."

"No big deal, son. Don't give a shit long as he doesn't sue, and he won't. Too red-faced after we had a private talk on what a damn fool thing he done . . . and what a great tale he can take home 'bout the mountain man he befriended. Tell Melissa hello and promise her Jackie and me will stop by after boating season is over." He let me push him away from the bank when he got situated in his raft. My wave was returned by a paddle held high.

With the fire out, I was ready to leave. First, I shuttled Tonto then Erlene to the river to slake their thirst. Julia learned by watching Scotty and Robin and followed suit with her horse and mule. She struggled with throwing a saddle I guessed was half her bodyweight over the pad on her mount. Resisting to help was difficult. Eventually, she got it in place with the cinch strap tight and the flank strap buckled. I thought her horse stuck its belly out, but it was a bridge we'd cross when we came to it.

I loaded the extra mule with empty panniers Scotty left behind. Reckoned he meant for me to fill them at Indian Creek. I learned during Julia's quiet conversations with the jack his name was Aztec, making me question everything I knew about Scotty. Why not Jumpy, Stubborn, or even Oh, Hell No? Erlene seemed the most even-keeled mule I'd handled and doubted if my pal would consider selling.

I led with Erlene ahead of Aztec, while Julia chose to ride drag. Knowing another rider followed seemed to keep the young mule in line. Neither Julia nor I spoke to the other. When once or twice I found reason to look back, she fell farther behind.

Midday caught us at the start of a climb causing us to leave the river because the shoreline became too rough for a trail. I knew by experience we'd lose sight of the fast-flowing water as we gained elevation. Rather than subject our mounts and mules to discomfort, I halted to water and allow them time to graze. They were already picketed and a baited hook tossed out before Julia appeared. She rode stiff as if afraid to fall. My answer came when she stopped. The belly strap was no longer tight. As her mount got used to the miles, its once distended belly pulled back and allowed her saddle to slip. One false move by either, and she'd lose her seat. Not thinking, I did the first thing to enter my mind. I tossed the spinning pole aside and hurried to the horse. "Kick both feet loose from the stirrups and fall out of the saddle. Don't worry. I'll catch you." I no more than reached out before she landed in my arms. Her saddle turned, but not enough to spook the appaloosa. I set her aside to strip everything but the horse's bridle. I got it watered and picketed before realizing I'd helped when I vowed not to.

A fish swallowed my bait of raw bacon while I listened to Jules going through my packs. Its size became clear when I set the hook and it caused my reel to scream as the trout took line. I tightened the drag enough to slow its rush to safety and tire it. Taking my time to fight the brute to shore, I was surprised to see its size. Perhaps twenty inches and deep through the belly, I guessed it weighed two pounds or more.

A voice startled me while stringing the rainbow on a forked stick. "Can I try? I haven't fished since Mom and Dad took me to Trinity River once. Didn't catch much, but I remember it being so much fun." I recognized a certain wistfulness and longing in her tone.

Impossible to stop myself, I rebaited with another piece of bacon saved from breakfast and gave it to her. She shook her head. "I never learned to cast. Dad always threw it out before handing it off." A sob catching in her throat caused mine to tighten. Flipping the bail open, I aimed for a calm spot behind a boulder. I hit squarely, and I locked the bail to hand it over. "Thanks." She gave a tremulous smile before directing her attention to the line.

I put together a fire small enough to be covered with my hand. It burned hotly as long as I added twigs regularly. Filling a soup pan and coffee pot with water, I used my ring of rocks to prop both atop the blaze. Four times I left our lunch to cast and sometimes rebait Julia's hook after she reeled in. Once the water boiled, I added potato flakes and set it aside with a cover. The skillet could barely contain the halved trout when I moved it over the flames.

Expecting to camp alone, I carried one plastic plate, an aluminum cup, and a couple steel forks. She gave up hoping for a bite and returned with the pole, while I loaded the plate with her half of lunch. Eating from the pan was fine with me. I'd done nothing else since leaving Falconberry.

Julia picked at the smaller piece of fish. Hungry as hell, I dug into mine with gusto, barely slowing until the pink meat was gone. I took time to wash it down with coffee before finishing the potatoes. She finally set her plate aside, and my guts tensed when she spoke. "We were having an end-of-year staff party. You probably got there after names were drawn from a hat. Didn't matter whose...man or woman...you danced with whomever got yours. A couple minutes sooner, you'd have seen Mrs. Robinson cutting a rug with Miss Cole." I smiled inwardly at the vision. The former was past retirement age—the latter a young woman engaged to be married. "I didn't plan to stay...just have a quick soda and tell everyone goodbye for the summer." She sniffed a couple times while I focused my attention on my cup. "I wanted to leave, but Thomas drew my name. They kept pushing me to dance, and that's when you saw me trying to keep distance between us. You turned on the barstool right after he got me onto the open floor." Her voice thickened as her nose plugged. "Now I know what people mean when they talk about seeing murder on someone's face. Nothing I could do would stop you. I almost breathed a sigh of relief when you ran for the door, because I knew then your gun was in the truck, not on your belt." Her story was painful to hear. How could I have been so foolish as to not believe in her? Was it a combination of her leaving me to pursue The Company alone and my personal animas toward Howell? "Another sixty seconds, and you would've met me walking out the door. Timing is everything."

I stood and brushed dirt and twigs from my butt before wandering to the river's edge. To have jumped to the wrong conclusion faster wasn't possible. It wounded me to know I hurt the love of my life so easily. Thin wiry arms wrapped around my waist from behind—her cheek rested against my back. "Saying I'm sorry seems pretty weak about now," I said quietly.

She sniffed before answering. "I don't want an apology. All I need is to know we're good. I haven't ruined what we've built, have I?"

I turned in her arms to face her. "You? You ruin it? I've broken some sort of record when it comes to mistakes. I couldn't be sorrier, Jules. My only hope is that you'll forgive me but understand if you can't."

She rubbed her snotty nose against my dirty flannel. "Of course, you're forgiven. It goes without saying." Julia took a deep breath and let it out slowly. She stared into my eyes and never blinked. "I can only hope you'll excuse the terrible way I treated you." She took another deep breath, with it catching as she let it out. "You were right. I planned to leave you behind in Laredo because I realized something after you saved my life. Relying on others threw me off my game. To continue signing those running The Company meant I had to call the shots. All of them. No one to decide my next target...to push me in a certain direction. Also, I didn't want to worry about your wellbeing or any of the rest. If one of us was going to get killed, it would not be you, my love."

We returned to the smoldering fire, where I leaned back against my saddle. Julia did the same against an old stump. "I understand. Really, I do. Problem is...was...it didn't take away the danger. If Al hadn't sent Ox and Jose to stay with Mom in Belize, she'd be dead. Our place got blown up and burned down. Plus, the Company damn near killed Jake and me." I went on to explain the pointer and my flight for safety through the wilderness. Nor did I forget to reinforce how closely my mother came to death. "You can't tell her, Jules. Promise you'll never let her know. She enjoyed herself a great deal in Belize, and I'm sure she'd never go back if she ever found out."

"Of course, I won't. Melissa is as much my mom as yours. Protecting her is as important to me as your safety." Julia sighed. "I'm shocked they sent ten men after you. I knew the possibility existed but didn't believe The Company would do it. My hope was their marshalling and focusing the bulk of their resources against me."

"Not ten men. Two women were included. I killed one not far from the cabin." Like J, killing a female didn't bother me if she planned to murder me first. "The last was left to freeze in the Bitterroots with her buddies."

Ferrying water from the river in my coffee pot took care of our fire. Stirring embers while pouring in the last drops, not even a warm spot remained when we mounted. Steep trail forced us to dismount and lead our animals in places. The river was visible far below at the path's apex when we stopped to rest. Jules passed the mules to halt her horse close to mine. "I wanted to tell you I understand why you've been so angry...avoiding me after I returned home. You were left alone without a word, and she...I-I didn't bother to contact you. My inaction is inexcusable." Jules sidled her mount closer to lay a hand on my

258

forearm. "I'll spend the rest of my life making it up to you if you'll let me."

I reckon my sigh was telling. She hurt me. Bad. "You can't imagine how hard it is to know your spouse is fighting a war in which you're not allowed to help. I thought about you every minute of every day. For a time, I could barely sleep. Then came nightmares, always losing you in the worst possible ways. Al and Robin were my only link to you. A simple phone call or text was all I needed." Memories of my fear for her caused my emotions to surface as I turned away.

Happy people floating the river no longer interested me. Instead of continuing on the trail, I turned Tonto's head and pointed his nose up an open ridge. As all mountains in Idaho, it was steep or steeper yet. Knowing Erlene and her lack of fear, I hoped Aztec and Jules would follow. "Hold tight to your saddle horn," I called. We stopped after reaching a high bench partially timbered with an hour of light remaining. The roar of the river far below was sometimes carried away on a rising wind. After stripping away the panniers, saddles, bridles, and lead ropes, I left the animals picketed in belly-deep browse.

Jules watched and helped where she could, while I devised my facsimile of a Baker tent. With a back, sides, and roof overhead, the front was merely a lip extending outward from above offering a larger shelter. Our gear got stored against the rear where it couldn't get wet. "Not a lot of food left," she mentioned after searching through the last pannier holding supplies. "If you can make a fire, I guess we'll eat pancakes and reconstituted eggs. No wonder you inhaled the trout today." When she lost her appetite and picked at her freshly caught lunch, I jumped at the opportunity to finish it when she offered.

Always cautious with a summer fire, I dug into the soil with the short-axe, forming a shallow hole I ringed with stones. A keyhole extended from each end, and she questioned their use. "To cook on," I explained. "Build a fire in the center, then rake coals outward to fill the extensions. Rocks give us a place to brace our pans over the heat."

I kept our fire small, letting the center burn hotly and produce coals. Julia waited with hotcake batter until time to cook. She found my method worked slicker than she imagined. Cleaning our plate and pans was simple—we used handfuls of pine needles to scour them. A wolf howled farther up the ridge after we retreated beneath the awning. Jules shivered and pressed against my side. "I'll never get used to that sound." Another answered the first, causing the hair on my neck to rise. For a moment I wondered if we should let our fire burn out or stoke it as a barrier. Didn't matter, we carried flashlights and were armed.

"I love to hear them," I said. "Problem is they've nearly destroyed the deer and elk herds in the Middle Fork. There's not a tenth of what they used to be. Moose are almost nonexistent now just to appease pencil-pushers living somewhere in a concrete jungle. Most of 'em don't know their asses from a hole in the ground." It wasn't easy to keep the bitterness from my voice. "Used to be near twenty thousand elk in the Bitterroot herds. Now, they're less than fifteen hundred." As both a sportsman and conservationist, I found the reality repugnant of wolves pulling a deer or elk down and eating its guts while the poor thing struggled to escape. "Do the world well if the self-appointed do-gooders got an opportunity to watch, listen, and smell actual brutality up close and personal." A sudden thought made me remember. "Where's Jake?"

"With Melissa. Once I discovered where you were and told her Scotty promised to pack me in, she couldn't volunteer fast enough to keep our boy." She bit a lip with a pensive look. "Better watch it when we get back. She's terribly angry with you."

Without syrup or jelly, we ate our pancakes rolled with an egg center. We let our fire burn out, rather than alert the forest service spotters with our smoke. A small hot blaze briefly burning would make detection difficult. I checked our livestock while Jules laid out our sleeping pads and bags. The horses and mules seemed content, but I moved them closer to our shelter. A wolfpack would have an easy time with tethered stock.

Our bags were zipped together when I returned, forming one large single. Barely able to see in the little light remaining, she waited for me inside our bed. I kicked my boots away before shucking out of my

260

clothes to slide in beside my wife. She gave me time to snuggle safely away from mosquitos before rolling against me and throwing an arm across my chest. With her head on my shoulder and a leg resting on my thigh, she brought us together again at last. "Do we finally get our chance to enjoy life?" I whispered against her crown. "You and me and Jake riding into the sunset?"

Her spontaneous giggle made me smile in the dark. "You paint a pretty picture, mister. I don't know about you, but I'd rather come home from a day in the trenches herding primary schoolers and get cozy on the couch with my hubby." She squeezed me for effect. "I haven't gotten a chance to tell you. Your Aunt Bess offered me third grade next year."

Julia's dream come true couldn't make me any happier than I was at the moment. "What'd you tell her?"

"Are you kidding?" Her voice lifted. "I accepted. Already signed my contract for next year." Pride oozed from her pores. "I start as a fifth-year teacher after they accepted my first four in Astoria. Pay scale is relatively low, but did I mention I'll be a teacher with my own room again?"

I could only chuckle at her enthusiasm. "You may have said something about it. Congratulations, honey. You've worked hard for this position. Who left?"

"Mrs. Wark. Her husband accepted a job in Missoula. They've been talking about starting a family since I've been at school. Sounds like she'll take time off, have their children, then find another teaching position after the little ones are old enough."

"Reckon I'm happy for both of you. Lucky you started substituting when you did."

"Uh huh. Our finances might be tight, but I think we can live on my salary if we're careful."

"Uh..." I struggled with how to explain. "We shouldn't have to. Neither of us use credit...we've always paid cash. Far as I'm concerned, other than this's your dream job, you don't have to work if you decide not to."

"I'd rather not spend money I made while working for The Company, except for emergencies or something really important. I know you have an income as a partner in Al's business, but I've never really been sure of your quarterly or yearly earnings." Jules left what I'd never bothered to share with her unsaid.

"Far as I'm concerned, it's a lot. Mom gets whatever she wants or needs...which is little, and the rest goes into a savings account. Probably ought to have someone take a look at it, maybe invest a little." I laughed quietly. She sometimes mentioned having a diversified portfolio but might as well have been speaking Celtic. Money meant little to me except to keep the farm ours and Mom happy.

"Could you be more specific?" she asked. "What's a lot? Fifty thousand?"

"I think our portion came to about eight-fifty."

"Eight-fifty...do you mean eight hundred fifty thousand?" She sounded incredulous.

"Yep."

"You can't let that kind of money sit in a bank and not have it work for you." I wondered if she realized how odd her declaration sounded with almost as much in cash at our house. "If you diversified with a higher rate of return, you could have increased your nest egg—"

"Jules, eight-fifty was last year's income before Uncle Sam got his grubby meat hooks into it. Mom does our taxes, so I'm not sure how much was left afterward."

"So much in just one year?" she whispered. "You've earned money like this for over a decade?"

"Our first few years were pretty lean. After giving Al my earnings from service, Mom and me struggled to get by. Sold four hundred head of beef, last of our horses, some equipment, and I took a job drivin' gravel truck. Wasn't until the third year before Al was better known. Only got about seventy-five grand the fourth, but it paid our bills. Still don't understand what it is he does, except mostly computer work and not all of it government approved. Keep in mind Al's portion is seventy percent, and he resides in a multi-million-dollar estate outside of Missoula along with the villa in Belize."

"You're telling me we're probably not going to be destitute anytime soon then."

"Nope."

Her voice was firm. "I'm still going to teach."

"Didn't expect anything different. You've worked hard for your position. Enjoy it."

"I'd better talk to Melissa about your money." Her fingers stopped running through my chest hair as her hand slid lower.

"Our money." She reached her objective. "But let's not talk about our mom now."

Chapter XVIII

Heavy fog kept us under cover the following three days. Our horses and mules didn't seem to mind so long as I staked them in fresh browse each morning. Evenings, I moved the four animals closer to our shelter for protection. Jules and I lazed about, venturing out only to relieve ourselves, get water from a spring I dug, or to replenish our wood supply. Time meant nothing outside of our dwindling food stores. It was either night or day, and we took the time to reconnect both physically and emotionally. Tears were shed on both sides while we worked through our differences.

We woke to blue skies the fourth morning. A hasty breakfast consisted of fried bread made of flour, reconstituted milk, baking soda, and salt. Normally I would have turned my nose up at such a meal, but anything tasted good with my belly button and spine about to touch.

We reached the river a few miles above Pistol Creek. From there we traveled downstream a short distance to Indian Creek where Scotty left supplies. Rather than chance fishing and striking out, we hurried to the forest service cabins. The fellow I spoke with didn't seem to want to part with our food until I showed him photo ID. Even then, he hemmed and hawed before Julia knocked on the door to see about the hang-up. Our dilemma was resolved when he recognized her.

She went right to a bag of candy bars as we loaded the mules. Snickers were a favorite of mine, too. My mouth watered over real potatoes, butter, home-canned sausage, even slabs of bacon ready to be sliced—our panniers fairly bulged when we left. "You should eat this orange, Dawson." Jules caught me to hand one over. She munched an apple to its core and carefully eyed what was left before reaching forward and feeding it to her mount. "An apple, too. We need more roughage in our systems."

Rather than camp at the mouth of Indian Creek where planes landed regularly, we chose to continue downstream to Marble. Wasn't much of a stream or camping spot, but we made the area work. My reconciled mate started potatoes cooking in tinfoil, while I watered the stock and tethered them in grass. She fixed a sausage gravy to spread over our spuds.

I took the time to toss my hook into the river. Periwinkles abounded, making perfect bait for big trout. When nothing took interest, I strolled back to the fire. Two large bakers waited for me—a third one for Jules—while she stirred gravy waiting for the milk to boil down. Gnawing at a corner of her lip when she glanced up, I was sure she needed to discuss something important. "I went to your cabin during my search for you." I knew immediately what she was concerned about. "There were papers on the counter..." She hesitated, appearing worried about overstepping personal boundaries. "I probably shouldn't have read them, but I hoped they held a clue to where you might have gone. Do I understand you and I have been granted some sort of clemency? Exonerated of any crimes up to the date of the signatures?"

I kicked myself mentally. Such vital subject should have been brought up much earlier. "Yep."

Her brow knitted while she spooned gravy over her potato. Handing over the pan, she sat cross-legged while I continued preparing my meal. "Who's behind it? And why? What does someone know about me and you that we aren't privy to?"

I could only explain what Will said when he left the papers at my place. "Sheriff Daugherty said state and local law enforcement don't seem to know anything. Can you think of anyone who might have someone on the inside? A person or persons connected to the feds?"

Jules didn't pause to consider. "No. Only Al and Robin. I signed everyone else."

A shrug and conjecture were all I could offer. "Somebody knows me, and they're aware of you. I can't even venture a guess as to why they would go to the trouble of dismissing charges."

I could sense her terror. "The government knows about me, Dawson. I'm sure of it. Enough to be aware I could be charged with signing clients but forgiven instead." Nothing struck more fear into Jules than the government. Why she chose to sugarcoat killing with "signing" was beyond me. She was a killer for hire but refused to call it by its gritty name.

"Ain't sayin' this is something we should ignore." I sampled a bite and burned my tongue on steaming potato flesh. Cold water helped alleviate the scorch. "At the same time, I'm not about to look a gift horse in the mouth. I suggest we take it at face value and return to the life both of us want."

We spent two days at Marble Creek before moving downstream to Thomas. Near a decayed trapper's cabin from a previous century was a natural hot spring. Folks utilizing it over the years arranged stones held together with clay to make a nice tub-sized pool. I'd been dirty far too long and needed a deep cleansing. We set up camp not far away. Although tourists floated the river below us, I didn't hesitate to strip and step in.

Jules wasn't willing to undress and join me in a wilderness bath. Appalled, she replied to my entreaties, "No! Not until you're done and ready to sit shotgun. I'm not getting naked where people can see me." The last was delivered with a quiet shriek. My beautiful wife never understood the depths of her allure and attractiveness.

My bath felt good. In our supplies were soap and shampoo designed for backcountry washing—supposedly environmentally friendly. I was never quite sure of the hype. After soaking for a half-hour, I used a washcloth and scoured my body. Julia enjoyed washing my long hair and doing it outdoors didn't seem to deter her. Any natural oils, sweat, and dirt were stripped away when she finished. The hot bath got completed in the old ways of my father's people when I rushed to the river's edge and plunged into cold water.

Jules followed my bath saying she intended to hurry until she felt the soothing qualities of the spring. Then she lazed about after making sure I would stop anyone coming near. Her fingers were wrinkled when she finally stepped out to dash inside our shelter for privacy. After we both were dressed, she took time to brush and braid my hair again. I'd often thought about cutting it—something I'd not done except for trims since returning home from the service long ago, only to have Jules beg me not to. She did a good job of binding it, almost tight enough to give me a headache.

We kept a smoky fire after a dinner of trout, rice, and fried apples. "Know what we should consider in the morning?" I asked after we were eating. Jules nursed the second of six precious containers of beer, while I sipped whiskey from a shot glass.

She waved her bottle—cooled by the river. "Don't care. I'm living the dream." Spending time in the backcountry was an aspiration she wished for far too long.

"Let's hike." I poked over my shoulder with a thumb. "There's a lookout up there...or used to be. Wouldn't take but a few hours to make the trek."

"Lead on, fearless master. I'm with you. Let's get an early start to beat the bugs, okay?"

"It's a date."

Tonto certainly, but I thought both our horses were disappointed not to be included. My mount nickered when we left and watched with his head high and ears forward. Jules brought a small daypack with water and a lunch. I carried my rifle in addition to the Anaconda on my hip simply because I didn't want to leave it behind unattended. A group of rafters camped the evening before—easy to see by their bonfire at the far end of the airstrip. Although we got a later start than I hoped, no movement could be seen around their camp. I located the trail and led the way.

We passed a herd of elk on the slope below as the elevation increased. Perhaps fifty or more, they seemed alerted to us before we were visible on the trail. With a gentle breeze blowing uphill, I surmised the outlying sentinel cows somehow got an earlier whiff of us. A few nice bulls were in the group along with healthy calves. The howl of a distant wolf drifted to us. "I really love that sound, except I worry about Jake," Julia said behind me.

I stopped to catch my breath and to help hers, too. "We should both be concerned about him. Wolves prefer elk calves and deer fawns, but dogs are also fair game."

"People?" She asked casually caressing the butt of her revolver.

"Probably not, although I've talked with a few locals who've had run-ins with 'em. At least one faced charges eventually dropped for killin' a brace while fearing for his life. The wolves didn't backdown even after he fired a warning shot. He potentially faced more time for wolficide in self-defense than murderers are sentenced to for doing away with their fellow man."

"Our judicial system in action."

"They're influenced by the loudest with the most money. Not so much by those who actually know what they're talking about."

"The squeakiest wheel gets the most grease."

We reached the lookout earlier than I anticipated. The moment we arrived there, the reason for an overall lack of wildlife to view—and the spookiness of the elk herd—became clear. Three women beat us to our objective, though not by much. They still breathed hard when we arrived. "Oh!" One of the trio said when she noticed us. "Linda, Bethany, we have company."

The group were in their twenties, certainly not yet thirty. Young and fit, they immediately voiced opinions of the firearms I carried. "Why the guns?" Linda asked.

I shrugged and smiled. "Why not?"

"Do you have a permit?" I guessed the second questioner to be Bethany. Her tone was rude—bordering on belligerent.

"Are you with law enforcement?"

"Give them to us," the first said. "We'll turn them into the authorities when we reach Salmon."

Incredulous at their demand, I could only stare. Jules harbored no patience for stupid adults. She stepped forward and turned enough so they could see the .38 holstered on her hip. "I don't think so. Frankly,

I'm astounded at your moronic demands. Besides, Sheriff Daugherty would rather laugh in your faces, then at us for putting up with your obvious insanity." My Jules, never at a loss for words.

The loud whap of rotators stopped our verbal sparring. Two military helicopters passed overhead. We watched them circle the valley twice before continuing downstream. Julia pressed against me while we watched them disappear. To her they represented the government.

"Don't think you can get away with this." Bethany said to us through gritted teeth.

"Get away with what?" Their arrogant outrage left me bewildered.

"Carrying a gun in the open."

The three left me exasperated. "Do you have any idea where you are? You're not only in Idaho where its people are still free, but you're in the backcountry with predators that don't give a damn how important you consider yourself. Not all of them are four-legged."

They pushed past us, eager to return to their camp. "You just wait," one yelled over her shoulder. "We're informing our guide about this and giving him your description."

"Who is your guide?"

"We're with Chuck Dotson, of Dotson's Family Rafting." My immediate burst of laughter stopped them cold. They turned in unison. "What?" came the snide question.

"You won't find Chuck ignorant of state and federal laws. Tell him Dawson Pelletier and his wife said hi. If you could, would you also let him know Mom would love to have him and his wife Cheryl over to dinner again sometime soon?"

Jules turned to me after they flounced their indignant selves out of sight. "Who's Chuck Dotson?"

"You remember the fellow I was with when you, Scotty, and Robin located me?" She nodded. "That's Robert Dotson, Chuck's brother. They co-own the rafting business. Both men and their families were friends with my folks. I pretty much grew up around them."

She could only snicker. "World's a small place, isn't it?"

* * *

269

We stayed at Thomas Creek three days before continuing downstream past more hot springs on our way to Lower Loon Creek. Early afternoon when we arrived, I suggested we spend the night before riding out to the trailhead where we could contact Scotty for a ride. Our camp went up quickly after days of working together. A deep fishing hole beckoned, and we hurried to toss in our bait. Julia looked skyward at what I surmised to be the same aircraft as before. "What's with the helicopters? I don't mind small airplanes flying the river. These machines with their extra noise are awful."

"Dunno. Mountain Home air force base is southwest of us. Might be flying maneuvers." Not long after their disappearance, a third and much faster corporate version sped over from the south. Our animals grew nervous when it banked and circled. "I watched an SR71 Blackbird zip past once while I hunted in here. Must've taken off from the same base. Broke the sound barrier before disappearing."

Our final evening in some of the wildest country the lower forty-eight has to offer was spent absorbing it. A nice breeze caused flying insects to work hard for their meals. Jules and I made ourselves comfortable against driftwood near our fire. A water ouzel landed nearby only to discount us as a threat when a meal presented itself. Diving into the water, the little bird came up ready to fly to the next partially submerged rock and any food it might harbor. We saved a bag of cashews, beer for Jules, and whiskey for me to celebrate our final backcountry hours. Her lids drooped with relaxation and contentment. "I get Robin now." Julia popped a handful of nuts in her mouth and chewed slowly.

She couldn't have caught me more unaware. "Whazzat?" I mumbled.

She smiled. "Robin. I understand why she gave up everything to move to Idaho. If this were my exposure to our great state, I'd never want to leave either."

I loved how she considered herself an Idahoan. Seemed her life started when she reached Salmon. Rarely did she mention California or Oregon unless prompted. "Don't forget there was more than one reason for her to quit and find Scotty. Yes, she fell in love with the area and planned to come back, but she was fired for hacking Manny's phone to warn you. You were someone she looked up to. I think she knew or guessed what might happen. We owe her a lot."

I missed her tears until Julia sniffed. She knuckled them away and finished drying cheeks with a sleeve while I waited. "She almost died on Falconberry." My wife never mentioned our attack. "We...I-I was convinced she was a part of The Company when I observed her speaking privately to the hunters in camp, and the four talked as if they knew her the night I listened outside their tent." I sat forward when the inadvertent *we* slipped from her lips. I was convinced more each day she understood another identity resided within her, a side of herself she sometimes fought with over control.

"You were right. They did know each other."

"Not like I thought. The information she provided saved her life." Julia's chin quivered when she looked at me. "I would have...I planned to kill her when we got back, and because we found him alive, it would have been in front of Scotty. Oh, Dawson, what have I become?"

Her cries broke my heart, but I kept my tone low and even. "A third-grade teacher with her own classroom. One who hopes to work another thirty-five years and retire with a state pension. A strong woman alone in the world who chiseled out a place for herself. How many could do what you have, Jules?"

She stared into the fire. "I'm not sure I made the right choices."

"Do any of us know? Think of life this way. A deck of cards is issued to every creature born. Every so often, we're dealt a cosmic hand. Sometimes it's four aces or a straight flush, other times a bust. All we can do is play the hand or bluff our way out." My arm squeezed her shoulders. "I think we can safely say you never use subterfuge."

She couldn't let it go. "He would have never forgiven me."

"He doesn't have to. You didn't follow through once you learned the truth. You're a good person, honey. Don't lose sight of who you are and what you mean to the rest of us. You're not alone in this world."

* * *

Jules was astounded and tickled when she caught me charging my phone. The same small photovoltaic charger for my tablet allowed me to do the same for my cell with an adapter. "You, Mister Anti-anything-digital, not only buys a device to download books, but now you can charge your telephone, too?" My solar panel got tied to my saddlebags and worked its magic with each passing minute.

I turned in the saddle, lifted my chin and sniffed, giving her my best look of indignation. "You can call me Mister High Tech. Lemme know when you have phone or computer on the fritz, and I'll take care of 'em."

I should have expected her snort of derision. "After watching you shoot your last phone, no thanks."

Damned thing possessed a mind of its own. Half the time it refused to alert me to texts—sometimes messages supposedly left by others were nonexistent. I finally got tired of it and tested the accuracy of my Anaconda at fifty yards. With little to salvage after five rounds, I proudly scraped the remains into a box to show Julia. Less than impressed, she explained a new one would set me back over five hundred dollars, maybe a thousand. After I sulked and refused to pay such an exorbitant price, she surprised me with a model costing even more and threatened me if I returned the technological marvel. I couldn't believe how much better it functioned than my old one. Tough for me to figure out its full potential, though. "Wait until we get to the trailhead, and my phone is the only one to get service."

My assertion was proven correct. Neither of our cells could reach out to make a call, but my text got through to Scotty. Although late in the afternoon, he was there to load the horses and mules before dark. Jules couldn't wait to shower properly in the trailer and relax on the couch.

He got out of his pickup slowly, watching us carefully. "You're talking," he said after taking the lead ropes of Aztec and Erlene. "Neither of you seem to be wounded. Am I to guess you've worked things out?"

Jules stepped down from her saddle. No more wincing or walking funny—she was finally in riding shape. "Threatened to shoot a leg out from under him, Scotty. Once he got the full story and ate crow, we were good."

I gave him a shrug of agreement. "She ain't far from the truth."

After our gear was packed and the loading ramp closed, we piled into the front seat of his truck. "Ready for civilization again?" Scotty asked. After so long in the wilderness with friends and then alone, the time spent with Jules couldn't have been better. No, I wasn't prepared to meet the world.

We didn't have to wait long for Julia's answer nor her excitement. "Yeah, but we've got to spend all of next summer in the backcountry! My clothes will be packed on the last day of school, and I don't want to come out until a week before teachers return to their classrooms. After finding my honey and making up, this was the best two weeks of my life."

For me, I wanted to make peace with Mom, see Jake, and sleep in my own bed. Yet my wife was right. An entire summer spent together in the wilderness would be incredible. "Dawson?" Scotty said.

"Think I'll buy a nice little ten-by-twelve wall tent, something easy for horses to pack. Jules won't want to come out until the snow flies."

"You're right," she said. "But I'm responsible for my own classroom now. We'll have to be content to have Scotty pack us in early, then return before September."

We told him stories until we reached his place. Didn't take long to unload the horses and mules before transferring our gear into Julia's wagoneer with Robin's help. Scotty's animals wouldn't have long to rest before hunting season. Nor did Julia have many days before teachers met, and the schoolyear began.

Our ride home from Scotty's was silent and filled with quiet introspection on my part. Spending so much time together free of most other influences left us talked out. Too late to stop for Jake at Mom's, we went straight to our place with few furnishing and stores. Barely two weeks remained of our summer before Julia reported back to class at the end of September's first week. A lot of work remained if we hoped to be moved from the travel trailer.

I'd not been in it since Laredo. Although Jules lived in it on the road and then at home for months, I wasn't surprised to find it clean and without clutter. Julia left it plugged in with the air conditioner running to keep the interior from overheating, but we opened the door and windows for fresh air. Taking turns in the tiny shower with ladies first, I found her sleeping soundly when I finished. The soft but firm mattress made me groan quietly in relief after too many nights on the ground. My head touched the pillow not an instant too soon.

Hotcakes with Mom's thick blackberry syrup was ready soon after I woke. A glance at the clock caught my attention. At almost nine, and my wife still wore her nightie. She was a vision through the short hall, standing over a hot pan on the stove, a spoon in one hand and a bowl in her other. I smelled breakfast at the first drizzle of batter. "You might as well get up," Julia said without glancing my way. "I know you're awake. Besides, you've got some serious ass kissing ahead of you."

I sighed and rolled to my side. Julia gave voice to a concern of mine. Making amends with my mother after I'd left her alone by running off into the hills. Oh, I'd left to go woods bumming before, just never without so much as a how do you do. "Pretty bad, huh?"

Her chuckle sounded grimmer than tickled. "I suppose after almost forty years you've seen her madder." She pointed a thumb at herself. "Not this kid. She almost made me cry while I was still livid with you."

"Huh." Took a lot to piss Mom off, but once there, all bets were open. "Might as well get it over with after we eat."

We took Julia's Jeep, knowing Jake preferred it over the new truck. Shouldn't've mattered. He still got the backseat and two windows to himself. Good thing Jules drove—if it'd been me, the trip would have taken much longer than the normal ten minutes.

Mom must've heard us drive in, because the door opened to an explosion of Jake rushing out. Mom stopped with a hand shielding her eyes. As usual, she wore a dress reaching past her knees, with an apron overtop I'd bought two decades before. Jake leaped into Julia's lap the moment she swung her door wide enough. "Let me out, boy," she managed to say through laughter.

Rather than provide a wifely unified front, Jules left me to it and held back. I took the stairs slowly, feeling as if the executioner awaited. Mom's lips were pressed into a straight line when I stopped at the top, staring at me and then Julia as she and Jake caught up. Mom and Jules locked eyes for a moment until I noted a nod from my wife. Brimming tears spilled over when Mom held her arms open. No punishment could be worse than holding my mother when she cried because of me. The last time was when I joined the army against her wishes and got ready to leave for basic training. "You're together? You've worked things out?" She whispered her question in my ear. I felt another arm and Julia pressed against us.

"You did a shitty job of raising a dumb kid, Mom," I said. "Jules got me filled in and thinking straight."

Mom didn't let me go, nor did Julia. "You're not dumb." She sniffled. "Bull-headed and prone to drawing the wrong conclusion, but you have your moments, Dawson."

Only Jake whining for his mistress brought my parent to her senses. Tears worried the poor boy. We traipsed inside only to have him land in Julia's lap the moment she sat. "It wasn't easy, Melissa." Jules talked around the dog mauling her in his relief. "I caught Scotty and Robin on Falconberry and rode out with them."

"Rode out?" Mom butted in before she could understand.

"Dawson borrowed a horse and mule to ride through the mountains in hopes of reaching the Middle Fork. Scotty was to have supplies flown in and waiting at Indian Creek if and when your son arrived." Uh oh, even my wife's tone took a southern bend, putting too much emphasis on *if.*

"No big deal," I said. "Mom, you know I've spent time in wild country alone on horseback." I felt at least a little vindicated when she nodded.

Jules's look told me to shut the hell up. "When I learned what a long trek Dawson faced, I talked them into packing me and the food into Indian Creek. Figured he'd either be waiting or would arrive soon after. No such luck. After waiting a couple days, we rode upstream to eventually find him camping with some rafters." I couldn't help but grin to myself when thinking about Mrs. Thurman. "Robin and Scotty left me behind to explain and work through things."

Mom fiddled with a sock with a big hole in the heel. "You've talked it out? Do I get grandkids anytime soon?"

I knew she wanted me to have kids. I planned to—Jules and I talked about it many times—except I wasn't yet ready to share my wife with even our children. We needed time together before I could imagine a little Julia or Dawson getting between us. Besides, Jules's new job would require a lot of effort during the first few years. "We're fine. When it comes to kids...not yet. Maybe in a year or two."

"What of your other problem," she said. "Will you have to whisk me off to South America again anytime soon?"

"Central America, Mother." It was too soon to roll my eyes, lest she throw a darning needle. "No, it's taken care of. You'll only see Belize again if you want to. Life should be fairly normal from here on forward."

Jules and I left knowing the world lifted from Mom's shoulders. I swear she looked a decade older than before The Company declared war on us. Jake was happy to ride home, his head hanging from the window one minute, the next shoving a cold nose inside Jules' collar. Afraid she may have disappeared again, I guess.

Without furniture or appliances, we were forced to tow my twenty-four-foot flatbed to Twin Falls the following day, where we spent more money than I imagined household items costing. Because I plumbed the new place for propane, we found what Jules thought was the perfect kitchen range and refrigerator, too. Our hot water on demand was already installed and connected to gas. Furniture, bedframes, mattresses, even a freezer, we were able to fit everything by putting some in the pickup bed. She already purchased area rugs soon after I started rebuilding.

Getting home late with Jake tired from riding and sitting all day, we left the trailer backed near the front porch. "It's going to look incredible when we move in, honey." Jules said while she crawled into bed. Jake waited with her while I brushed my teeth. He groaned when she shoved him over to make more room.

I joined her, my feet hanging from the end after stretching full length. The travel trailer served us well, but I was ready to see the last of it. Perhaps sell it on consignment if not outright. Before turning the light off, I saw where J once stood and watched coldly as Jose and I pored over maps, while Ox sat where we were lying. I reached above us to hit the switch and throw the interior into darkness. "I can't wait until everything's inside." Made my back ache just to think of what was in store. "After what we've been through, I reckon tomorrow will be the first day of the rest of our lives."

Chapter XIX

Moving our possessions inside proved as exhausting as I feared. We got our furniture into place, the beds assembled, and even the dining room table and chairs ready for use. Although I looked through the garage, I couldn't find tape to attach the refrigerator and stove to our gas line. Thoroughly worn, we retired to cook and eat in the trailer. Where Jules and I hoped to spend the night in our house, a bed already made beckoned after eating and relaxing. Another day of hard work lay in store before we'd be ready.

We finished breakfast and moved the new washer and dryer into place before eight. I plugged them in and stood back. "Gonna run into Salmon for propane tape. You stayin' or ridin' along?"

"I'm staying," Jules said, peering into the washer. "No, changed my mind. I'll go if you can wait for me to change clothes."

The hardware store stocked what I searched for. Jules roamed the aisles far too long and found a pair of lamps she thought would look good in the loft sitting room. Then a stop at the antique store relieved us of more cash for a big-ass oak roll-top desk. I'd noticed it getting covered with other items for sale over the years. Thought was it sat around too long due to its two-thousand-dollar price tag. Once I realized Jules was serious about it, I haggled urgently. Mrs. Martinez agreed to fifteen hundred after I tried to cut the damage in half. Now I needed to somehow get it upstairs. Five feet wide and taking three men to load it, I wasn't sure how that would happen at home.

Julia could barely contain herself until we were leaving town. "Thank you, thank you, thank you," she squealed and scooted next to me before attaching the center restraint. "I've always wanted a desk like this. We can pay bills, I can correct homework...oh, we can use it for anything we want. Dawson, you don't know how much this means to me."

"Happy wife, happy life," I said, quoting centuries of wisdom.

She giggled. "Don't you forget it, mister."

Racket drew my eyes skyward to a corporate helicopter. Salmon rarely saw rotor-driven aircraft with the exception of Al's. The low-flying bird traveled the same direction as us and was soon followed by two Bell ARH-70 Arapahos. Both disappeared in the direction of the Bitterroots and Missoula. "What the hell's goin' on?" I wondered aloud. "We normally don't see the like around here." Jules seemed far too content with her purchases and where to put them than to pay attention to my mumblings.

I was turning slowly into our driveway to avoid shifting the desk in back, when an even louder roar shook the truck. The gauges read normal as I searched for the cause. I kicked the transmission out of gear and revved the engine as the sound grew worse. Catching sight of an enormous shadow from something huge overhead, I slammed into drive and gave it the gun to race to our house. Jules squeaked and grimly braced a palm against the dash.

We never stood a chance. A 'copter swooped forward and spun to face us while hovering ten feet from the ground. Pilot and copilot were visible through the canopy. We could see the 30mm cannon aimed at us, and four ready rockets mounted on each of its stub-wing pylons. I guessed the pilot read my mind when I got a warning headshake. The barrel went side-to-side with the movement, and I knew the gun was slaved to the helmet. Eyes behind the darkened face shield only needed to look at something to kill it. Something told me the team wasn't flying a training mission. Hurricane force winds from the rotors blasted debris into the air.

"Can you go around?" Jules shouted above the din.

I put the transmission in park and shut off the engine. "We're looking at a fully armed AH-E-64 Apache," I hollered back. "Nothing gets around it. Nothing. All we can do is stay still and wait to see what happens."

We didn't have long to sweat it out. The huge machine drifted backward, never letting its cannon muzzle waver. A mic keyed before a female voice blared over the loudspeaker. "Driver, exit the vehicle." I wasn't surprised to find a woman piloting an Apache. In my experience riding gunships, most proved as ferocious warriors as the machine's namesake.

Julia didn't worry me, but a return of J did. "Jules, do exactly what you're told. Don't deviate an inch from their orders, okay?" Her frightened nod didn't set my mind at ease.

I stepped out to wait without bothering to close my door. Behind the truck landed what I assumed was the same corporate version we'd seen earlier. Two Arapahos set down a hundred meters away, one on either side. The Apache slid sideways without letting us from her sights—I assumed to stop collateral damage of those behind our truck. Her action merely drove home these people were seasoned professionals. A half-dozen armed troops exited each transport and took up positions around us.

She ordered Jules out next. "Passenger. Exit the vehicle. On your knees, fingers laced behind your head," the booming voice commanded. I hadn't hesitated to follow orders and prayed Julia wouldn't, either.

Watching through the open cab, she did as well as I could have hoped. Our wrists were restrained after being relieved of our weapons. They searched the truck before the Apache pilot saluted and powered away. I could only pivot on my knees and let my back take the brunt of the rotor wash. Our eardrums weren't quite so lucky against the roar. A short, burly soldier marched Jules to my side of the Ford and pushed her roughly to the ground, drawing a quick protect from me. "Knock it off, asshole." My rebuke earned a boot shoving my face into the dirt, then Julia's.

Soldiers parted to let a man through, his importance obvious by his Wall Street business suit. He was bracketed by two in civilian black fatigues, both well-armed. With army enlisted men at each of our elbows, Jules and I were dragged to our feet to face the slender newcomer. Rather than meek, my wife stood erect with eyes blazing. Shit. Bastards woke J. I craned my neck to identify the soldier throwing her to the ground and using his boot against both of us. J followed my gaze. I inclined my head toward the stout soldier behind us and looked back to my wife. She nodded.

Laughter wasn't what I expected from the handsome civilian. "Julia Marie Hampton, now Julia Pelletier?" She lifted her chin in a defiant affirmative before he turned to me still chuckling. "You must be Captain Dawson Pelletier?" His eyes narrowed when I didn't answer. "Anything happens to my corporal, I'll hold you personally responsible."

My turn to chuckle. "Then someone better plan on holdin' me responsible." My grin couldn't possibly show the rage I felt.

All mirth was gone this time. "Don't worry, I will."

"Not you, laughing boy," J said. "You're mine." The gray woman— too fearless for her own good.

I was sure he knew who he faced when the civilian recoiled. The soldier manhandling us stepped closer only to be waved off. "It's possible we got off on the wrong foot," he said with far less bravado than moments ago. "This may have been a little overkill. I merely wished to secure a safe environment to speak with both of you."

"You have no idea what you *may have* done." I mocked his choice of words. "A phone call or knock on our door, and we'd have gotten through whatever this is about with minimal fuss. Now?" I tipped my head to indicate J. "Too late."

The civilian spread his hands wide. "I was ordered to contact Julia Pelletier and offer her a job. That's all."

I didn't let Jules answer, even if J desired. "Ain't interested. She's got a job. Besides, she's never served."

"My orders aren't to argue with you. They're to make her aware she's needed by her country. It's the reason for all this military presence...to demonstrate what she'll be part of."

I didn't hold back my laughter. "She's a schoolteacher, Einstein. Teaches third grade. Unless you're expecting her to handle a classroom of nine-year olds, you're barking up the wrong tree."

My heart dropped at his next words. "I'm here to employ the services of the gray woman."

* * *

J sat rigidly at the kitchen table while I made coffee. Our unidentified and unwelcomed guest took a chair across from her. Ten soldiers surrounded the house with the brace of civilian guards stationed inside the kitchen blocking entry. Both were armed and appeared willing to use deadly force. At instructions from their boss, they'd unload our handguns and brought them inside. Most of our other firearms were locked in the master bedroom safe, but Jules's newest suppressed Ruger MK IV lay loaded inside a nearby kitchen drawer. Thus, it was lucky for our interlopers when their leader apologized profusely to us for his ill-considered amusement and his overzealous military helpers. I considered him too arrogant and good-looking for his own good, but cooling J off a bit was a smart move.

As if we'd been granted pardon, he said, "A letter exonerating both of you of any crimes committed before the serve date was delivered by local law enforcement. It's legally binding no matter the decision Mrs. Pelletier reaches." His earlier smirk gone, he looked over J's head to me. "Our government is sincere in its need for the services your wife can provide."

"Who are you, and what branch do you work for? Judging by your weaponry and troops, it's army."

"We're unaffiliated with any branch of military. Whatever equipment and manpower are needed, the closest assets are ours for the asking. What we do is protect the United State and her people from within. You've never heard of us—few even within the halls of Washington know of our existence. Our job is to monitor and nullify threats to the homeland with minimal public exposure or scrutiny." His gaze dropped to Julia. "It's where you come in."

"Why me?" She delivered her question in a flat and emotionless tone.

He didn't hesitate. "You went by J while employed by The Company, terminating those who imported and dealt poison on our

282

streets." Our guest noticed my eyebrows raise. "Oh, yes, we knew very well their undertaking. My superiors made the decision to monitor the group and their employees rather than stop them. We've admired your work for quite some time, Mrs. Pelletier."

When she didn't respond, I was sure Jules didn't know how. I couldn't see her facial reaction while standing behind, but her worst nightmare had come true—the government was specifically aware of her. "What if we say no," I asked.

"Then we leave. But know this...someone not far from where we sit...an unsung war hero and his family...will likely die at the hands of America's enemies. I can't stress the importance of the strengths your wife can bring to bear in this case, not the least of which is simply going unnoticed." Ah, he truly understood the gray woman.

J found her voice. "One job and I'm done?"

"Dammit, Jules," I said.

She raised a hand to silence me. "Well?" Her appearing to acquiescence caused acid in my stomach to rise.

He wanted to lie—I could see it plainly. It was probably a big part of his job, and I had to give it to him for fessing up. "I'd like to say yes, but I won't. Maybe is the best I can do."

"I get my own classroom this year. I've worked hard for it. Do you expect me to give my dream away so easily?"

"No reason you have to. We'll speak with your administration when the time comes." He glanced at me. "We understand Bess Mueller is your aunt. I'll approach the superintendent and board."

"You're not expecting me to leave with you today?" Her surprise was obvious.

He shook his head. "Normally, we immerse a candidate into our program, instructing him or her on what to expect and how to approach a mission. Hone their reflexes and sharpen their skills. Not so in your case. The gray woman works best alone as we saw in Chicago." J cocked her head at his acknowledgement. "Who do you think redirected law enforcement's attention from groups of fleeing men and women to reports of a fire breaking out on the twelfth floor? You disappeared into an alley only to reappear in northern California for a short time before returning to Salmon."

I moved enough to see her lips pressed into a colorless line as she considered his admission. "What incentives do you offer if I agree?"

"Not as lucrative as The Company, but we'll make it worthwhile."

"What of Dawson?" I guessed she didn't need to hear numbers. Knowing targets awaited J was enough.

He shrugged. "Use him or don't...however you see fit."

"If I'm wounded or killed?"

Our guest didn't hesitate as if he anticipated the question. "You'll be treated by the best doctors in the profession. If you..." He grimaced. "...die, we pick up the tab from the time of your death until after burial. Your husband will receive a substantial amount in non-taxable spousal benefits."

"Can you tell me a little of what to expect...what you plan for me?" Her question let me know the decision was already made. Eagerness now showed.

"An honorably discharged army sergeant wears a ten-million dollar bounty on his head. It seems the enemy either located him or has mistaken someone else for their target. We've intercepted transmissions leading us to believe at least three kill teams plan to infiltrate our country with the plan of collecting. Perhaps a fourth, although we're not certain as yet. One group will arrive by air, another by sea, and at least one...perhaps two...will slip through our northern or southern borders. My guess is both."

I couldn't believe the story we were being told and slammed my cup to the countertop, coffee splashing to coat and drip from cabinets I'd paid a fortune to have installed. "What do you want from my wife? Work as a part of some team, or is she supposed to take on these cells alone? A better question is do you expect surveillance or termination?" Truthfully, I couldn't wrap my head around what I was hearing.

"We expect only one outcome when the skills of your wife are required. Termination with extreme prejudice." His eyes never left J, and I guessed by his smirk, he approved of her reaction. "We expect her to follow directions as best she can, improvise where she can't. No others will be involved. She goes alone or with anyone of her choice." His gaze finally rose to meet mine.

"How many in each group?" My mind's eye went back to what I once watched—J taking on Benton and her thugs. "Will they all arrive and converge at once?"

"We can only guess, but each team may well arrive with seven. It holds particular significance to their sect. We hope to better answer your questions after learning more over the next weeks."

"Where do these *teams* as you call them originate?" J asked.

The bane of my existence blew across his coffee before taking a sip. Easy to see he stalled for time to formulate his thoughts. He swallowed and returned the cup to the table before answering in a low tone. "From northern Africa, the Philippines, and Middle East. They're followers of ISIS." My immediate fear and rage fought for mastery, and I took an angry step only to stopped by the rising muzzles of two rifles, both with their safeties disengaged and barrels trained on my chest. The civilian waved both guards back. "I understand. Please believe me when I say I do."

"Our government's aware of Islamic infiltrators and doing nothing about it?" I shouted, doing my best not to hurl my cup as a weapon.

I couldn't miss the hard edge in his voice. "We are doing something about it, Mr. Pelletier. It's why we're here."

* * *

Julia swept through the house after her first day of the school year on her way to the bedroom. "Hi, honey, I'm home," she said to where I washed potatoes in the sink. After going outside to meet his mistress, Jake trailed her through the kitchen and into our room. I followed suit to watch from the threshold. She hung her jacket in the closet and removed the harness for her Glock and spare magazines, tossing it to the bed. Jules saw me ogling when she kicked her shoes off and shimmied out of her dress. I loved her cheesy grin. "You like?" She cocked a hip and posed for me.

"Like? Nope, I love." I drawled in my deepest bass.

She stepped into old jeans and tugged a ratty sweatshirt missing both sleeves and most of the collar over her head. "Did you get the potatoes dug? Supposed to get a rainstorm tonight."

"Out yesterday, brushed off and boxed today. They're in the garage storeroom. I figure the rest of the garden can wait a few more weeks." My goal was for her to help me harvest carrots, beans, onions, and a multitude of other vegetables. Mom promised to preserve whatever we brought to her place.

"Mah hero," she said threading the Colt on her belt and tightening it around a waist not even twenty inches. "I stopped at the feed store and picked up six bags for the chickens. Can you pack it to the coop for me?"

She stood outside the pen watching her hens and rooster pick at the cracked corn she threw them, while I moved the fifty-pound sacks. Four of the little mommas were each trailed by eight rapidly growing chicks. Without any adults to butcher for winter, I contacted a neighbor for help. After making a deal on some of his pullets, eighteen were in our freezer—the last one in the sink for supper. "Gonna take 'em all winter to finish what you brought home."

She nodded without looking away from her birds. "Yeah, didn't want to worry about running out when it gets cold." Blamed little things were still filling up on grasshoppers and maturing grasses. Until the first frost hit, they wouldn't eat more than a couple cups of grain each day. Most would be butchered after Jules kept some to replenish her flock. "What's for dinner?"

"Left a chicken out to fry. We'll also have spuds, green beans, and sliced tomatoes. Mom sent home an apple pie after I drove her to a favorite hair salon."

A quizzical look caught my eye. "You've been practicing?"

I nodded slowly. "Uh huh." Leave it to her not to miss a significant depletion of .308s. A short wall in our bedroom was shelves of ammunition reaching from floor to ceiling. My AR-10 was capable of half minute of angle. I'd be foolish not to keep my capabilities of wringing every bit of accuracy from the rifle up to par. A stack of perforated targets on my bureau told the story. One three-shot group at seven hundred five yards went three and fifteen-sixteenths. I'd never make a fast and furious up-close assassin, but I could guarantee a target was usually dead shortly after I squeezed the trigger.

She smiled before looking away. "Guess I will, too." I expected no different and followed her into the house. She could shoot while I started our meal. I was sectioning our chicken to fry when she stalked past the kitchen ignoring me. I wasn't surprised to see her carrying only the suppressed Sig-Sauer rifle gifted from Al and Ruger MK IV .22. With its minimal recoil and short barrel, it seemed Al's rifle was becoming her go-to as much as the handgun. No sense in speaking to her before the backdoor screen slammed with J already firmly in control.

Forecasters were partially correct. We got rain, but instead of one day, it lasted a week. Julia loved her classroom and spent too much time in it as far as I was concerned. She left our place at six-thirty for a job starting at eight, then was tardy in returning home at five-thirty or later. I'd given her a day of help in arranging her room and appreciated her excitement. Each evening was filled with the sharing of her daily experiences. I finally understood her hunger for teaching when she could talk of little else but her kids. Twenty-four of the little buggers, and there was this cutest little redhaired girl...Mrs. Pelletier loved to share the idiosyncrasies of each student.

I perceived Jules—and J—better as each week drew to a close. Doing each job well drove her to excellence. The teacher was no different than the gray woman—one a master killer—the other adept at instructing. A few hours each evening were spent upstairs at the desk we purchased and coerced our army visitors into moving for us, once we'd sorted who could or couldn't be manhandled. The burly corporal who'd been slow to agree smiled despite his taped nose. She invested another four or five hours each day of the weekend making lesson plans even with Jake ready to hunt. Pursuing pheasants, grouse, and quail was left to me and him, giving Jules plenty of time alone to work.

Of course, all good things must come to an end. Texting with Mom and making plans for the upcoming holiday season, I noted Julia parking. Without an automatic opener, she was forced to do it manually before driving inside. I'd offered to have it open and waiting each evening, but she worried about mice getting inside. The extra minute of work needed to keep her mind at ease didn't seem a bother. Rather than hurry into the house as usual, she stood outside the garage door and waited. My curiosity lasted only until a white SUV drove into our yard.

I stepped onto the front porch to stand with Jules and provide a unified front. Wearing camouflage fatigues, the driver exited and opened the rear door. He was the burly corporal I'd convinced to apologize to Julia after treating her rougher than I thought he should. I noted his chest patch showed he was now a private. The warrior dressed as a civilian stepped out, as did his same two contractor security guards. "Mr. and Mrs. Pelletier," my nemesis greeted us. Other than tipping my chin, he got nothing from me. The army driver stayed with the car, while the remaining three stopped at the steps. "May I come in?" Although my Anaconda lay coiled against my hip, he made no mention of me being armed. Whether he knew Julia carried a gun to school, I wasn't sure. My bet was he did. A cool wind created a dust devil in the dirt behind him as I considered my answer.

"Just you." I didn't wait to see if he agreed or not and turned to guide Julia inside before me. "Got a name?" I asked when he closed the door. The two in black fatigues lurked ominously outside the window.

When he smiled, I saw my initial impression was wrong. He didn't smirk. A deep scar on his upper lip caused it to twist. "Call me Kevin."

"What can we do for you...Kevin." I figured it was an alias to placate me.

He looked from me to Julia and back. "May I speak to your wife? She's the reason I'm here."

I nodded slowly, taking his measure. This man was at our house to ruin our lives as we knew it. "You're talking to both of us...*Kevin.*" I purposely emphasized his name a second time.

He successfully battled back a smile. "It really is my given name. May I sit?"

"Sure. We're all out of coffee." I'd be damned before making his second visit enjoyable.

"No problem." Bare-headed both times we met, he removed his coat and hung it from the back of his chair. No way was I going to take it for him. My job wasn't to make the man comfortable, nor was I his lackey.

Kevin didn't look as if he'd be out of place at a state dinner. Impeccably groomed, not a hair was out of place. Other than his lip, he could have graced the cover of a men's fashion magazine. I figured him about five-ten and a buck seventy. "Floor's yours."

Dismissing me immediately, he turned to Julia and didn't waste time. "We've uncovered a successful incursion. At this point we're not certain of their objective. A dozen possible targets exist within US borders. Any are feasible hits...along with others we aren't yet aware of." He squinted awaiting her reaction.

"What do you expect of me?" J answered. Julia made her personality switch—no wonder he stared intently.

"Your help to keep what many of us who served consider a national treasure safe. Problem is...we don't know when, where, how many, or their identities. Our adversary is known only by their digital footprints."

I stepped in to interrupt. "Hold on. You know absolutely nothing except the bad guys are here but expect my wife to keep this..." I pantomimed quotes. "...'national treasure' safe?"

Kevin nodded seriously. "Not only our man with his wife and children but extended family, too. They're all in jeopardy."

I couldn't allow him to destroy my family, marriage, and future so easily. "No." His eyebrows raised as I shook my head. "No one is important enough for me to lose my wife and eventual family."

"Are you certain, Mr. Pelletier?" Kevin's tone stayed frustratingly calm. "Not even one who may have single-handedly started events leading to the destruction of ISIS as we know it?" He sat back to cross his arms and await my response.

It took a moment before I understood. "You mean..." I wetted dry lips with my tongue, remembering a fellow soldier known only by reputation. "...are you talkin' about our guy in Syria? One the army planned to prosecute for whatever happened before suddenly dropping the charges?" Media outlets reported what they learned differently. Even the least outlandish story strained credulity. Then one day, the media firestorm simply vanished. The American public—and the world—knew him only as the shooter on Sziria Hill—or the Sziria Hill shooter.

Kevin didn't blink, nor did his facial expression change. He simply waited for me to assimilate and digest the information presented. "How am I expected to keep your man alive if we know nothing except some may have entered the US?" J said. "No photos, ages, or even names. You ask the impossible."

"You don't need *me* to tell *you* how to do *your* job. We'll provide names and addresses of those we wish to see protected. From there it's up to you."

"What of law enforcement?" J asked. "Daily expenses, housing, vehicles...do you even have a plan to deal with bodies? You're asking me to terminate average-appearing men or women at any given time. I could encounter them in a crowded mall or on a busy street. Bystanders could be wounded or worse."

He nodded. "We'll cope with the worst-case scenario when we come to it. Know this, Mrs. Pelletier. You have the full faith and weight of government behind you whether they know it or not. Expenses are expected to be reasonable. I suggest you avoid the lavish five-star hotels causing a spotlight to be shined upon us, although money isn't an issue. Stealth and nerves of steel are what we're hiring."

"Bodies?" she asked again.

"We'll have cleanup teams available around the clock."

"If I'm arrested?"

For the first time since accosted by Kevin, I saw real humor in his smile. "I'll be there to bail you out."

"If no bail is set?"

He laughed—he was so arrogant I don't think he could help it. "Have faith. You'll never spend a night behind bars."

I'm not sure what he saw, but all humor on Kevin's face evaporated when J leaned forward. "I'll never believe the government has my best interests at heart," she said. "Impress me."

* * *

I leaned back in a chair dragged into our bedroom to watch Jules pack. "Any idea of where you're going?"

She glanced to where I sat and grimaced. "I do. Don't ask me to say, honey."

So many things I wanted to verbalize. Some to shout angrily into her face—of what she seemed too willing to give away. Potentially, she risked removing herself from those who loved and would miss her—her students, friends, dog, and most importantly, her husband. I'd lose everything if she didn't survive. Yet the gray woman was in a class of her own. If anyone could do what Kevin and those above him asked, it was J. She knew I was against what she agreed to with every fiber of my being. Yet she seemed incapable of missing an opportunity to work at a profession I was assured she hated. A long-term substitute teacher would stand in for her classroom while she moonlighted as a killer. Aunt Bess was not a happy vice-principal.

Three firearms accompanied Jules. Al's rifle in 9mm with a new EOTech scope in addition to open sights, her father's Glock 17, and the suppressed .22 Ruger MK IV. Three guns, only two calibers to feed. Two were already packed in the government-provided Chevy Suburban with the Glock holstered beneath her left arm. "I won't," I assured her. "Do your job and get your cute little derriere home as quick as you can." I swatted at it as she passed me with a bag.

She chuckled when her attempt to twist her bottom out of range wasn't enough and my palm connected. "Be a good husband and get my last two suitcases, will you?"

"No." My answer was firm. Jules stopped in her tracks to turn to see if I joked. "I'm against this. Ain't no way I'm gonna help you leave." I shrugged. "Sorry."

The screen door slammed behind her as she carried her load outside. Jake padded in to see if I remained. "Momma's leaving us again, boy." I scratched his chin and rubbed the pointer's face until we heard her again. When she passed with the final bags, I stood to follow with Jake at my side.

The moment she closed the back end, Julia came to me with her arms outstretched. Strong limbs went around me for a hug she needed. We clung together with Jake watching and waiting anxiously. She finally lifted her face and puckered. "Kiss?"

I pulled away and stepped back. "Nope. Ain't doin' it."

She was hurt. A blind man could see it. "But why? I'm leaving."

"Because I'm not telling you goodbye."

"But...but what if the worst..." She trailed off without finishing.

"Then I make do with what we've lost, Julia Marie Pelletier."

At least she hugged and kissed Jake before blowing one to me after fastening her seatbelt. After a little wave she was gone. Our pointer stood and followed his mistress to the edge of the garage before stopping to look back at me. One gesture, and he heeled to the house. Taking a seat at the table with a fresh cup of coffee, I opened my cellphone case to send a text. *The hawk has flown the nest.* No longer was Jules my wounded dove. She flew free with talons extended, and I almost felt sorry for her prey.

Ten minutes passed before I heard the croak of a bullfrog offering an answer. *She's moving south. Will contact when I know more.* Nothing to do but wait. I didn't expect another missive for hours if not days.

Jake enjoyed our trip to town and waited patiently during a stop at The Jumping Salmon for a late afternoon meal. We were low on groceries at home, but I didn't plan to purchase more. Instead, I got their twenty-ounce prime rib with eggs and hash browns. Damn near ordered it rare in honor of my bloodthirsty wife but relented and got it medium rare instead.

Twenty-four hours later, I was contemplating another jaunt for a hamburger and fries when I got my answer. Sitting at the table with a *Field & Stream* and Jake lying close, the croak of my phone startled me. This call I answered. "Yeah?"

"Got her, sir. At least, I think I do. She stopped in Jackson Hole, Wyoming, late last night. This morning she drove southeast to Pinedale, spending a couple hours driving north of the town before returning to Jackson. Since then, she's moved around but always returns to where she started this morning. Dawson, I believe G-Dub's targets are expected in the general area."

My initial burst of elation throttled back to an excited hum. "Can you tell me where she's staying?"

"Yes, sir. I've already identified the hotel as the Come Horn Inn, a high-end place but not exorbitant. Give it another day or two before making any decisions. We need to ascertain if she's staying in the general area."

I grinned at Jake after ending the call with Al. "Guess you'll spend some time with Mom again, little fella." I pulled him against my leg and stroked his side and muzzle.

Thirty minutes later, I drove away from a place both Jules and I loved, one I feared we'd never live to see again with first Missoula, then Jackson my destination.

Get ready, my little sparrow hawk, because I'm coming. Your falconer's got your back and is on the way.